AIRSCREAM

Sam saw. He saw quite clearly the Cessna crossing his path, but he was an ordinary man with an ordinary man's reflexes, a shade faster, perhaps, but not much.

As his mind raced to avoid the impact, Sam sat transfixed, immovable in shock, his body waiting for orders his mind wasn't able to issue quickly enough.

The Cessna grew and grew: he'd never seen one so clearly before. He saw the line of rivets in the air-frame below the pilot's shoulder. Then he saw nothing. The screen went black, the film broken.

The impact was appalling . . .

JOHN BRUCE

Airscream

FONTANA/Collins

First published in 1978 by William Collins Sons & Co Ltd
First issued in Fontana Books 1978

Made and printed in Great Britain by
William Collins Sons & Co Ltd, Glasgow

DEDICATION

Privately and primarily to Sandra,
without whom, in the words of the
cliché, this book would never have
got off the ground—truth.

and

Publicly to 'Godzone'—small
enough, potentially, rich enough
and intelligent enough to reverse
the 'Events dictate to man' syndrome
and come to show democracy the way
in the decades to come—truth?

and

Thanks to Gwyneth Callen, Peter Moyes
and the New Zealand Air Traffic
Services, Air New Zealand and the
Chief Inspector of Air Accidents
for New Zealand

'The crimes of extreme civilization are probably worse than those of extreme barbarism, because of their refinement, the corruption they presuppose, and their superior degree of intellectuality.'

Jules Barbey d'Aurevilly, 'La vengeance d'une femme', *Les Diaboliques*, 1874

GLOSSARY

ADF	Automatic Direction Finding Equipment
ATIS	Aerodrome Terminal Information Service
ATC	Air Traffic Control
DME	Distance Measuring Equipment
EPR	Engine Pressure Ratio (between inlet/outlet)
FIO	Flight Information Officer
IFR	Instrument Flight Rules
ILS	Instrument Landing System
GPU	Ground Power Unit
NOTAM(s)	Notice(s) to airmen (in changes in operating conditions)
PAR	Precision Approach Radar
POB	Person(s) on Board
QNH	Actual air pressure at sea level
RPM	Revolutions per minute
RT	Radiotelephony
RTO	Released For Takeoff
RCC	Rescue Co-ordination Centre
SAR	Search and Rescue (Operation)
TMA	(Airport) Terminal Control Centre (ATC)
V_1	Point of no return on take-off (speed/position)
V_2	Speed point on take-off to attempt lift off
VFR	Visual Flight Rules

PART ONE

Chapter One

God, she felt tired.

As she waited for the lift she eased the heel of her right shoe and grimaced to herself as her fingers found the little blister. She looked down at it and decided to pop it directly she got in, and to stretch the shoes before tomorrow's flight.

'Evening, Miss Carol. Good trip?' The Irish brogue, which had survived years of exile caused her to look up to see old Mr Bates, and just for a second she envied him the tranquillity of a janitor's life. No sweat, just a nice new twenty-storey all-automatic apartment block to care for. But then she wondered what there was to do day in and day out in Wellington if you weren't tired, retired, or making it tick. So, looking at him again more carefully, she substituted boredom for tranquillity, and decided that she would take blisters any day if that were the price for a bit of action.

'Super, thanks, but I've got a blister.'

'Ah, take good care of it. They go septic, you know.' He scratched his chin as he stood in front of her. Class, he thought to himself, real class. Blonde, 23 or so, five seven, about 120 pounds, beautiful legs, and a body which from time to time he had raped from his armchair, eyes closed and a *Penthouse* pet almost forgotten on the floor beside him.

'Mrs Bates OK?' she asked.

'Oh, fine, to be sure. Yes indeed, much better now, thanks. She's out shopping today, first time since she became ill,' he confided.

'That's good, isn't it?' she replied brightly.

'Oh yes indeed, but it does worry her so, you know, having her breast off. I keep telling her it doesn't matter, not at all. I tell her that after all, it's not like she was doin' something like you, or young. And I don't mind, but she still goes on worrying. She's a great one for worrying, you know. I say to her, "You're 57, Martha, and it isn't that important to us any more, so quit your worrying," and I tell her, "It isn't like you was Miss Carol. Now, if she got a growth, she mayn't be able to go on being an air hostess but you, you're OK, so there's nothing to worry about, nothing at all." But she still worries.' He fell silent for a moment and Carol felt sorry for the poor old bugger.

'She just worries, Miss Carol, just worries and worries and I can't think of anything, anything at all to say to help her.'

Always the same whenever she saw him. Polite – a little distant, though never this familiar before. She felt that she was seeing him for the first time – a real human being with feelings and a problem – not just any old guy in a blue serge suit. Suddenly she felt a pang of pity for him. She reached out and took his arm as she said in a quiet voice of sympathy, 'Try not to worry. Give it time and she will begin to see it your way.' She gave the 'will' emphasis as she spoke and his arm a gentle squeeze of reassurance. She glanced round to see if there was anyone else about but they were still alone. She didn't want this. She was tired and had her own life to lead. Jesus, would the bloody lift never come? She looked at the floor indicator: just five more floors to go and she'd be off the hook. But then, she thought, she couldn't just walk off and abandon the old guy.

'Mr Bates, are you OK?' He looked so very miserable.

'I'm sorry, Miss Carol.' He managed a slight smile as he added 'I know I shouldn't be worryin' you with my troubles.'

'It's OK,' she smiled back. 'It's better than getting all uptight, isn't it?'

As the lift doors opened he said, 'Yes, I suppose that's right, and thanks. But I'm grateful to you, indeed I am.'

She smiled reassurance again before, with a small wave, she entered the lift, to sigh thankfully as the doors closed behind her. In a way, she was quite pleased to have been able to help the old guy. At least she had done something today which hadn't been bought and paid for, smile and all.

As Mr Bates went to his reception desk he was thinking he might – just might – with sympathy swing her into bed. After all, he thought, it wasn't exactly like she was a virgin or anything. His mind went back over the men she had shared the flat with over the last few years. To be sure, they had pretty well all been aircrew, but the present stud was bloody well nearly old enough to be her father – a DC8 captain, Harry James Standard. Yes, he must be 48 if he was a day. Sitting at his desk, he noticed very little, for once, as his imagination began to paint the fantasy of the future.

Most of the tenants would have been appalled by what the janitor knew of them for he missed almost nothing of interest, and particularly Harry James Standard.

The lift had seventeen floors to travel, and, as always, Jenny turned straight to the long mirror opposite the door. She knew her good points and how to treat them – all part of the initial training which managed to turn girls who might not turn a head in the street into those who could be sure of it. She wasn't beautiful, if beauty was in terms of flawless perfection over a perfect bone structure, but she had the sort of face which would still be pretty in middle age. Her blue eyes were wide-set and had a frank appealing innocence about them – lovely expressive eyes. Innocence was reflected in her 'little girl's' nose – *retroussé* and a trifle short, giving a slightly short upper lip which was very attractive with such good teeth as hers. Her jaw was perhaps a trifle pronounced, but not over much so, with the fullness of her wide lips to catch the eye. But as she turned to the lift's mirror it was her eyes she concentrated on after the briefest of glances at the rest of her face. Quickly she touched up her eye shadow before pulling the big purple comb through her hair – long, naturally blonde, thick hair. Then as her stomach told her that the lift was slowing down, she put the comb away and turned to wait. It was moments like this, she thought, moments of anticipation, that made life really great.

Harry had been fantastic from the beginning. There was something different about him. It wasn't only that he was always intuitively right in sex, that if she wanted it gentle then he was gentle to the point where she just couldn't breathe for the height he got her to before she came crashing down, or that he could hit like lightning. No, he was super in bed, but it was only a small part of it. He seemed to be tuned in to her. She'd think or wish and he made it happen. A night free and somehow he just knew what fitted. And somehow they just didn't clash; she didn't have to fight. He was the only man she had ever felt completely at ease with; with whom silence – if she wanted silence – could last for as long as she wanted it to without it ever becoming too long.

Now, as she waited, her tiredness seemed to be slipping away and she began to feel a little sexy and to build on it. As she stepped from the lift she stopped, across from the door to her apartment, prolonging the moment of delicious anticipation. She glanced at her watch, 5.15, and she wondered whether Harry would have remembered the new schedules. She was about to take the last steps across the hall when the apartment door opened. She stopped, wondering who was going to come out. Then she froze as she heard Harry's voice.

'Be good, my little boy, and I'll give you a ring, OK?'

'Sure, Harry, but aren't you forgetting something?' The tone of voice was soft.

'How do you mean, forgetting something?' The reply perplexed.

'Money, Harry, some money.' Soft but insistent.

The boy's back was in the doorway, obliquely across from her.

As she gazed with almost unseeing eyes at the back of the leather jacket, taut over the boy's wide shoulders, and at the flares which did nothing to disguise the slim hips and good legs, the words 'little boy' pounded through her mind. 'Little boy!' Oh God, dear God! It just couldn't be true. She felt numb – no shock, no nothing, just disbelief. She didn't know what to do. 'Little boy.' Oh God, his little boy!

'C'mon, Harry. No money, and no me again.' This time there was a touch of cold steel in the insistent softness.

'But Phil, I thought . . .'

'What, Harry? What did you think? Not for love! Do you think that, that it was for love? Christ, you should have been a vicar.' The boy laughed as he went on, 'Oh no, my dear Harry. A boy's got to make a living and if you want a boy then you've got to see he lives right, OK?'

'But . . .' Harry blurted. 'I thought . . . I mean, you didn't ask for any money before.'

Harry's 'little boy' had hit her hard after the first numbness had left her stunned, with just the sort of shock which everyone knows who's ever had a near miss. The shock of driving along and suddenly, from somewhere, a kid appears and it's too late to miss. You're going to smash life into a pulp like a hammer into fruit, then for some reason – nothing to do with you – it just doesn't happen. No kid, no accident – just you in the car reacting, blood draining from your head, gut screwed up, legs out of control, tingling. Beginning to breathe hard in a cold sweat as your hit brain begins to take over again. Then as the full impact of what might have been shoots through you, you gulp and feel sick. Jenny felt sick and faint as the full impact of what Harry – her fantastic Harry – really was. Oh dear God! A fag. Gay! She didn't know the words but the picture of him in bed 'wifing' it – it had to be that way round somehow – suddenly nauseated her. But still she was frozen to the spot. Still she heard them, and at Harry's submissive wheedling tone of voice she nearly threw up. But still she couldn't move.

Then: Oh God! she thought, as the 'before' sank into her brain. How many times 'before' she wondered as anger grew. Anger and sheer disgust at the filthy thought of her defilement by these 'men'. But though her anger grew it still wasn't enough to unroot her: so she just stood there, unconsciously waiting for her brain to cloud sufficiently to make her act as she never would normally – in violent outrage.

Philip James – not his real name, of course – leant against the doorway and looked with arrogant distaste at Harry. This was the fourth time he'd serviced him, and Harry was hooked; another old fag to add to the small but select list of his 'reliable clients'. But like them all, dear old Harry didn't like the moment of truth. Philip smiled to himself as he looked at the man in front of him. To think he'd nearly missed him. Just shows how wrong you could be. But Graham never made mistakes, so he had stuck with Harry for the evening, trying to work him out. And sure enough, as the evening had gone by the bits had begun to fall into place, and he'd got Harry typed. One of the 'ashamed' brigade – timid and frightened of it. A good guy to hook into: someone who would pay well for silence in the long run. Once hooked, the innocent little touch on what happens to airline pilots if . . . ? That would be enough. Strange the way he really liked so much pain though, he thought. Still, made him more dependent, so why worry.

'Harry, old thing, I'm waiting. You'd better make up your mind soon.' He looked at his watch before adding indolently, 'Isn't your girl-friend due in soon?' Then slowly he started to light a cigarette. After the first long draw he said, 'All right, Harry, I'm off, but I was wrong about one thing. It's not just for the money. Of course, I need it, but with you . . .' he paused. 'Well, Harry' – the change in his voice was plain – 'I could become very fond of you – very fond, Harry. But you must see that I can't live without anything . . .' He saw he had made the point. It always worked; with the promise of love payment became a present and the fag's pride was salved.

He watched Harry reach into his pocket.

'I don't want much, Harry. Just enough to get by for a few days, and you'll ring, won't you? I really want you to. I mean it. Last night was lovely, wasn't it?' Then to give it emphasis, he added quietly, sincerely, 'Honestly, Harry.'

Jenny found it almost unbelievable – a terrible dream of nightmare emotion. God! How could anyone have so little self-respect? she wondered. It was as though part of her had taken one step back and become a cool observer of some sort of slow-motion dream with her powerless to move or take part. She heard the boy continue, 'It's been getting better, Harry, hasn't it?' He knew his technique well enough to be sure of it, and his voice took on a slightly pleading tone as he added, 'Please, Harry. I need you. Look, I'm sorry I said anything about the money. Look, forget it.'

Harry was confused. But then, of course, the kid had to live, and he owed him – well, something – but money! He had decided to get a present, but then you couldn't eat presents so perhaps the kid was right. Then suddenly the boy was coming towards him. They were in each other's arms.

Jenny, aflame with emotions stronger than anything she'd known before, simply didn't know what to do as the boy just stood there and they spoke. But then he moved, and she heard them kiss. At that – unmistakable as it was – reason fled in a wave of horror that this obscenity was actually taking place in her apartment, had taken place in her bed. And something suddenly snapped deep, deep down inside her and she moved. As she did so, tears started to her eyes and she had no idea that she screamed as she began to vent her anguish.

Both men went rigid at the first scream. The boy, still with his back to the door, had no time to unfreeze before she had blindly thrust her right hand in amongst the hair which fell so attractively to his shoulders. It was all so quick. His head was jerked viciously back, hard and fast, and in agony he gave birth to a yell of fear and pain to mingle with her screaming in a cascade of sound.

'Get out . . . get out . . .' The same thing over and over again. He would have run but he couldn't. Christ, the girl had strength, and he yelled again, and tears of pain whipped across his face as she kept jerking his head as hard as she could. Vaguely, she knew she was hurting him badly, that the hair was tearing from his scalp. Yet it wasn't enough. Her left hand found his face, and with a wonderful feeling of release she felt her long, strong nails bed into the boy's face, and in an ecstasy of revenge she raked savagely down and exulted in the noise of agony torn from him. He shuddered, the pain of his scalp eclipsed by the torture of laceration, then he ducked in desperation. He went down in near oblivion while she still grasped his hair and tore more from his head, and his blood smeared her uniform as his face swept down and bumped off her thigh to freedom. He ran. But he needn't have bothered – she didn't follow. Suddenly it was over, and she was standing still with her hands hanging, blinded by the tears streaming from her eyes. Vaguely, she heard a voice whispering, 'Oh get out, get out, get out . . .'

It had been all very much too sudden and shocking and unexpected for Harry. He'd hardly been aware of the boy being torn from his arms, had hardly seen what happened next. His brain reverberated to the noise yet all he could understand was that something awful was happening. As Jenny had come through the door he was looking wide-eyed at her, yet he had hardly recognized her as she'd leapt at the boy's back. Then something had joined the terrible sound in his mind but it wasn't until it was nearly over that he had heard himself saying, 'Stop it, stop it,' powerless to do anything. He'd been powerless when, so very slowly that it would always be etched on his mind, he'd seen the girl's nails, like an eagle's talons, bed in and tear down the boy's face. It was terrible to see – that strength of unrestraint. With the sinking of her nails into his flesh the blood had come and welled into four parallel channels down the boy's face before, finally, the corner of his mouth had been torn. It was the final devastation to which Harry reacted, and in reaction he had retched before spewing in horror on to the hall carpet. He retched and retched long after there was anything left in his stomach to bring up. He continued to try to be sick long after the boy had fled and all that was left of the noise was the girl's whisper, punctuated by long shuddering gasps for breath as she cried, and his own quiet odious noise. Each heave of his stomach ended in a strangulated, pointless effort which racked him with pain and bent him double over the pool of vomit he had made on the floor.

Slowly, Jenny's mind began to clear as, emotions spent, she

became aware of the nauseating noise behind her, and her whisper. She stopped whispering, falling silent as she turned. In a glance the sight of Harry revolted her. His semi-crouch of apparently abject submission suddenly filled her with loathing for this miserable creature. The emotion gave her strength – this pitiable man! The word 'pitiable' stayed in her mind. New thoughts began to churn in her mind: no wonder he was so good with women. It tainted her pity for him, which again became tinged with anger at his betrayal, his concealment. The fact that he had successfully passed himself off as an acceptable counterpart for herself, when all the time . . . Her mind shied away from the reality of all that she had done with him in bed; shied away and began to close off the past. At the release from the rat-trap of contemplating the past, the present suddenly hit her and she smelled the man's vomit and saw the sickness.

She was one of those people who could never see another being sick without herself reacting to it. She fled to the bathroom.

Bates, sitting at his resplendent reception desk noticed the lift indicator moving and wondered who was coming down. He saw it pass the hall for the car park below. He knew his residents and thought it odd. Too late for anyone to be on the way out to shop, and too early to go out for the evening. And no one was visiting so far as he knew. His curiosity aroused he got up and went out of the main doors to the side exit of the park. Very strange, he thought. He had been down to do his late afternoon parking check just after Miss Carol had gone up. No strangers there then. He was turning the corner of the building when the young man ran into him. 'Hey, steady on,' he shouted. The young man crashed off him, and staggered before falling a few paces on. Bates went up to him, holding his shoulder which had taken the impact of his ricochet into the wall.

'You stupid bast—' His voice trailed off as he got a good look at the young man. 'Oh mother of Jesus!' he whispered to himself, seeing the blood pumping from the torn face, the blood-sodden handkerchief lost in the fall. 'Oh mother of Jesus!' he said again, as he bent down to help the young man up. 'Here, hold this to it.' He placed the pad of his own handkerchief gently against the torn flesh, took the other's hand

and put it to the pad. 'Now, just you hold that there for a moment.' Unthinkingly, he bent down and retrieved the sodden handkerchief, not noticing his hand crimsoning as the blood drained out of the handkerchief and began to drip from between his clenched fingers.

'Now, tell me then, are you all right to walk a bit?' he asked.

The young man didn't seem to have heard him. He just stood there.

'Oh mother of Jesus, oh dear, oh dear, what a mess you're in. But now, what shall we do for the best?' he asked himself. 'Yes, I think you'd better come in. Yes, I think that's best,' and as he put his arm around the young man to guide him back the way he'd come, he said again, 'Yes, I think that's best.'

Together they traversed the underground car park to a small door at the back, with the older man supporting the younger. Through it and up the stairs they went, and all the time the old man was talking to himself – making his decisions. 'Yes, that's what we'll do. Get the doctor. Yes, I'll give you a brandy first of all, and then . . .'

'No, no doctor.' Though muffled by lips that hurt too much to move, the words were sharp and clear enough to stop Bates: too loud for the small passageway.

'What's that you say? No doctor? No doctor! That's bloody madness. Of course you must have a doctor . . .'

'No doctor,' the young man cut in. 'You clean it up. I don't want a doctor, understand, I don't want one.'

The young man had stopped, and seemed to be hesitating on the point of running.

'All right then, no doctor, but you must be a crazy fool not to want one – have you seen your face?'

The young man murmured, 'No, I haven't, but if it's too bad I will go to my own doctor later, understand.'

'No, I don't, that's for sure, but have it your own way. Now in here.' He opened the door to his apartment and guided the other into the kitchen.

'I'd be takin' you into the sitting-room,' he said, 'but the wife would never forgive me for blood on the carpet. Now sit down there. I'll be back in a moment.'

He was, inside a minute. 'Drink this.' He held out the glass. In his haste to swallow the brandy the young man slopped it across the torn corner of his mouth. 'Aaaah-oh, Jesus fucking Christ. Oh sweet Jesus, that hurts.' He moaned to himself, slowly shaking his head to rid himself of the pain. Then at the sink, looking round at Bates he said, 'Have you a mirror so I can see it?' But the question was lost in the rush of water, so Bates merely shook his head before turning the tap off.

'Hey!'

'I'm not bloody deaf. Now, what was it you were wanting?'

'A mirror.'

'In a minute. Meanwhile hold still while I have a look. Lucky for you I was once in the ambulance service. Now hold still – it's going to hurt some – are you ready?'

'No, get me a mirror first, please.'

'Well OK, if you must see it – but you stay there now.'

When he came back besides the mirror the janitor had a handful of things from the bathroom cabinet. He handed the mirror to the young man who, as he looked at the mess, drew a sharp intake of breath before whispering, 'I'll fucking kill him, I'll kill him, I swear it. I'll fucking kill him . . .' Then his voice broke as tears began to course down his face to mingle with the blood. 'It was his bastard fault – I'll kill him . . .'

'All right, all right, steady now,' the janitor broke in. 'There'll be all the time in the world for that later but just now we must clean you up, so hold still now.'

The boy nodded and Bates enjoyed reliving a slice of the past. After a few minutes he said, 'You know, boy, that tear in your lip should be stitched. How about it now – you say no doctor, and if that's what you want –' he shrugged – 'well then . . .' He paused to look once again. 'But it should be stitched. If it isn't,' he went on, 'you'll have a mighty big scar there for the rest of your life.'

'Couldn't you do it?' the boy asked.

'Ah, to be sure, yes, I could, and I'd make a good job of it for you, but I've no anaesthetic. Without it, it'll hurt, hurt real bad. Enough to make you wee yourself – now is that what you want? Or would you rather I called this doctor friend of mine? I could soon get him and I don't think he'd say anything. Or of course I could take you to the hospital – you could call yourself whatever you liked there, I suppose. Now how about that for an idea?'

Philip James thought it over for a few moments but decided that once someone had seen the wounds he'd be marked and remembered. Only nails would leave marks like these and he didn't want any tie-in. It was a muddle, it all hurt too much. But the burning idea of revenge in some undefined way beat through his brain. The pain couldn't be worse than it had been and this old guy seemed to know what he was doing, but oh Jesus Christ, would they pay for it! He sat in silence thinking about it and as his mind turned to the future he began wondering how he'd manage for the next few weeks while his face mended. He'd see Harry and he'd pay, and pay good – yes, he'd sort that out, and then Harry would go on paying and paying and paying. No, he wouldn't kill Harry, he was worth much too much alive. But he would kill the bitch – do it so she'd know all about it. He almost smiled to himself at the thought. Oh yes, he thought. . . . The janitor's repeated question broke his train of thought.

'. . . Hospital? No, no doctor or hospital. You do it.'

'Well, if you want my opinion, I think you're bloody mad, but if that's what you want I'll do it, but hold on tight. It's going to hurt something terrible, I'll tell you that.'

It did – terribly.

Tenderly the janitor tied the last suture, then, a routine almost forgotten, he mopped the sweat from the boy's brow. 'There now, that'll do very well.' He stepped back to admire it. 'Oh yes,' he said to himself, 'the old hands haven't lost their cunning, oh dear me no.' Then to the boy, 'Right, I'll cover it up now and you'll be as good as new – well almost, but you'll always have a bit of a scar there.'

The boy nodded and the old man carried on until the job was finished. 'There now. How about another brandy? I think you've earned one.'

In the sitting-room, with brandy in their glasses, the janitor began to lead the young man on to tell him the tale. He made the telling easier by remarking casually at the beginning, 'You needn't worry at all, I know how you make your living, and to be sure I've nothin' against that.' He leant back, and, having a fair idea as to what happened and what this kid's feelings were, he added, 'And she's a right little bitch if ever there was one – but then I never talk about anything that's not my business, you know. Anyway, you were saying. Did she catch you at it? Was that it?'

Philip James hadn't been saying anything, but he needed to talk and the janitor seemed to know the score, so he began to talk.

She locked the bathroom door behind her, leant against it, and, gulping air, tried to stop herself being sick. Then as the need to throw up receded she began to weep. Crying quietly and miserably, she got herself a glass of water. Without thinking, she sat on the edge of the bath, and, cradling the glass between both hands, sipped the water. The water finished she went on holding the glass, sitting there, drained of feeling, until, emotionally exhausted, she stopped crying. It had ceased to help. She felt suddenly unutterably alone, but just wanted to let it stay that way.

Harry walked past the door. Hearing him, she wondered vaguely what he was doing. A flicker of disgust made her wrinkle her nose at the memory of him in the hall. She shuddered, but got up. Suddenly, filled with resolve, she felt a compelling need to get rid of him right now. Looking at herself in the mirror, she couldn't help a wry smile at the wan, tear-stained face looking back at her. She smiled again at the thought of passengers' reaction to it. Then feeling a great deal better she washed her face and re-made up. Ten minutes later, cool and calm in her resolution, she left the bathroom.

'Hello.' He saw her before she saw him. He was sitting on a hall chair and, thank God, he'd cleared up the mess. She didn't answer but just turned and stood looking at him.

In her new-found objectivity she took him in. The face was almost strikingly handsome: thin, but firm, with a good nose and eyes beneath the intelligent forehead and thick dark hair, just streaked with the distinction of grey. But the mouth gave him away, of course. She had always thought of it as sensitive – now it was just weak. She turned her gaze to his chin and for the first time saw its weakness, clear to her now despite the virility of his six o'clock shadow.

He was watching her and suddenly she noticed his beaten-dog gaze. It made trouble with her, prompting a wave of anger at his weakness, prompting a need to punish him before she got rid of him. 'You disgust me.' She said it with clear emphasis and he flinched. 'You're nothing – less than nothing – you should be flushed down the pan like shit.' There was scorn and the need to goad and hurt in her voice. 'But I suppose you like shit. Tell me, do you enjoy wallowing in it?' The hurt she saw was good and drove her on to wound still more. She wanted him to bleed, to be scarred deep down. 'God, you pathetic, weak – miserable fag! Is that the term for hybrids like you? What are you anyway?' Her whiplash rhetoric came faster as words became easier. 'Tell me, is it nice to be fucked by your little "Phil"?'

'Please don't say anything more.' His voice was flat in defeat, but it merely goaded her further.

'Please don't say anything more,' she mimicked. 'Christ, you should have heard yourself out there with that little prick!' And irresistibly, she found herself mimicking him: 'I thought . . . I mean, you didn't ask for any money before.' She laughed harshly.

'God, you make me want to spew.' She'd seen him flinch as she mimicked the boy's words, and wanting to hurt yet more said them slowly again.

'You didn't ask for any money before.' Each word a twist of the knife of her disgust turning in the wound.

'Jesus Christ, and to think that I – I thought that . . .' She choked and the words caught in her throat, before bursting out, 'Oh for Christ's sake, just what are you? Are you really so incredibly fucking gutless!'

She stopped, then paused, the pressure of poison almost gone. Suddenly it didn't seem to matter any more. Anyway, what was there to say? Why try and hurt the poor sod any more?

Before she realized it the touch of pity was out as she heard herself say, 'You're just a poor miserable sod – gutless, sexless, and I suppose there's nothing anyone can do about it.' She paused as she stood over him, then in dismissal she turned, but as she walked away she said over her shoulder, 'Anyway, just get out. I don't want to see you again, now or ever.' But then the dregs of poison turned her again.

'And there's just one more thing. If I ever see you with any of my friends, then I warn you, I'll tell her, by Christ I will. Now just get out of this apartment. Go on, fuck off! Get packed and get out.' But he didn't move. So in sudden exasperation, she yelled at him.

'Hey –you, you little fag – can you hear me or are your ears blocked with shit? Go on, fuck off, just fuck off – get out of my life.' And with the final drop of poison at last spent she turned towards the sitting-room again.

She didn't hear him get up. It was the noise of his tread that started her turning, but she didn't make it. Her head exploded as the slap whipped it round. Stunned, she fell to the floor, and as she shook her head trying to clear it she began to hear him.

'. . . understand. I really thought you were someone. Yes, I was going to tell you. I don't like it – I hate it, and I thought that here, at last . . .' He strangled for a second as the tearing sob was wrenched from him. 'But you're like all the rest. You wouldn't recognize a human being if you saw one. When did you last do anything, anything at all, that wasn't either for you – number one – or wasn't bought? Yes, I've got a problem. It's me – what the hell am I? You're right. Just what the hell am I?'

It was agonizing, his crying more than his words. He just stood there, shaking with each great sob that seemed to be tearing him apart. Blankly she looked up at him, her mind in a turmoil. She felt that she ought to be tearing his hair out or something. But as she lay there she didn't feel any of the poisonous anger of just a few moments ago, or even outrage at the vicious slap. She felt pity – deep, deep pity, for she had never seen a human being disintegrate like this before and it was so awful that it hurt her. In the hall he had been abject, or seemed so, but whatever he had been it was still something to fight, to hurt, something to absorb punishment. But who killed a corpse! Without thinking about it she got up. The pain of the slap lost in the overwhelming emotion that here was something without rights or wrongs which just had to be stopped – this mental bleeding of the man – something no less real than a flow of blood from slashed wrists. And who stood by and just watched then?

'Look, sit down and I – I'll get us a drink, and we'll talk about it,' she heard herself saying uncertainly as she moved to him.

'Harry – Harry?'

She gave him a shake.

'Harry, listen to me. Are you listening?'

She could see he was trying to control himself. He nodded as he sat down. Thank God for that she thought as she went to the drinks tray. 'Here you are.' She wasn't sure how to handle it and it made her brusque. He took a long pull at his drink, then looked at the glass cradled in his lap. She watched him in silence. What the hell does one say at such moments? she wondered, but was relieved of the problem as he said, 'Jenny, I'm sorry. It's inadequate, I know, but I'm sorry.'

'What exactly are you sorry about?' she asked. She didn't mean to sound hard, but couldn't help it as pity for the man falling apart began to ebb away now that he seemed to be getting a grip.

'For you,' he replied. 'I'm sorry you had to see and hear and learn like that – must have been a horrid shock.'

She laughed, but without humour, as she said, 'You can say that again.'

'I'm sorry for what I am, and for involving you in it.' A prick of annoyance stirred in her.

'Harry, let's be clear. I am not, repeat not, involved. Whatever we had going for us just stopped. I'm sorry for you, and bloody angry, but that's it. You're just a guy I made a mistake with, so we split.' She made it as final as she could.

'But the future, Jenny. We can't just ignore it. What are you going to do?'

She misunderstood him. 'Do? What the hell's to do? You go, and that's it.'

'You won't tell anyone?' he asked.

Oh God! she thought, as she heard the pleading weakness in his voice. 'Who is there to tell? I shouldn't think you're the only pilot who's as queer as a crooked orange!' She regretted it the instant she said it – unnecessary now – so she added quickly, 'Sorry, I didn't mean to say it quite like that. What I mean is that it's none of my business.' Then she remembered her threat in the hall. 'But, as I said, you're not going to mess up the lives of any of my friends, so stay clear.'

'But you won't tell anyone, will you?'

'Oh for Christ's sake, of course not and stop sounding so bloody –' she searched for the word – 'oh, I don't know, so bloody impotent, or something – so beaten. Jesus! There must be thousands of people with your problem.'

'Thank you,' he said as he finished his drink. 'I'm just sorry that I couldn't get it sorted out without losing you.' Then looking down he began to add in a lower voice, 'You know he was the only one while we've been together, and I didn't go looking . . .'

'Stop it,' she cut in. 'I don't want to know. I just want you out of here. Do you understand?'

'Yes,' he said as he was getting up. 'Yes, OK. Yes – I'll go and pack – Jenny.'

She wished he hadn't used her name. As he went out of the door she called after him. 'And if I find anything of yours after you've gone, it goes straight out.' She didn't wait for a reply but got up to pour herself another drink.

She could hear him moving around as she sipped a scotch and soda, stretching out on the settee looking out from the big windows – out and over the city which, as an earthquake zone, had few high-rise buildings. She noticed the Bank of New Zealand building away to her right. One of the new universal images of success – expensive vanity units – to be found in all large cities. The inane death to cities as people were driven out, she thought idly. And Jesus, who in their right minds wanted thirty-storeyed buildings in Wellington? She gave it up with a mental shrug: some people would never see what was worth seeing. She raised her eyes to look across one of the best harbour views in the world, the line of hills beyond wonderfully beautiful in the clear golden light of the setting sun.

She was still gazing across the bay when she heard the door to the apartment close quietly behind Harry. She breathed a sigh of relief and idly fingered the little blister she had discovered – well, a lifetime ago – all of half an hour. Then, as she continued to sip her drink and gaze out at the hills over the water, etched sharp in nearly impossibly beautiful colours in the clear air, the thought struck her that she had a problem. She needed a flatmate to keep this pad on. Bugger Harry, she thought.

At the thought of Harry another entered her mind and she said quietly to herself, 'Oh God in heaven!' as she remembered that under the new schedules she would start to fly with Harry again on the Nandi run – the first of them tomorrow. It made her feel ill and miserable. And she began to worry about the next day. . . .

Rather later, as she poured herself a fifth drink, the janitor in the basement apartment closed his diary with a smile and locked it away.

She took her third sleeping pill at 2.30 in the morning. She knew she'd be hung-over the next day, but sleep, she had to have sleep. Anything to stop the merry-go-round of her mind. Other people, Nandi, Harry, other aircrew to pretend to. That prick – perhaps he'd bring charges. Was it legal to assault someone who upset you? Was it a criminal offence for men to kiss in private? Was it 'private' when they could be seen and heard, as she had seen and heard them? She kept seeing his back, but what was his face like? What had she done to him? She felt exhausted: had done so when she had gone to bed four hours ago, but her brain, oh God, why couldn't it just go to sleep and leave her alone? Then as her mind at long last began to fuzz, she saw Harry, in surgical white, and wanted to laugh – but she slept.

Chapter Two

Suddenly it was all a sickeningly spinning noise, falling and falling into a black, bottomless, sideless pit of enormous sound. . . . And she was wide awake in terror, heart pounding, sweating, her hand instinctively reaching out to the alarm, but unable to reach, held fast by her tight twisted sheets. Then she hit the off switch, and trembling slumped back for the last wisps of clear remembrance to sweep from her consciousness in her waking to reality. And in reality wet and windy Wellington was caught in its usual weather and she heard the gusting wind, the slap of rain. She looked out of the window at the rain being swept across the balcony in wild gusts of shifting wind. Then, the dream gone she held the present and found misery in anticipation of the inescapable nearness of Nandi – Harry. Sick nervousness caught her stomach, dampened her palms, and a stress headache twinged at the thought of meeting him again, her strength of yesterday gone with the night.

Captain Harry Standard looked at his watch. With relief he saw that at long, long last, it was almost 7.30. It had been the time he had set himself – oh so long ago – to ring room service. And he had waited and waited, conscious of every passing minute during the long stretch of the night. To begin with, as he left Jenny's sitting-room, his mind had been so troubled by the turbulence of conflicting emotions and thoughts that nothing had really registered beyond the stark facts . . . all too vicious, quick and shocking for contemplation at first.

In a daze he had packed with meticulous care and had become quite upset when he couldn't find a sock. In its escape into trivia his mind had seized upon the sock and been almost frightened of finding it too quickly. But in the search other trivia had arisen to the surface to bring postponement of the moment – perhaps when he left the security of the apartment – when the meaning of these stark facts would be unavoidable. And that he dreaded, for he feared the conclusions, and worse, the thought which would prompt them. So having found the sock he searched for something else to fill his mind.

When finally, reluctantly, he was packed, he spent time considering what to do with his key to the apartment. Of five possible places to leave it – he had carefully narrowed it down to five – he chose none, preferring to post it. Another triviality for later. Milk – perhaps he should leave a note reminding her, but after careful thought, he decided not to.

Then, almost suddenly, with no further excuse for delay he was standing in the hall, bags in his hands, yet still unable to face what might await him outside – Phil perhaps, maybe the police, certainly the beginnings of thought. But then the image of Jenny – hard, remorselessly hurtful Jenny – flooded his mind. The pain in her face and the obscene, destructive truth from her lips echoed in his mind. So he left, and shut the door as quietly as he would have done on death.

To avoid Bates he left the block via the car park below. Fearful that someone who wanted him might see him, he strode quickly with his head down, looking neither right nor left. He walked, intent on just one thing, and in his concentration on it was able to continue to avoid thinking about what had happened. He wanted to disappear, as wounded animals run to hide when hurt, to lick wounds and be safe until strong enough again to survive in a predatory world.

Soon he found himself passing the James Cook, a hotel used by stop-over aircrew though not by him. He stopped, wavering and uncertain, as a need to hide did battle with the risk of recognition, before he turned into the entrance. He avoided the receptionist's glance as he gave his name as William Barrett – the first that crossed his mind – then he looked away in his attempt to remain unknown. Covertly he glanced around, almost wishing he had kept on going and sought a place without any risk. But it was too late: he heard his room number and felt the key in his hand. His shake of the head at the offer of someone to carry his bags was almost lost as he fled. As the door of the room closed behind him it was just after 6.15 in the evening.

Within seconds, now hidden and alone, he abandoned himself to himself and cried his heart out. A psychiatrist would have said he was crying as a necessary prelude to rational thought – a catharsis which, if strong enough, would leave him capable of beginning to deal with the situation without professional help. The cause of grief: probably self-pity. The inescapable reality of exposure of self; his façade torn down by a normal girl in outrage. And so he wept bitterly. This left him comforted in exhaustion on the normal side of sanity, and not far from sleep. That had been at about 8 o'clock. But where peace of mind is an illusion, so is it tenuous. A single shaft of unbidden appreciation of reality was enough to destroy it and drive sleep away. The citadel of his mind was recaptured by the cohorts of doubt, fear, anxiety which marched in to torment him. But at least he had specific problems to save him – at first – from the wholly destructive torment of aimless, speculative worry.

Face to face with his homosexuality – what did it really amount to? Certainly nothing worse than, in fact not as bad as, his old self-deception that he really wasn't queer but just catholic in his tastes. A doctor, and perhaps a bit of treatment. Yes, he would do that, he thought to himself, as he remembered past pangs of fleeting self-disgust. And surely I wouldn't feel like that if I really weren't essentially male, he rationalized. And in the comfort of this logical and sequential conclusion, the problem seemed just then to be nothing to worry about.

Jenny. He thought about Jenny and equally swiftly skated over the harm he might or might not have done. He remembered some of what she had said – selectively. Invective to be expected from 'a woman scorned' he thought. And smiled grimly as the safety to himself of the corollary struck him: that a woman scorned would keep it to herself if she could, and Jenny would. And if tomorrow passed off OK, well then, she probably wouldn't even bother to get herself off his flight, and if so, well then there wouldn't even be that for anyone to wonder about. But even in his optimism it was a worry which, as the night went on, ate up optimism. For, unlike his homosexuality, her reaction was beyond his control. Yet though it was worrying, he tried to dwell on other thoughts – but couldn't.

So at last control gave way and Phil took over. Not the mild innocuous youth he had taken him for but a hard, ruthless, young man on the make, who had been damaged, and badly damaged – a young man he hadn't heard the last of. Of that he became more and more disturbingly certain as the hours of the long night ticked painfully past.

What might Philip, or whatever his name was, do, if only later? And in the knowledge that the young man could hurt him in many ways, Harry began to worry. Worry in the true sense. To know what harm might be ahead and to consider how to avoid it would have been OK. But not to know left Harry with only speculation, fear and then destructive, pointless anxiety. From time to time, in search of relief, his thoughts returned to Jenny – certainly a lesser worry, but as the minutes became hours, so it grew. And what of his homosexuality – was it so simple? What if it all got out? Life had been so bright until that afternoon.

It was a little after midnight that he first really needed a drink. But for fear that in some way he might betray himself, he hadn't tried to get one. Water didn't help. Then, for no clear reason he'd set himself 7.30 as the time he'd call room service, and in the hours that passed, that hour became his time of hope and release – he came to long for 7.30.

But now that the time was approaching to see Jenny again he began to feel increasingly nervous. He had felt sure that a light breakfast and a shower would release him from the troubles of the night. But as he looked out of the window, he didn't want a shower or breakfast, and the future even less. He felt cheated that 7.30 when at last it came had been irrelevant. He sat on the bed staring hopelessly out and let five minutes pass. Then, with a sigh, he finally reached for the phone and ordered coffee. Wearily, he then rang reception and told them he was checking out within forty minutes and arranged for a taxi. He had to be at the terminal by about 8.30. As he left the hotel he thought: so this is what the sword of Damocles is like. He felt exhausted, but it didn't help to dull the flutterings of nervousness in his gut. He hardly noticed he was already late.

Walking through the departure lounge on his way to check

in he didn't see Jenny. If he had seen her he knew her well enough to have been able to assess her mood at a glance, even her feelings. But she wasn't there. He must see her. He had taken half a dozen steps across the departure lounge when he faltered and stopped, the blood draining from his face as the awful thought cut through all other feelings that perhaps Philip had had his revenge, though not directly on him. Worse than that. Perhaps Philip's revenge was to burden him with the vicarious guilt of what had been done to Jenny. Oblivious of all around him, the thought took hold and his imagination began to dwell on what a ruthless young man could do to a girl who had scarred him for life and hurt him as he had never been hurt before.

'Oh God!' The words were torn from him in his sudden certainty that something dreadful had happened and Jenny wasn't going to turn up – wasn't able to turn up – perhaps would never be able to again.

Instinctively he walked on towards the line of airways check-in points on the way to the area manager's office. As he passed through the line one of the girls smiled at him. Mechanically he smiled back, but didn't really see her. She noticed it.

Almost unaware of it, he swung into the general office – big, and with Harry's flight due to roll in forty-eight minutes, busy in orderly chaos as everything from seat allocation to baggage, health, catering, weight, fuel, documentation and all the rest of the administrative nuts and bolts were tightened up by clerks in a hurry; people intent on making sure that forty-eight minutes would be just that, and not forty-nine.

The senior despatch clerk looked up as Harry came in and remembered the message on his desk. 'G'day, Captain,' he called out. But Harry didn't hear. He strode across the office to the smaller one off it which the senior clerk usually occupied. But now he was out in the thick of it, trouble-shooting. As the Captain brushed by him he looked up, nodded briefly, then returned to the problem of the heart case.

'Hey, Captain!'

This time Harry heard, and turned. 'Morning, Frank,' he said, striving to look normal as he recognized the clerk. 'Want me?'

'Yeah.' The clerk's New Zealand inflection was strong. 'Got this message for you.' He held out the bit of paper. 'Sounded like a bit of a weirdo to me,' he commented as Harry took the paper.

'Thanks.'

Giving the Captain another quick glance the clerk turned back to the manifesto. Aw well, can't be a dag every day, I suppose. Then work reabsorbed him.

The slip of paper shook in Harry's hand as he forced himself to be calm. To hide his feelings he walked on into the smaller office, glad that it was empty. Over-casually, though everyone was too busy to notice, he put his briefcase on the worn desk before sitting on the corner of it to face the door. Only then did he look at the piece of paper, his heart thumping. 'Call me 386460 by 9 or too late – Phil.'

It hit him hard, but no one noticed. He dialled the number, and shrank inside as he waited for the phone to be answered.

Philip let it ring, enjoying the sense of power it gave him. He could almost see the old fag sweating, praying even, that it wasn't too late. He looked at his watch. Seven minutes to nine. He sat back and the phone went on ringing.

He had slept well. His earlier blind rage had been swept away as he had begun to weigh up the possibilities of the thing. Played right, he finally decided just before going to sleep, he was on to the best thing that had ever come his way. His excitement had woken him early: woken him to lie in bed smoking and enjoying the thoughts of his revenge. At eight, he'd phoned the airline with an 'urgent family message' for Captain Standard. He'd dictated the message carefully and had it read back to him before getting the man's name and promise that Harry would have it. Then, the call made and still in bed, he had carefully checked again for flaws before, satisfied there were none, he relaxed to enjoy letting the time tick by, savouring the moment when the phone would ring.

Well, better put the fag out of his misery, he thought, as finally he stirred himself – but not with any great haste.

Harry looked at his watch. 8.54. He felt hot and clammy and the phone was damp in his hand as he held on. Oh for God's sake, answer, you little sod, he thought; but it just went on ringing. He looked at the message in his hand. Nine. But it wasn't nine. Dear God, make him answer . . . make him. The ringing stopped and all he could hear was his own breathing – too loud.

'Jesus, you been running, my old thingy?' and the boy laughed.

'Phil, I . . .'

'You what, Harry?' he cut in. 'You what? I'll tell you what. 'It's "you" nothing. It's me now, Harry, and it's going to be me for you for a long time to come, Harry. Can you hear me, my old thingy?'

'Yes, I hear you, Philip.'

'Now listen, old thing – you list'ning?'

'Oh for God's sake . . .' But then Harry stopped as he realized how bloody stupid it would be to antagonize the little sod further.

'Oh for God's sake what, my old Harry?' the boy purred. 'C'mon, what, my old thing? What d'ya wanna say, old thing? I'm listening.'

'I'm sorry, Phil.' The tone was conciliatory, almost pleading, as he continued. 'I'm sorry but I've got a flight out in just over half an hour and I'm behind on briefing already, so please, just tell me what it is you want.'

'Oh my dear old thing, how dreadful for you.' The boy was enjoying himself: it was lovely. 'Now, as I said just listen and answer a couple of questions – will you do that for your little boy? I am your little boy, aren't I? I mean, you won't mind my face will you, or the hole in my head your girl-friend made, will you, old thing?'

Harry's nerve snapped. 'For Christ's sake, just tell me what you want!'

'Well, let's see, old thing.' He pretended to think. 'Yes, first you mustn't lose that nice fat job of yours, Harry. No, that wouldn't do at all, would it?'

Harry looked at his watch. 9.01. He felt like yelling down the phone: God, it would slip from his trembling hand in a moment.

'OK, Captain?'

He looked up to see the area manager looking at him intently. He hadn't heard the man enter. Anxiously wondering whether the man had heard anything, he managed to reply 'Oh yes. Yes, thanks.' But the man went on looking at him. 'My father died,' he said in near desperation.

'What's that?' he heard down the phone.

'Hang on a moment,' he replied, as the man continued to stare at him.

'You going to be all right for this flight?' the manager asked.

'Oh sure. We weren't all that close, but still, it's a shock, just to hear suddenly – no warning, you know – best thing really.' He realized he was babbling, so forcing himself into an easier tone he added, 'Been ill for a long time – in his sleep last night – couldn't get me before.' He forced a smile while he tried to remember what he had been saying just before he had been noticed by the area manager.

The manager weighed it up. He hadn't in fact caught anything the Captain had said on the phone, but instinct told him that if he had any sense he would pull the Captain's relief in; he looked bloody awful. Harry could see that he had to do something to stop the decision, or the lie might come out and with it the truth. He felt sweat begin to trickle down his neck as, desperately, he tried to think. Then it came, and he heard himself saying, 'No sweat, don't worry, when I'm in the air I'll be fine . . . give me something to do . . . funny thing, really, the way it hit me. Must be the surprise, I s'pose.' He smiled as he added, 'To tell you the truth, the old man couldn't stand me. Haven't seen him in over a year.' Then, his bolt shot, and with a last smile to the man he returned to the phone. Philip was saying something, but he couldn't take it in as he waited to see what the man would do.

The manager looked at Harry, undecided. Perhaps it was OK. Harry Standard was as reliable as they come, but all the same he looked a bit crook. But the tone of voice as he heard Harry speak into the phone again and the smile made their point. With a shrug and a muttered 'All right, if that's what you want it's OK by me,' he left the office. He had problems enough as it was without making more.

With the man standing undecided Harry had turned back to the phone to say, 'Sorry, I didn't hear that. Would you say it again, nurse. Something to do with the body, was it?'

'Too bloody true, old thing. It will be a body if you don't fucking well watch it. Now, are you listening again?'

From the corner of his eye Harry saw the manager go. 'Yes, but quickly – please.'

'OK, OK, old thing. Now the second thing I want is for your girl-friend not to become the body you were on about, understand?'

Harry felt ill as he replied, 'No, I'm not sure I do.' But he felt relief at the same time – at least she was still OK.

'Oh, come on, Harry. You've got to protect her. That's obvious, isn't it?'

'From what?'

'Do I really have to spell it out, old thing?'

No, Harry thought. No, the little cunt didn't have to spell it out. So he said with weariness in his voice, 'No, Phil. No, I suppose not. How much do you want?'

'What you've got, Harry.'

His last bank statement had read $11,539 in savings and a small overdraft. 'I think I've got about $5,000 saved. I'd have to check, but it's about that.' He paused, with no intention of adding anything, but it was out before he could stop it. 'Will that buy you off, you miserable little bastard? God, you're . . .'

But the boy cut him off. 'My dear old thing, now you really mustn't work yourself up like this. You should leave that to me.' The boy laughed. 'I mean,' he added, 'I must do something for my money, mustn't I, and I do know what you like, my dear old thing. I can say that without a word of a lie, can't I, Harry old thing?'

'Stop calling me that!' It had snapped out before he could stop it.

'Temper, temper. You know you really must try to keep your cool, my dear old thing,' he said with cruel emphasis. He was enjoying this more than he thought he would.

'That's it then. I'll send you a cheque when I get back tomorrow, OK?'

'Five grand? Oh dearie me, no – you must be out of your tiny mind. No, no. But it'll do for starters, and keep the girl-friend all right till we meet again. Anyway don't worry, I'll be in touch, old thing.' And the phone went dead.

The area manager saw the Captain come out of the office and wondered whether he had made the right decision. But the Captain caught his eye and though the smile did nothing to erase the pain in his eyes, he was too far away for the manager to notice. And so he was reassured.

If the seething pit of the greater part of his mind – like a child with an adult's problem but no parent to solve it – was at all evident in pre-flight briefing, it showed in a slight coolness to those he had to deal with: the absence of the usual smile or little joke when it might have been expected. But, as the clerk had thought, so did others. Even a dag wasn't a dag all the time. Then, later, understanding came to the few who wondered further. 'Poor guy's old man died, what d'you expect?'

No one knew that his father had died eighteen years ago.

As Jenny looked out of the window at the squalling rain the nervousness of the unavoidable meeting with Harry began to churn inside her. The thought crossed her mind that it might be best to ring in sick. But then why the hell should Sheila – or whoever was her relief – be dragged in for the flight? If it had been her she would have kicked like hell. No, it wouldn't do, she thought. But even if it did and she escaped today, just how long would it be before she had to meet Harry? Days, at best. No, it would be better to go in and get it over with today, she decided.

To give herself strength, she reviewed the events of the past evening and worked up a few remnants of the strength of her feeling at the time. It gave her courage to say, 'He's nothing but a queer and you weren't to know,' and she said it to herself aloud. She avoided her own part; failure to think about Harry and put two and two together. For appreciation of her failure to herself wasn't what she needed right now, so the word 'queer' dominated her mind and she began to draw from it the strength she needed to meet him again. 'Pitiable, miserable sod', a 'fag', 'crooked orange': the words helped and she hung on to them as she dressed after an unsatisfactory shower. Surprisingly, she didn't feel particularly hung-over from the Mogadon, just a bit light-headed.

Despite the dampness in the city air, the Mini started first time. She noticed old Mr Bates on the steps to the apartment block as she drove away. Ignorant of his knowledge, she waved to him, and he waved back. The normalcy of it and the drive through the city – on and out past the Basin Reserve cricket ground – all helped her. The world was so normal: he wasn't, but she was. As she passed the roundabout into Cobham Drive she caught a glimpse of the Tower and was reminded of her last dinner at Plimmer House with Alex Granger. Plimmer House, a little timber-framed colonial house now nestling in a concrete jungle. Her memories of evenings spent there with other people carried her to the terminal car park, and drove away much of her nervousness.

Once in the building she was carried along by the chatter

of friends and the pre-flight work she had to do. You never know, she told herself almost cheerfully: perhaps you won't see him till Nandi. Suddenly, noticing the time, she realized that she was running late. Christ, she thought. At this rate the passengers will be on the plane before I am! She thumped the papers down on the desk and fled, Harry completely out of her mind for the first time since the evening before.

She beat the passengers to the DC8 by a couple of minutes but was late, which earned her a scowl from the Purser between professional smiles to those who paid for them. Later still he cornered her in the little galley.

'Well, where were you then? You were ten minutes late.'

'Oh, you know, last-minute things. I had to take some bumf up,' she said airily.

He wasn't satisfied. But worse, she wasn't satisfied, and became even less so as she realized she had deliberately been late so as to try and avoid Harry. The thought kept bugging her behind the calm tranquillity of the lovely smile she handed out to the paying herd as they flew north.

Chapter Three

'Morning, Captain.'

Half bent over the pre-flight briefing documents, the co-pilot continued to watch Harry Standard walking to join him.

'Hi, Sam.' Being behind schedule, he added, 'Got snarled up on the phone.' Nodding towards the documents, he asked, 'Any curlies?'

'No, pretty well OK. Just a med and a VIP on board – LeRoy. Apparently he's the Financial Director. Never met 'im myself. Know him?'

'No.'

'Anyway, I've checked this lot out.'

'OK, you go on out. Won't be long.'

'Right.'

Sam Meadows, short, dark, with a mop of hair and a chubby, handsome face in a rather unexpectedly beaten-up sort of way for someone of twenty-eight, nodded and turned to walk away.

'Oh by the way, Sam, who's our Flight?'

'Flight? Harvey. You know Harvey Jones.' He looked at his watch. 'He went out 'bout ten to, I s'pose. OK?'

'Oh yes, of course – stupid of me.'

Walking away, Sam wondered to himself. Not like Harry to forget who his engineer was. In fact, come to think of it, he really didn't seem all that bright. Still, he smiled to himself, the old ram's probably feeling the strain. But funny about the engineer.

Left to himself Harry turned to work – a welcome escape. He worked quickly, following the route through the met print-out. Blocks of figures in squared segments of the flight path: wind speed, direction and temperature to be expected en route; pressure taken to be the international flying standard; 1013 millibars to ensure standard altimeter readings for all aircraft flying at 11,000 feet plus. He was due to cruise at 35,000 feet. Below 11,000 and the QNH – actual pressure at sea level – was what was used to calibrate the altimeter. He noticed it was 1013 millibars.

He flicked the page over to look at Nandi Terminal local weather, then Sydney Airport local, the divert if Nandi closed in-flight. It could happen, and the thought of the guy who had bailed out into the violence of a cumulo nimbus tower crossed his mind. The guy'd been two hours on the end of a chute. At times he'd been rocketed up at 200 feet per second. He'd survived – just. Comforting to have weather radar aboard.

He flicked over to the next page of the met report; as on TV, a graphic of fronts – lows and highs showing wind and cloud expectations as well. That's OK, he murmured to himself, now for the flight plan.

He glanced at the in-flight info sheets. A plan to be followed. Fuel usage to elapsed time and spent distance on predetermined tracks – headings from beacon to beacon in the hands of Air Traffic Control. The aircrew's job was to fly the plane under precise instruction from the moment of starting to taxi, to shut down. Deviate from those instructions and there'd be an inquiry, fire or emergency the only excuses, and even then no change in altitude or course without clearance from the ground and new instructions (except in the case of the immediate necessity of a cabin blowout).

With care, customary care, Harry followed the plan through before turning to the latest and special ATC briefing prepared on the most up-to-date information covering each point of flight reference. Nothing to worry about there, except the Nandi NOTAM where the ILS was on test. Not that it mattered: with the weather good, they'd land visual. Satisfied, he turned to check the fuel rundown. Most documents he merely signed as read, understood and accepted, but he had to fill in that requisition personally.

Flight time, anticipated, 3 hours 38 minutes – 1654 statute miles – ramp weight of the DC8 217,000 lbs, subject to minor corrections when the final all-up accurate load sheet was brought out to the flight deck minutes before rolling.

Cruising speed 470 knots. Fuel usage in cruising – the most economical usage in flight, save on descent – 6300 lbs per half hour, give or take a bit on wind and current engine performance. Burn-off before take-off 1200 lbs. The data mounted up to a fuel requirement of 42,420 lbs which was about 3-5 per cent generous. But with the extra holding reserve for an hour at Nandi in the event of trouble before a final divert to Sydney, and enough for an hour stoodging around there as well, and the figure came to 64,800 lbs of fuel on board.

As Harry worked through the pre-flight briefing info, the fuel was being pumped under high pressure into six of the nine tanks. 64,800 was well below the maximum load. The restricted articles sheet read nil. He signed it, glad he wasn't carrying explosives or uranium 325 or whatever. With time now pressing and the fuel requisition dealt with, he glanced quickly at the passenger information list. One special diet – the Purser's problem. And, as he picked up his bags he hoped the heart case wouldn't have a coronary and the guy from the company just wouldn't bother him.

As the Captain made up for time lost in the office, Harvey Jones was busy. Small, dark and wiry, with eighteen years behind him in the job, he'd known DC8s for years. This old girl, he thought as he walked out to the plane, must be twelve years old, but not in bad shape really. So used to the roar of the GPU supplying power to the systems he didn't notice the noise as he stepped over the umbilical cord of thick power cables – cables which were only unplugged when the plane came under power, all engines spinning, removal of chocks the last job.

'G'day.' So used to it that he didn't realize he bellowed, he greeted the gas bowser chief. The man raised a hand. They'd have a moment together later on the flight deck after the refuelling to compare gauge readings. Out by a few hundred pounds, and the plane would be grounded. Leaving his bags at the gantry, he started his external inspection for oil and fuel leaks and damage, and anything else he didn't like the look of. Tyres OK, he thought, as he noticed the radial rings were still nice and deep, but habit forced him to stop as he noticed the heavy scuff on one nose wheel. OK, he thought, but wondered who'd let the old girl down heavily. Walking under the wings he misjudged the melting ice from the last in-bound flight and swore as a drip smacked his neck. Going on round the gear he looked carefully between each set of four main wheels for hydraulic leaks. Finally, happy about the external, he climbed the steps into the plane to begin his internal. As he put his briefcase on his seat to the right and back of the cramped flight deck behind the co-pilot's seat, he said 'Wotcha.'

Sam twisted his head round. He'd come on board while Harvey had been aft. 'Hiya.' He smiled briefly and nodded before going back to making up the NavLog, the blueprint for the flight. It was used leg by leg to feed the Doppler, a square box overhead on the console between the pilots. Five windows. First, the across track, and then the two legs, each with its two windows. Miles to fly, which would tick back to zero on the pre-set direction track for the leg, then the second leg, then the third on one again and on till flight's end. He began to set the first leg and figures twirled in the windows. Foolproof point-to-point navigation, and Air Traffic kept the other buggers away. The Doppler, he noticed from the report, was reading point six left of heading – something to be allowed for.

The Flight Engineer started to walk through the cabins. They had to be clean and tidy, but most on his mind was the equipment check, including eleven oxygen bottles. He glanced at each gauge to see that all were in the red. He hoped the heart case would be OK. Not the worst thing that could happen, of course. Far worse would be a quick blowout – abrupt and devastating loss of cabin pressurization – rare, very rare. In fact he'd only ever heard of it happening a few times over the years, but still, just like this old crate, planes got older. If not too sudden it would merely be serious but still safe. As cabin pressure sank to below the ambient pressure of 11,000 feet the little doors above each seat would automatically spring and masks would drop. He opened the door in the roof just short of the aft galley and looked at the two large oxygen bottles. Readings normal: oxygen enough for all on board for half an hour. But then, with a wry smile, the thought struck him that they probably wouldn't be much of a life-line if the worst happened – a sudden and complete blowout at 35,000 feet where pressure was down to about 300 millibars – less than a third Ground QNH.

He wasn't a very imaginative man, but fleetingly caught hold of the sudden vision of passengers near the blowout being sucked like malleable sausages through the rent and others, shocked, gasping for air not there, strangling red, blue, then death. Bloated tongues, rupturing ear drums, blood pouring out of noses, sightless . . . his mind shut it out. It wouldn't happen. Door chutes checked, he went back to the flight deck. In striding through the first class cabin he met the Captain coming up. 'G'day, Cap'n.'

But as old friends, the greeting suddenly became personal when he saw Harry's face. 'Hey, Harry.' He went up close to him so that none of the white-overalled ground crew hurrying by would hear him. 'Harry, you OK?' There was concern in his voice. Harry turned a haggard glance towards the Flight Engineer.

'Oh Harvey, good to see you again.' Then, as the question sank in, he raised a smile. 'Sure, fine. Just didn't get enough sleep last night. Guess it shows at my age!'

'Yeah, well it looks like you had one hell of a night,' he grinned. Harry laughed – or part of him, the façade, did as he went on into the flight deck. 'How goes?'

'OK,' Sam replied from the co-pilot's seat as he held out the NavLog to Harry who was settling himself in the Captain's left-hand driver's seat. Harry took it and began to check the figures. He glanced up at the Doppler to check, then back to the sheet.

Meanwhile, Sam set up both comms boxes to frequency 118·7 for first check-out to the Tower. Harvey was doing the fuel systems integrity checks: tanks to tanks to engines.

'Flight – your input figures.'

Harvey glanced up at the bowser chief and taking the figures checked them against flight-deck readings. 4 was down 80 lbs and 8 up 40. 'OK.' He signed the chit before going back to the checks.

The passengers were walking out to the plane as the bowser drove away. The noise of the roaring GPU pouring its power made some of them turn their heads away as they passed.

The first class hostess, cool and beautiful at the beginning of the trip, a petite, slim, auburn-haired girl who made the uniform look good, came on to the flight deck to ask 'Cold drinks?' 'Aw, not for me, thanks.' Harvey never liked anything to drink before the routine 'top of climb' coffee. 'Yeah, please.' Sam gave her his brilliant, full-of-promise, 'I mean it' smile. Pretty well all hostys got the benefit of it, but she hadn't exactly danced around in its warmth he thought as he went back to checking the flight-deck voice recorder. Every transmission in or out, every word said on the flight deck – all recorded.

'Captain?'

'Great,' he flung across his shoulder. Thank God Jenny wasn't on first, he thought.

He went back to checking the performance requirements for take-off. The load sheet had just arrived. He noted the temperature of the day on his flight pad clipped to the stick. Total load, head winds element on take-off – an extra 20 knots and the plane would lift an extra 12,500 lbs with the same power setting – and he noted the QNH at 1013. Turning from the data, he began to compute figures from the performance tables and scribbled down the answers on the pad. That completed he leaned forward and set the little white indicator bugs on the air speed indicator.

The co-pilot followed on to make his own independent analysis, and the Flight Engineer continued to check the progressive servicing data on the engines and made a note to keep an eye on the vibration indicator on starboard 2. A little concerned, he also noted that port 1 had shown an excessive fuel usage on the last trip of 3·8 per cent. Over 5, it would mean an engine replacement: an eight-hour job, though the engineers reckoned on less than six and a half, a matter of pride and job satisfaction.

'What do you make it, Sam?' the Captain asked.

Sam looked at his pad. 'Check at 80.' Both men looked at the little white bugs they had set on the speedo.

'Check,' Harry said.

'V1 112.'

'Check.'

'Rotate 127.'

'Check.'

'V2 141.'

'Check.'

'Pitch 12 degrees.'

'Check.'

As the first and second class stewards closed and locked the exit doors, the Purser came on to the flight deck with the drinks. He liked to meet his flight crew and it was an excuse.

'Here you are, Captain. I don't think we'll have any trouble with the heart case. Says he's pretty fit. Flew in two days ago.'

'Thanks, Purser. Any trouble and you know where to come.'

In the tourist class, Jenny, bright, cool and with a comforting smile for the obviously nervous, was down the aisle giving out sweets and checking seat belts, determined not to even think of Harry. He was just a captain, and, thank God, she'd swapped with Viv to take the tourist. Viv had thought her mad.

Harry sat back for a moment to think if there was anything to do before he started the checks, and remembered the new bit of gear on board.

'Sam, ever heard this—er—ground proximity warning system?'

Sam shook his head and Harry reached up to the test button and pulled it. The cabin was suddenly filled with a high-pitched WHOO WHOO followed by a noise that only Lee Marvin at the bottom of his range could have made, BUUURRP BUUURRRP.

'Jesus! What the hell was that?' Harvey asked, as he jerked his head round in surprise.

'If we're in trouble, that's it,' Harry replied.

'Jeez! I wonder how much it cost them to discover a noise

like that,' Sam laughed. Unable to resist it, worries forgotten for a second, Harry smiled and pulled the tit again.

In the first class cabin, LeRoy beckoned to the Purser.

'Purser, what was that?'

'Oh, just part of the checking of flight equipment, sir,' he replied blandly. As far as passengers were concerned, all noises were this. But as the airline's Financial Director settled back again to return to the distribution cost profile, the Purser wondered what on earth the noise had been.

'OK, Sam? Harvey?'

'Ready,' replied the co-pilot.

'OK,' replied the Flight Engineer, and they all looked down at the DC8 flight checklist, Part B. Volume 2, Section I. A wire-spiral bound aircrew bible headed:

NOTE: ALL ITEMS MUST BE CHECKED AND THOSE IN CAPITALS MUST BE READ ALOUD (CHALLENGE AND RESPONSE).

Each of the crew would have his section to go through and each response carried responsibility. In its red card pages were the emergency drills.

'SEAT BELT AND PEDALS'

The Captain and co-pilot adjusted theirs to give them comfortable pressure on the pedals – big pedals to either side of the stick. Pressure on the toes, and the mammoth disc brakes to the wheels were brought on; pressure at the heels operated the rubbers.

'Check,' replied the co-pilot. The engineer didn't have to respond.

'PARKING BRAKE AND PRESSURE. . . .'

Sam's response before start-up completed, he made his first check on the radio.

'Wellington Tower – this is Paranational Zulu Delta. How do you read me on box one?'

'Paranational Zulu Delta – reading you five this frequency – weather Juliet current – QNH 1013 – time check 21 and 15 seconds.'

Sam glanced at his pad and confirmed 1013, then at the altimeter to confirm correct for take-off. He noticed that the synchronized dash clocks were out, and corrected. Harry nodded.

The time was just after 9.21.

'Paranational Zulu Delta starting in three minutes – testing box two.'

'Paranational Zulu Delta – reading you five.'

As the checks went on between pilot and engineer Sam switched box two to frequency 120·3 for contact with the Departures Director at the Centre for identification of the new paint on the Controller's screen after take-off.

'PRE START CHECKS COMPLETE.'

'Check.'

'Check.'

'Paranational Zulu Delta starting engines.'

'Paranational Zulu Delta' replied the Tower Controller, turning to the Tower Coordinator for confirmation, which was given with a nod 'cleared to start'. Then he flicked the console switch to the Terminal Procedure Controller in the hushed cavern of the IFR room at the Centre of Control, half a mile away; a room without windows, only radar screens on which the controllers watched the airspace for miles around.

'Yep?'

'Paranational Zulu Delta starting.'

There was a pause as the Procedure Controller checked for conflict in terminal airspace, the flight progress strips giving the up-to-date position of everything in the area. Briefly he conferred with Departures radar.

'Yeah, Paranational Zulu Delta cleared Nandi Flight Plan route 35,000 feet – maintain 5000 feet to Porirua North,' and reaching across for the flight progress strip made out for the DC8, he marked it RTO (released for take-off). Then he turned to the Departures Controller in front of his screen and told him of the clearance. Departures entered it on the identical strip in front of him. He'd see the plane within ten minutes on the screen and, as a matter of procedure, be contacted within three miles of take-off while it was still below 1500 feet for positive identification. He leaned back in his chair. He wasn't very busy.

In Comms, at the Centre, a Decca 25-channel recorder turned with a constant hum in its air-conditioned room, recording every spoken word.

On the flight deck the 'starting engines phase', a ten-point procedural checklist, was almost complete. Just the last engines to start.

'PORT OUTER CONTACT.'

'Contact,' replied the Flight Engineer.

Its isolation cut, power fed into the starter motor, the noise from the GPU still connected to the jet by its umbilical cord now lost in the overwhelming whine of the other three engines spinning on power towards operating parameters. The port outer turbine began to spin – an engine so well-balanced that, at rest, a 10-knot wind would stir the blades to be seen in the nascelle. As operating speed approached, the starter disengaged and the engine began to whine to a high pitch to join the others. Pending all engine operational parameters mark-up, there was a lull on the flight deck. Almost idly, the pilot and his co watched the centre console gauges.

The lights for FASTEN SEAT BELTS and NO SMOKING were on in the cabin; the passengers murmured amongst themselves, pretended to sleep, chewed sweets, or just sat and looked vacant, or read. But some were excited. Children, constantly finding things to point out to parents, longed to get going, hardly able to wait for the next deliciously scary experience, though some were quiet: wide-eyed they sat in nervous trust of 'grown up' capability – and one small boy cried in his naked fear.

'OK, Harvey?'

'OK, Skip.'

'Right, we'd better be on our way,' Harry said. And Sam took his cue.

'Paranational Zulu Delta requesting taxi clearance.'

'Paranational Zulu Delta cleared to holding position, runway 34. You're second to go after the Cessna.'

'Paranational Zulu Delta.'

As the passengers, or some of them, were surprised at the bumpiness in taxiing, the taxiing checklist – all systems go – went on on the flight deck: a 39-point checklist – the longest of them all.

In the Tower, the Coordinator watched the DC8 roll slowly on whilst the Controller dealt with getting the Cessna off the ground. Funny little things, the Controller thought, as the Cessna set off. A short run, and it seemed to hop into the air, wobble a bit as the pilot caught a bit of Wellington's venturi effect wind, then it was away. As it went he took the strip off his board and concentrated on his next customer. Glancing out from the height of the Tower over the panoramic spread of the airport, he noticed that the DC8 was about halfway to the holding point.

'Paranational Zulu Delta, your clearance available. Are you ready to copy?'

Sam flicked the switch on the left horn of the half-wheel which topped his stick. 'Paranational Zulu Delta affirmative.'

'Paranational Zulu Delta is cleared to Nandi – Flight Plan Route – level 35,000 feet – depart Porirua one – maintain 5000 to Porirua North.'

Equally clipped and concisely Sam read back the clearance from the note he'd made on the pad clipped between the horns.

'Paranational Zulu Delta clearance correct. When airborne, contact radar on one two zero decimal three. You are cleared for take-off.'

Sam glanced at box two to check the frequency as he acknowledged.

Now that they had about two hundred yards to run to the runway start Harry flicked his intercom button. 'Cabin crew to take-off stations.'

Jenny was about to strap herself in at the back of the tourist cabin when to her horror she saw a thin, spiralling telltale tendril of smoke rising from one of the seats near the front. She was up like a shot. Then, obeying the first rule, 'Never upset the passengers', she forced herself to walk calmly down the aisle towards the offender. 'Jesus Christ,' she thought to herself as she approached the little, fat, bald Englishman, 'can't the idiot read?'

He looked up at the nice little girl beside him, so pretty in the uniform, and not hearing what she said smiled benignly at her in encouragement. More loudly, and with her smile still just hanging on, she said, 'I'm so sorry, sir, but you'll have to put your cigarette out. No smoking is allowed until the sign goes off.' She pointed to the illuminated strip. Blankly he looked at his cigarette. She felt the aircraft begin to turn on to the runway. Oh for God's sake, put it out, you silly little bastard, she thought, as she watched him grope for understanding. 'Oh! Oh yes, I see now, yes. Out, you say? Yes, very well.'

She felt the plane stop. Come on, come on, she thought. Then finally she saw him begin to grind it out. Yes, she'd remember him, she thought. First that damn fool question when they were demonstrating the use of the life jackets and now this. Drinks slopped with a smile for you, she thought, as she went as slowly as she dared back down the aisle. She reached her seat as the plane began to strain on take-off power, to go at any second.

On the deck, Harry watched the ERP settings being reached by the engines: the pressure difference between engine inlet and outlet. With concentration he made some fine adjustment to the throttles. It looked good. He even felt good. Phil couldn't get at him in the air. As soon as he remembered, he wished he hadn't, because unbidden, the thought followed that he'd be back in Wellington within thirty-six hours or so, and then what? Mentally diving away from it he shot back to lose himself in professionalism but didn't make it before a final thought came and went. OK now, busy: but in the air – oh God!

'Ready to roll, Captain.' The Flight Engineer's unnecessary comment brought him back and he realized they'd been over time on position. 'Bugger,' he said to himself. Usually he told his passengers, all 158 of them this time, that they had been cleared for take-off, etc. He'd forgotten.

Jenny noticed the omission, and despite her determination not to think about Harry she couldn't help wondering how he was up front. A flicker of fear went through her as, for the first time, the thought went through her mind that perhaps Harry was in no fit condition to fly. The problem was that really, in practice, it was the captain who decided whether or not he was fit. True, other people – his aircrew – could ground him, but it would have been a brave guy who did it. The area manager could, but again it would take some guts. So theoretically a captain could fly when sick, and as long as he wasn't paralytically so he might get away with it. Fleetingly she wondered about Harry. Could it be that he was sick but so subjective as not to know it? She tried to remember who the co-pilot was. She knew his face but not much more about him. He looked young, and she sent up a silent prayer that he'd have the guts to make the decision to take over if Harry packed up. NO! Christ, no, long before that, she amended her prayer. But then she smiled at her fears; so far as she knew he was OK and whatever else he might or might not be, he was a bloody good captain.

'OK. Rolling.' Harry let the brakes off and the big plane began to roll. As they started Sam and Harvey checked power settings – more critical now than at any other time. Then Sam turned to the airspeed indicator and watched the needle begin to rotate clockwise from the one o'clock position. As it tipped the first bug he called 'eighty knots'. Harry had seen it come up on his indicator. It was the only check they could do on the instrument in front of them. In fact it was only in flight that several instruments could be checked. Speed increasing, Harry concentrated on keeping the plane stable as it arrowed down the 6350 foot runway, too short for jumbos.

'V1'. Sam's voice was crisp as he notified his captain that they were now past the point of no return. V1 was passed at 112 knots – airspeed. Harry's eyes didn't flicker, but for all it mattered he could have been blind. His feet, hands and senses told him all he needed to know to keep the plane stable and straight down the runway. It was all 'feel' – the brain sensitive to every movement of the vast, rushing body of the machine. He sensed VR was about to come up and waited for it.

'Rotate.' Sam's voice was sharp, and Harry, like an automation – large part of a pilot's job – hauled back on the stick. As the nose rose its first few degrees he lost visual and switched his eyes to the green ball of the altitude indicator. It swung on its axis one line past the black reference etched on the instrument's glass. 10 degrees of inclination, and as it passed the point he eased a trifle and held it at 12. Speed 127 knots.

'V2.' 35 feet off the deck and speed 141 knots. 'Flaps retracted.'

He saw Sam reach forward to deal with the heavy landing gear lever. 'Gear up.' The wheels obediently bedded into the body with a sigh from the plane's hydraulics. Then climbing away Harry set the plane up for a climb of 700 feet a minute – a standard 3-degree climb. Stabilized, he relaxed as he heard

Sam make his first contact with Departures.

'Paranational Zulu Delta establishing contact.'

The Departures Director had seen the paint begin on his screen.

'Paranational Zulu Delta – identified on Departure – now cleared to 35,000 feet and at Porirua North contact Wellington Airways Control on one two three decimal seven.'

'Paranational Zulu Delta.'

Cleared now to above 5000 feet over Porirua North, 46 miles north of Wellington, Harry stepped up the rate of climb, then settled back to the next procedure, the after take-off checks – fourteen of them. Still something to do, thank God, he thought. Sam was resetting box one to Airways on 123·7.

On the Airways, the flight strips for Zulu Delta were marked with its ETAs at the next three beacons. Anticipated overhead Porirua now in four minutes, then another 90 miles north at Waverley in another eight minutes, then Ohura 150 miles on in another eleven minutes. All monitored, all seen on radar.

The plane's DME homing in on Porirua gave a dead reckoning distance to the beacon of eight miles. The Captain's eyes switched to the ADF, its needle slowly pivoting to the downward vertical to indicate overhead the beacon. It was superimposed on a needle, which swung against a degree scale. Pass left or right of the beacon and it would tell him his degrees away from centre overhead. When computed with his height, he'd know his precise position and could check for straying.

They passed directly overhead as the needle hit bottom with no deviation. As the Captain's first leg, he made the transmission. Sam, he noticed, was deep in a book. Not permitted, of course, but aircrew are human, flights long and usually tedious.

'Paranational Zulu Delta Porirua North at this time through flight level 17,000 for flight level 35,000 feet. Estimated time Waverley 46.'

He was glad they hadn't been late on take-off. Bang on 9.30, a few seconds past perhaps, but what the hell. Yes, he thought to himself, he'd be at Waverley by 9.46, sixteen minutes' flying time and 136 miles outbound.

'Paranational Zulu Delta – roger,' Airways confirmed.

*

Slowly they went up to 35,000 feet. Coffee came as he made his cruising transmission, which almost coincided with coming up to the end of Wellington Airspace.

'Paranational Zulu Delta now flight level 35,000 feet.'

'Roger Paranational Zulu Delta. At Ohura contact Auckland one two six decimal seven.' He made a note and switched box two to the new frequency. Auckland Airways next.

The Captain stretched and as he drank coffee he told the passengers a bit about the trip, as captains do. Coffee finished, they did the short cruising flight checks.

Auckland Airways waited for Zulu Delta to enter their airspace.

Well north of Wellington now, the ADF needle again bottomed on Ohura beacon. 'Auckland, this is Paranational Zulu Delta – crossing Ohura at this time, flight level 35,000 feet.'

Because he wanted to be busy, Harry made it a long leg out past Auckland Oceanic Control, through Cauldron, and then the 296-mile leg to Cascade, the next reporting point. En route from Cauldron to Cascade, between New Zealand and Fiji, Auckland Oceanic transferred the flight to Nandi Oceanic Control. The DC8, 301 miles on, passed Crater Lake and the Control Oceanic Boundary and so into Nandi hands. Sam reset the Doppler for the last leg in from Silver Fern, waited till he could report the overhead then passed control to his captain.

But Harry didn't hear. He was lost in the morass of misery which yesterday had brought him and this morning had confirmed. If only he knew what the little sod wanted. But it was the uncertainty of the future which really bothered him. He had repeatedly shied away from thinking about it, but he couldn't, so the thought kept tormenting him. More as wishful thinking than anything else, he'd toyed with the idea of going to the police – blackmail – but rejected the idea as he realized that though he would be Mr X in court, the police would know and somehow it was bound to get out, if not to the general public, then certainly to those who mattered in the airline. With nothing to do on Sam's leg his mind seethed with the problem.

'Captain!' The unaccustomed sharpness in the co-pilot's

voice brought the Flight Engineer's head round. For a moment he looked at the two backs and faces turned in profile to each other, then he shrugged and turned back to his tall, vertical instrument-studded console.

'Sorry, Sam. Miles away.'

'Your leg.'

'Oh. Right.'

Sam could see – and it was very puzzling – that Harry had missed Silver Fern. 'Just reported Silver Fern,' he said. At first the Captain merely nodded.

Chapter Four

The nod was instinctive and so much easier than the near physical effort required to blot out the misery from his mind. To help reorientate himself he looked up at the Doppler. 'Right. Taking over – I have control.' But try as he would, he couldn't avoid occasional bubbles of worry bursting through the morass seething just below the surface of his mind.

The formality over, Sam looked covertly at the Captain. He was not particularly concerned, but obviously the guy was being bugged by something. But not to worry, he thought to himself as he returned to his book, he seems to be OK.

Harry didn't want the flight to end; he wished he could do a turn-round instead of a slip. He worried about living with Jenny in the same hotel; he wondered how to deal with Phil back in Wellington. That is until the job and descent checks brought relief again as the DME, locked into Nandi, told him it was just 119 miles away now.

12 miles from touch-down, Sam said, 'LANDING GEAR DOWN – THREE LIGHTS,' to complete the landing checks.

'Check.' 10½ miles to touch down. The altimeter, corrected on descent through 13,000 feet on to actual ONH of 1004 millibars, read 2340 feet. A touch high went through Harry's mind as he eased the stick fractionally forward. The descent went on without a hitch. With full flap now and airspeed at only eight knots above landing speed, the big plane swept down and Sam concentrated on the altimeter. Little was said between the aircrew as the plane continued to lose altitude through 1000 feet and on down.

They hit 500 feet with their descent rate standard at 800 feet per minute and it was then that Sam began to call out altitude deviation. At the 400-foot target 'plus 10' – altitude 410 feet.

Harry eased the stick a shade forward, the throttles slightly back, then called the Tower on box two.

'Paranational Zulu Delta making contact.'

In the Tower, the Controller, who had been watching the jet's approach, acknowledged. 'Paranational Zulu Delta roger.'

'Plus 2.'

150 feet, Harry leaned forward to the throttles as they passed over the end of the runway. Marked by more black rubber slicks than bands of white at touchdown he throttled back with 133 knots registering before lifting the nose. After a moment's hesitation, the wheels touched to the screech of tortured rubber to set them spinning.

'Spoilers,' Sam called, as they triggered to the impact of landing. Tightening his grip on the knuckle bar the Captain prepared for reverse thrust, waiting for the co-pilot's call. 'Four lights.' Then Harry pulled it over. The jet tails blanked as the side vents opened and the plane began to brake as it swept down the runway in the shuddering roar of reverse. Finally with speed falling away to last transmission of the flight. 'Paranational Zulu Delta – request taxi clearance.'

The Tower Controller answered 'Paranational Zulu Delta – cleared via north taxiway to gate 3. Welcome to Nandi.'

To dying engines, they began the final shutdown checks on the flight deck. 'Flight library and desk stowage items' – the clear up.

Harry didn't hurry. In the brilliant glare of the sun he noticed the GPU in position, the ground crew and engineers outside, and the first straggle of the passengers walking away, some talking, some solitary souls, some swallowing, their ear-drums still a little painful; businessmen in light suits carrying jackets, already sweating in the humid heat; children, trailing along reluctantly, clutching bears and bits. He noticed the high loaders coming out, the baggage trucks. All the activity to finish the flight; all the activity to prepare the plane for the slip crew's return run in the early afternoon. He noticed the Purser hovering at the back of the flight deck. 'Ah! Purser. OK back there?'

'Our VIP asked me to thank you for a pleasant trip. Apart from a couple of kids sick I think that's it.' Then he added with a smile, 'At least our heart case held out.'

'Very good, and thank you,' he said in dismissing him.

At last he saw what he was waiting for: the cabin crew walking away. He gave an exaggerated yawn and rubbed both hands down his face to let them gain a few more yards. Then, unable to delay Sam and Harvey longer, he got up and picking up his gear followed them out of the plane. The job done, he felt unutterably weary: so tired, suddenly, that his brain just crumpled. He completed final administration almost in a daze.

The time was 1.33 and the day was February 7th. As he was driven the half a mile to the Gateway he decided to have lunch sent along to his room and to try to sleep, and so avoid Jenny.

Jenny had left the plane as quickly as she could. Her fears of being 'turned over' by Customs proving groundless, she had got out of the terminal quickly. In the taxi with Viv she felt dried up inside. Perhaps it was the Mogadon, or too much anxiety, but for once the purples, mauves and impossible pinks of the Bougainvilia passed by unnoticed. She barely noticed the jolt the taxi gave as it drew near the main road it had to cross before arriving at the hotel, the jolt over the narrow-gauge tracks connecting the sugar plantations to the refinery with its ever-present smell of molasses.

The taxi swept round the drive to the hotel. As she paid the driver it struck her that all the *entrepreneurs* in Fiji seemed to be Indians. She wondered why. She smiled, tiredly recalling the taped greetings to passengers as they entered the terminal at the end of a flight *'Ni Sa Bula.* Welcome to the holiday islands of Fiji'; the Indians did well out of it. Odd about the Indians, she thought, as she waited at the reception desk, shivering because of the sudden drop in temperature. It was quiet in the hotel.

She rang the old-fashioned reception bell in irritation. The girl came out from the office with a bored yawn. The hostess seemed familiar. The yawn was replaced with a bright smile. 'Good afternoon. You must be off the flight from Wellington,' she greeted Jenny.

'Yes. Jenny Carol.'

The receptionist consulted the bookings register. 'We've put you in 36.' She indicated the left-hand wing corridor. 'It faces out on to the pool.'

'Thanks,' Jenny replied as she took the key, with a smile.

The pool looked like the most wonderful thing in the world as she stepped out of her french windows on to the patio that surrounded it. The heat brought little beads of perspiration to her upper lip. How cool and inviting it looks, she thought, and its tranquil blueness beckoned and promised release from tiredness, tension and the past. She wanted a swim, but not exposure to Harry.

She felt quite irritated. To hell with him, she thought. Why should I worry? Oddly enough it was Harry, and not the boy, who worried her. Perhaps it was because the boy was a stranger. In her room she stripped off. In the long mirror she regarded herself critically, and pirouetted on her toes. You've got a super figure, kid, she told herself. It wasn't vanity, or even narcissism. She was a very lovely girl.

As she stepped out of her room, Harry was checking in. Soon afterwards he heard the splash. His room was almost opposite hers. He watched as she swam to the side of the pool: took in her loveliness while she walked back to the board to stand poised for a still brief second before running to hit the board hard. He watched her arrow up and away, and jacknife into a straight, clean entry. It was beautiful, and his heart ached for what he'd lost. He cursed himself and in mounting bitterness and despair, drew his doors closed on the pool and in on himself and lay down on the bed. He cursed whatever it was that had blurred his sexual definition, cursed his hateful aberration. Then he turned his hatred on himself, and felt deep hatred also for the man who had robbed him of Jenny, and was forcing him to suffer blackmail. And all this welled up in him until he lost all perspective and was overwhelmed by an acute sense of depression. Then tears began to flow through his tight-shut lids. He could do nothing about it. Quietly, but with huge, uncontrollable shudders, he cried.

Jenny, feeling much better for the swim, went along to lunch in jeans and a shirt. Harry didn't turn up, but she couldn't get him out of her mind.

As the afternoon passed by she tried to read, but it was no good so she decided to have another swim.

'Hi!' She shielded her eyes to see who it was in the water. Recognizing the young co-pilot, she called back, 'Hi.'

Sam continued to swim gently on his back as coolly he surveyed her. 'Beautiful!' He made the word a long drawn-out sigh of appreciation. 'Yes, it looks it,' she said. He laughed.

'I kept a space for you,' he said. Four couples were around the pool and three kids were in at the shallow end.

'How very thoughtful of you,' she replied lightly over her shoulder, making her way to the springboard. Aware of his eyes on her, she walked slowly and languidly round the end of the pool. Rather nice, in a way, she thought. Anyway, if you fall off a bike . . . She gave him a nice, natural smile and dived in.

'What's your name then?' he asked.

'You should know your crew,' she retorted coolly.

'Yeah, but a bit of a rush this morning. Skipper was late. Any idea where he is?' he asked innocently, gently probing their relationship.

'Absolutely none.' It had meant to come out lightly, but her voice got it wrong.

'Hey, none of my business, but I thought you and he were organized at the moment?'

'You thought wrong then, didn't you?' She paused, then added, 'Anyway if you're just going to talk about Captain Standard then I'm off, OK?'

He raised his hands in the water, a shrug that said 'Whatever you say', and sank. As he came up she was laughing.

'That's better. You looked worse than 20,000 feet of CB for a second.' Before she could answer he went on: 'Has anyone ever told you that you have the most beautiful smile, such lovely teeth.' His voice had become mock-serious. 'And those eyes, those eyes, such depth, such soul, such poetry, oh! and your hair . . .' She was blushing just a little through her laughter. 'And you,' she said, when her laughter subsided. 'Whoever you are . . .'

'What the hell do you mean "whoever you are"? Don't you ever look at the crew sheet either?'

'*Touché*,' she smiled.

'Well, let me introduce to you this magnificent man of the

flying machine – tarantara! Samuel Everard Neverwrong Tries-all-the-time,-but-with-little-success, Meadows!'

'Yes, yes,' she said with mock solemnity. 'I feel deeply for you in your affliction. Tell me, did you get the number of the bus that did those terrible things to your poor face, Mr Little Success?'

And the ice broken they began to get to know each other as the sun passed across the sky to the roof-ridge of the hotel. As she went in to change into something for the evening she felt mildly frustrated that she'd got the 'curse'.

The only thing that bugged Sam as he shaved were her silences. Like she had a problem or something. Oh well, he shrugged, he could always opt out. He looked at his watch as he went along to the bar. Seven. He bet himself she would be at least ten minutes late – and lost. 'What'll it be, Jenny?' 'Gin and tonic, please, Sam.' They had a couple of drinks in the bar then left the hotel for the Meke at the Mocambo up the road.

In his room Harry wearily answered the phone. He'd put in a call for seven, but hadn't slept. 'Yes. Er, look, send me along a bottle of scotch, some ice and soda,' he said.

Four large scotches later he ordered sandwiches. What the hell, he thought to himself. No rules about hangovers. So what the hell. Get bloody well stoned. You never know, old thing, you might even get a bit of sleep. He laughed, but it wasn't funny and the laugh was a bitter parody.

The Meke, 'under the dark blue velvet of the tropical sky, beneath palms whispering in the cool breezes of the night', was all the islands cracked it up to be.

The Fijian music was as nostalgic as ever. And the bamboo drumming! Well, it was something you had to go to the Isles for – quite unforgettable. So intimacy grew, and they were cloaked with the romanticism of the night, the place, the music, and the dancing – all the stuff of honeymoons. The barbecue was super, they agreed, though neither fancied the palusami. But the chicken, pork, ham, and the fruit, super, as was the walu. And there was something about the spit of oils on to hot charcoal, to waft in rising fragrant smoke in the night, that was the stuff of memories. But it ended too early – at 10.30.

He went straight into routine in the taxi: the long kiss and tentative caress. The response seemed full and he thought for all of thirty seconds he'd make it before, surprised, he heard her say, 'Don't.' And he was even more surprised when she added, 'I mean yes, but not tonight, I've got the "curse" so all I want is a drink, then sleep. Got it?'

He laughed. 'Christ, I've never won and lost so quick in my life!'

Back at the hotel they went and sat in an alcove in the bar to talk quietly – until Harry appeared.

Harry had spent the evening in his room killing the bottle, until the thought had at last struck him that if she hadn't been so bloody early she wouldn't have found out anything. The change in her schedule had escaped him. By 10.30, drunk, and with some vague idea of confronting Jenny, he wasn't quite clear with what, he left his room to look for her. Eventually, he tried the bar.

He saw her before she saw him. He didn't see Sam sitting in the alcove as he made his way with the unsteady grandeur of the drunk, and with infinite dignity, towards her. Little slut, he thought to himself, drinking alone.

A couple across the way in the bar noticed him. The barman saw him too and smelt trouble, but he didn't get out from behind the bar quickly enough to stop it. Suddenly Jenny became aware of Harry's presence.

'Oh Christ! Not now, Harry, not here. Go away, just go away, please!'

'I'll fucking go away when it pleashes me to go and bloody well not before, d'you hear? You little slut, d'you hear?' Slurred though his voice was, it brought a deathly hush to the room.

'Please sir, if you will come with me . . .'

Harry looked blankly at the little Indian barman for a moment, then knocked him away. The force of the blow made Harry stagger a bit but he held his ground, though the barman, caught off balance, fell to the carpet.

'S'll your fault, Jenny. Shouldn'a come when you did.' It struck him as funny. 'You hear that – come – you coming . . . very funny, that.'

Sam was on his feet now, aghast that the Captain wasn't only drunk but offensive too.

'Jenny, you're a bitch.' The words were said with complete clarity.

Then Sam hit him. Slowly, the Captain's eyes rolled up until the whites showed, as he rocked with the blow. Then with blood beginning to ooze from the little cut to his chin, he began slowly to collapse. By the time he hit the floor he'd been out cold for about five seconds.

Jenny watched as if mesmerized, then, as Harry hit the floor, she burst into tears. Sam, seeing the barman had been joined now by two members of the night staff, said curtly, 'Take him back to his room and put him to bed.' Then he turned to Jenny. 'Come on, Jenny.'

Blinded by tears she let him put his arm around her and guide her away. In the lobby, the receptionist came from behind the desk.

'It's room 36, sir,' she said as she handed over the key. 'Ring if you want anything, won't you, or would you like me to come with you?'

Sam shook his head, and they walked away from prying eyes.

'Drink this – it's water, or would you like something stronger?'

She shook her head as she took the glass. 'No. But oh Sam, I'm so ashamed.'

'Well now, how about telling me all about it. Never know, I might be able to help.'

Jenny hesitated: her desire to share conflicting with the damage she might do to Harry. Finally she asked, 'Did Harry fly well today?'

'OK, I guess.'

'Well, if I tell you will you promise to remember that?'

'Yes.'

'You could ground Harry, couldn't you?'

'If he was unfit to fly, yes I'd have to.'

'But nothing happened during today's flight to make you think him unfit?'

'No,' he replied. 'Nothing much today, but after tonight, well,' he paused. 'Well I don't know. For all I know, he's gone round the twist.' He paused before adding, 'I think you'll have to tell me now, don't you?'

'Yes, I suppose so,' she sighed. 'But I want you to realize that he's been flying with it for years. And tonight was – oh, not important – something between Harry and me. If he'd seen you it probably wouldn't have happened. Do you understand?'

'OK, Jenny, I understand that. Pity, though, that it was all so public. Anyway what's it all about?' he asked gently.

'It's very simple. Harry's queer, I found out, and we split and it's upset him a bit.'

'Harry! Queer! Oh, come on!' His voice was incredulous.

'It's true, but it's not really that dramatic, is it? Must be thousands of them; in important jobs too, I suppose.'

'Yeah, but in flying?'

'Why not? It's not something you'd exactly shout about, is it?'

'No, no I suppose not,' Sam replied slowly. He paused, then added ruminatively, 'He's a bloody good pilot. I'll say that for him. But Jesus! It's unbelievable,' he paused before adding, 'And that's it?'

'Yes that's it. You won't tell anyone, will you?' she asked.

'Dunno.'

'But if you don't have to and he flies all right tomorrow?'

He thought about it. The guy was paid to fly, so if he passed the medicals and psychs each year, who was he to pass any sort of professional judgment? 'No. Anyway not before I've found out about it. It's OK', he quickly reassured her, 'no one will connect it with Harry, and if I don't have to tell anyone, OK, I won't.'

'Thanks, Sam,' and she let out a long sigh before adding, 'And now I think I'd just like to go to bed. Oh God, the last couple of days have been bloody.'

'Yeah, I can believe it,' he said as he gently rubbed her shoulder. 'But OK now?'

'Mmmm.' She put her hand over his. 'Yes, fine now. And until Harry came along, it was a super evening, Sam.'

'See you tomorrow then.'

'About 9, OK?'

'Super.' Sam kissed her on the forehead as he might a child, and left.

He walked pensively back to his own room. Queers he really could not stand. As a small boy, he'd been offered two bob in a department store. It had frightened him. Still, I suppose I'll fly with the bugger if he's OK, but to hell with the 'comradeship in the line' bit, he thought as he went to bed.

Jesus! A fucking queer! Who'd have thought it!

During the morning of the next day, February 8th, neither Jenny nor Sam saw the Captain. Nor did he appear at lunch. Twenty minutes before the slip crew were due to check out, Sam went to the Captain's room, unable to delay any longer finding out if he was fit to fly. Harry had been waiting for it. Yet when they met it seemed to Sam as though Jenny just had to be wrong. He seemed so much as usual. The little cut could have been a shaving nick, the bruise six o'clock shadow. And the Captain was obviously stone cold sober.

'Are you fit to fly?' He hadn't mean to put it as bluntly but the customary air of authority had thrown him, somehow he'd expected something different. It was as though last night just hadn't happened.

'I have had no alcohol during the last twelve hours and I am perfectly capable of flying, First Officer. But you are quite correct to ask.'

'I see.' All that he had decided to say evaporated, and he stood silent.

'Am I to take it that Miss Carol has discussed me with you?' the Captain asked.

'Yes, she has.'

'And?'

Sam wondered. The question floated in the air. And what? And nothing he supposed. The guy was fit to fly – it was as simple as that. 'And nothing. I just wished to make sure you were fit.'

'I see. Well, as you no doubt can see I am perfectly fit, so shall we go?' Distaste must have shown in Sam's face, for the Captain added, 'Unless there's anything you wish to say first.'

Woodenly, Sam replied, 'No. I'm paid to fly with you and I will. It's a job.' And he turned on his heel and left. As Harry Standard followed, it was with a sense of detachment from the world, but he didn't really notice; he had been feeling that way all morning.

Chapter Five

The phone rang just once, in the stillness of first light. His wife didn't stir. She only answered calls at night if the phone rang more than once; for then Frank wasn't in, and the second ring would tell her subconscious this. But she never heard the first ring.

It was a delayed reaction partnership which started in the bleak dales of Yorkshire when, as a young vet, he had taken her from her parents' old farmhouse. The move, after their marriage long ago in that summer of 1944, was to a little cottage in Brawton barely four miles down the road.

Theirs had been a delicious but slow courtship of two years or more. At first Frank Newton had just been a name on the lips of a reserved community, close-knit in its isolation and in the relentless task of making the Dales yield a living. As with all newcomers, the locals just waited. But he had had, it was soon grudgingly conceded, 'summat abaht 'im'. Eventually, 'summat abaht 'im' became ''e'll do', and so old Meadows handed over his practice to him. It was badly run down, and the twenty-three-year-old vet spent the next five years winning the fight for lost patients. Farmers and smallholders were persuaded by his patience, availability, good work. Chance meeting and chance words all played their part. And so as time passed he was tentatively accepted as one of their own.

Grace had first seen Frank to speak to when her pony had got sick. She had been terrified that it would die. Her dad had found her in the barn wondering whether to call him or not. One look at the pony and he'd gone to phone the new vet. He got Frank instead who was covering his colleague's practice for the evening. At seventeen, she had been very reserved. She was well-read and well-versed in the ways of the world, but at only second hand, the Dales being all the world she knew except for occasional family visits to York. She was very shy when she first met Frank. He had told her what a pretty girl she was. He would have been bolder, but as he saw her his heart had flipped over, and he felt awkward. He didn't remember what he'd said. Though now, over thirty years later, it was still in her diary to read. On reflection she could still feel the blush his words had brought to her cheeks, could still recall her first impression of the tall young man with blue eyes and blond, crinkly hair.

After that, her dad hadn't bothered to continue with the new vet. So Frank Newton started to stay for a cup of tea when he could. And from a cup of tea he had started to come out specially to see her. They could go for walks together, finding reflection in each other of the strength and beauty of the Dales. Their intimacy grew until he was taking her out to local hops. They held hands, danced, and in the excitement of each other, laughed at silly things and forgot what they were going to say. Such evenings ended in a kiss, and finally, he asked her to become his wife. It had been a courtship of innocence, appropriate to the time, the place, and the people.

Then her dad died; their baby was stillborn; and finally, in the expected chapter of threes, both his parents had been killed on their way to visit them in Brawton. So much sorrow, so quickly, unsettled them, and when the advertisement for a vet with good sheep and general experience to join a partnership near Masterton, in New Zealand came up, they jumped at it.

Now, some twenty-seven years after emigrating, they were a prosperous, happy couple with two sons and a daughter. The eldest son and the daughter were married and the younger boy, now twenty-four, would be coming into the practice next year. The lessons of the Dales had been well-learned and money had kept its place. They could have done without the night-calls, but no one's life was perfect. It was the imperfections which gave quality to the rest of it. They were a very ordinary couple, insulated in the enjoyment of a good marriage. That Frank was still a 'pommie bastard' to the few people with whom he was intolerant, well, it didn't bother them. That he worked too hard was merely the price for their way of life. And if Grace was thought of as 'a bit too pushy' on local committees she wasn't aware of it.

'Frank Newton here. What can I do for you?' Though fast asleep ten seconds ago, the voice was crisp and ready for work.

'G'day, Frank. Bill Hulman speaking. Can you come up?'

'What's the trouble?'

'Dunno how she's done it, but one of me cows split 'er teat.' His voice was faintly apologetic. Twenty years ago he wouldn't have bothered.

'Sorry to trouble you, Frank, but it's a helluva mess,' he added.

'Not to worry, Bill. Be with you in about twenty minutes, OK?'

'Right.'

The Range Rover sped forward. As Frank drove over the deserted roads he thought about Bill. Second generation on a farm, which had just grown and gone on growing. A big stud and now sheep spread the land. Christ knew what he was making in a good year these days. But Bill was still Bill, and kept a few cows for old times' sake and still chose to get up for milking each day. But to see him in Masterton, you'd think he was a smallholder down on his luck. Nothing about him to show ownership of a stable worth well over a million bucks, let alone what the farm must be worth.

He drove past the main farmhouse and through the big yard, and pulled up in front of the model milking parlour. Frank smiled to himself as he saw Bill coming out. 'G'day, Frank. Thanks for coming so quick. She's in 'ere.' Together the two men looked at the beautiful Jersey. Her eyes wide and frightened by the pain, she turned to them and a clout of saliva elasticated to the ground as she gave a rumble in her throat. Blood and milk dripped from her udder. 'Like you said, a hell of a mess,' Frank said, as he went over to have a look. As he got near he reached out his hand and rubbed her head, making quiet little noises. 'Right. Hold her, will you, Bill.' He bent down to examine her. 'I reckon she must have trodden on it,' he said as he leaned against her hind leg to keep it steady. Not that it would have stopped her lashing out, but it often did.

'All right, old dear, take it easy, that's a good girl. That's it.' He kept on murmuring quietly to her as he examined the wound. Her hind leg quivered. 'Steady on now,' he murmured. 'Have to stitch it up, Bill. Nasty long tear right into the milk channel, I'm afraid.'

'OK. Be all right, will she?'

'Oh yeah, she'll be fine.' The local jiggered her, but the pain over, she settled down as he bathed, sterilized and stitched her up. Finished, he scratched her tailhead. 'There you are, old girl. But be more careful next time, eh?'

They were walking outside now to the Range Rover. 'I've got a teat syphon, s'pose I should use it for a bit?' Bill asked.

'Yes. Poor old girl'll be sore for a while. About a couple of weeks. Yes, do that and I'll look in sometime to see how she goes.'

Frank put his bag in the back of the pick-up and the two men looked at the morning about them for a moment: one of the little pauses to be enjoyed in full days. The sun was bright and strong now; early morning mists, chased from the hollows, remembered now only by the glistening dew in curves of grass yet to be explored by the rising sun. Sheep gently on the move, punctuated the quiet of the morning with their bronchitic coughs. Far off, the sound of machinery came and went on the morning breeze, and near at hand a radio accompanied the bang and clatter of pans. The rich smell of fresh coffee and bacon and eggs wafted across the yard. The day had begun.

'Stay for breakfast?'

Frank looked at his watch. 'I'd like that. Thanks.'

'You'll want to wash.' Together, in companionable silence, they walked across to the back of the farmhouse. As Frank cleaned up in the bathroom at the back, he heard Bill say: 'Millie? Frank's staying for breakfast.'

'Morning, Mr Newton,' Bill's housekeeper greeted him. 'Thought you'd be staying.'

'Thanks, Millie. And how's it with you, then?' he asked as she plumped a large plateful of bacon and eggs down in front of him.

'Couldn't be better, thanks,' she replied cheerfully. To the background noise of kitchen bustle they ate breakfast, their conversation confined to the odd comment. The last of his coffee poured down his throat, Frank sat back, stretched appreciatively, and said, 'Great, Millie, just great.' She smiled back over her shoulder from the sink as he looked at his watch. 'Well, Bill, I must be away,' he said, getting up. 'But first, I'd like to use the phone.'

'All righty, but there's just one thing I was going to ring you about anyway.'

Frank nodded, 'Yes?'

'A stallion. Moonlight II.'

'Yes, you interested in him?'

'Maybe. Won't run again but he'd pay his way in stud.'

'Who's got him?'

'Joe Marks over Nelson. I'd like you to have a look at him for me.'

'Fine. Any hurry?'

'Matter of fact yes. Heard there's an Aussie interested and'll be there tomorrow afternoon.'

Frank rubbed his hands down his face as he tried to remember what his schedule was. 'Tell you what, I'll phone Grace and see what I'm doing.'

'All righty, but if you could I'd appreciate it. Parsons is OK, but well . . .' he shrugged.

'OK. See what I can arrange. Phone's just down the passage, isn't it?'

'Yeah, you know yer way.'

'Hallo, Grace Newton here.'

'Well, by all that's great, what a strange thing, but it just so happens to be Frank Newton speaking.' She laughed as he continued, 'First, darling, and how are you this beautiful day?'

'Like the weather, Frank dear, just beautiful. And you?'

'After one of Millie's breakfasts, couldn't be better.'

'So that's where you are. I wondered. What happened?'

'Sorry, must have forgotten,' he replied, but then, remembering the morning call, he added, 'Come to think of it, I didn't forget: I just couldn't find the pencil.'

'Oh dear, yes, sorry. I was using it for the crossword in bed. Which reminds me: do you know you went to sleep with your glasses on again?'

'I thought it was probably all my fault,' he agreed equably. 'Any calls?' She repeated a few messages. 'Right,' he said. 'Now where am I meant to be this afternoon?'

'Today, my dear,' and she put on her 'patient' voice, 'you may remember that we were going into Wellington after you had finished, which you thought was going to be about 11.30.'

'Oh Lord, yes, of course. Well I'm afraid we can't, dear, something's cropped up . . .' He waited for a reaction. 'You still there, Grace?'

'I'm here. It's just that *you* never are. Frank, this is the third time we've planned this trip!' The tinge of her exasperation was inescapable.

'I know, darling, but this is important, and it really can't wait.' He paused. 'Look, I'll make a solemn promise. Next time we'll make it, OK?'

'If you say so, dear,' she sighed. 'If it really is a promise and you're not just saying it to get off the hook?'

'I promise. In fact, look in my diary and put a line through the next free day. It's all yours.'

'Why not let's make it a night as well. It's been a long time and *Coppelia*'s on a week next Friday. It would be fun.'

'OK. Great idea. You fix it.'

'Lovely. Now where will you be going and what's so special about it?'

'Bill wants me to go over to Nelson this afternoon about a horse. And time's a bit urgent. Come to think of it, why not come with me?'

'Will we stay the night?'

'No, we'd have to come straight back I'm afraid. Rather a lot of money involved, so I want to put it in writing.' The litigation after a phoned report some time ago, though unsuccessful, still rankled.

'All right. You go alone, but get back as soon as you can. In time for dinner do you think?' she added.

'Yep, pack me a lunch and if I get going at, say, about twelve, I'll . . .' he broke off, as he remembered suddenly. 'Oh, damn and blast! No, it's no good,' he said down the phone. 'Look, forget packed lunch; I'll be in for it, and probably won't be back till latish.'

'What's the problem?' she asked.

'Just remembered the radio's crook. You remember I told you.' He thought about it for a moment. 'Look, will you do something for me. I'm running a bit late, so ring Peter at the club and get him to give a message to the guy who's coming to hurry up with it. Tell him I'll be going through to Wellington Terminal and don't want to be silent VFR, OK?'

He could hear her scribbling at the other end of the line and could picture her bending down to hold the pad with a little finger. Ought to fix that pad sometime, he thought. 'Got it?' he asked.

She read the message back. 'No, not G,' he corrected her, 'but V for Victor, F for Foxtrot, R for Romeo – Visual Flight Rules.'

'Ah yes, got it now – whatever that means. Yes, darling, I'll do that right now. Anything else?'

'Yes, will you call Joe Marks and tell him I'll be flying over but don't know when. Probably late afternoon, and can I land on his strip?'

'OK, and while I'm about it, I'll ask Cathy . . .'

'Sorry, darling, must dash. Arrange what you like with Cathy, but tell her I won't have time for a meal tonight. She's bound to suggest it. But must go now, darling, bye.'

'Bye, darling, see you.'

'Oh, there you are,' the vet said as he walked towards Bill's Range Rover.

'It's OK. I'll let you have the report first thing in the morning.'

'Beaut. Want me to get one of the lads to pick it up?'

'I'll drop it in. I'm going into town first thing anyway.'

'All right and thanks, Frank.' And with a 'see ya soon' and a wave of his hand, he gunned his Range Rover away.

He'd wanted to have a word with the radio guy before lunch but a glance at the dash clock ruled it out. It had been a heavier morning than he had anticipated. Anyway, he'd have to drive past home to get there so for once he was home just in time for a beer with Grace on the wide verandah in the sun before lunch. Far and high, over to the west, he noticed cloud.

The time was 12.48 and the day February 8th. As Frank sipped his beer, the P4 Air Traffic watch were driving, riding or walking to work in the Tower, or the Centre for Wellington International Airport.

In far-off Nandi, the Paranational DC8 which would do the return flight with Captain Harry Standard and his crew later that afternoon was just letting down at the end of its morning run.

The beer tasted good. 'You know, Grace darling, I reckon we have it pretty good really, don't you?'

'Hmmmm.' The voice wasn't wholehearted agreement.

'What's that supposed to mean?'

'Well, a lot of men would be taking their wives into Wellington as they had arranged to,' she replied.

He laughed. 'But a lot of guys have boring jobs and their

wives don't have all this.' He waved his hand vaguely around.
'More beer?'
He looked at his empty glass. 'It'd be welcome,' he said. Her shadow falling across him, he looked up into her large brown eyes. 'Reckon you don't change much, do you? Still as beautiful as the day I first saw you.' She smiled down at him and he reached out to take her hand in the moment of quiet intimacy. He looked at it as he held it in his. 'Do you know you've got the most lovely hands?' he said. 'Not bad,' she agreed. She took her hand away and, the beer still unpoured, put her hand lightly on the back of his neck, caressing him gently. 'Cold lunch in there,' she said. 'Nothing to spoil.'
'Well fancy that,' he said with a slow smile as he got up.

In the bedroom with french windows wide to the view and the gently stirring air of the noonday heat, they undressed, she slowly and he quickly. She had a nice figure still. It showed her age, of course, but women wear age in different ways and hers was nice. She was still desirable; just a little plump, as it's best to be in middle age, but fit and firm. She did a lot of work on the fifteen acres that were theirs. At seventeen, she'd been shy – still would have been with any other man, but with Frank to 'show off a little' had become natural and as it aroused him, so it helped set and heighten her mood. She was deeply in love with Frank, perhaps never quite equated to him, wanted to please him and so please herself.
He enjoyed watching her undress, unselfconsciously, to please him, and it did. She wasn't tall or short, fat or thin, but though very average in many ways, she had something for him which was special to her and he found her exciting at moments like this. Unpremeditated mutual affection, given the little spur of time to spare, and desire, still stirred in them both.
Later, he raised himself on the pillows to study her face in the soft green light from the grass beyond. She gazed back at him as tenderly he traced out the network of the little lines on her face which told the story of their years together. He loved to look at her. And as a blind man comes to know the face of another by gentle touch, so he felt as well as saw, and had advantage over the blind man. And all the time, as his fingers traced the shape of her broad forehead beneath its strong brown wavy hair, the long eyebrows above her widely-spaced

eyes, then down her straight nose, her eyes stayed on him. Her mouth was generous and she lightly kissed his fingers as they passed. She moved her head a little, just as a cat might when stroked beneath the chin, as he ran his hand along her delicate jaw back to an ear. 'Yes, darling, you're very beautiful,' he murmured.

'So are you, Frank, very.' For a further second they gazed into each other's eyes, the moment captured. Then it was time for lunch.

Later, as he drove to the field he thought back over the last couple of hours, and wondered whether the odd hours he worked weren't a blessing in disguise.

Chapter Six

James Barrymore, P4 Supervisor for the Centre, sighed and looked at the Gent synchronized clock on the small panel of Comms switches in front of him. 1.23. Twenty-three minutes of an eight-hour watch gone. Idly, he supposed that there must be some sense in it. Someone had to say 'OK, Bill, Frank, Bert, or whoever, your break', or whatever. And he supposed someone had to fill in watch sheets and all the rest of the bumf of officialdom to keep a bureaucratic mountain alive with a semblance of justification for its monumentally inefficient size. Yet he wondered whether that was really sufficient justification for his inevitable boredom.

The phone rang. Almost too quickly, he picked it up. 'Centre Supervisor here.'

'G'day. Pete Phillips here. Look, I'm on A46 Airways tonight, but I'm crook. The doc's told me to keep out of it for the next three days.'

'OK, rest up, Pete. Leave it with me, all right?'

'Thanks.' He had desperately wanted to go on talking to use up a few more seconds, but as with most men bored in their jobs the world over, he automatically adopted the habits of under-employment. Brief, sharp and to the point. The illusion of a busy man under pressure was crystal clear, and fooled all the right people. Wearily, he turned to the roster charts and sorted out Pete's duty times over the next three days. That done, he turned to the recall roster. The Gent ticked up 1.58 and 20 seconds when he looked at it again.

He sat back and said to himself slowly and softly enough not to be overheard, 'Now, my Barryboy, what next? Tour the dump or pick up that dreadful book and try to get lost?' But the book really was just too much to face yet. No, I'm not that desperate, he decided. Lazily, he got to his feet to do the rounds. Just to the right of his desk ran the long desk of the assistant busy filling in flight progress information strips so that no one would be unbriefed on anything which came into their area of control.

'OK, Mary?' he asked.

The forty-six-year-old woman smiled briefly up at him. 'Bit busy,' she said, then returned to work. A little irritated at her slightly offhand manner, he said, 'I'd like a coffee when you can, OK?'

'Milk and two sugar isn't it, Jimmy?'

As she went back to the strips, he strolled from the shrouded IFR (Instrument Flight Rules) room and out into the brightness of the VTR anteroom with the tickertape and incessant quiet, rushing noise of the vacuum inter-departmental tube system, and big windows that looked out on a sunlit world. As he walked in the system gave a thump. Absent-mindedly, he took the message pad and passed it through the slot to Mary for action.

'OK, Charlie?' The ding dong of the FIO's phone interrupted him.

'FIO . . . Right, special weather Nelson cancelled . . . right, thanks.'

'And how is the Flight Information Officer of the watch dealing with the problems of Visual Flight Rules today?' he asked grandiloquently.

'Oh hi, James. Nothing much doing really. Police have informed me that a dinghy's loose off Paraparam. I'm asking people to keep a lookout for it. You might pass it on next door. Other than that, all's quiet on the western front, as they say.'

'Did you find out what happened to that Cherokee?'

'Oh yeah. The guy decided to stop at the club for a cup of tea and forgot to let us know. Might have known it. Anyway, I bollocked him.'

'Good.'

The ding dong sounded again, and the FIO picked up the phone. 'FIO.'

For a moment the Supervisor stood behind the man's back listening. Nothing important, but then there never was here. The job could easily be done by an assistant, he thought, and glanced across at Jean Parker. Like Mary, she was a married woman doing a job but not as a career. But then, he thought, as he listened to her taking down a flight plan, probably somebody's quick flip for a drink, no doubt she finds it interesting.

On his way back into the gloom of the Instrument Flight Rules cavern – a place with its walls lost in the dark, but with its ever-sweeping radar scans, pinpoints of motion before quietly concentrating controllers, a place of incessant muted RT clatter – he tore off the latest print-out from the ticker-tape. Confirmation of a cancellation of a NOTAM, he noticed. Well, they all know that the end of runway 16 was clear now after the repairs. As he went back past Mary he dropped it on her desk for ex *post facto* action. Then he decided to tour the radar positions.

He stopped behind the Airways Controller in time to hear him pick up a Friendship inbound from Christchurch. 'National 985. You are identified. Wellington landing report is Lima – QNH 1015 millibars. When ready you are cleared for en route DME descent to 7000 feet. Report . . .' The Controller's voice carried on with instructions but James had heard it all too often, done it all too often in the past, to be interested. Nevertheless, his eyes switched over to the Airways radar. Its indigo screen was constantly being brought to life by the sweep of the scan as it went round and round from its eternal bright point of centre – Wellington International. The range it swept on Airways was 93 miles and he noticed right at the bottom of the screen, just in now from the 90-mile range circle, the paint of the Friendship. Just past Cape Campbell. He watched for a moment as the scan came round again. Every twelve seconds it picked up the descending aircraft to make a new paint in briefly brilliant orange a point ahead of its past fading positions.

'OK, Arthur?' They had known each other for a long, long time. With a pang of pity, for he knew Arthur very well, it struck him that in about six months Arthur would be made Supervisor and he'd come bitterly to resent the job. Poor old Arthur, he'll be a pain to everyone, James thought.

'Hiya, Jim boy.' Arthur leaned back in his tilting chair, and stretched. 'Nearly had an accident on the . . .'

'Wellington Airways, this is Alpha Charlie . . .'

'Oh hell, tell you later,' he said, as he turned to deal with the transmission. 'Alpha Charlie Foxtrot. This is Wellington Airways . . .'

In walking across to the Arrivals Director, James thought to himself that Arthur was about ready for a change. Bit lax in procedure lately. Good, but a bit too informal perhaps. He looked back at him for a moment and heard 'and contact Terminal on one one nine decimal three.'

'Alpha Charlie Foxtrot,' came the acknowledgment.

Funny how some radios seemed to be so much better than others, he thought as he stood beside the Arrivals Director, the guy who saw them through the last 50 miles of descent and on track for a ten-mile precision radar or routine instrument and visual approach.

'OK, I've got him,' he heard Rod Stringer reply to Arthur on takeover. For some indefinable reason he found he could never like Rod Stringer.

'Alpha Charlie Foxtrot. Good afternoon. This is Wellington approach. You're identified . . .'

Perhaps it was the guy's voice he didn't like, he thought to himself as he listened. But surely one didn't dislike someone solely because of his voice.

'Hey, Bert?' Bert Lifelong on the Precision Approach Radar for talkdown looked across to the Arrivals Director.

'Yeah, Rod?'

'I've a guy here who wants a PRA, can you handle it? Not much different, I should think from a PAR once you get the hang of it. Just change the words around a bit,' he added with a laugh.

'OK. PRA it is, if that's what the guy wants.' Then seriously, he asked, 'Time?'

'Oh, he's got 45 miles to run, or so. 'Bout twenty minutes by the time I've got 'im lined up, OK?'

'OK.' And Bert went back to writing whatever he was writing.

'Charlie Alpha Foxtrot . . .'

James went on to the Departures Director. Same SD 1010

display unit as the rest, but set, as with the Arrivals Director's radar, to a 50-mile scan. He liked young Steven Ring. A bit on the sensitive side perhaps, but a bloody good Controller. Newly rated for the job and inclined to be a bit serious, perhaps, but he'd get over it.

'Wotcha, Steve, bach!' For some reason Steve always reminded him of the Welsh, but he would have been too timid a member of the breed, too quiet and too sensitive; not typical at all.

'Hello, James. Busy?'

'As a Supervisor! You must be joking, dear boy. Just here in case you lot can't cope, you know.' He laughed at the parody.

'Well, just because no one's pigged it today, doesn't mean it'll never happen.'

He could sense that the boy was serious, so replied, 'No Steve. You're quite right, I suppose. Now, what's happening?'

'Couple there.' He pointed close to the screen. Two flyovers were going on, both well painted. '707 away there,' he remarked in pointing to the 707 which was just making its prescribed first turn away from take-off.

'Happy with it?' James asked.

'Yes, thanks.'

'OK, but let me know if anything bothers you.'

''Course.'

'Oh, by the way, Steve, Mary and I were . . .' And he stayed chatting to Steve for a few unprecious minutes before, at the end of the line, he stopped to watch Bert begin the precision. Just as he stopped he noticed Alpha Charlie Foxtrot begin to paint on the right of the tubes.

'Alpha Charlie Foxtrot, this is Wellington Precision. Continue descent to two one zero zero feet – turn right on to heading one seven seven – you are 8¾ miles from touch down. How do you read me?'

'Alpha Charlie Foxtrot – turning right on to heading one seven five – reading you five.'

'Roger – do not acknowledge . . .'

Satisfied that all was well, James returned to his desk; just in time, as it turned out, for as he sat down, Mary arrived with his coffee. Sipping it, he looked around again. He'd visited all four radar positions, but not talked to the tactical 'generals'. Now he noticed the two of them at their desks in front of their flight information boards made up of the flight progress strips. No radar to think about, theirs the job of marshalling it all and foreseeing conflicts in the use of airspace. A military Starfighter 150 miles out, and not painting on the Airways Controller's radar yet, but at a speed and on a course to come into conflict with the Friendship coming in from Cape Campbell would have been his problem to solve procedurally before giving instructions to his Airways Controller. If done properly, the Star, when it began to paint, would be on a course out of conflict and/or with a safe altitude separation. James didn't know the Airways Procedures guy particularly well, so he made a mental note to have a chat with him when he was free.

On Terminal, as the 'general' in charge of the immediate airspace around Wellington, radius fifty miles, Andy Burt was quietly getting on with it. James could just hear him giving clearance to the Tower for a take-off, having satisfied himself there'd be no conflict.

Good Terminal team this, thought James to himself. Andy was one of the most reliable guys he knew, and below him in the system, Rod – he wondered again what it was about the man he didn't like, before dismissing it with the thought that, like him or not, he was a bloody good Controller. Then, of course, young Steve looking after departures and overflys: the Procedures Controllers' job to give him the correct information for crossing separations and courses. Then Bert on the PAR.

He smiled as he heard the slightly formal tone of voice of the new guy on Airways Procedural in contrast to Arthur on the radar. Arthur was, of course, responsible to the new guy, but listening to them who'd have known it.

Spinning out the time, he glanced through the big window separating the Visual from the Instrument Flight Rules room and at the back of the FIO. Staring out at Charlie's back, he wondered how long it would be before Charlie made his usual beef (it always came at some time during every watch) that the job was an assistant's one and a bloody waste of time for a Grade 4 Controller.

Pity he couldn't bet on it, he thought as, putting his feet up on the desk, he sipped his coffee again and pondered on the system. Strange, really, that there were still near-misses. Like the 707 which somehow found itself going over the hill 150 feet above the ground and not 950. God knows how it could happen, but somehow it did from time to time. But not on my watch, please God, he thought. Not on my watch.

As James Barrymore managed to avoid reading his book Arthur Brighton's mind was disturbed again and again by the near-accident. The thing that kept recurring to him was that the young bikie could so easily have been John, his eldest son. John had been doing well until some fucking little bastard at the university had got him on drugs. So now he was a bikie on drugs and due to appear in front of the magistrate next week. What a bloody mess! He tried to keep his mind off his son as he looked after the safety of the aircraft that came and went across his Airways, but at times it wasn't easy.

Rod Stringer disliked James Barrymore with a much greater intensity than James disliked him. But whereas James didn't quite know why he didn't like Rod, Rod knew very well why he didn't like James. Not that the knowledge helped any. James was on the Air Traffic Central Executive as the branch representative, and three times now the Executive had refused to take any action on things originated by Rod. Rod blamed James, quite unjustly. That was part of it. The rest? Well, James had been made Supervisor and he hadn't. Silly things, but for some reason, they disturbed Rod, and being on watch under Barrymore was one of life's pinpricks Rod could well have done without. Not, of course, that it made a blind bit of difference to his competence as an Arrivals Director.

Steve Ring had no immediate worries, other than money; a constant sore that they, the people upon whom lay the greatest burden of safety in the air (they considered), were paid a great deal less than aircrew. Nonsense really with modern congestion and the closing speeds of modern aircraft. Steve, however, wasn't thinking about money. He was new to Terminal Control and it had his undivided attention. Departures and those who flew through Terminal airspace couldn't have been in better hands.

Two o'clock ticked up on the twelve synchronized Gent clocks. And as the clocks in the Wellington Central Air Traffic Control passed the hour, far away to the north, winging its way back, was the DC8 Paranational Zulu Delta.

In walking out to the aircraft, just before one o'clock, Sam had caught up with Jenny. With the rest of the cabin crew present, it hadn't been possible to say much, but it had been enough, and in her heart of hearts, she was really quite glad that Harry had regained his cool. Not, as she told herself, that it was really anything to do with her any longer, but it would have been a bit sad if he hadn't made it.

Having given the word on the Captain, the co-pilot added casually, 'Oh by the way, whatcha doing tonight, then?'

'Don't know, really, can't remember. What did you have in mind?'

'Well, one thing's out,' he smiled, 'but how about dinner?'

'Hmmmm, could be interested,' she replied.

'Plimmers?'

'It's getting more interesting.'

'Pick you up at, say, seven?'

'Know where I live?'

'Dare say I can find out,' he replied.

'Well, if you find it too difficult here's my number.' She held out a slip of paper. He laughed – rather a nice laugh, she thought to herself as he turned towards the flight deck.

There is rarely much pre-flight chat on a flight deck with so much to do, that it wasn't until after the cruising checks that Harvey first began to wonder what was wrong between the Captain and his co-pilot. Sam's hostility was scarcely veiled; not that it was really registering with Harry whose almost total withdrawal, save at the purely functional level, came over as an icy reserve.

Sam had wondered how they'd get on during the flight. He'd been prepared for coolness from the Captain. After all, he had slugged the guy, and the guy knew that he knew about him. But this acting like he just didn't exist, like he was just another bloody instrument for the Captain's use, made him angry.

As the flight went on the misunderstanding grew and no word which was not strictly necessary for the piloting of the plane was said between them.

Frank Newton swung the Range Rover off the main road and

down to the club. He'd been flying from Wairarapa or Wood, as it used to be known, for years. Leaving the Range Rover, he went into the clubhouse, which seemed to be deserted, and had a look at the info board to see if there was anything new posted. The 'Beware Soft Ground' notice he saw was beginning to go yellow and curl up at the edges. One day, he supposed, they'd get around to doing something about that corner, but, nothing else catching his eye, he forgot about it.

From the clubhouse he swung left and over towards the hangar. Entering it, he heard a spanner drop.

'Hi, there!' he called out cheerfully.

'Oh, yeah. Over here.'

He went off in the general direction of the voice. It had seemed to come from the 172. Bloody radio shouldn't have gone, he thought. 'How's it going?'

The mechanic looked out from the cockpit, and raising a hand, wiped it across his forehead before giving his head one of its habitual shakes to get the mass of red hair out of his eyes. 'Yeah, what can I do for you?'

'My plane you're working on.'

'Oh, yeah? Nice. When'd you get her?'

'A few months ago.'

'Like her?'

'Great, when the radio works.'

'Yeah, well, I've found your problem.'

'You know I want to get going as soon as it's OK?'

'Yeah,' the guy said. 'She'll be fine, four at the latest.'

Frank went round the other side to get some gear. If the truth were known, he didn't really mind the delay all that much. It gave him time to do one or two things he'd wanted to get around to doing, and anyway he could do his daily inspection and dab the fuel for water.

At twenty to four Frank finished and looking into the cockpit saw things were looking pretty good. 'Still OK for four – that's in about twenty minutes?'

'Oh yeah.'

Strange character, Frank thought as he went into the club to file his flight plan. As the toll call was being put through, he wondered whose bright idea it was to make the government pay for calls on flight plans. Probably frightened that if the pilots had to pay, no one would bother, he smiled at the thought. 'Oh, put me through to Met, please.' There was only a slight delay.

'Met here – can I help you?'

'Yes, I'm just going to file my flight plan, Masterton to Nelson VFR and I'd like to know the weather.'

'Right. Hold on, please.'

As he waited, he saw someone he didn't know wander past. They exchanged nods.

'You there?'

'Yep,' he replied, as he clipped the old envelope beside the phone. 'Shoot.'

'General synopsis. Weak cold front lying mid Cook Straight travelling north west at 10 knots, giving rise to a band of low cloud, average base 2000 feet from Cape Edgmont to Cape Campbell. Tends to break east of the Tararuas. Perhaps light rain associated with the cloud later. Nelson good with broken strato cumulus at 2500 feet. Average wind north westerly at 15 knots.'

'And the QNH for the area?'

'QNH? 1018 millibars.'

'Right, and thanks. Now, would you put me back to the exchange?' As he waited, Frank gazed out of the window to the west. He could see the band of cloud over and beyond the Tararuas to the west, which he'd be passing through. Be OK when I've got well out to sea, he thought, but decided that he'd ask for radar guidance through it on the way.

'Exchange.'

'Put me through to 822, would you?'

'Hold please.'

'Flight Information Assistant speaking.'

'Afternoon, I'd like to file a flight plan.'

Jean Parker picked up a biro and drew the pad in front of her. 'Go ahead please.'

'VFR – Echo Lima Sierra Cessna 172 – I'll be leaving at about 16.15 at 130 knots – time en route to Nelson 1 hour 20 – alternate Paraparam. 3 hours' fuel and I'll be going straight via the Brothers beacon in the Straight – radio and compass – I POB. My name is Frank Newton and the plane's private.'

Jean glanced through the entries she'd made and then said 'Stand by, please.' Then, handing the plan to Charlie Walker, she added, 'The FIO will brief you now.'

'G'day, Mr Newton. Have you checked with Met?'

'Yes.'

'When were you last at Nelson?'

'Three days ago.'

'Right. There's no new NOTAMS. Are you familiar with Wellington Airspace?'

'Yes, but Met advise me of bad weather in the Straight so I'd like to go to radar for marshalling through TMA.'

'Charlie, I say . . . Oh! didn't see, don't bother.'

The abortive interjection interrupted Charlie for a moment, before he continued. 'Sorry, Mr Newton. Did you say radar through Wellington Terminal area?'

'Yep.'

'OK. I think that's it.'

'Fair enough,' Frank replied.

'Right, call me on frequency one two one decimal three when airborne, and again when changing to radar, OK?'

'Sure.'

'OK have a good trip.'

As Frank replaced the receiver he had no idea how boring Charlie Walker, a Grade 4 Controller, had found the whole business. And Charlie Walker, suddenly realizing how bored he was, nodded to Jean before getting up to have a word with the Supervisor about it all.

And James Barrymore smiled as Charlie started to wander through to him.

Frank Newton had been talking to Met at nine minutes to four. At that time, 15.51, the DC8 was 376 miles north of Wellington on a heading not far off due south on 127 magnetic. In Auckland Central Control, the Airways Procedural Controller, realizing that in about twenty minutes the DC8 would be crossing out of his Airspace and into Wellington Airways, made his contact. The new guy on Procedures in Wellington took the transfer (still procedural at this time) for the plane remained Auckland's responsibility for the rest of the 160-odd miles into Wellington Airspace. In Wellington, having marked the flight information strip in front of him for the DC8, the new guy looked to his right and at Arthur on the Airways radar.

'The Paranational's up in Auckland, Arthur. Be with you in about 40, OK?'

'OK.' He turned back to his strips, the composite giving the overall picture of activity. Mentally, he tracked the 8's path and saw no conflict. Frank Newton's flight path, though filed, had yet to be formalized by Mary on a flight strip, or, more correctly, procedure strip, so it hadn't been distributed around the Controllers yet.

On the flight deck of the big jet, still cruising at 470 knots and with about one hour ten to run to Wellington International, the atmosphere could have been cut with a knife, at least by Harvey and Sam. Harry wasn't aware of it. Cruising in now, he was beginning to feel something akin to serenity: a totally unreal detachment. He was long past any objective appraisal of the blackmail threat to himself, long past any capacity to think realistically at all. His mind, blocked off by worry, left only the shell of his professionalism in operation, and it was now only a very thin shell. He was at the point at which a human being is near complete breakdown. All it would take was just a little more pressure. He was very, very ill in his euphoric abandonment of himself to fate, but he had no notion of his illness; he had not the slightest idea how easily the wafer-thin shell could break.

Sam was a very angry man. He'd had two and a half hours of Harry's detachment, olympian in its disregard for Sam, and he'd decided that never, but never, would he agree to fly with the sod again. And, by Christ, it would only need just the slightest hint in the regulations, or just the slightest persuasion in the advice he had decided to get when they got in; anything which would cause him to construe it as his duty to make a report on the Captain, and by God, he would see to it. Just the smallest peg of 'done in the proper course of duty in ensuring the protection of the aircraft and/or safety of it or its passengers' to hang the coat of justification on, and he'd do it.

As the two pilots flew the plane, Harvey felt worried. It'd be OK, he supposed, but two guys up front who hated each other's guts was bad news – any time.

In the Tower at Wellington, the only two Controllers who could actually see the outside world, the Controllers who had to conduct the business of immediate flight in and out and ground movement, weren't busy. On the airport spread out at their feet, nothing much moved. Alan Bell was the Coordinator, and Alan Samuels the Controller, the guy who carried out the Coordinator's instructions. Between them, they avoided snarl-ups in landing sequences and take-offs. If they had been busy, they might have had half a dozen planes in circuit, stacked waiting for landing clearances, and some on the ground burning up gas as they waited for their turn to become airborne.

They had all the flight progress strips, of course, for anything that would need their attention, long before the event. They knew that the 8 would eventually pass to them, but not for another hour or so: ETA 16.55. The only responsibility which was theirs, and it was the Coordinator's, was the Automatic Transmission Information Service: a tape deck which endlessly ran a loop transmitting the Wellington weather carried on frequency 112·3. At the moment, weather 'Mike' was current.

Frank, flight plan filed and cleared to go, went for a pee and then back to the hangar. At the doors, he met the radio man. 'All right now?' he asked as he looked at his watch. 15.58.

'Yeah. What'll I do, bill you?'

'Yes, thanks. Can you spare a minute to help me roll her?'

'Yeah, sure.' One on each wing they ran her out of the hangar. Then with a brief 'cheery' the Comms Tech walked away. The time was 16.02.

The Comms Tech wearily climbed the final and third flight of stairs into the Tower, glad it was four o'clock. Just the ATIS to do and he could shoot through and miss the traffic home.

'Yep?' The Coordinator's voice was sharp; too many people just wandered up to the Tower these days.

'Comms Tech – come to have a look at the ATIS. Due for its monthly.'

'Right, but be careful with the tape.'

'I've seen 'em before,' the young man replied, without any real interest in whether the Controller heard him or not. The Tech stopped the machine and carefully hung the loop up on the nail someone had thoughtfully provided for it. It took him five minutes to clean the head and deck. 'Any trouble with it?' he asked, as he looked at the servicing log. 'Nope.' Taking the tape from the nail, he carefully threaded it back on to the deck and switched the ATIS back on, listened to 'Mike' on check, then, satisfied, looked over at the Coordinator. 'That's it. Be seein' yer.' And he turned to go.

'Thanks.'

'OK, mate,' and he was gone.

The Controller turned the next page of the car adverts. The time was 16.11.

Cruising at 36,000 feet at 470 knots, Sam reached out and switched box one on to 112·3 to receive the weather. Having had his last contact with Auckland Airways, he switched box two to 123·7 in readiness for first contact with Wellington Airways. He'd make his first contact over the beacon, New Plymouth north, the physical transfer point Auckland to Wellington Control. But now he leaned back again for a few more minutes; the beacon was still 60 miles on. Once it was reached, they'd be about 37 minutes from touch down at Wellington. He glanced at the clock in front of him. It read 16.14.

Frank didn't bother to strap himself in as he set the fuel mixture in the Cessna and started her up. While she was spinning, and he was waiting for the operating parameters to come up, he set his altimeter with the QNH given him, twirling the little knurled head until the figures appeared in the window. Then he sat back watching the temperature gauge swing up and the oil pressure gauge become steady in the green, having risen through the orange and red arcs. He ran her up to 2900 rpm, brakes on, and checked the mags. Beautiful, he thought, as he throttled back and, releasing the brakes, taxied over to the pumps. There he switched her off, filled her up with the 100/130 octane, and noted the 28 gallons on his flight pad. He was taxiing down to Vector 28 for a north westerly take-off and strapping himself in at about 16.15.

Now 180 miles out, Sam switched in to the ATIS and began to note weather Mike on his pad. 'Good afternoon, this is Wellington Terminal – Mike – runway 16, surface wind 160 degrees magnetic 15 to 20 knots, visibility 25 kilometres reducing to 6 kilometres, continuous light rain, cloud 7 opters at 2500 feet, temperature 15 degrees, QNH 987. Expect twin

NDB approaches, the 2000 foot, wind on 180 degrees magnetic, 35 knots. On first contact with Wellington Control notify receipt of Mike.'

As Sam switched from 'receive' he noted the time – 16.18 – then switched box one to 119·3 for use after Airways had seen them through from 151 miles down to Arrivals at 51 miles or so at New Plymouth south. One more frequency change after that on box two to the Tower, and they'd be home and dry – or wet, in Wellington's bloody weather.

Nothing much stirred on the green grass of the field, though the wind sock billowed gently from time to time in the gentle breeze. The grass, Frank noticed, was a little longer than it should be. In the waves of gentle wind, each blade bent compliantly as it marked the passage of the eddying breeze. Across the field the tops of the trees gave a quietly swaying token to the light winds. All was quiet, except for the drone of the little aeroplane as Frank made his final pre-flight checks at the beginning of Vector 28.

In the clubhouse the Comms Tech leaned on his elbows against the window surround, and, watching the little plane, sipped coffee from the Thermos beside him.

It was a beautiful day over the east of the North Island of New Zealand. Lined up to take off Frank looked about him, more out of interest than as a final check. Seeing it was all still deserted, he decided to get going. He flicked the mags switch and checked out the drops again, set flaps to 10 degrees, and checked the radio. Then, as he ran the revs up to 2400 his eyes swept the instruments once more, and seeing them all in the green let the brakes off to roll. Air speed built up and when he saw it hit 55, he pulled back and effortlessly the little plane soared into the air. Climbing through 450 feet, he swung off to the left and on to a heading of almost due west. As 110 knots came up, he brought the flaps in and, glancing at the dash clock, noted 'Airborne 16.20' on the flight pad clipped to the stick. Then he settled back to climb 3000 feet. At 1000 and about four miles from the field, two minutes after take-off, he would make his first aerial contact with the FIO on 121·3. As he thought about it, he pre-set the radio in anticipation.

The Tech in the clubhouse watched the take-off before

reaching for the Thermos for a refill.

In the DC8 it was Sam's leg into Wellington. Pure routine. Not a lot to think about. Almost without seeing it he watched the ADF needle creep towards dead bottom indicating overhead New Plymouth. Clearance from there, and he'd begin to think about coming down, expecting a descent clearance fifty miles and about six minutes on, as they went over New Plymouth south. But just now his anger was eating him up.

In the Centre, the DC8 had yet to paint on Airways radar still over ninety-three miles to the north.

'Arthur, look after the shop for a minute will you. Must have a slash or I'll burst. OK?'

Arthur looked up at the new guy. 'Any problems?'

'No, the only thing not on the radar is the 8 – here,' and he indicated the progress strip on his board.

'OK.'

'Thanks.'

James looked up and over his feet resting on the edge of the desk as the new guy went past. He had been on the point of starting to read, and nodded to him as the guy said, by way of explanation, 'Just off for a slash.' Then he looked at his feet and wondered whether anyone would ever in his lifetime replace the Supervisor's desk, scratched and scarred from countless heels that rested on it, day in and day out. His eyes strayed down, and then the phone rang. Christ, that was close, he thought, as he put the awful book down.

As the ADF bottomed Sam pressed the tit and began his first exchange with Airways, and Arthur. Time of the transmission 16.22. 'Wellington this is Paranational Zulu Delta crossing New Plymouth north this time.' Arthur noted 22 on the strip.

'Flight level 35,000 feet, estimated New Plymouth south at 28,' Arthur noted.

'We have copied weather Mike,' and the voice flicked off the air.

'Paranational Zulu Delta – roger – report New Plymouth south.' He hadn't noticed the assistant come up behind him, but as she placed the slip of paper in front of him he glanced down while he continued his transmission. 'At Wellington weather Mike current.' Suddenly his eyes took in the fact that amongst other writing on the slip of paper was 'John'. Oh Christ, what now, he thought; then, where the hell was I? Oh, yes. To a listener there was hardly a pause in the transmission. 'Initial wind as follows: 160 magnetic 15 to 18 knots, swings 150 to 180 maximum 20 – over.'

'Paranational Zulu Delta – copied.'

Arthur turned back to the screen to wait for the plane to begin to paint at the limit of the 93-mile scan.

As Frank Newton's Cessna passed through 1000 feet he made his first contact. 'Wellington Information.'

Charlie Walker, still on FIO ('this menial task') and still irritated with it, put down the paper and listened, for menial or not, lives up there depended on it.

'This is Echo Lima Sierra, airborne Masterton 16.20. Climbing to 3000 feet, VFR to Nelson.' Charlie made the note on the procedure strip, correcting the 16.15 phoned-in time of becoming airborne to 16.20 actual, and ticked the flight as effective.

'Echo Lima Sierra – roger – Wellington area QNH 1018 millibars.'

'Echo Lima Sierra – roger – 1018 millibars,' Frank replied and checked the window of the altimeter.

The time was 16.23. As he flew steadily on, still climbing, Frank felt the still fierce, exultant joy of flying he always experienced, the freedom of it all, and saw the mountains ahead. Jesus, they were beautiful. Off to his right was Hector, a bit over 5000 feet, lovely in the afternoon sun this side of the cloudbank he was running towards. Looking down, he saw an old fellow walking a cow and tried to recognize him. He must belong to the practice. One of the nice things he liked about the Cess was that no wing got in the way over the side. The climb giving him better visibility, he looked at the bank of cloud ahead. Through it or under it? he wondered to himself. But he'd said 3000 so perhaps he'd better stay there. Anyway, it was good instrument practice.

At 16.28, 51 miles on and still cruising at 35,000, the DC8 closed on New Plymouth south. 'Wellington – Paranational Zulu Delta – just passed overhead New Plymouth south at 28 – requesting descent clearance – estimating Wellington at 55.'

Arthur, looking at the screen and to the peripheral top, thought he saw a faint paint. 93 was the official range, but, well! As he transmitted, he looked hard at what he thought might be a paint. 'Roger – Paranational Zulu Delta' . . . but it wasn't. 'Er, oh yeah, cleared to 11,000 feet.'

'Roger – Paranational Zulu Delta – flight level 35,000 descending to 11,000.'

'Roger, Paranational Zulu Delta.'

With the 8 now ninety-four miles away, Sam eased the stick forward and with icy formality they went into the descent checks.

Arthur was just about to reach up to note the reported progress of the 8 when the new guy returned. 'How's Zulu Delta getting on?' he asked resuming his seat.

'Beaut,' replied Arthur. 'Over south at 28 and out of 35,000 now.' The new guy marked the strip.

Arthur leaned back and read the slip of paper the assistant had given him. 'John asked you to ring home, 16.20.' Did he indeed! Well, the little bugger could bloody well wait. He crumpled it up and threw it in the wastepaper basket before turning back to the tube. Ah there you are, my beauty, he said to himself as he watched the paint, strong and clear now closing the 90-mile radial ring to the north.

At the 80 he decided it was time to get the formal identification done. 'Paranational Zulu Delta – for identification report your DME distance to Wellington.'

Sam glanced at the Distance Measuring Equipment reading. 'Paranational Zulu Delta – roger – we're showing 79 DME.'

'Roger, Paranational Zulu Delta – you are identified.'

Yes, Arthur thought, there it is, and he marked the strip beside the radar as he informed the new guy who transferred Zulu Delta to Procedures on Arrivals. 'She'll be with you in about nine minutes, I should think.'

'Right,' Andy Burt replied.

The Arrivals Procedural Director started to check the 8's passage as clear through to touch down with nine minutes for decision if needs be to achieve effective separation, and noticed the conflict between the Cessna and the 8 immediately. They'd cross tracks just north of Titahi Bay, about 20 miles north of Wellington. Yes, he thought to himself, and, coming to his decision, gave it to the Arrivals Controller, his eyes and ears for the 8 on the 50-mile range Arrivals radar. 'Rod?'

'Yep?'

'The DC8 Zulu Delta?'

Rod looked at the strips beside the screen. 'Yep.'

'Right, a couple of miles north of Titahi he'll be crossing a Cessna flying at 3000, so when you give him clearance, keep it to 4000, OK?'

'4000 it is,' he checked back to Andy.

Andy then switched to Steve Ring on Departures, who would take responsibility for the safe flyover by the Cessna. 'I've got an 8 coming in and at, oh about 45 it'll just be about to cross the coast at Titahi. Now, you've got a Cess about there then, I think?'

'Yes, I have.'

'OK. Keep the Cess at 3. I've cleared the 8 only down to 4, but let me know when they've crossed, OK?'

'OK, but at the moment I haven't been given the Cessna. Guy said he'd want radar, but he hasn't come up yet.'

'Not to worry. They're not due to cross for another 15.' Rod thought for a moment, then added, 'Let me know if you don't get the Cess within 10.'

'Right.' And Steve made a note on his strip.

At 16.32 Frank, cruising at 130 knots, give or take a bit, was enjoying Hector and the range of hills he was over. To his front the cloud was piling up. By his reckoning he'd been airborne about twelve minutes now. On a good day he would have been able to see the coast passing beneath him in about thirteen minutes' time. But today, no way, he thought to himself.

He began to set himself up to get radar and go IFR. As first step on IFR he set his ADF on to the Brothers in the Strait, those two little islands of very little importance to anyone but pilots flying through Wellington Airspace, on the way through to the South Island. Direction finder on them, he thought to himself, and at least I'll know what direction I'm on in this bloody cloud if the radio does go crook.

Set to frequency 317 the ADF responded to the beacon's transmission. OK. Now for radar, he thought. 'Wellington information, this is Echo Lima Sierra, position 10 miles south east of Paraparam, 3000 feet and wish to remain at 3000. Am requesting radar assistance to Nelson via the Brothers.' Charlie noted it on the strip.

'Echo Lima Sierra – contact Wellington Departures on frequency one two zero, decimal three.'

'Echo Lima Sierra, roger.'

As Frank selected the new frequency, the FIO notified the expectation through to Steve Ring and Procedural.

'Wellington Departures, this is Echo Lima Sierra – position 8 miles south east of Paraparam – 3000 feet – homing in on to the Brothers – request radar assistance en route to Nelson until clear into IV Airspace.'

Steve had him on the radar and the thought went through his mind that the guy wouldn't be clear to visual until well out to sea. It would be pure instruments in the cloud.

'Echo Lima Sierra – you are identified at 7 miles south east of Paraparam – maintain 3000 feet and continue homing on to the Brothers – check QNH 1018 millibars.'

'Echo Lima Sierra, roger.'

Steve leaned over to Rod on Arrivals and, putting a finger on the screen, said, 'That's the Cessna.'

'All right,' Rod replied. His DC8 hadn't begun to paint yet. 50 plus miles still to run. The time was 16.35.

James felt the need to stretch his legs and decided to do another tour, and perhaps have a bit of a chat with the new guy, make him feel a bit more at home, perhaps.

On the flight deck of the DC8, now passing through 13,000 feet, Sam reset the altimeter from the note on his pad: 13,000 corrected to 12,220 feet actual. Technically, no one flew between 11,000 and 13,000 feet.

Rod watched north on his 50-mile range ring for the 8 to begin to paint.

Arthur, having watched him in from the periphery of his 93-mile scan and now down to approaching the 50-mile range ring, decided it was time to follow the earlier Procedural transfer with the physical. 'Paranational Zulu Delta – contact Wellington approach – now – on frequency one one nine decimal three and report your DME distance.'

Sam acknowledged briefly, and went straight on to the other channel he had pre-set on the box. 'Wellington approach Paranational Zulu Delta – 48 DME Wellington – establishing contact.'

Rod had had him on his screen for twenty-four seconds –

two sweeps of the scan: it was enough. But before he replied, he had a word with the Procedural Director. 'Still to four zero zero zero for the 8?'

'Yes, no change,' Andy replied.

Everyone knows the slightly disturbing feeling of being watched. James, standing behind Rod and listening, gave Rod that feeling.

'Paranational Zulu Delta – g'day – you are identified – continue descent to 4000 feet and home on to Porirua.' It was the last beacon on the DC8's plan from which it would be taken into the Terminal Airspace.

And it was just at this moment that Rod, glancing over his shoulder, saw James and registered a flicker of irritation sufficient to break his concentration before finishing his transmission with 'Expect no delay for a twin NDB approach on to runway one six.'

I wonder why I can't stand the fellow, James was thinking to himself as he turned from behind Rod to the Procedural Controller. Andy had been speaking to him, but in his preoccupation with his dislike of Rod he hadn't heard. Just as neither of them had heard what Rod was saying – it was his job, not theirs – so neither of them heard Sam's brief 'Paranational Zulu Delta' acknowledgement from the 8. The time of that transmission was 16.38.

As James drifted away with the Procedural Controller, Rod and Steve watched their screens as the paints made by the Cessna and the 8 converged towards each other. No worry, with a separation of 1000 feet.

In the Tower, at 16.43, the creed buzzed to attract the Coordinator's attention. It meant that the guy in Met had decided to change the weather a bit. To let the Tower know, he merely started to write on the strip of tape on his machine, and half a mile away the creed duplicated it by singeing the tape feedout in copy as the Met man wrote.

Alan Bell got up to read it off. 2 degree temperature change, a bit of a shift in the wind, 20 to 25 knots now. Having marked the data down on the white record sheet which, with the creed, were permanent records of the ATIS transmission, he picked up the microphone and started to correct the ATIS. 'Good afternoon, this is Wellington Terminal.' He glanced down at the copy board to make sure that the last ATIS had been 'Mike' . . . 'November', and continued. The dictation completed, he played it back, carefully checking it against the board, then switched it on to 'transmit'.

The other Alan in the Tower looked up and with a smile, said, 'With a voice like that, man, you could make a million.' They both laughed. They had nothing much to do, pending the arrival of the DC8 in about ten minutes; ETA 16.55.

16.45. In the Centre, Rod turned to Steve as the two paints were still just separated, and cracked the universal joke, 'Well, at least they've got frequency separation, if nothing else!' Steve, new on the job, dutifully laughed at the old chestnut. Next sweep, the two paints would superimpose.

In the tourist cabin of the DC8, Jenny was making her way down the aisle checking seat belts preparatory to landing. She was glad she hadn't been lumbered on the return flight with a pain like the fat little Englishman on the way out with his silly questions and cigarette-smoking. For her, unworried by Harry and ignorant of Phil's threats, it was a good flight. With the prospect of Sam, she was looking forward to the evening. It would be fun.

PART TWO

Chapter Seven

At his feet, the quiet oily swell of a lazy sea swept by the rock on which he stood. In the passage of each incipient wave the seaweed caught, floated, then waved farewell to take rest again, almost motionless, waiting for the next swell to pass it by. The noise of the water was an endless suck and gurgle in the crevices in the rock. An endless repetition beneath the clouded sky.

Harry William Trevor Stevens, a man of peace these days, and far away from the world where you struggled with your neighbour or fought for a buck, stood fishing. Beside him, laid out to dry, was some of the bright green seaweed peculiar to the water line. Dried and lightly boiled, it was like cabbage with the delicacy of lettuce. And with butterfish, it was *cordon bleu.*

Once, and not so very long ago, Harry William Trevor Stevens had been a very, very successful solicitor and barrister. With the arrogance of youth, excited by his own potential, for he had a good forensic brain which combined the natural talent of the advocate with the necessary flair of the actor. He gradually became aware that he was in fact leading a parasitic existence on the corpses of dead goodwill. The excitement of gaining a good divorce settlement soured when he saw the cases for what they really were: fights between greedy, selfish, immature people. And he gave up the sacred cow of divorce.

There was always crime, one of the preoccupations of a sick society which considers it no offence to safeguard dishonesty. It also had the merit of the endemic cut and thrust of Court work and it paid well. A hugely exciting game, until one day he got fed up with it also. From criminal law, he turned to mere inhumanity: avarice, greed and stupidity. Neighbours too stupid, vindictive and immature to settle their differences over who owned a strip of land but a foot wide; who should pay what towards drainage; or those who stole another's cow for getting through a fence which, one year and

$6000 later, was held to be theirs to mend. His reputation grew. The bigger companies began to take note of the young lawyer. Insurance companies began to use him to evade payment to men and women who had lost an arm, a leg, were paralysed, or were merely killed. His job, and he was good at it, was to show that the loss was the victim's fault, but as case succeeded case, it was borne in on him that in reality his job was simple: define the reasonable man and show that the victim had been more stupid than the reasonable man, and so win the case. Not a matter of justice, but a matter of technique; the quicker lawyer, cool in his natural environment of the Court, dissecting the lesser mental calibre of the disorientated witness. A game. The price, a family's misery.

He had given it up, but not without a flicker of hope for the future. In New Zealand, perhaps, it would be different. But, as so often in a new milieu, the bliss of ignorance can only last so long. For a short space of time, he was permitted to rest, observe, and enquire, as he found his feet. But when he found them, he saw that he was standing in a muddy pool.

He turned his back on it. He could afford to: he was only 33.

He'd bought the bach, a two roomed weather-board place, facing on to Titahi Bay near Wellington. And he had discovered music and reading and philosophy.

In his hands the rod rested easily, and he wouldn't have changed it for the wheel of a car, homeward bound in the evening fight, or for anything anyone could have offered him. Behind him rose the swell of the land – bleak here, except for the native bush, in a country where people were lost within yards of a main road. Towards the top of the hill behind him were a few houses hewn into the hillside. Over the hill many more nestled in sheltered seclusion from the winds of the ocean. More trees there, and Porirua Bay, alive with boats and people; and beyond the bay was the rising ground of Belmont Hill. All very beautiful in its way, but he preferred the west side and the sea to look out to. Among his greatest joys were the flaming sunsets over a quiescent water, or the rollers driven by an offshore wind, their crests swept back into long streams of spray.

But now the sea was quiet, as if in reflection of the low cloud in sympathy with it. Far away on the horizon he had been watching a fishing vessel, small at this distance, and wondered where it came from. Above the boat, he could see the end of the cloud layer sharply defined against the clear blue band of sky beneath it. He had been keeping an eye on it for some time, and had come to the conclusion that it might yet become a golden evening; an evening to eat out in front of the bach, hopefully on butterfish with a glass of Velluto d'oro. Nice but a bit sweet, he thought, as New Zealand wines tend to be.

He felt a bite and struck with satisfaction, but was disappointed to find that it was just a leather jacket. All right, he thought, as he slit across the tough skin before peeling it back from the white flesh, but not what he wanted. Then, with hook rebaited, he cast again. By his watch it was 4.20, but it was five minutes slow.

A few hundred yards behind the fisherman, that solitary figure on the rocks, Susan Arnold glanced out of the picture window of their new house and wondered what the weather was going to do. Almost like winter, she thought. It wouldn't be so bad if it actually rained. In fact she hoped it would rain as the newly-sown grass badly needed it. Sitting on the floor playing with Charlotte, and thinking about the grass, the new house, Dirk and his appointment as chief accountant to Shreibers, and the future, Susan was very happy.

The rod dead in his hands, Harry William Trevor Stevens puffed on his pipe in a contented sort of way. He'd caught two more leather jackets, but still no butterfish. He was debating with himself whether, in the event of catching a butterfish for himself, he should take the leather jackets up to the new couple. As he turned it over leisurely in his mind, he unconsciously eased his back muscles. In arching his back, he raised his head and heard the far-off drone of a light aircraft, faint but distinct in the shroud of low cloud. Aircraft had been his only complaint about the bay, they had just become part of the scene, sometimes noticed, but more often not.

Now as he listened, he heard the drone loud enough to place it. On a good day, he reckoned, he'd see it just about to cross the coast to the north.

Then another noise in the sky impinged on his consciousness, easily recognized as a big jet coasting in on approach to Wellington. All very unremarkable, and, his back eased, he turned to concentrate on catching fish.

*

In her house Sue wasn't listening. Something much more exciting was happening. She might have been mistaken but could have sworn that Charlie had said 'mamma'. 'That's it, my baby, say mamma for Mummy. Come on, darling. Say maa-maa.' The baby gurgled and Sue giggled as she went on playing with her.

Frank, flying on instruments, concentrated on his artificial horizon and the track homing in to the Brothers. As he flew through the cloud, it wisped thinly past in its linking of puffs of thicker mist for him to burst through in ever-changing light. About five minutes, perhaps a bit more, and thank God, he thought, he'd be through cloud and out into the clear sky and the late afternoon sun. Never any fun flying in cloud.

It was the last thing that went through his mind. In the space of a millisecond, much too brief for consciousness to comprehend, he ceased to be a sentient being. More than that, he ceased to be anything more than a red mist, as his body splattered and was torn and pulped and disintegrated in the collision. At a mere 130 knots and in the space of just seven and a half seconds, his plane had sped the final 500 yards to that precise point in the sky to be occupied by the big jet. He would have seen it fleetingly, as a ghost growing in terrible substance in the mist, had he looked to his right and seen what there was to see: the nose of the DC8 boring out from the mist towards him. He would have watched it grow larger and ever larger, fascinated in immobility, until he was at one with it. He would have watched it from the limit of visibility in the cloud – the last 60 yards of its flight – for an interminable one-third of a second. But had he done so, his fate would still have been inescapable. However, not seeing it, he was spared the terror, and was extinguished in peace. His last thought: Never any fun flying in cloud.

Harry was sitting in his Captain's seat. The plane flew through the cloud. But, had Harry been struck blind and asked what it was that he had seen before the blindness, he wouldn't have known. At best, it would have been a vague idea of wide blue sky stretching into infinity. For as the seconds towards their arrival at Wellington ticked by, he had begun progressively to shut down. He was sitting in hell, but so isolated from himself that the searing flames of his incipient breakdown were almost unfelt. He was merely in an agony of spirit; his mind had nothing to do with it, for there was no real thought, just the nightmare sensation of confused mass within him. Yet at this moment he was strangely at peace, detached from reality.

His eyes must have seen the Cessna, for they were fixed ahead, but if they did, it did not register in his consciousness. Suddenly he was relieved of life.

Sam was flying the DC8 on instruments, and had been for some time. But his concentration was broken as his vision flickered in glancing at the clock. 16.46 and 7 seconds. It happens to all eyes that have concentrated for too long. Drivers on long straight roads don't realize, and sometimes crash in the mesmerism of the way ahead. Sam relieved his eyes by looking out at the cloud in front; they flicked momentarily out of focus. Many pilots in war die because of this, for they don't see what is immediately near them. But this time Sam saw. He saw quite clearly the Cessna crossing his path, but he was an ordinary man with an ordinary man's reflexes, a shade faster, perhaps, but not much. Before the collision his hands had just received the message from his brain – but it was too late. But though he had no time to act he saw and appreciated what it meant.

When faced with emergency, it is a strange thing, but often the mind acts as a camera speeded up yet playing back to the intellect at comprehensible speed. In the result, what he saw was in agonizing slow motion. At one moment there was merely the greyness of cloud – then there was something in it, something crawling not many yards off centre from his left. A very small plane, a Cessna. He could see the pilot, a man with blond, crinkly hair. As his mind raced to avoid the impact, Sam sat transfixed, immovable in shock, his body waiting for orders his mind wasn't able to issue quickly enough.

The Cessna grew and grew: he'd never seen one so clearly before. He saw the line of rivets in the airframe below the pilot's shoulder. Then he saw nothing. The screen went black, the film broken.

The impact was appalling. The nose of the DC8, in advance of the wing of the Cessna, hit the engine nascelle. And the engine of the Cessna, all 300 lbs odd of dead weight, tore through the nose of the DC8 and smashed all in its path; it carried Sam, in a lightning slaughter, to dismembership, instantaneous bloody gore and unrecognizable fragmentation of what, but an instant before, had been breathing and whole. Then, in its awful passage, it smashed Harvey. He knew nothing of it as he was splattered as a fly is obliterated in the path of a fast-moving car.

But its carnage not yet done, the engine carried the bulkhead on and into the first class cabin, through which it passed leaving in its wake the offal of those six passengers who had been seated in its path. A carnage of blood, splintered bone, torn flesh and shattered seats. Finally, it tore through the division to the tourist class, to come to rest on the only bodies not to be extinguished by it. These it crushed and broke. But they didn't die immediately, and theirs was a worse fate.

Those who had been killed instantly had given up life without any knowledge of what had happened. But these other poor tortured souls knew searing agony for all the time it took for the plane to plummet to earth. Only then were the screams of the child stilled in its final release from pain too great to bear. Only then was the mother allowed a swift end to the terror of seeing the blood pumping from the place where her leg had been, blood spewing in endless spurts from her femoral artery.

But the engine alone was not all that shattered the flight deck. The Cessna, wrenched from the sky, slewed as the nose of the big jet opened for the engine to be engulfed, and Frank Newton, as a body still, hit the inside of the light airframe of the Cessna as it swung round to meet the jet in front and a bit to the side of Harry. Then as that impact joined the initial impact Frank's body was ripped to shreds to give up blood in a red mist as the mess of lacerated flesh tore into the front of the instrument panel in front of Harry, tearing it away and back into the Captain. It is doubtful whether there was a bone left unbroken in Harry's body at the impact. And the flight deck was no more. The big jet with its human cargo, torn open at the front, had no one to try to save it.

But dreadful though the first impact had been, it wasn't the end of that first damage. For, as the nose of the jet and the cockpit of the Cessna merged in crumpled metal, torn and unrecognizable, that part of the Cessna aft of the cockpit was carried into the port wing of the DC8. The fuselage of the

Cessna disintegrated as the knife of the big jet's wing carved into it. But it was a blunt knife, which crushed and broke the body but itself survived. Not so the port outer engine. Its nascelle was torn away by the tail plane of the Cessna, or part of it, as it smashed into the pylon connecting the jet to the airframe of the wing. That massive hammer blow twisted the jet which, in seeking escape out of its operating line, writhed for a suspended second before shearing its pylon. Then free, the engine began a lazy, flaming rotation as it fell away from its broken wing, to begin its free flight through the low cloud: a flaming, broken mass shedding pieces as it arced down through the all-enveloping shroud.

The port inner engine held in the impact, but debris from the Cessna was swept into it to break turbine blades and mash fuel lines before the engine was swept with fire which began to trail in the blackness of free-burning fuel oil.

It was all the work of less time than it takes to blink. Then, slowly, carrying much of the Cessna with it, the big jet began to arc, almost gently, out of flight. It took just 93 seconds before the greater carnage happened.

In the tourist cabin, shock stultified all who saw. Dreadful, horrified shock and utter disbelief. But some didn't see immediately. They heard, and were held fast, rigid in their terrified fright, to be transfixed as shock took its place and indeterminate realization swept through them that something beyond redemption was happening. And a few knew the fear of death. But most dreadful was the fight for breath in the sudden compression as the air forced itself through the shattered gaping flight deck, and eardrums burst and blood flew from noses, and many were blinded. Then, as reality fused with comprehension, the passengers shrieked and screamed in their utter and pointless terror.

Jenny was mercifully released. The shock wave hit her as she was walking up the aisle. Twisted in mid-step and flung back, her head hit the arm of a seat and she knew no more.

Harry William Trevor Stevens heard the crash, or was it an explosion? He wasn't sure. That it was near and to the north was certain: but whether in the air or on the earth, or past the point of the bay, again he couldn't be sure. His uncertainty, however, was shortlived. Immediately following the sound he realized that the noise in the sky had changed. The jet's customary noise of descent sounded different. He looked up. The sky was still clear, save, as yet, for the undisturbed low cloud. But as he looked he saw to the north a plummeting orb of fire. Then he realized that it was still arcing through the air, and was far from falling straight. Instinctively, he realized that something truly ghastly had happened; he turned his back to run up the hill to the house, his mind crystal clear. A warning must be given: the machinery of catastrophe must be set in motion.

The plummeting engine fell nowhere near him or any house. It missed falling into the sea and fell with a dull, reverberating thud into the ground away around the bay to his left as he ran. He didn't stop, but as he ran he turned his head and saw flames in the bush to the north, flames spreading to within yards of houses, not merely on his side of the hill but beyond. He forced his body to move still faster. Houses made all of wood: the thought hammered in his brain, one small but appreciated part of a greater, yet uncomprehended disaster.

He ran, gasping for breath and oblivious to the sharpening pain of tortured lungs in straining towards the goal of the house on the hill: oblivious of the burning wreckage with its agonized cargo sweeping down towards final revelation. His concentration was fixed on getting to the house. The need to get help was so overpowering that as he ran and the noise of the DC8 grew, he continued to remain unaware of it until his senses could no longer shut out the screaming whine of the approaching plane. Then he was almost overcome by it and was forced to turn.

He saw the plane break cloud. Instantly he took it all in; the fire in the wing, the shapeless mass of the nose, the certainty of the crash. Then, in incredulous disbelief, he saw two more things. As the plane was dropping lower, looming larger, he was standing in line with its descent. And it was on fire, and spewing fire behind it. He wasn't to know, but a main tank was blown and fuel was gushing out to fall in a trailing rain of fire. He was horrified, and then panic came to root him rigid to the spot.

Unable to move in the fascination of pure terror, so strong and so overwhelming, that for a time he was no longer conscious of his physical self at all. Then came the first reaction. Had he lived, his accurate phrase to describe it would have been 'it scared the shit out of me.' In fact, it did just that. In an unconscious and uncontrollable bowel movement, he soiled himself as the anticipation of what was to happen physically shook him, but with it came a release from paralysis. The plane was now very near and hurtling unerringly towards him but still a few seconds away from impact. But where? Where to escape? The plane was weaving slightly in its descent.

He started to run to his left, his face turned to the monster sweeping towards him. But it seemed as though it was in the hands of some malevolent guidance, and to swing towards him as he ran. Now in uncontrollable panic he turned and fled back the way he had come. But then it seemed as though it would be there that it must surely land. So in a desperate and final instinctive contortion, he sought to turn and run to the sea, but he slipped in his panic and so gave away any chance of survival. And he knew it, as he became motionless in the eye of his disaster.

The plane swept down. Yet even as he died inside, at the seemingly certain belief in his fate, he was reprieved. Perhaps it was the profile of the wind, who knows, but at the last moment the gigantic wreckage, still on the wing, lifted and cleared him to soar on for yet another 100 yards before it hit.

But Harry William Trevor Stevens still died. And in the few lucid moments of the agony he suffered he yearned for a quicker extinction, for as the plane swept up and over his prostrate form the burning petrol spewing from the tank soaked him. And he burned. The unbelievable but mercifully brief exquisite agony allowed him to scream just once, but to him the scream encompassed all eternity as it measured the excruciating torment of a ghastly death. In his death, he was that scream.

Startled, wondering fearfully whether there had been an earthquake, Sue looked up and out of the picture window and saw the plane on fire flying towards the house.

When faced with danger and devastation, people often react in what seem to be the oddest ways that later one sees to have been inspired. When the shredded blanket of her body was lifted from the bath the bloodied baby beneath was found unscathed, alive. The plane struck just where she had thought it would and it was at that point that the belly had been torn out by the small outcrop of rock. The terrible trail of human carnage had spewed out from there as the greater part of the plane had ricocheted up the hill to demolish Sue's house and beyond. In reconstruction it seemed that the plastic bath itself had taken a scything blow and it was this which had killed the girl. But quite what happened in that instant was never known. Similarly, why the house escaped fire was never certain.

Through the house the breaking wreckage had gone, scattering and taking debris with it, until finally the trail ended with a wing, still with its two engines in situ, not far up the hill above the house. That was before the final explosion as the wing tanks went up in flames.

Then minutes passed and in what seemed near silence after the awful cacophony the dust settled and the return of peace was broken only by the crackle of flames in the bush, and the thin screaming of the child. And in the distance, smoke billowed up to join the cloud rising from where the first engine had ploughed into the soil. And the child went on screaming.

In the space of less than two minutes, one hundred and sixty-eight men, women and children had died, including Captain Harry James Standard of the inbound DC8, his First Officer, Samuel Meadows, the Flight Engineer, Harvey Jones, the girl Jenny Carol, and the other cabin staff.

No passenger survived, and Frank Newton, veterinary surgeon, died as well; so did Susan Arnold and Harry William Trevor Stevens. The crying baby was the first mourner for them all.

And the quiet oily swell of a lazy sea still swept by the rock on which the fisherman had stood, heedless of the affairs of man.

Chapter Eight

'Frequency separation, if nothing else!' In Wellington International Air Traffic Control Centre, Steve's face relaxed from the dutiful laugh. Few days passed without someone cracking the old chestnut as paints crossed. But it wasn't an aimless joke, for frequency separation, if nothing else, crystallized the fear without which no controller would keep his edge. The perpetual nightmare that one day something would go wrong and the sick joke would become terribly true. The fear was real, ever-present, and necessary.

As the line of light swept past the point just north of Titahi Bay, it left a single spot of light. Two aircraft, stacked one on another, painted as one though a thousand feet apart. Steve followed Rod's old chestnut with its companion piece, 'Crunch!' It was quietly spoken. Rod heard and smiled at Steve before returning to his newspaper. Then Steve leant back in his chair, the job all but finished: all requirements met, save final reassurance to that part of human nature that worries about Friday the 13th and black cats. So he watched for the tube to demonstrate another triumph of logic over superstition.

The scan swept inexorably on round the tube. The seconds ticked by, neither fast nor slowly. Round down past the six o'clock position the scan swept, sweeping past the point again to show separation. But separation didn't show.

Steve's immediate reaction was 'something crook with the radar again'. There was the paint of the 8 . . . but – then – was it? The question forced itself upon him as, unwillingly and fearfully, he began to interpret the tale being told by the screen. And suddenly, in stunning certainty, he realized he was looking at the one thing in the world that controllers fear more than anything else, something for which they would probably rather die than see happen.

He had seen it once before, long ago, in training on the simulator. Now he remembered, and, more than that, it was as though he heard the voice of his instructor again. Words stored in some recess of his mind seemed to well up for him to hear with unnerving and frightening clarity: 'And if you ever see that, lad, then it's gone so fucking wrong that you might as well be dead!' The words had been said as he looked at the screen, which had been frozen in mid-scan, so that they could study it. He studied it and had seen the paint of an aircraft disintegrating in the sky. The paint had its centre – a centre body – but no more. There were pinpricks of other light trailing behind it. The radar was picking up the debris torn from the planes in collision: the engine, a torn plate from the nascelle of the big jet's port outer engine, and all the rest of the mayhem.

From blank disbelief, an almost physical pain shot through him. Without realizing it, his mouth opened to give a strangled, choking recognition of disaster. He rose to his feet and blindly backed away from the horrifying screen. The chair fell with a quiet thud to the carpet. Still he backed away from the awfulness of it. His was the responsibility for over-flight of a small plane. All planes relied on controllers for safe passage. Commercial pilots didn't cause disasters. Guilt and shock flooded through him.

Rod spun to the screen in front of him. By now the last paint had nearly faded and it was difficult to make it out. He went closer. Then, faintly, he saw the fragmentation of the paint. But it only got finally through to him as the scan swept past again and then, in all its vividness, he saw more clearly than Steve what had happened. The debris was separating out as it fell. The mess on the screen was unmistakable.

'Oh Jesus Christ!' he whispered almost inaudibly. Then instinctively he shouted the first of the emergency messages which, were he the Supervisor, would have headed his list of procedures on the Ground Safety Alerting List. Perhaps it wasn't training, but merely a statement of fact. 'Crash! Crash! Crash!' 'Bravo Tango Sierra.' The words fell from the RT into the pool of appalled silence within the Centre. They were unheard and unheeded as all heads turned to Rod.

The unbelievable had happened in quiet Airspace. How? Well, that was to be the work of months to decide. But even in this first instant, the fear of a mistake on his part touched the heart of Arthur on Airways. He couldn't think of anything he could have done wrong, but fear was there merely because, earlier, he had handled the 8.

And even as he heard himself calling out 'Crash', Rod suffered the first sharp pang of personal doubt in his dealing with the DC8 at over flight. And fear, like cancer, grows.

But whereas Arthur, on later reflection, and Rod too, after looking at their flight progress strips before they were taken away for the record, found a measure of peace of mind, Steve didn't. After his first instinctive guilt, he considered it again. Probability gnawed at his mind. He knew that of the thousands of near-misses each year, the greater percentage by far were where both heavy and light aircraft were involved. And ultimately, the cause was found to be error on the part of the amateur pilot. The thought was followed by the knowledge that he, and he alone, had been responsible for the safe passage of the Cessna, and its passage had not been safe. Guilt had been his first subconscious reaction, and now conscious logic drove home the sledge-hammer blow of certainty. Shock, of course, rendered the whole of it illogical, but he was in no condition to perceive this, so under its weight he crumpled in the dazed darkness of a mind filled with fault and failure for which others had suffered. The only sound from the crumpled figure in the chair was a low, monotonous, toneless repetition 'What have I done? Oh God, what have I done, what have I done . . .' It didn't help really, but he needed some outlet. 'Oh God! What have I done, what have I done!'

'Crash! Crash! Crash!' hit James Barrymore startlingly hard, but he acted without hesitation. On his feet in an instant, his priorities clear, he began to deal with the situation. In a voice compelling in its authority, his words turned heads back to the business of safeguarding the Airways. One crash was one crash but neglect of duty could make things worse. In the instant he took to glance round the room, he saw Steve away from his position: no time to deal with Steve now, but Departures had to have a Controller. The sound of Rod String's voice had hardly died in the appalled silence before James Barrymore shouted, 'Charlie!' The tone was imperative and with a muttered 'Back in a tick, hold this guy,' to Jean Parker, he strode next door. As he entered James said, almost conversationally, 'Take over Departures, Charlie.'

What's wrong with Steve? rose to his lips, but wasn't uttered. Something in James's voice kept him silent as he went straight over to the position. In a glance he saw what was wrong. The DC8 was in the last stages of its plunge to the ground. Then he looked up and saw Andy, the Terminal Procedural Controller, who began quietly to brief him on current Airways traffic in Terminal.

No one appeared to notice Steve as they got back to the job after the jolting dislocation. But all were aware of him and pitied him. Experience provided protection, of a sort, in personal terms. Had it happened to Andy, Arthur or James their intrinsic faith in their own professionalism and in their inability to make an error would have led them to the immediate conclusion that it was a pilot who had been at fault.

But Steve, newly rated on Terminal, hadn't had the time for the protective carapace of experience to grow, harden and protect him; he was searching for his fault and finding it in the realization that he had not told the Cessna pilot that he was about to fly beneath the 8. It would almost certainly turn out that the Cessna hadn't held to his prescribed flight level.

And Steve wished with all his heart that he had thought to say just those few words: 'Make sure you keep at 3000 feet; there's a DC8 to overfly you at 4 over the coast.' How easy it would have been. Not, of course, that it should have been necessary, or was procedurally laid down as a required transmission of information, but amateurs were amateurs.

He began to be overwhelmed by the feeling of guilt; too shocked to be able to think objectively, too inexperienced to be self-confident, he had no weapon with which to fight the accuser who rose in his mind and said clearly, 'You have killed!' A terrible sentence, passed and acknowledged by a mind rendered unbalanced by a single heavy stroke of fate and not far now from that state recognized by coroners in the phrase 'While the balance of his mind was disturbed'.

Having satisfied himself that the Controller position was in hand again, James started on the rundown in crash procedure. With his sheet for the job on the desk for reference, he lifted the phone, noticing that the Gent synchronized clock in front of him was just seconds short of 16.48. The DC8 was still just airborne as he made his first call. Charlie was in Steve's place covering departures; Andy instead of Rod was on Arrivals; and Rod, at James's side, was writing down the distance and vector of the crash. Then, taking a chinagraph, he marked the position of the crash on the map with a circle.

Looking down at it, James said, 'Operator, this is a priority "flash" crash situation. Clear all outgoing lines for my use. And no routine incoming calls to this desk; please divert them to 884, the Airways Director. Do you understand?'

'Yes sir, I'll get your first number, then ring you on your alternate to take your other numbers for contact and hold them till you're ready.'

Thank God for a good girl on the board, he thought as he heard himself being put through to the police.

'Wellington Police.'

'Crash alarm Aviation here. Your senior officer on duty, please.'

As the phone rang in the Chief Superintendent's office, James was dictating numbers to the girl over the other phone.

The Chief Superintendent was about to leave; he had reached

the door in fact, when the phone rang. Conflict between the desire to leave and the call of duty held him uncertainly at the door for a second, but not for longer. And anyway, strictly speaking, the office day still had ten minutes to go.

'Yes?' he said.

'Hold please,' the operator said as she switched straight through.

'Yes?'

'Supervisor Air Traffic Control speaking. We have a crash. A DC8 with some 160 lives aboard and a Cessna have collided at 16.46 approximately 3 miles north of Titahi Bay. Position of wreckage whether on land or sea unknown at this time, but almost certainly on land. I'm just about to set up the Rescue Coord Centre here.'

The Superintendent took a little time to get into gear. 'Is this an exercise?' he asked. 'Good thing, of course, but you could have picked a better time.'

But the stone-wall voice over the phone shrivelled hope. 'No, it's not an exercise. There's been a crash, and a very bad one.'

'Oh Jesus Christ!' Then, to gain time for thought, he added, 'I was hoping you were kidding.' It gave him the time he needed to grasp the fact before he could begin to function. He was one of the first to suffer short paralytic shock as a prelude to efficiency.

'Right. What are the coordinates?'

'Approximate position . . .' and James reeled off the coordinates for a point just east of Titahi Bay.

'OK, I've got 'em.' The Chief Super traced the spot on the map. 'Grid reference N21 and about 38, 47. Correct?'

'Correct,' James replied as he nodded to Rod to go back on Arrivals.

'There's just one other thing,' James added. 'Could you send a car to pick up our Regional Airways Officer? He'll be coordinating.'

It was a spur of the moment decision prompted by the thought that Duncan Freemantle was not a guy who drove fast at the best of times, and minutes might count.

'Right, and I'll have our SAR man up at the Centre as soon as I can.'

The line went dead; a second later it rang again.

'Hello. Did I hear right that we've got a crash?' the

Regional Airways Officer asked in his habitually quiet voice.

'Yes sir, and there's a police car on its way to you now.'

'Set up the Centre then.' The call was complete.

Duncan had been in the shower when the 'flash' priority came in. All his wife had said was 'There's a girl on the phone and she said to tell you just "flash SAR 3" whatever that means,' and wet, he'd fled to the phone. It had to be serious. 'Flash' – the highest telephone priority in the system, and a Search and Rescue 3! All services, a major calamity. It was his job to take the situation in hand and to deal with it. The prospect frightened him. He dressed nervously, his clothes dragging because he had hardly bothered to dry, and he was still putting his shoes on when he heard the wail of a police siren approaching fast. As he rushed down the stairs, his wife called out to him, 'Duncan, what's happened?' 'A major air crash – I'll ring later,' was his terse reply and then he was gone.

The police car, lights flashing, wailed into view, took the corner at speed, roared up to 14 Milburn Way and came to a screeching halt. Barely did it stop to pick up Freemantle before it did a screeching U turn, to bounce, then rocket off the opposite pavement. If he hadn't been so preoccupied with the task ahead, Duncan Freemantle would have been bloody frightened at the driving. As it was, he hardly noticed the journey, a fast hard drive through Island Bay towards the Centre, the way clearing to the urgency of the siren. The near-collision with the old car coming out of Alexandra Road, just by the old fire station, caught his attention. But with a flick of the wheel, and a crisp 'Fucking idiot, must be deaf!' the police driver was by. Silent again in his concentration, they swept up and over the hill, the wide road verged by pines. Then they were swerving, with screeching tyres barely holding on a bad camber, to the left, off the main road, and into Ruahine Street. A short, hard bend to the left followed by a quick hard right. As they took it, Duncan was flung across the seat. Deep in thought, he'd been taken by surprise. After the car took the final hard left hand hairpin off the main airport road and up the short slope to the Centre, Duncan had looked at his watch. He'd taken the 'flash' at home at 16.52, standing wet at the phone: the drive of just under 11.4 kilometres, had taken exactly eleven minutes. He entered the building at 17.03.

In that eleven minutes, James had done a lot.

Strictly speaking, having notified the police and the Regional Airways Officer, he only had one more job to do: to set up the RCC next door; lights on, maps laid out, initial report and action taken on the Coordinator's desk, Comms and teleprinter ready to go. But he'd done better than that. The Wellington Marine Superintendent was on the way to his office. The Wellington Fire Brigade had been alerted and were pulling in men. They were doing so because James hadn't been the only man to ring in.

As smoke had begun to fill the sky, people in Titahi Bay had seen it. The local fire brigade's Chief Officer breasting the hill on his way over the unmade road to Sue and Dirk Arnold's place had been shattered by what he saw. Great waves of flame were shooting into the sky from at least four separate fire points. In a glance he had seen the menace to the community. He'd called for assistance and, closely followed by the appliance, he'd taken his first decision to evacuate the seaward houses at the top of the hill. No way to save them, he thought, but lucky there weren't many. His order, which set two of his team running to the cluster of doomed dwellings, was the first of many to follow.

It was then that he was joined by one of the residents, a middle-aged woman who had run up the hill and panted out what she knew of the disaster. His eyes followed her pointed finger and he saw what in his preoccupation with the fires had escaped him till now.

At first glance, at this distance, there didn't seem to be much to see. With binoculars, however, it was all too clear; so fearfully, terribly clear that as he looked from the lower fire, and up through what had been the Arnold's house, and on the fire above, in which the remains of the wing and engines lay in shattered, twisted metal from the final explosion, he was suddenly forced to take his binoculars away from his eyes as his stomach churned in revulsion. The blood fled from his face, and he found himself trembling.

He'd never experienced anything like it, nothing so brutal, nothing on this scale.

In his second call for assistance he specified ambulances: perhaps a lot would be needed. He would report further after he and his men had been down. Ghastly though the idea was, there was no other way to find out how many people were injured. However, in his own mind, unprepared and suddenly scarred for life at the sight of white torn limbs and the bloodied dismembered remains of humanity strewn in the path which linked the fires, the real question was, could anyone have lived? Not that this helped. He would still have to go down to look for life, and his stomach churned over again.

He hardly noticed the police car with two men in it draw up, the first police on the scene. He was summoning the courage to walk down to the area, the courage to call the rest of his men to join him in something no one should ever have to face, but which had to be done quickly before the fire became a black, oily, smoking funeral pyre.

With the benefit of his knowledge of the size of the catastrophe, James had contacted Wellington Home Command. The Wellington Brigadier Commanding was away, but Colonel Plumpton, the Chief of Staff, had acted on his own initiative. The Wellington 7th and Hawkes Bay Regiment were coming to stand by at Arnold barracks in Lower Hutt, their commanding officer awaiting orders. The army's role, as set out in the manual, was to stand in readiness in civil disaster to provide a base camp to cater for up to a hundred men. He had understood that the requirement would be exceeded.

In the barracks, men prepared to move out and Bedford three-tonners were mobilized in the square.

The Station Commander at the RNZAF Airbase at Ohakea was contemplating a round of golf, well, perhaps nine holes, as the phone rang at 16.59. He was in his quarters. Ohakea, with Auckland in the North Island and Wigram in the South, were the three stations with an SAR role in civil emergency. Ohakea was 130 kilometres north of Titahi Bay.

The Commander weighed the situation up, and decided that to cut delay in flying time, he'd swing the Search and Rescue team into action straight away. He could always recall, but not make up for minutes lost.

Within ten minutes four choppers were on their way; also two seven-man Iroquois and a couple of Sioux two-man scouts. Unsure of the position, he also gave the order for an Orion with its airborne radar to take off.

James was about to contact the navy as Duncan Freemantle came through the door. At his entrance, only one of the Comms team looked up from the equipment. The time was

17.04. An orderly chalked his name on the watch roster board.

As James Barrymore had set the wheels in motion, each move had been recorded on the activity boards, and was noted in a glance by Duncan, striding across to his desk to join James.

'Thank God you're on, James. Now, what's the position?'

'Fire brigade, I've just heard, is on its way in strength; four appliances which, with the local, makes five. Others are being turned out now. Apparently it's bloody bad. Police alerted – don't know who their SAR rep'll be. Should be here in a moment. Ohakea on the alert.' As he said it, a Comms operator called out.

'Sir. Four choppers airborne and an Orion on take-off from Ohakea.'

'Good,' Duncan nodded. James continued, 'Marine Super is on the way to his office.' He paused to see if he had overlooked anything. While he was thinking about it, the Coordinator was reading the bare facts of the disaster on his desk.

The door opened and the Assistant Commissioner of Police, in civilian clothes, came in. No one knew who he was, but the air of authority was unmistakable; plainly he belonged. At the desk he stopped in front of Duncan Freemantle.

'You Freemantle?'

'Yes, and you?'

'Gainsway, Assistant Commissioner of Police. When I heard of this one I decided to handle it myself.' He smiled as he extended his hand to the Airways Officer, adding, 'Pity we had to meet this way.'

'Yes.' Duncan briefly acknowledged this before going back to the position, which had been clarified by contact with the local Fire Chief. Nine men, policemen included, were now on Titahi Ridge.

The Police Chief took his place at the long desk beside the Comms Chief who was sitting to Duncan's right. The team was growing. The time was 17.07.

Next door, James resumed the job of ATC Supervisor. His first job was to deal with Steve, who, quiet now, dry-eyed and bewildered, was still sitting in the same chair he had crumpled into. Gently, James leaned over him and said 'Steve?' The response was nil. James took his arm and spoke his name again. Slowly Steve looked up as a child might at a complete stranger. James had seen shock before, but never anything quite like this. For a few moments he pondered what to do. Then, with a word to Steve to stay where he was, he rang home. Mary Barrymore answered straight away.

'Mary, are you doing anything important right now?'

'Well, I was going out. Why, what's happened?' He could hear the sudden alarm in her voice.

'There's been a crash, a bad one. You remember young Steve Ring?'

'Yes.'

'He was on radar at the time, and it's hit him – very badly, I think. He isn't in a fit state to be alone just at present, so I was wondering whether you would come down and pick him up, and call the doctor or whatever. Can you do that?'

'All right, darling, if you think so.'

'I do. Anyway can't think of anything better, can you?'

'No, probably not. But what about you, darling?'

'Oh I'm OK. Be home I suppose about the usual time. I've done my bit now.'

'OK, poppet.' He smiled. She always called him 'poppet' when she was worried about him.

'Don't worry, it'll be OK. See you in about ten minutes?' he asked.

'Yes, about then if the traffic isn't too ghastly.'

That done, he reviewed the position and realized that he had forgotten the strips for the 8 and the Cessna, which were still sitting on his desk. Better take them down to the safe, he thought.

Supervisor Comms looked up as James came through the door. 'Hiya. What a hell of a thing to happen,' he greeted James.

'Yeah, bloody. Just too bloody to be true,' he grimaced. 'Anyway, I came down to check up here and ask you to put the strips in the Comms safe.' Then, as the thought struck him, he asked anxiously, 'You have taken the tape off, I suppose?'

'Yep, whatsisname, your new guy, told me. Said you'd asked him to – right, I hope?'

'Yes, you know the procedure.'

In the safe, as it was opened for the strips, was the 25-track tape. An accident, and everything froze. In months to come it would be played again and again as the Air Accident people slowly pieced the whole terrible thing together. As a matter of policy, for they shied away from anything to do with courts, they would probably lay the blame with no one, but the facts would all be there for whoever wanted to make something of them.

James had forgotten he'd asked the new guy to contact Comms for him.

Tired, he walked slowly back along the corridor in the Centre to the Air Traffic Control set-up. Reaching a window, he paused to look out at the world outside. It seemed too peaceful, he thought, for such a terrible thing to happen. And in his mind's eye he saw far and wide and was suddenly conscious of the enormity of it all. That thousands would be affected in the days ahead caused him to shake his head. He thought of the phone calls, telegrams, visits by kind policemen – all bearers of tragic news to husbands, wives, fathers and mothers, brothers and sisters, and all the rest of those set down for the record as 'next of kin'.

Dear God, what a dreadful, dreadful business, he was thinking, while wandering back towards the VFR room. Once there, he noticed Jean was alone, and recollected he'd moved Charlie to Departures. 'Jean! I forgot all about you! I am sorry, but could you look after it for a bit longer?'

'Yes,' she smiled back, noticing how old and crumpled he was looking and feeling a pang of pity.

'Right, but if anyone wants a briefing, I think you'd better tell me. I'm sure you'd do it very well, but you know . . .' He shrugged his shoulders. However experienced assistants were, they did not do briefings.

Back at his desk, he had a look at the recall roster and phoned for a replacement FIO. That done, he saw his wife enter the FIO's office before coming on in to him in IFR. James took her over to where Steve was sitting. She'd been a nurse, and gently she led him away. 17.27, James noticed, as he signed Steve off sick. Suddenly, with nothing really to do any longer he leaned back wearily, his feet instinctively coming up to rest on the old scratched desk. He cast his mind back. So much had happened in just forty-one minutes. He tried to recapture it all, but already it was assuming a dreamlike quality, the fabric of nightmares, but not real life. He looked around the quiet cavern at the quiet men in front of silent screens, painting bright; the only sound was an occasional quiet, competent voice, it seemed almost impossible that it had happened at all. Steve's absence was the sole reminder.

Next door, with all the reins in his hand, Duncan Freemantle began his general briefing. There was joint consultation on further action to be taken; joint because Duncan, though Coordinator and ultimately responsible for the SAR Class 3 operation, fully realized the validity of the experience gathered to aid him in his attempt to mitigate the disaster. The briefing finished by 17.15: just twelve minutes after Freemantle's arrival.

Feedback was coming in and was very helpful. At first it was coming mainly from the local Fire Chief, whose men, with the two policemen on the spot, were still working to clear the houses to the seaward side of the unmade road down to what had been the Arnold's house. They were working now almost with relief, the earlier awful task having been completed. The Fire Chief's information pinpointed positions on the map and defined the dangers and the need for men, and still more men, to stop the fire spreading east and south towards the city suburbs. The prospect was real and frightening. It had to be stopped at all costs before it broke out of the peninsula of Titahi, a peninsula about 2 km wide and 7 long. To the west the sea, to the east, Porirua Bay. The dense native scrub was tinder dry; the only method of stopping the creeping carpet of intense flame was bare earth in fire breaks, wide and well-manned.

At first the local Fire Chief had thought that if he sacrificed the houses now being cleared he'd have a chance, given men and equipment, of saving the other property within the peninsula, but the afternoon brought a freshening wind, and with it came doubts whether the fire could be contained in the peninsula at all.

'Right,' Duncan concluded. 'You know the task. Now let's get on with it.' The task elements were delegated and things began to move. James Barrymore, next door, was instructed to reroute civil aviation round, and not over, the peninsula. The Orion was recalled as there was no need for airborne radar. With no role to play the two big choppers were recalled but the Scouts were retained. Two RNZ naval fishing protection vessels set off from Wellington Harbour, their speed a little over 30 knots. They came into the sea search area one hour and twenty-three minutes later.

They had set out accompanied by three fast, privately-owned sea-going launches. Only Steve Forde's *Ariadne* still had the naval vessels in sight as Titahi Bay was broached. But in creaming into the bay, the navy found the water already being combed by small craft from the local boating fraternity. The yacht club commodore, following the request for assistance from the Marine Representative after Duncan's briefing, had worked tirelessly. But there had been little in the sea to find; what there was had been landed and the position of finding marked.

So the naval craft swept on out of the bay to the north to extend the search back over the path flown by the 8 after impact. Nothing was found. By 20.00 hours the sea search had been called off. It was plain it would yield nothing more from the surface.

But the army had a major role to play. The Chief of Staff was instructed to take command of all services on the spot and set up the Area Control Base at the neck of the peninsula. His task: to evacuate the peninsula and contain the fire within it if possible. The method: a 30-metre fire-break, running from the ocean due east over the hill and down to the waters of Porirua Bay on the other side.

As Colonel Plumpton set off in his staff car to the area, the Wellington 7th were roaring out of the barracks in a convoy of thirty-six vehicles, the route down the motorway kept clear by specially drafted police.

But at an early stage, Duncan Freemantle and his team had realized that 600-odd men alone could never do the job.

City police, assisted by the scout helicopters, were assigned the task of bringing in all the earthmoving equipment they could locate, big or small, it didn't matter. Time was the enemy, and drivers of heavy plant couldn't, with the best will in the world, move fast. Only three pieces of heavy gear arrived on the scene within the hour. The military had been there for about thirty minutes by then, and were working flat out.

Colonel Plumpton took command at 17.32. The situation on his arrival was that the houses in immediate danger had been cleared. The search for survivors had necessarily been brief. The ground, from the point of first impact to the highest debris – no more than a swathe 100 metres wide and 400 long – was being menaced by fire even as the local Fire Chief and his men had first approached it.

They had found a survivor, the only one, Charlotte Arnold. Of the team of seven firemen and two policemen who had to carry out the task of the search for survivors, five had been physically sick. No man should be called to squelch through the muck of human debris that these men had had to walk through with eyes not averted, but looking, taking it in, in their search for signs of surviving life.

The first of the very courageous men to fight back his nausea at what lay at his feet was the man who found the burned body of the lone fisherman. It lay unrecognizable on barren rock, the body of Harry William Trevor Stevens. But at least it was dry, relatively whole and recognizably human. It hadn't been too bad, and, knowing life was extinct, the man had walked up the hill and past the rock of first impact. The trail of grisly carnage ran from there.

The plane, its belly ripped away, had mashed much of its human cargo in tearing, bounding onwards. The scene was a nightmare. But, just as some of the first civilized men to enter Belsen after the war were ill at the atrocities they saw, but though ill and horrified went on and did the job set before them, so these men found the courage to continue. As at Belsen, there was no alternative. The flames were consuming the first of the carnage as the men finally beat their retreat. The child alone was recovered.

It had been a task beyond description for all of them, and few even tried to describe it afterwards, for it was an experience to put to the back of the mind, to try and forget, only to be horribly relived from time to time in nightmare, or in the officialese of reports.

Now, the first houses cleared, and the reality of the search over, Colonel Plumpton found the small group of men standing back from the road, powerless and helpless: so small a number in the face of the fire. And as he looked, he saw that the fire below the Arnolds' house had passed it by and had joined the fire above. A front of flame 600 metres long was sweeping towards them, distant now no more than about 400 metres, and the wind, as it blew towards them, was warm and the sky filled with whirling, floating specks of white-edged black ash from the burned bush. The smoke was thick, but nowhere near as solid as the oily, thick, black smoke joining cloud to the earth: the dense fat rolling pall of the funeral pyre.

Plumpton noticed the insignia of the Fire Chief. 'As briefly as you can tell me what you've done.'

The man turned with shocked eyes towards him as he answered, 'Aw, well sir, we've, er, been over the area where anyone might have been alive.' He jerked his head towards the child, now being taken into the first of the ambulances to arrive.

'That little kiddie was all we found – mother dead.' He scratched his head as he thought what else had been done. 'Called up the ambulance people. Not that they're needed,' he added. 'The two cops,' again he jerked his head 'are about to get down to the road junction a couple of kilometres back and seal it off and set up, er, whaddaya call it, a road base?'

'Road end base,' Colonel Plumpton murmured.

'Yeah, that's it, and the lads and me were just about to go over to there,' he stretched his arm out and pointed to the greater number of houses, the roofs of which could be seen behind and to the east, overlooking Porirua Bay. 'We've cleared those,' he said, his arm swinging round to point to those he had decided to evacuate straight away.

The Colonel nodded. Some way back he'd seen the small knot of people standing staring wide-eyed in the realization that there was no way of saving their homes.

'That took a bit of time,' the Fire Chief continued. 'People never want to leave, and when you do get them out the door they remember something they've got to take. Anyway, they're all there now. Only two people not accounted for. The father of the little girl – poor sod's still at work, I s'pose. And the other, well, I guess he was caught in the crash – body's probably over there – used to live in the bach down there. Weirdo or something.'

The Colonel waited patiently for the shocked fireman to finish before he put some vital questions. 'You arrived here when?'

'Well, let's think. We got a call out from one of the locals at 4.49. I noted that and I s'pose we made it here by 5.' He looked at his watch. 'So we've been here thirty-five minutes I s'pose.'

'And how far has the fire come this way in that time?'

The Chief scratched his head as he tried to recapture what he'd first seen. It wasn't easy: he'd seen too much in the interim. But then it came back and he looked down the hill to the Arnold place, shimmering now behind scorched air fanning up from the front of the leaping sea of flame.

'Give or take a bit, I s'pose it's come on about, aw, say a bit under half a kilometre. But it's been freshening up a bit.'

'I see. Right. Now what else have you done?'

'Kept the RCC informed, called for men, and that's about it. Oh and plant,' he added.

'Good. And well done, Chief.' Then he raised his voice so that the men could hear. 'Yes, very well done, all of you. But now I want more, just a bit more, from you. Your chaps must go down and clear those houses, that's the first thing and it won't wait. Can you do that? But you stay with me please, Chief.'

Exhorted by their Chief's 'OK lads, get on with it,' and 'Edmonds, you're in charge – right?' they started running down the hill to the houses overlooking the bay on the landward side of the hill.

'Now, you people,' the Colonel moved to the small knot of people behind them. 'I'm terribly sorry about your homes, but I want you to get out of here now. Go back to the main road and wait there. But remember this: it's important. When you get there, get your cars well away from the road. It must be kept clear.'

As they began to get into their cars, he turned back to the Chief. 'I'll come with you in the engine, OK?'

And they all started down the road, with the fire engine bringing up the rear.

'Right, Chief, we can't stop this without a break. That's obviously right isn't it?'

'Yep, I had in mind one back there – would have saved those,' and he gestured to the houses down the hill to his left, 'but it's come too quick.'

'Right – so we try and stop it back a bit. Now given say 600 men, we've got two kilometres to cover . . .' He was talking to himself more than to the fireman now, as he considered practicalities. 'That's a space apart of about a man to every two and a bit metres.' He pictured the job. A man with a hand tool and a section of scrub to clear two metres wide and thirty deep; the fire about 3 kilometres an hour, but more, perhaps, and the wind could freshen up still more, of course.

As they drove back, he considered his strategy until they drove past the police car at the main road junction. 'Well, I reckon we'll just have to try, Chief, but it'll be bloody close. What do you think?'

The Chief had come to the same conclusion. 'Yeah, mightn't cut it off right across, I s'pose.' Then, as he braked to a halt, he noticed the head of the army convoy appearing. It was 17.44.

With nothing in its way the fire joined up with itself. That part started to the north by the engine swept over and around the ridge behind the Arnold house to meet the flames that came over the hill. It was all seen through the eyes of one of the scouts, returned now from the search for plant and reporting progress.

The fire reached the second community at a little after 18.30 hours and roared to savage new height and intensity as it fed on the dry, wooden houses which heated each other in their close proximity to give devastating heart to the fire.

At the front which the Colonel had established, the ranks of toiling soldiers were swelled by volunteers. As more earth-moving equipment arrived the pace of the race against diminishing time stepped up. As more volunteers arrived the uprooted brush was cleared away and a long, thin line of naked earth began to appear from sea to sea across the mouth of the peninsula, everything to the north already committed to the flames.

Back at the command post, police were now surrounded by milling people drawn to the spectacle. Volunteers were allowed through the cordon, but once through a few just stood and watched, enjoying their better view undisturbed, with everyone else too busy to bother them. And seeing their homes go up in flames, people wept.

The press, in force, notebooks in hand, interviewed people who would have been best left alone. But a story is a story and papers sell in competition; the winner is the one with the greatest capacity for the most vivid portrayal of other people's horror, the greatest capacity to pep up breakfast tables with the taste of other people's misery, blood and fear. There was money in this, and editors sent their best men in the hope of world syndication. If the disaster was bad enough, it might be done. As one editor put it, 'Report it, but remember, I want to cry when I read it.'

And over it all, the TV watched with several eyes and concentrated on close-ups of a house consumed by the flames, then panning out, if lucky, on to the face of the owner, so that people at home could study misery and let it touch them, preferably in colour and on a big screen.

One of the policemen, a compassionate man, realized that Dirk Arnold should be stopped before he drove into all this. He was stopped, and quietly told, and he had enough sense to allow himself to be directed to the hospital where his daughter was. He was spared public curiosity, though as the story about the mother – 'cut right in 'alf, she was' – got out, two reporters putting two and two together, weren't long behind Dirk in getting to the hospital for an exclusive. But they were disappointed. He'd see no one.

And as the flames inexorably advanced on the puny line of defence the question was 'Will it check it?' Thirty metres was beginning to seem a very narrow strip to stop such an awe-inspiring wall of shooting flame and billowing smoke, alive and strong, a raging, sweeping, curling inferno, near which the air was scorching hot. Men sweated and steamed as they worked harder and harder to beat the clock.

Then the waves of searing flame began to lap the long, straight strip of bare earth. In great waves fire gouted, billowed and plunged in seeking to cross the narrow strip. In places it succeeded. Then men and appliances swamped the place to beat and kill the flames before they caught and spread on to the south.

It was 20.07 when the news of the final last-ditch stand against the fire began to come through to Duncan at the RCC. From the moment he had entered the Rescue Coordination Centre at 17.03 he had been working non-stop. By the time Colonel Plumpton had established his Area Control Base Duncan was mobilizing forces for the Colonel's use. To the 600 troops first drafted to the danger point Duncan had been steadily adding public employees. It wasn't until it was nearly all over that Colonel Plumpton had realized he was in command of a force of some 3000 men. The Colonel had known nothing of the commandeering of public transport in Wellington, the clamp down on telephone operator usage as names and numbers were fed into the system and specialized men recalled, the traffic rerouting for miles around to clear the way to the danger area.

The work of the Coordinator had been enormous as he and his team had planned and tried to foresee what would be needed. The scouts flown in from Ohakea had been invaluable in searching for plant and equipment and reporting progress and problems, conditions and movement. And the police and fire brigade had never been more heavily committed. The result was that Colonel Plumpton had the men he needed, and the tools for the job.

The only problem encountered by Duncan Freemantle which he couldn't handle were the politicians. Four, under the SAR Manual, had to be contacted. They were duly advised, and, thank God, before the first news flash, Duncan thought as he spoke to each in turn.

But it didn't stop there. Two of the Ministers failed to realize that their importance, for once, was secondary, and Duncan had to assign his assistant to the sole job of keeping these inflated men happy and off his back, or at least (the thought brought one of his rare smiles) he was buggered if he cared whether they were happy or not as long as they kept out of his hair.

As Coordinator, Duncan's job hadn't stopped at dealing with the actual fire. He had also the greater responsibility of foreseeing what it could become and preparing for the worst that could happen. Should the fire break out of the peninsula and surge south, the capital itself, surrounded by wooden suburbs backing on to bush, would be endangered. He listened intently as the Colonel quietly, almost casually, spoke on the air through to the RCC, giving an accurate account of the stand against the spread of the fire. And as he listened, he hoped to God that the contingency plan would remain just that.

In the space of half an hour, the climax was reached and passed. In three places along the 2-kilometre line the fire seriously breached the gap, caught on, and drove the nearest men back. But in each case, men of the fire brigade, seemingly oblivious of the risk, sped along the bare earth track to the new danger. So no new outbreak had established itself to the south of the line. Fire engines were seared and blackened by the fire they had skirted, but fortunately none caught fire.

So as the fresh dry tinder of the bush gave way to the line of bare earth the fire was finally consumed, and with no fresh fuel to feed on, reluctantly writhed lower and lower, to become spasmodic before sinking into dying defeat. And all that was left of Titahi was scorched earth, black, stunted stubble of what had once been native bush, and gaunt skeletons rising from the ashes of what only three hours earlier had been a secure community. All that was left of the fire were wisps of smoke rising from the area, and occasionally, as twilight approached, the eye would be caught by pricks of light from spasmodic flickers of flame as something left by the inferno finally caught, burned and died.

The Wellington 7th made camp and watched as night began to fall.

Then, as Sue had hoped it would, finally it rained. And Harry William Trevor Stevens, had he lived, would have seen that he had been mistaken. The sun didn't set on the scene that evening. The clouds didn't go, but gathered to blanket the sky from horizon to horizon, as though in mourning, and, as though in sympathy, tears of rain fell. Only then was the danger finally over. The time was 20.38. Only an earthquake of an intensity to shatter a city could have been a greater disaster.

In the small Porirua hospital, Dirk Arnold didn't sleep. He would later, but now he sat at the bedside of little Charlotte. A cold cup of coffee (coffee had been all he would take) was on the table beside him. But he was as oblivious of it as he had been of its arrival. Grief had shut him off from the world. He hadn't cried; had shown very little of what was in his heart. To some, grief is too personal to share: they carry it alone and cope. He was one of those. But just now, after the numbness of the first understanding of it was passing, he thought his heart would break. In life, he had loved Sue. In death, he was coming to realize just how much.

Sedated, Steve Ring slept.

The Prime Minister, appraised of the situation and deeply troubled by it, stated his requirement for an interim report from the Minister of Transport. He smelled trouble. The report had to be on his desk inside a week.

'But Prime Minister, no one can deal with it that quickly.'

'They had better do so this time, Christopher,' the Prime Minister replied.

'Well, of course I'll push it along. My people are probably up there now. But I can't promise anything.'

'I don't want the frills, but what we must have at the very earliest is a definite cause of this terrible accident.'

The Minister of Transport wrinkled his nose at the quotable quote. 'Yes, I appreciate that, and you will have a report the minute I've got the facts. But I would rather they took twice as long and got it right, than rush it and get it wrong. I'm sure you'd agree with me on that?'

'Yes, of course, but I can't express it strongly enough that we do need positive action.'

'I assure you, all that can be done will be done, as quickly as possible.'

'All right, Christopher. Good night, but remember, I am relying on you.'

As the phone went dead the thought crossed the Minister of Transport's mind that that was presumably why the PM had given him the job in the first place. But then, of course, he was himself new to the job in a new administration, a little naive, perhaps. But obedient to his master, he had a call put through to the Chief Investigator of Air Accident's office. As he expected, it was manned. The girl, a trifle overawed at speaking to the Minister, told him that the full team, headed by the Chief Investigator personally, were all at the scene now. Satisfied, he left a message for the Chief Investigator to contact him as soon as he got back and then returned to his dinner.

With the peninsula declared safe, the Chief Investigator with the help of lights was walking with his team of four into the area. The investigation had started, even though the ground was still warm beneath their feet.

Chapter Nine

Grace Newton decided not to wait any longer. Humming to herself, she prepared some bacon and eggs. Then she heard the car drive up outside, the step on the verandah. Puzzled, she put down the egg she was holding. She hadn't been expecting any callers that night. They were to have been in Wellington, as most of her friends knew. She opened the door and saw Sam Coles, a policeman she knew slightly.

'Why, hello, Sam. Come along in. Frank's not home, if you've come to see him.'

Suddenly aware that Sam hadn't started to follow her in, she turned.

'I'm terribly sorry, Mrs Newton, but it's about Frank I've come. You see, there's been an accident.'

He watched her to see how she was taking it. She didn't move – just stared at him, then in a low voice, said, 'Is he . . . is he . . . badly . . . is . . .?'

'He's not coming back, Mrs Newton. I'm very sorry, but he's . . . well, been killed.' It sounded too brutal as he said it.

Her hand went to her mouth. She murmured, 'Oh my God! Frank, Frank dead, you say?'

'Yes, I'm so sorry, but, well, there's no doubt about it, I'm afraid.'

For a moment she stood there, then just said, matter-of-factly, 'Dead.'

Sam felt very awkward. Didn't know what to say or do. But he had an idea that she really ought to be sitting down. 'Come on, Mrs Newton. Let me get you a drink or something.' Unresisting, she let him lead her back to the kitchen. 'There now. What can I get you?'

'I think I'd like a cup of tea, please.' Then it hit her, and she doubled over in the plummeting certainty of the meaning of the words 'Frank dead'. And grief began to take its toll.

As Grace Newton wept, Sam Coles made the tea. He didn't hurry it. He let it brew, stretching the time, waiting for the poor woman to absorb the thrust of fate. Frank dead. Knowledge, but no pain. Shock, as a stabbed man knows it, but no pain. Then the first sharp terrible pain; then the knife withdrawn, leaving only the wound itself and the beginning of the dull ache which only time can cure. He watched her and watched the ache begin.

The policeman was beside her with a cup of tea. She looked at him, nodded, took it, unfroze, as time moved forward once more.

She had always hated flying and had dreaded that this moment would come. Yet in a way her expectation had built strength against the day: that and age now helped. She grieved as she sipped her tea, and would further grieve. But she was a realist. She hadn't lost, as a younger woman would have, the possibility of shared achievement, but merely its extension into the contented reflection of old age. It could have been even worse, and even as she sipped her tea she knew it subconsciously.

'Strange, in a way, but I think I knew this was going to happen.'

'What made you think so?' the young policeman asked gently.

'Oh, nothing special. I've always hated the idea of Frank flying. Dreaded it. Always wondering whether something like this would ever happen and praying that it wouldn't.'

'He was a good pilot.'

'Was he? I was never sure. People said he was, but of course, no one would have said anything else.'

'It was true though. I'm learning myself, and he took me up once about a month ago. Everyone at the club knew he was good.'

She took it in, then asked, 'What happened? I'd like to hear it from you, not the papers.' He told her what little he knew, and so they talked for an hour or so, until he thought she'd be OK. Rising, he asked her, 'Is there anything I can do? What about the family. I could get in touch with them for you if you'd like?'

'No. I'll do it a bit later on.' The policeman gone, she sat a while composing herself for the phone calls she'd have to make.

Within two hours her middle son – 24 and on a Postgrad at Wellington – was with her. The next day the rest of the family arrived; Henry, her eldest with his wife and two young children; Maggie, married eighteen months before, came alone; her husband was tied up on a project in Sydney. They took the weight of it and she began to live again.

There was a mass funeral in Wellington. Her private grief was almost eclipsed by the misery she saw around her. The enormity of the tragedy almost overwhelmed her. With the feeling came another; a slight worry that perhaps Frank hadn't been such a good pilot as people said.

At first she kept the worry to herself. Henry and his family had gone home and two days later, Maggie had to get back to her job in Auckland. Graham stayed. He'd decided to move into the practice now, a year early. In some ways things were little changed by the tragedy. Instead of Frank she had Graham to care for. It was for Graham, not Frank, that she now carried out her part in a vet's life. If the phone rang twice at night, she answered it.

She began to do her own things again and found it wasn't too bad once first meetings with her friends were over; the hardest part to bear was their sorrow for her. But in a way it helped, for once acknowledged the tragedy became almost forgotten by those who did their best to draw her back into active participation again.

But the fear she'd first felt at the funeral didn't leave her. She tried to ignore it, but it remained. It was a few days after the funeral that she first tentatively voiced it. She and Graham were settling down with coffee one evening.

'Graham? It couldn't have been your father's fault, could it?'

It was the question that had worried them all. Before the other two had gone back they had discussed it. Henry had been in touch with Air Accidents and got nowhere. A report would be published in due time, but until then the Chief Investigator would make no comment. Not satisfied with this, he had insisted on speaking to the Chief Investigator. It had been very unsatisfactory, but, under pressure from Henry, the Chief Investigator had admitted that so far nothing had come to light which indicated fault on the part of Frank Newton. They had had to be satisfied with that, and a promise to let Henry know what was happening as the investigation went on. But they had heard nothing else before Henry had gone. Graham tried to reassure his mother.

'They didn't think it was anything to do with Dad.'

'Everyone says he was a very good pilot, you know.'

'I know. Anyway, Mum, you know Dad. Would it be likely he'd do anything stupid?'

'I suppose not, dear, but it would be terrible if it was anything to do with him.'

'He was all right when you last saw him, wasn't he?'

Her mind went back to that afternoon so long ago now, and the image of Frank's face over her on the bed, the touch of the gentle exploration of his fingers on her face came back to her. 'Yes, darling, he was all right.'

'Well, I wouldn't worry then. Hey, Star Trek's on. Want to see it?' She smiled as she nodded, the subject forgotten for the time being.

But the next day it raised its ugly head again. Graham was out. In fact, he was having a look at Bill Hulman's cow. Grace was having a morning cup of coffee on the verandah. It was a beautiful day, much like Frank's last. She looked out over the mountains to the west, and felt her sadness as she gazed at the route of his last journey, but it was a gentle feeling now, no longer something to make her cry, at least, not during the day. Sometimes she still did weep, but it was always in the loneliness of her bed in the dark of the night, like last night. She had come across his spare glasses, and had sat on the bed and wept as she held them.

Her thoughts were broken as she heard a step on the verandah. Looking up, she saw a man of medium height and build in a light grey suit coming towards her. She noticed he was slightly balding, had a nice smile and wore glasses. Perhaps he was about forty-five, maybe a bit more. His self-assurance said more, his smooth face less.

'Mrs Newton?'

'Yes, I'm Mrs Newton.'

'I rang at the door, but I suppose you couldn't hear me out here.'

'No.'

'My name's Mark Simpson. Your husband was insured by Pacific Guarantee Life and General, as I'm sure you know.'

She nodded, as she motioned him to a chair beside her, which he turned a little before he sat down so that he would be looking at her. He continued: 'I'm a loss adjuster – do you know what that is?'

'I don't think so.'

'Well, your husband had a pretty big policy out on his life

with the Pacific and in cases like this the company employs me to see that the claim is properly met. I would just like to ask a few questions.'

'I don't understand,' she faltered, unsure and alarmed. 'My eldest son saw our solicitor and I thought the company had been contacted and the claim made.'

'Yes, that's right. But you will appreciate that the company wants to be quite sure of the facts before it pays out a hundred thousand dollars.'

Grace Newton felt herself chill inside. She felt she was up against something she didn't understand, something to be guarded against. 'Would you mind, Mr er . . .'

'Simpson – Mark Simpson.'

'. . . Mr Simpson, if I just gave my solicitor a ring about this? I don't understand it. My husband was insured if he died, and, well, he has. I don't know what there is to ask questions about.' By now, she was out of her chair and turning to the door behind her. 'Please stay there – I'll be back in a moment.'

'Certainly. If you would like your solicitor to speak to me I'd be glad to do so,' she heard him say as she was going through the door.

Marty Chalmers, now the senior partner of Snell, Burton & Chalmers, was seeing a client when Grace rang. Normally, he didn't allow any interruptions.

'Hello, Grace. What's the problem?'

'There's a man here, a loss adjuster I think he called himself, and he says he's here to ask me some questions from Frank's insurance company. What should I do? Shouldn't you see him or something?'

'Well, that depends on what he wants. Which company is this?'

'Pacific Guarantee.'

'I see. He's with you now, is he?'

'Yes.'

'I think I had better have a word with him, and then I'll speak with you again, Grace. OK?'

'Yes, hold on.'

'Mr Chalmers would like to speak to you.' She showed him the way. 'Phone's there. And would you like a cup of coffee?'

The man thanked her as he picked up the phone and Grace

went into the kitchen. 'Hello, Mr Chalmers?'

'Yeah. You're for the Pacific who held Frank Newton's life covered, is that right?'

'Yes. Mark Simpson of Stanley and Partners, loss adjusters, Auckland.'

'What's the problem, Mr Simpson?'

'Nothing to worry about. But it's a fairly substantial claim so the company just wants us to confirm it for payment. The policy barred suicide and I must check the proposal and so on. You know the sort of thing.'

'I see, and what have you covered so far?'

'You know as well as I do, Mr Chalmers, that I can't discuss the company's business with you.'

'OK, but I'm not going to advise my client to speak to you unless I know what's going on. Let's face it, suicide's absurd. Even if he knew the other plane was in the vicinity, how the hell could he fix himself in front of it in a cloud?'

This was in fact Mark Simpson's own opinion. If Newton had wanted to kill himself, he'd just have done what they all did – fly into a hill. As the thought went through his mind it was followed by another. The insurance company would be a long way from pleased if they were seen to pay out only after a writ. Bad for the image, especially in something so public.

'All right, Mr Chalmers, of course I agree with you. So now I just want to have a word with Mrs Newton to button it up, and finally I want to come and see you.'

'What do you want from me?'

'Would you tell me if he was in any sort of jam which was worrying him?'

'If he was, I'm not sure I'd discuss it. But no, he was OK.'

'Splendid, that's all I wanted to know. Now will you advise Mrs Newton for me?'

'What do you want to ask her?'

'Whether she knew of anything which was worrying Mr Newton, what he was like when she last saw him, that sort of thing.'

'Right, put her on again. And tell me, when do you anticipate payment?'

'I've got an acceptance form with me for the full amount. If you advise her to sign it I don't think she'll experience any delay at all.'

'What's on the form? I think you'd better read it to me.' The loss adjuster read it and, satisfied that it was the usual, the solicitor advised Grace Newton to answer questions and sign the form, but to ring him back straight away if the man started to raise problems.

'Now, Mrs Newton, there's very little I want to ask. First of all, did your husband have any worries?'

'No.'

'Health good?'

'Very.'

'What was he like when he left for the airfield? I'm sorry to have to ask it, but how were things between the two of you?'

'We loved each other very much.'

None of it was what he'd come for. All the answers were predictable, but they served their purpose and broke the ice. Now that they were talking he began to get down to the business of the visit. Grace Newton thought he'd finished and spoke more readily, now it seemed on a social basis.

'Lovely place you've got here.'

'We love . . . we were very happy here.'

'I suppose you'll be moving to something smaller now? It must have been hard work looking after it all even with the two of you, or have you someone who comes in to help?'

'Yes, someone helps but I've always done most of it.'

'You do a great job. Must take up most of your time?'

'No, far from it. I play golf twice a week and then there's the church and the guild and, oh lots of things. I think I worked pretty well as hard as Frank.' She laughed in self-depreciation. They talked a bit longer, then he took his leave.

In the report that he filed with his recommendation to meet the claim there appeared the following paragraph:

'. . . I am satisfied that the deceased had no major worries on his own account. Upon further investigation into the health of his wife, I discovered she had not been in professional contact with her own doctor for three years and two months. I found nothing to indicate she had consulted any other doctor during that time. On a personal investigation, I found her to be an active, pleasant person and I have no doubt that she is in good health. Further, I find from my investigation that she was happily married. In the result, I conclude that there is no possibility that the deceased was concerned for himself or about her health or the possibility of any breakup in the marriage. I conclude that this is not a possible suicide case and full and accurate disclosure having been made by the deceased in his proposal form this claim should be met in full.'

Perhaps it was nothing specific that Mark Simpson had said that caused a ripple of unease to go through Grace's mind, but the fact of his visit brought it home to her, as nothing else had, that people she knew nothing about were involved in the investigation of the accident. And there was big money, other people's big money, at stake. As she thought about it, it dawned on her that it might suit some people very well if Frank were found to blame. It worried her, and as she worried about it, she told herself she would watch for any sign of it.

No one, but no one, she decided, was going to blame Frank.

The cheque from the Pacific came through three days later – a good company not seeking to maximize earnings by delaying payments. With it, her heart lifted. No one, she thought, could blame Frank now. As she understood it, no insurance company paid out if the person who had died was in any way to blame.

Steve Ring watched mesmerized as the sweep of the scan swept remorselessly on; he watched it sweep down and round and begin the upward climb. He tried to get to the set to switch it off, but couldn't move. In the fascination of growing terror his eyes watched the spot. It grew, the screen itself grew; it was all he could see, and then the scan swept past. And the spot burst as a star shell, and he was looking at a growing flame in the sky. He wanted to shut his eyes but couldn't; wanted to look away but couldn't. Wherever he looked it was there. Then he heard a little sound like the sighing of trees in the wind. He strained his ears to catch it and it was faint screaming in the sky. He wanted to shut his ears but couldn't.

Then came a head streaming fire: legs, arms and torsos, all streaming fire. They fell away from the flame in the sky and screamed and screamed as they moved with infinitely slow precision towards him. And he heard on the wind 'You . . .' He felt the scorching wind of their passage into oblivion, the fiery blood spattered him. He tried to wipe it away but couldn't move. The noise in his head was unbearable, yet there was no escape.

And the blood, the screaming, the fire, the live dismembered parts of dead bodies, grew and engulfed him and drew him into that indescribable screaming: 'You did this . . . you did this . . .' He awoke screaming his torment into the night, as though he could scream himself away and out of hell. He wasn't aware, in his terror, that he had defecated, urinated; whether it was night or day, light or dark. He was anguish. He was terror. He was guilt. And he screamed and screamed in an agony of spirit.

Steve Ring lived with this dream for several days and nights, and the Barrymores lived through it with him.

After she had brought him home, Mary Barrymore had sat him down and given him a drink. He was quiet and withdrawn, and seemed hardly to hear what she said to him. As they talked she felt her concern growing. He told her that he had been on Departures. Flatly, unemotionally, he spoke of the flyover, and the fact of the accident. But it wasn't the Steve she knew speaking to her. His degree of irrationality only began fully to dawn on her as in answer to her remark that there was absolutely nothing he could have done which would have prevented it, he'd replied, 'Nothing,' before he'd paused to drink some of the brandy and then, in the same toneless voice, said, 'You know, I killed a lot of people today.' It was said conversationally, yet with complete detachment.

'Steve – are you listening to me?'

'Yes.'

'You did not kill anyone. Do you understand? It was not your fault. Do you hear me?'

'Yes, of course. I wonder how many people I killed today. I don't kill people often, Mary.'

'Steve. Look, dear. Will you listen to me?'

'Yes.'

'Try to understand what I am saying.'

'Yes.'

'You killed no one today!' She spoke with firm emphasis.

'But they must have told you. Didn't they tell you? I killed a lot of people at work today. That's why I'm here, isn't it?'

'No, it isn't. You are here because there was an air crash and you were on duty and it upset you, so James asked me to come over and bring you here to stay with us for a bit. But

Steve – and you must understand this – the crash was not anything to do with you.'

'I'm not upset, Mary. I'm here and not at the Centre because I killed a lot of people.'

It was the beginning of a nightmare for the Barrymores. James got home a little after seven and took up where Mary had left off. But it always reached the same point, the toneless statement of fact, unreal and unemotional. By eight Mary, now seriously alarmed at Steve's mental state, called the doctor. He spoke to Steve and then to the Barrymores. 'I don't know how this is going to go, Mary.' They had known each other from her hospital nursing days. 'At the moment he's deeply shocked. That'll pass, but this "I killed" bit . . .' He shook his head. 'I just don't know. James, could there be anything in it? Could he have done something wrong?'

'I don't think so. But I suppose it's just possible. He might, I suppose, have written one thing down and said another to the plane.'

'When can you check that?'

'Ah well, the problem is that after anything like this all the tapes are taken into custody. I s'pose I could try tomorrow.'

'Do that, James, and when you are sure, let me know. I'll come round again and we'll see if we can't get through to him. Meanwhile, two of these three times a day and two of those at night should help.' Mary nodded.

They had been asleep for a couple of hours when the screaming from the spare room hit them. Mary was out of bed in an instant. When she saw Steve she was horrified. The smell in the room was bad, but forgotten when she looked at him. Eyes wide open, arms stretched behind him on to the bed, neck muscles taut, head rigid and flung back, and his screams, each cascading into the other, all frightened her badly. 'James! Come here. Hurry!' she cried but he was already there.

Steve was oblivious to them. Mary put her face in front of his and grasped his arms, but he neither saw her nor felt her grasp. She shook him, but still he screamed. Then she hit him, a sharp quick hard slap across the face. It broke the hysteria, and there was silence. He saw her then, saw James, realized it was night. He looked around, taking in the strangeness of his surroundings. Then memory hit him. They watched powerless as he gave a racking sob, buried his head in his arms, and started to cry. Four and three-quarter hours later, finally he slept. Mary had given him four more Mogadon and he'd been exhausted. Neither of the Barrymores got any more sleep that night.

The next two nights were as bad, and the days not much better. James tried to get an answer from the office of the Chief Investigator of Air Accidents. There was sympathy for his problem but no, they were not in a position to know how it had happened nor could they disclose any information yet.

The doctor called four times. They tried to get through to Steve, but he was hardly there. On the fourth day he was finally admitted to Bramley Mental Hospital, certified under the Act by two doctors. Steve was alone in the world: both parents dead and no brothers or sisters. He hadn't married and there wasn't a girl in his life of any importance when it happened. So the Barrymores stood in as proxy parents. But in the weeks that followed he hardly knew them, and knew even less of the events of the outside world. He wouldn't have comprehended them.

The greyness of pre-dawn began to filter into the room. Dirk Arnold had eventually drifted into sleep after midnight. The light penetrated the barrier of sleep, just as a dozen little things had disturbed its tenuousness over the past four hours. Quiet sounds of the night had startled him into bewildered consciousness and almost at once bewilderment had given way to the awful blanket of misery as the meaning of this strange room with the sleeping child made its impact.

Sue. Darling, dearest Sue. God! Why did it have to be Sue? And every time silence had mocked the question. At first the shock had made it seem an alien thing, but with each awakening his consciousness had imperceptibly come to accept that the tragedy was real, his to bear.

As he awoke he yawned and stretched, and his mind began to turn to the immediate future. For himself, he had wished many times in the night that he had been at home when the plane hit. But now as he lay watching the faint grey of dawn strengthen into light, a small part of his spirit seemed to share the day's rebirth. There grew a determination, rock solid, to go on and bring to fruition the plans that he and Sue had made for Charlie. Charlie! The first small island of resolve in a sea of grief, for as yet there was no hope nor desire for himself. But in Charlie, Sue lived on.

In his anxiety for the child he started to operate again. His parents lived in the States, but Sue's were in Upper Hutt, outside the city. He decided that the child should go to them. But as he thought about the arrangements to be made it struck him that they might not yet know of the disaster. It must have been on TV and the radio, he thought next: surely they would have heard. On the other hand, if they didn't know yet, then Charlie mustn't be around when the first shock hit them.

It was too early to phone. Just 6.20. But with his mind fully alert came the need to get out of bed, as though to leave the misery of the night behind. Silently, so as not to wake Charlie, he dressed and left the room to look for the phone. He couldn't use it until later, but he felt the need to know where it was. In the corridor, the Night Sister looked up. 'Did you manage to sleep at all?' she asked kindly.

'A little. A bit disturbed, you know.'

'You should have let us give you something' came to her lips, but remained unsaid as she substituted for it 'I've just made coffee. Would you like some?'

'Yes, thanks.' He felt relieved that she hadn't tried to commiserate with him.

'You just sit down there while I get it. Won't be a sec.'

She came out of the small side kitchen with the coffee and handed it to him without a word. He shook his head as she offered him sugar. She waited as he sipped his coffee, well aware that until now he had had no contact with anyone. He had been completely shut up in himself since he'd arrived the evening before.

'I'm very sorry.' She said it softly, to be taken as a statement of fact, or as an invitation, it was up to him. And because there was no pressure in it, he suddenly wanted to share the trouble. So, as the minutes passed, he told her about Sue, the new house, and Charlie. And in simply listening, the nurse helped him. It helped him also to know the size of the tragedy, and the fact that he wasn't facing something alone, as she told him about the suffering of others.

They discussed the decision he'd come to about phoning Sue's parents. He looked at his watch again and saw that it was just coming up to seven. He wondered whether Dorothy and Arnold were asleep still in their neat little timber flat, sleeping away the last few minutes of the night before the alarm rang. Or were they awake and deeply troubled, after spending a night much like his own? The hour came that he had settled on for the phone call. But he postponed it with the thought that he would wait until a quarter past, so as to give them time for their morning tea. Waiting, he suddenly realized the responsibility which rested on him and wondered what he would say. 'It is right to ring them, isn't it, before going there?' he asked the nurse in his doubt.

'Yes, I would ring them.'

He rose from his chair and she watched him go down the corridor to the phone. As it rang for the seventh time, he became sure they couldn't know. If they did, they would have been waiting for it. It was lifted two rings later.

'Arnold Lamont speaking.' Dirk was relieved that it wasn't his mother-in-law.

'Arnie, it's Dirk.'

'Hi there Dirk. Wotcha ringing us up at this hour of the morning for? Only just got out of bed. Still, glad you did. Dorothy wants to come up to see you all on Saturday and perhaps you and I could get a few holes in. Whaddaya think?'

'Arnie. There's something I've got to tell you.'

There was a pause at the other end of the line. 'I see. Well, you'd better tell me about it. What is it? Trouble between you and Sue? We've always thought you two were fine together.'

'We were. Arnie, look, I'm afraid it's going to be a shock, but, well, something's . . . well, something awful's happened, Arnie.'

'Yeah, but what? Has something happened to the baby?' His voice became sharp as he added, 'Or Sue?'

'The baby's OK, but yes, something's happened to Sue.' He paused, not sure how to break it. 'There was a plane crash, Arnie. Two planes hit north of Titahi and well, you see . . . er, they came down near us. I was at the office, you see. And, er . . . Sue and Charlie, well, they were at home, you see. And the plane . . .' he drew a long shuddering breath. 'And the plane, it, or both of them, I don't know, but they . . . hit the house, Arnie.'

There was a long silence at the other end of the phone.

'Are you there, Arnie?'

'Yes Dirk, go on. What's happened to Sue? Is she badly injured?' The awful possibilities ran through his mind. 'Or is she . . . was she . . .' He baulked at the words before forcing himself to say, 'Is she dead?' And dread as the answer was clear in his voice.

'Yes.' Dirk quietly answered.

'She's dead?'

'Yes, Arnie.' His breath shuddered again before he added, with flat finality, 'Yes, Sue's dead.'

And as he heard himself crystallize the fact, the impenetrable loneliness of it all finally caught up with Dirk and brought tears. He cried, and, crying, whispered down the phone, 'Oh God! She's dead, Arnie, dead! And I can't bear it. We loved each other so much!'

The night sister was walking down the corridor, and as she passed the room in which Dirk Arnold was making his phone call she heard him crying. She drew a quiet sigh of relief. His unreal calm when they had spoken earlier had worried her. Now that at last he was giving up his grief in a normal way it was OK. The danger period was past.

'Dirk? Now listen, where are you?' As Dirk told him, the numbness of Arnold's shock gave way to compassion. 'OK now, don't rush it. But when you're fit I think the thing to do would be for you and Charlie to come on down to us. Would you like to do that, or shall I come up there?'

'No, I'm OK and I'd thought of that. If it's not going to be too much for Dorothy, it's what I'd like to do.'

'Right, well, you get on down here, but don't hurry it. Have you had breakfast?'

'No, no, I don't feel like it.'

'Now come on, Dirk. You'd better eat. You have something there then come on down. I'll stay home and we'll see you at say, about 9.30. I don't think I'd come before then. I'll have to tell Dorothy and er . . . you know.'

'Yes, of course, I understand, Arnie.' Then Dirk added, 'And thanks Arnie. Don't worry, I'll be OK by the time I get down there.'

'Yeah, well don't you worry. We'll see this through together, Dirk, OK?'

'Yes, OK.'

'Now, have you got a nurse there? I'd like to have a word with her.'

'Yes, she's around somewhere.' He found her with Charlie, who was having breakfast. The child didn't seem too upset.

Dirk stayed with her as the nurse went off to speak to Arnold. He didn't know it at the time, but for him the very worst was nearly over, and he was to come through it all and live on to love and be happy again.

Chapter Ten

At about 8.35 that morning the accident team were up at Titahi. The pressure from the Prime Minister for an early report had resulted in policemen being added to the team. The first task, a reconstruction. Every piece of wreckage was photographed where it lay before being entered on a grid plan of the immediate area. Then, piece by piece, it was brought in and the jigsaw began to take shape. And as it began to take shape answers emerged and the report grew into a three-phase document.

By day 3 the air impact analyses were almost completed. The facts for a composite report on immediate damage were all there: The paths of the aircraft, the points of collision, the effect of the collision and the entry of the Cessna engine into the DC8's flight deck and its final resting-place amongst the child and her mother. The broken pylon of the port outer told its own story, as did the remains found where the Captain of the DC8 had been sitting.

By day 10 the team had finished its on-site investigation. To get that part of the report into final form for the Minister would take months, but as the team returned to the office they knew already that though they would be able to say what happened, they wouldn't be able to answer the question 'why?' This was fairly rare. More often than not, reconstruction yields up sufficient clues to answer the question 'why?' A type of metal fracture raises suspicion of metal fatigue; an odd angle of impact from scars on metal; cockpit photos, which could raise a doubt on instrumentation accuracy: all these little points help to clarify the picture.

In this accident the team drew a blank. They should have had the benefit of two 'black boxes' from the DC8 but in this case there was nothing of any use. After a crash the procedure is to photograph all instruments on the flight deck. But there was no flight deck left, either on the DC8 or the Cessna. The photos taken merely stated wholesale, inexplicable disaster. So the question 'why' stayed open.

The preliminary report from the team leader was on the desk of the Chief Investigator of Air Accidents within thirteen days of the accident. Having read it and discussed one or two points with his immediate subordinate, he picked up the phone to contact the Minister of Transport.

'Good morning, Minister. Weller, Air Accidents here. I've now got the preliminary site report.'

'Bring it straight over, will you? The Prime Minister wants to see me at ten. We can have a chat before I see him. Come to think of it you'd better come with me.'

He rang off. Ten minutes later Christopher Silaman, the Minister of Transport, looked up as the Chief Investigator was shown in.

New, in a new administration, and not yet quite at ease in a field which had little to do with his earlier supermarket background, he felt the need to assert himself. He didn't rise as Weller entered, just smiled briefly as he waved the Chief Investigator to a seat across the desk, before reinforcing his point by reading and signing something of very little importance. Having thus dealt with the feelings of inferiority which characterize many a politician, he buzzed through to his secretary and looked up briefly, to say, 'Must just clear this up, then I'll be with you, OK?' On cue, the door opened and the girl came in. He handed her the memo without a word, before becoming apparently lost in thought again until she closed the door. It was only then that he turned his ostensible attention to the grave and weighty question of the accident. Very good, he reckoned, for the image. 'Well now, Graham. Let's have it.'

As the Chief Investigator ran through the report, the Minister nodded from time to time, and asked a couple of minor, safe, questions. It didn't worry him that a great deal of what the Chief Investigator said made very little sense to him. He knew his Prime Minister well enough to know that the part that he would have to play in the interview at ten would be more that of interested spectator than participant. But to listen and appear to understand was important to his keen intellect. After a while he looked at his watch and thought that they had better be on their way.

'Yes.' He drew the word out with gravity. 'Yes, I see. I think you'd better tell me the rest as we go over, but I would like to ask just one question that comes to mind from what you have told me so far. As I understand it, you say that there was no indication from the on-site investigation as to whether one or other of the aircraft was flying at an angle of inclination other than that to be expected. Is that correct?'

'Yes.'

'I see.' The two men passed through the door. 'Well now, what else arises in the report?' As they walked together up to the Prime Minister's office, Graham Weller continued to speak. He wasn't sure whether he was talking to a very clever man who had seen a major point straight away, or whether he had just had one of the old 'feed back for effect' tricks in the game played on him. He decided to reserve his judgment on the Minister until he had had more time to assess him. Together, they entered the Prime Minister's suite, to be met by his private secretary. 'Good morning, Minister. He's expecting you, so I don't think he'll be long.'

'Morning. I don't think you know Graham Weller, do you?'

'No, I don't think we've met.' The tall man glanced keenly at Graham. He was the sort of man who'd remember if he'd met someone. The pointless expression of untrue uncertainty irritated Graham, who by instinct and training was a man who saw things in black and white, and he began to feel vaguely uneasy in the presence of the 'corridors of power' indirectness of these men. But the smile was pleasant, and the handshake firm. 'Graham's having a hell of a time of it just now, you know, sorting out this wretched crash,' said the Minister.

'Interesting work, I should imagine,' the tall young man observed. 'Tell me, how do you set about it?' Graham felt a prick of annoyance at the suspicion of offhand patronage for his one-track expertise in the young man's voice. But of course there was nothing to get hold of, so polite conversation filled the gap as they waited to go in. While they were chatting, the little light on the young man's desk came on. Graham thought he'd missed it and was about to draw his attention to it, but was forestalled as, with practised ease, the young man disengaged himself from the conversation. 'I think he's ready to see you now. I won't be a moment.' The words of personal depreciation in the near presence of an unseen but great power lingered in the air as he walked across to the heavy doors. As he reached them, one door opened to let quiet conversation ebb out of the room for a moment, and then two people, recognized by Graham as the Ministers of Defence and Finance, came out. Then the door shut again behind the tall young secretary. With brief nods to Silaman, the two Ministers left the outer office.

Suddenly, in the silence between the two of them, the Chief Investigator of Air Accidents realized that the Minister of Transport was nervous. In his experience very few politicians were ever prepared to wait in silence. As he glanced at the Minister, his suspicion was confirmed. The man was decidedly nervous. Then the doors reopened and the secretary was smiling as he said, 'The Prime Minister will see you now, gentlemen.' The tall young man stood at the partly open door and showed them in. 'The Minister of Transport, and Graham Weller, Chief Investigator of Air Accidents, sir.'

'Ah. Good to see you, Christopher.' Walking towards them, the Prime Minister indicated that they should sit on the sofa at one side of the room. 'Coffee for both of you?' It was hardly a question. 'So you're our Chief Investigator of Air Accidents? It's good work you do,' he observed, 'but sad that it has to be done, hummm?' He smiled at Graham, briefly but firmly shook hands with him, and then took one of the armchairs. Graham couldn't help but smile at the basic psychology.

'Right, Mr Weller. What have you got for me? How did this terrible thing happen so near a major airport?'

'I regret that just at the moment I can't tell you that,' Graham replied.

'What do you mean, you can't tell me? It's nearly two weeks now. Surely you've had adequate time to prepare some sort of interim finding?'

'Well, I can tell you *what* happened, but not yet *why*,' Graham said.

'I see. Well, I suppose we'd better start with that.'

'Briefly, a Paranational DC8 in-bound from Nandi to Wellington collided with a Cessna 172 bound from Masterton to Nelson at just about 16.46 on the afternoon of the 8th, about eighteen miles north of the airport and just north of Titahi. The collision was right angle, nose to nose. The

Cessna's engine entered the flight deck of the DC8 to the front of the co-pilot, that is to say, to the front right of the flight deck. The Cessna was flying left to right across the nose of the 8. Sequentially, after that the body of the Cessna pilot, a vet, entered the flight deck to the front of the Captain of the 8. The flight deck was more or less destroyed at that time. As this occurred, the fuselage of the Cessna was torn away and fell back towards the port, or left wing, of the 8. It caused the support pylon to the port outer engine to twist and shear. That engine fell to earth north of Titahi Bay. Debris of the fuselage entered the air intake of the remaining port engine, damaging it badly and setting it on fire. Upon ground impact, the under part of the remains of the 8 was torn out. Important for two reasons; the first, it was probably at that stage that most of the passengers died; and secondly – and it's worrying from an investigation point of view . . .' and here he paused to give the little dry cough for which he was well-known, and which he used when in full spate to punctuate a point of importance. The Prime Minister merely found it annoying. 'Yes, you were saying,' he said, with a trace of asperity.

Unused to interruption, and unaware of this habit of his, the Chief Investigator looked momentarily perplexed. 'Ah yes. Yes, I was saying that secondly, and worrying . . .'

'Yes. You've said that.' There was no mistaking the mood of the Prime Minister. He had hoped for, in fact, badly needed, an answer.

'. . . black box, vital from a determination of causation point of view. In this case, we found the box but so damaged as to prove useless as a record of the flight. The damage to the flight deck was so severe that no instrument readings were possible and further, the in-flight flight deck recorder, another black box, was also destroyed. Needless to say, the remains of the Cessna cockpit could tell us little or nothing. And that's about it at the moment, Prime Minister.'

'And it has taken you two weeks to prepare this?' The Prime Minister's voice was silky.

'Yes, and if I may say so, it has only been possible by reason of very long hours put in by my team, helped by the outside assistance arranged by the Minister.'

'And were you out there leading your "team"?' The word carried an edge.

'I wasn't on the ground, as it were. As a matter of policy, I assign my inspectors to their tasks, and apart from supervision and guidance, I leave it to them.'

'While you remain on your backside doing bugger all in your office, I suppose?'

The Chief Investigator of Air Accidents was scandalized. 'My job . . .'

'Your job, sir, is to do as you are directed. I made it crystal clear to the Minister of Transport here on the night of the accident, and repeatedly thereafter, that I required a preliminary report on this matter within seven days. And what do you give me, one week late? Not much more than I already know from the papers. Anyway, tell me what else you have done apart from look at the bits?'

'Well put like that sir, nothing completed. Quite a lot in hand, of course. But, well, it's not the procedure . . .'

'Damn your procedure. Did I not order extra men to assist you? Did you not get them?'

'We had assistance, as I mentioned.'

'I see. In that case, tell me why you have not at least the foundation of a full report, or enough at least to indicate why this accident occurred.'

'Prime Minister, I think it right to say that if you have any criticism, then you would be more proper in addressing it to me than to the Chief Investigator of Air Accidents.'

The Prime Minister raised his eyebrows in surprise as he swivelled to his Minister of Transport. 'Why?'

'It is my departmental responsibility, and I chose to direct this investigation along the lines normally pursued. To do otherwise would, in my opinion, not have helped.'

The Prime Minister pondered for a moment, before changing tack. 'You will remember, my dear Christopher, that I specifically said that I wanted this to be cleared up quickly. A great deal may be at stake in a national sense, as you well know.'

'Quite, but I think in fairness to the Chief Investigator that it is being cleared up quickly. The report you have just been given usually takes much longer. We should remember it's not two weeks yet.'

'So that's quick is it?' he paused. 'But with the men available, explain to me precisely why other lines of investigation have not been going along concurrently concerning the aircrew, Air Traffic Control, the vet, and the rest of it?'

'Well, as the Chief Investigator here pointed out to me, there is no point in digging into a great number of things when the answer may easily have become apparent during the work in hand.'

'I see, Christopher. Yes, I understand. Hmmmm, I think I would like to discuss this further with you later today. Shall we say 2.30. And as for you, sir,' he said, turning to Graham Weller. 'May I ask for your explanation as to why you have seen fit to delegate this, the worst air accident in our history, to men junior and presumably less well-qualified than yourself?'

Graham had been watching and listening, fascinated. At first he'd been nervous of the Prime Minister, sympathetically nervous, as some had rubbed off from the Minister of Transport as they had waited outside. Then he had been appalled to see an aspect of the PM which was never known to the public. He was angry at the attack, then sorry for the Minister of Transport. Finally, he was vaguely amused at the idiocy of the whole set-up. 'Prime Minister, may I ask you a question?'

A little taken aback, the Prime Minister said, 'Yes. I suppose it can't do any harm.'

'Do you know anything at all about the investigation of air accidents? I would hasten to add that that's not meant to be impertinent, but it is important to make the point that I've been in it all my life. So I'd ask you to accept that there are valid reasons for the procedures, including my so-called delegation. I have to remain completely objective so that I can assess the work and the conclusions of my people.' He noticed the Prime Minister nod grimly. 'Now, as for concurrent activity, when we know what we should be exploring, we investigate several things at the same time. In this case, the next phase of the investigation is clear. Since we've no other lead, we must check over all the information given to these two flights – pre-flight, in-flight, right through. In fact, we are already well into the transcripts of every Air Traffic procedure followed for the flights, and that's a hell of a job, involving not merely Wellington, but Nandi and Auckland as well. And it's slow work. But I think we'll be in a position to start checking out the Air Traffic Control side within a couple of days or so. Also as a concurrent activity, we are checking all ground information fed to the 8 Captain and First Officer, and the engineers' data. And there's a lot more I won't bother you with now, but it can't be done thoroughly overnight, sir. All I can say is I will do my best to do it as quickly as I possibly can.'

This speech had its effect. Suddenly, as a cloud clears the sun, the well-known smile appeared on the Prime Minister's face. 'I see. Well, I suppose you people are doing what you can. Hmm, if I was a trifle hasty, you must forgive me. But you know, this terrible business weighs heavily with me.' Then he added, with winning candour, 'And between the three of us, you know, I find the pressure of the Press very trying. They just don't seem to begin to appreciate the difficulty of the task facing you chaps. Anyway you'll push ahead, won't you, Weller?' He paused for a moment to think as the Chief Inspector nodded. 'We must say something to keep people happy. Yes . . .' he paused again, before continuing. 'Yes, I think you'd better hold a Press conference, Christopher, otherwise everyone will begin to start getting a bit uptight. You know the sort of thing needed – investigation going ahead, difficult task, an answer will be given, but not the wrong one, etc. You needn't say anything much, just generate confidence. Tell them a bit about Weller here. Say that the public will be kept informed of progress.' He leaned back in his chair. 'Yes, something along those lines, I think, don't you Christopher?'

'Yes, and come to think of it, I rather think it wouldn't be a bad idea if Graham here was with me.'

The Prime Minister looked at him carefully. 'Hmmmm. Got the right sort of face, I should think.'

Graham laughed as he said, 'Well, if you want me along, I'd be happy to come.'

Then the Minister of Transport with one of those inspired touches to which he owed his place in the Cabinet, blandly murmured, 'Perhaps the best time for this little affair might be 2.30 this afternoon, Prime Minister?'

Sharply, for a second, the Prime Minister looked at him. Then, abruptly, he laughed. 'Yes, all right. The sooner the better I suppose. 2.30 today then.' And he smiled again his 'no hard feelings' smile which reminded Graham of a crocodile, before adding; 'I really can't impress on you both strongly enough the urgency of getting an acceptable answer, and getting it quickly.' He paused to let it hang in the air to gain weight.

Instinctively, they both nodded, though, for the life of him Graham didn't see what the great rush was. Still, as a public servant it wasn't for him to reason why, so he didn't ask the obvious question. The Prime Minister continued. 'Now, bearing it in mind that there has got to be an answer, I would like to explore, on a purely ex-hypothesi basis, of course, the possible answers. Now, Weller, in your experience, what would run through your mind?'

'Well . . .' he began cautiously, for speculation wasn't something he liked. 'I think we will be able to rule out mechanical failure. If it had been that, I think the on-site investigation would have shown it up, but I'll know for sure in a week or so when the results of one or two tests are back with me. Apart from that, had any failure occurred, I'd have thought there would have been a fair chance of the Air Traffic Controllers hearing about it, unless it was all very, very sudden, and there's no indication of that. So that really only leaves two possibilities: a mistake by one or more of the Controllers, or, alternatively, pilot error. And I'd add that I doubt, frankly, if we'll find anything wrong with Air Traffic procedures. So that leaves us with pilot error.'

'I see,' murmured the Prime Minister. 'Can you be satisfied that the altitude of one or other of the aircraft wouldn't have been affected by the weather.'

'No, almost certainly nothing to do with it. Low almost static cloud. No, certainly nothing to account for a thousand feet.'

'Why do you say a thousand feet?'

'Oh! I should have mentioned it earlier. The DC8 had been cleared over the area to 4000 feet and the Cessna to 3000 feet.'

'Hmmmmm, I see. So tell me, what does this all come down to?'

'Well, with no mechanical failure, no switch in the weather, and no failure on the part of Air Traffic Control, we're left with pilot error, as I said. On the one hand, you have the well-instrumented flight deck of the 8 with two highly experienced pilots working together, each checking the other with instrument duplication; while on the other hand you have a vet who, as I understand it, appears not to have owned his 172 for very long.' He smiled as he added, 'But, thank heavens, it's not part of my job to do anything more than state facts.'

As he stopped talking, silence fell on the room as the two

ministers considered what he had said.

Eventually, the Prime Minister broke it. 'You will of course be looking into the question not only of experience, but into background as well?'

'Yes, we always do.'

'Not just the vet, but the aircrew on the flight deck of the DC8? Must reassure people eventually you know.'

'I understand,' replied the Chief Investigator, 'but I must also make it plain that if any of them were in any, er, personal difficulty, it will have to come out in my report.'

'Oh, my dear man, I wasn't for one moment suggesting you avoid mentioning anything which you discover, merely that what you have to say could well be a trifle more than purely negative. Then it is up to the Minister here to come to policy decisions as to what findings are in the public interest to publish; and he will be helped if, for instance, he can state categorically that the DC8 crew conducted their flight at the highest level of professional competence. And as part of your investigation you have satisfied yourself that they weren't worried or under stress of any sort.'

'Yes, of course Prime Minister, I quite understand.'

By now the Prime Minister was on his feet and Graham Weller rose, the interview nearly over. Walking with him to the door, the Prime Minister continued, 'Well, thank you for coming to see me. Very interesting, and I am very glad to know that everything is in such capable hands.'

At the door, but before he opened it, the Prime Minister stopped and, turning to the Chief Investigator, asked his final question. 'Just to make sure I fully understand, it is correct, is it not, to say that, for whatever reason, the only possible cause of this accident is that one of these planes must have been flying at the wrong height. That's it, isn't it?'

'Yes, unless by some extraordinary coincidence one was high and the other low, but it's so unlikely I'd discount it. And I also discount the DC8 being damaged and diving on to the Cessna. They'd have contacted Air Traffic long before that.'

Opening the door, the Prime Minister said, 'Hmmm, thank you. Now, you'll want a word with the Minister about this afternoon, but while he's here I would like to have a word with him about something else, so if you wouldn't mind waiting for a moment.' And he smiled in dismissal. Graham nodded and the heavy door closed behind him. 'How'd it go?' the tall young man asked.

Returning to his chair, The Prime Minister sat and pondered for a time. Then, with a sigh, he looked up at Christopher Silaman. 'Chris, old thing, we could be in the most awful trouble here, you know. And you're the only chap who can fix it for us. And,' he went on gravely, 'I feel bound to say that if you fail, well . . . I doubt if we'll still be in office in twelve months from now. I think you know what I have in mind?'

'The Attorney General did mention something about insurance cover, a decision taken by you, I think, which I wasn't in on.'

'I think we can forget for the moment, Christopher, who took what decision, though it was a Ministry of Transport matter. However,' he added lightly, 'that's not important at the moment. As you know when we entered office we were short of cash – we blamed the Opposition. Dare say we did ourselves a bit of good with the electorate there. But, of course, we had to keep the bad news in bounds to avoid people asking what the hell were we doing in letting them make quite such a mess without screaming about it in Opposition. So, we played it down the middle. Now we went in for a good deal of pruning on public expenditure, most of which, thank God, didn't attract too much attention at the time. But now we've got a problem. Because we never thought there'd be a big claim, we decided not to go on diluting the Paranational premium income to Merlin Mutual Ltd by reinsurance with Lloyds. In the result, we persuaded their board to raise their risk from the first 10 million, to the first 100 and saved a premium to Lloyds or whoever of in the region of 12 million a year. Seemed a fair risk at the time.'

He paused, as he thought about how bloody unlucky it had all turned out to be, and smoothed the hair on his head. 'But, there we are. If that got out we are, to coin a phrase, in the shit. And, I fear, the Opposition would make it stick.' Again he paused, as though it was all very painful to him, which indeed it was. 'But, Christopher, I fear that's not quite all. For you see, we have no cover on public servants' liability. Claims in the past had been so very small relative to reinsurance premiums that we decided to discontinue. It saved several million a year. But now, of course, if the Air Traffic Control people are found to blame, then, well, I fear we pick up the bill and heaven help us if that state of affairs became public.'

'Yes, I see the problem, but what can I do about it?' Silaman asked.

'We can all pray that in the course of the investigation clear evidence emerges that it was the vet's fault. Yes, we can all do that. But you can do more. I want you to assume that your Chief Investigator of Air Accidents doesn't find anything concrete, so it'll point to the vet. With that in mind, I want you to pave the way for it, so that by the time it becomes clear, it will come as no surprise to anyone. Now, in starting on that, you'll be helped by this' – he handed over a single sheet of paper – 'at your Press conference today, all right?'

'It hardly seems particularly ethical . . .'

'Perhaps not, to the purist, and I don't s'pose you would think it particularly ethical, Christopher, if for one reason or another it became necessary for me to rely upon you to shoulder the blame for the insurance decisions I mentioned. After all, my dear Christopher, the question of adequate cover in the fields we're in, and advice to the Government and the Merlin Mutual Ltd would have been essentially a Ministry of Transport matter.' He paused before adding quietly, 'Wouldn't you think?'

The Minister of Transport was astounded. 'You'd never get away with it!' he said.

'My dear boy, that, if I may say so, is a trifle naive. But no, you are correct in the sense that it might see us out of power for a spell, but the public memory is very short, and it wouldn't destroy us. But you, my dear Chris, you would be considered unfitted for Government for ever more. A pity, but there it is. And I think I should make it plain that, if it came to it, I'd do it, I'd have to.'

'I bloody well wouldn't stand for it. I'd publish!'

'Would you? Well, that would be a matter for you, of course, but I rather feel that it wouldn't achieve anything. Lots of Ministers sacked over the years blame their downfall on everyone but themselves, and nothing smacks of sour grapes more surely than that. And, of course, I and my – I should say, our – colleagues would hardly be able to agree with what you had to say. Hmmm, yes, I think I can say that it would emerge fairly clearly that the decisions were yours, as would be expected. And I would emerge as a Premier sufficiently strong and substantial to be able to look facts in the face and not afraid to rectify a mistake when it came to my notice. Played right, you know, I might even survive a vote of no confidence. No?' he added, and his voice was soft.

Appalled though he was, Christopher Silaman realized immediately that if he wasn't to turn his back on politics for ever he would have to play along and hope it all came out OK. And he comforted himself with the thought that at least the PM hadn't asked for an undated letter of resignation. But Jesus, he thought, what a hell of a frightener. Then with no real alternative, he replied, 'I understand.'

'Good, good. Now we've got over that, I think we ought to think about what course of action ought to see us continuing in office and to see you with an extremely bright future, hmmm? Don't worry Christopher, everyone has to earn his spurs at some time or other, so don't worry about it.' Christopher nodded.

'Right,' the Prime Minister continued. 'We start forming public opinion, and also I think we should give a little thought to our Mr Weller. You must make it all a little difficult for him. I suggest that you keep looking over his shoulder to hurry him along but be very helpful. Make sure he doesn't get the thing out of perspective, stop him digging into things too much. You know the sort of approach. Now the reason for this is that the Solicitor General tells me that from a legal standpoint a judge has to work on probability. Get Weller to think along those lines and I think you'll find that if he comes to the private conclusion that the vet was to blame, he'll inevitably try to find something to support it. This is what you must encourage. Now, what else is there?' He paused, lost in thought for a moment, then added, 'No, I can't think of anything else at the moment, can you?'

'No, but I'm not quite sure that I see where all this is going.'

'Oh, in general terms, simply getting the vet's insurers to accept liability, or at worst, a contribution from us which won't attract attention. An over-simplification, of course, because we'll also probably have to sort out the Merlin Mutual Ltd people a bit but I dare say it'll all work out.'

Then, voicing his uncertainty as to quite how it would all work out, he added, 'We can always modify the plan of campaign as we go along, if necessary, so we must keep our options open.'

'Well, I don't pretend to understand quite what's in your mind, but I'll do as you say.'

'Good.' When they reached the door, the Prime Minister suddenly laughed and, just before he showed his Minister out, said, 'You know, Chris, if you did understand it all, perhaps it should be me and not you leaving to go back to your office!' And the Minister couldn't help smiling as he left.

Walking back to his office with Graham Weller, the Minister talked about the Press conference. It would be small and in his office. They could syndicate afterwards. Just before they parted the Chief Investigator asked: 'Is the Prime Minister always like that?' Christopher smiled as he replied, 'Lord no! He was rather pleasant today!'

Two o'clock was striking. Christopher Silaman was on the first of the steps leading from the street into the Ministry when his PPS finally caught up with him.

'Minister.' His voice was sharp and turning, the Minister saw an agitated secretary hurrying towards him. 'Don't go that way.'

'Why not?'

'Word got out and I'm afraid there's hordes turned up. And rather than start a row I've had to let them all in. I hope that's OK?'

The Minister frowned.

'I couldn't see what else to do.'

The PPS was plainly very concerned at upsetting his Minister.

'Well, not to worry. Did you, er, have a word with . . .'

'Yes,' the private secretary cut in.

'Good, is Graham Weller here?'

'I hope so. Perhaps if we go up the back way we'll see. I rang him.'

'OK, up we go.'

Graham Weller was in the office. The time was 2.10.

'Any worries Graham?' the Minister asked.

'I thought you said it would be a small occasion!'

'Aw, don't worry about that – the more the merrier.' Then more seriously he said, 'Now if you get worried about anything then all you have to do is push one of the pieces of paper forward on the desk in front of you, got it?'

'OK.'

'And if I do it – and for heaven's sake, watch for it – then shut up, I'll deal with it.'

'But surely I should finish anything I start?'

'Not so, Graham. Remember this is no more than an exercise to put the public mind at rest. You must appreciate that one wrong word and in a political sense great harm may be done. So you'll be guided by me. Is that clearly understood?'

'Well, yes of course, Minister.'

'Good. We'll be going in in a moment, but just one last thing. It's unlikely, but should you push a paper forward and for any reason I decide that you must continue, I shall lean back. If it happens, take your time but go on dealing with it. Right?'

'Yes, if you say so.'

'I do. Are they ready for us?' He turned to the secretary.

'Yes, Minister.'

The Minister straightened his tie as they walked through to the doors to the large conference room. As Graham followed the Minister in, he saw him raise his hand and heard the breezy 'G'day to you all. Glad you could come. Look, you at the sides, if you start to get short of air, just bellow and I'll get the guys in the middle to breathe out. That OK?' The murmur of laughter was just what the Minister wanted. As they sat down, the Minister began. The note struck was grave but informal.

'OK now. I've called this conference because the Prime Minister and myself, and all of us in this Government, were not only deeply, but terribly, shocked by this air disaster, the first we've ever had, mainly I think because we as a country put safety right up at the top of our priorities. But now we are determined on two things: one, we are going to get to the bottom of it, and quickly; and two, we don't believe in keeping the public in the dark about the steps being taken.' He paused, stretched the silence for as long as he judged he could to deepen concentration, then continued: 'Now, as I've said, we want people to be well-informed about this thing, and with this in mind, I've asked Mr Graham Weller, here,' he motioned to Graham with his hand. 'Weller, with a double "l" that is.' Someone murmured thanks. 'Yeah, we even help with spelling here.' He let the short laughter linger for only a moment.

'Yep, I've asked Graham to leave the investigation and come here this afternoon in case there's any point where I need his help. He, as you should know, is the Chief Investigator of Air Accidents. He's been on the job for thirty-seven years and during that time he's been involved in practically every accident we've ever had. But the question that some of you may have in mind is, is he qualified to look into anything on the scale of this disaster? After all, it's the first we've had, please God, the last. Well, I can be brief, yes he is. You could go around the world and you wouldn't find better experience or expertise. Graham has been to all the main international courses up to the very highest level. In fact, he was in the States as recently as last year on a refresher at Oklahoma. And many of his staff have been too.'

Graham smiled a trifle grimly to himself as he remembered the battle about it after he'd had a directive to cut his budget by no less than 30 per cent. But that had been under the previous Government. Amusing, he thought, how glibly the Minister took credit.

'OK, over to you.' The Minister finished. A small dark man raised an arm. The Minister nodded to him.

'Maclaren, *Globe.* Can you tell me, Minister, why, when you want everyone to know just how things are going, you forget to tell three-quarters of the people in this room to be here now?'

'Tell me, Mr Maclaren. If your wife buys a pink lavatory roll, do you have that nasty sneaking suspicion that she's becoming a Commie?'

The roar of delight was quickly silenced by the Minister. 'But I'll tell you. Only this morning did I receive Graham Weller's first report. And I didn't leave the Prime Minister until nearly midday . . .'

Graham smiled again to himself – he could have sworn he had been back in his own office by 11.15.

'. . . and then it was all go. OK, so some of you weren't able to be contacted, but we knew word would get around. Right, who's next?'

'Irene McCoy, *Evening Star.* I wonder whether Mr Weller could tell us what caused this accident?'

'No, he can't just yet, but Graham, tell them what you've got so far.' Graham began to give his summary of the on-site team's findings. When he'd finished he sat back, quite pleased with himself.

'Sam Stanford of Associated Press. Mr Weller, will you please run through what possible causes there could be?' Graham was about to open his mouth, when he saw the piece of paper slide forward.

'I don't think, Mr Stanford, that we should ask the Chief Inspector to speculate here. But would you be happy if your question was in the terms of what other aspects concerning an inquiry of this sort Mr Weller will be looking into?'

'Guess I'll have to be, Minister!' A ripple of amusement went through the journalists.

'OK Graham, shoot.'

'We have teams from my office and other government departments concerned with safety in the air, now working on Operations, Air Traffic Control, airworthiness; teams established for the DC8 and the Cessna in flight, and of course, we will be concerned with . . .' from the corner of his eye he saw the piece of paper begin to move, '. . . many other matters.'

Stanford came to his feet again when it was clear that Graham had finished. 'What other matters, Mr Weller?'

The Minister went straight in. 'I think you must appreciate, ladies and gentlemen, that there is a distinction between what is always covered initially as a matter of procedure and what is then covered as a result of findings from the first stage of investigation. But to speculate on what might have to be covered as a result of findings not yet made is a waste of time. Next?'

'Beaumont, NBC News. I'm not familiar with your country, Minister, but I guess people would like to know just who handles things of this sort here.'

'Experts in several departments. Next?'

Beaumont was up again. 'I guess that will mean something to someone, Minister, but not to me. If I may, I'd kind of like an answer to my question. Departments of what?'

'Government departments, Mr Beaumont.'

'Back home, we have a Board to deal with things like this and to that Board is given the help of bodies outside the Government. Do you have that here, Minister?'

'We would, naturally, involve anyone who we think could help.'

'I see. Do you have a Board here?'

'No. We've found that the task is best contained within the office of our Chief Investigator of Air Accidents. He makes the final report.'

'To whom, Minister?'

'In the first instance, to me.'

'And what do you do with it, Minister?'

'Mr, er, Beaumont, there are a lot of people with questions besides yourself. But if any of my staff can help instruct you in the workings of our investigation procedure then I'm sure it can be arranged for you. You sir?' he nodded to a man at the back.

'I've got a question for your expert, Minister. Harding, *Triumph*. Mr Weller, as I understand it, there are thousands of near-misses a year?'

'Yes.'

'Often between big and small aircraft?'

The Minister sat silent. 'That's true,' Graham conceded reluctantly.

'Would I be correct in saying that as a statistical fact world wide, such near-misses have usually been found to have been caused by the private pilot, rather than commercial aircrew.'

Silence settled on the room as Graham gently pushed his piece of paper forward. The Minister eased himself further back in his chair.

'Mr Weller, that's a statistical fact, isn't it?' the man persisted.

'Yes.'

'I would like to go a little further, Mr Weller. I believe that the Cessna in this case was flying at a lower altitude, supposedly, than the DC8. Can you confirm or deny that, please?'

Graham saw that the Minister was still leaning comfortably back in his chair, and irritation swept across him as he replied, 'I think, Mr Harding, that it would be best if I don't pre-empt my report on the matter.'

'Oh, I don't think we should avoid giving out a clearly established fact, Graham,' interposed the Minister blandly. 'No one knows how this accident happened, but as I see it, Mr Harding isn't asking you to speculate on that, is he?'

'Well, in that case, Minister . . . Yes, Mr Harding. I can

confirm it as a fact that the DC8 was cleared to a height of 4000 feet and the Cessna to 3000 feet. I cannot say at what height the collision occurred.'

'But you could confirm, Mr Weller, that the Cessna's wing runs above the pilot's cockpit which restricts upward visibility?'

The small fidgets in the room fell still, and the answer 'Yes' fell like a small hard stone into the limpid pool of silence. The Press conference broke up half an hour later.

After Graham had left, angry but impotent in the face of the Minister's bland assurance that 'Really, it went rather well, I think,' the Minister contacted the Prime Minister.

'How'd it go, Christopher?'

'Oh, rather well. Harding came nicely up to scratch. In fact, that's why I'm ringing. I owe him for the favour, and thought he might be interested in our tentative views on the question of extending permissible road haulage distances, as a non-attributable leak, of course.'

'Why not? We can always decide later that we were tentatively wrong!' They both laughed. 'By the way, Chris. I've decided to give an interview this evening on TV. Will you let me have the transcript of your Press conference as soon as possible?'

'Yes. It's being done now. I rather thought you'd want to follow it up.'

When Grace Newton read her evening paper later that night her eye caught the story on the front page. And as she read it she knew that her worst fears were being realized. Trembling with anger, she screwed the paper up and went to ring her solicitor. As a result she missed the news on the telly, but thousands didn't.

'Later, we have an exclusive interview with the Prime Minister, but first, some of the background . . . Ian McCrea reporting.' And in hundreds of thousands of homes, people who normally used the news as 'get up and do' time between two popular programmes hurried back to their sets to hear the first public statement on the crash.

The picture picked up Ian McCrea outside the concrete nonentity in which, on the tenth floor, the office of Air Accidents Investigation was housed. A veteran in the art of the build-up, he had dressed soberly for the role. A heavy, big man, he let gravity show on his face as he began his spot.

'I'm here, for what has been going on here for the past thirteen days is of national importance. Inside this building, in the heart of the capital, all day and late into the nights since the afternoon of that terrible air crash men and women have been working to give us an answer to the question . . .' He paused, looked down, then with a renewed keenness in his glance, continued, 'How could such a disaster have occurred?' He let it sink in. 'A question we have a right to have answered at the earliest possible moment. But – and you may think, wisely so – no one has been saying anything so far, for what could be worse than an answer which could be wrong? So we have waited. But today the Minister of Transport held a Press conference and with him he had the man who has had to shoulder the enormous burden of this investigation, the Chief Investigator of Air Accidents, a man who, at last, in public this afternoon spoke about this disaster . . .'

The picture switched to the video of the Press conference and panned the crowd in the room to pick up Harding of the *Triumph*, and viewers heard the first of his questions. Then the Chief Investigator of Air Accidents filled the set as he answered the questions until the psychological moment of the third question. Then it came into remorseless close-up as the final devastating question – the fourth – hung in the air.

'Mr Weller, which restricts upward visibility?' the man persisted.

Weller's face, large in filling the TV screen, showed his unease. And the camera continued to hold him in close-up until the last answer was given – the 'yes'. And it was damning.

At home, Graham Weller squirmed in his chair as he watched. He hadn't realized that he had looked so much like a man with a guilty secret being wrung from him.

'That was this afternoon.' Ian McCrea in head and shoulders close-up filled the screen again. 'But this evening the Prime Minister has agreed to speak to us further.' The shot switched to the Prime Minister in his office, seated in the armchair he favoured for informal comment. Legs crossed, one arm casually draped along the arm of the chair, the other supported the elbow with the hand resting lightly on the top of the uppermost thigh. He had found it an effective pose.

'Prime Minister, it's correct to say, I think, that we in this country have never suffered anything on this scale before?'

'That's right. I believe we have probably the finest safety record in the world. We have always spent a great deal of money on ground staff and equipment and, as you know, Paranational have a record second to none. The two together have made for a very, very high safety level in the past.'

'You say "in the past". Does that mean that you think that there was a failure in the airline or on the ground here?'

'No, it doesn't, Ian. I think that flying is safer today than it ever has been.'

'But an accident has happened. Do you attribute it to any failure on the ground or with the pilots of the DC8?' McCrea pressed.

'Well, I don't want to pre-empt our Chief Investigator's report which will, of course, become a matter of public record, but I think I can say . . .' and he gave the camera his candid smile, 'that I saw the Chief Investigator of Air Accidents today and I don't think he considers there is any probability of the accident being found to be anything to do with pilot failure or the Air Traffic Control Service.'

'You say "pilot failure". Would you be specific on that. Are you talking about the pilots of the DC8 or the Cessna?'

'We were talking about the commercial airline. But I think you'd better ask the Chief Investigator about the Cessna.'

'But you have seen them both today?'

'Yes.'

'At today's Press conference the Chief Investigator said that usually the pilot of a small aircraft was to blame, and in this case he was flying a plane with a wing which would have obscured his vision upwards, and he was the lower of the two in flight. Do you think that was the cause of the accident?'

'There has to be a cause, of course, but . . .' again he brought the disarming smile into effect with a shrug, 'as yet we simply don't know what it was.' He paused, as though reaching a decision. 'But to avoid speculation perhaps I should add there was no mechanical failure involved. That much we know right now.'

'So, would it be correct to say that the Cessna was probably at fault?'

'I can't answer that, Ian, and we cannot afford to speculate. The investigation has a long way to go yet and I think that I have said as much, probably more, than maybe I should have done already. But it is important for people to know the negative findings I've mentioned so they can go on using air transport with confidence. I say that sincerely. Operating conditions have always been good but even so the Minister of Transport has already put into effect measures to ensure that there is greater separation between aircraft in the future. We are determined that this type of accident cannot possibly happen again.'

'Does that mean, Prime Minister, that the view has been taken that the height difference between the two aircraft is now considered to have been too little?'

'No. In the absence of a mistake it was one hundred per cent safe and more than met international requirements, but . . .' he raised his hands to give point to it, 'we have decided to set our own standards for the future.'

'Thank you, Prime Minister.'

The fadeout in zoom to close-up for the final two seconds left the Prime Minister's smile etched before switching back to Ian McCrea.

'Well, there we have it, as far as it goes. No one is saying quite how this accident happened. At the Press conference today the Minister of Transport . . .' Christopher Silaman's profile was shown, 'said, and I quote, "The Chief Investigator here has dealt very fairly with the questions about what the statistics may indicate, but I am bound to say that they don't necessarily give the answer in all cases. In this case, as yet, there is no suggestion that the pilot of the Cessna was at fault." ' The Minister's profile switched back to the reporter. 'Added to that the Prime Minister has ruled out pilot error on the DC8, mechanical failure, and failure by the Air Traffic Services. If it wasn't such a terrible catastrophe one might feel it was a mystery more intriguing than in any novel. But this is too terrible to speculate on. So now we will have to await the final report from the office of the Chief Investigator of Air Accidents.' For a second he was still and silent, moving towards the closedown. When it came it was in a quieter tone of voice and very earnest: 'And then, and only then will we know whether this unfortunate veterinary surgeon was in fact to blame. Meanwhile I will remind you of the Prime Minister's words: "We cannot afford to speculate". On that final note, this is Ian McCrea reporting from the capital. Good night.'

Chapter Eleven

The questions from Harding at the Press conference hammered in Grace's mind as she waited for the solicitor to answer the telephone. Marty had just got in and was passing through the hall when the phone went. 'Marty Chalmers here.'

'Oh Marty, they've done it. What I feared. They've blamed Frank.'

'How do you mean, Grace?'

'The paper. There was a Press interview today and they blame Frank. Oh Marty, we must stop them. It wasn't Frank's fault, I know it wasn't. And the insurance have looked into it and they must have decided it wasn't his fault. So how can they say . . .'

'Now Grace. Easy, dear. Just calm down. I'm quite sure you've got it wrong. No paper would say it's anyone's fault unless it was quoting a Government source, and I know for . . .'

'But they have!' she broke in. 'I tell you, they have. I've read it, you haven't, so how can you say they haven't?'

'All right, Grace. Just take it easy. Have you got the paper with you?'

'It's in the other room. I was so angry that I screwed it up.'

'Well, go and get it and read me what it says.'

'Don't hang up on me, Marty, will you?'

He chuckled. 'No, Grace my dear. Just go and get that paper.'

Patiently, he waited for her to return. Her voice was clear and steady down the phone as she read.

'. . . "Also at the meeting, the Chief Investigator of Air Accidents . . ." then it gives his name,' she interposed, ' "confirmed that a Cessna of the type involved has its wing above the pilot's cockpit, and of the two aircraft it would have been flying lower than the DC8. In answer to a further question, Mr Weller conceded that statistically it had been found more usual for a private pilot to be at fault than a commercial pilot in past near-misses between big and small aircraft . . ." ' She didn't finish the paragraph. Instead, she added: 'That's as plain as could be, isn't it Marty?'

'Well, from what you've read me, it does seem to point a finger . . .'

'Exactly. And it's just not fair. Frank's dead. How can they do this sort of thing? I don't understand. We must stop them, Marty. Can we stop them? I mean, it's wrong, isn't it, to print things like that? Oh! What am I going to do, Marty? I'm not going to let them . . .'

'Grace! Now stop it, there's a dear. It will do no good, not the slightest, to get all hot and bothered over the phone.'

'Can you come over? You could read it yourself then, couldn't you? I've only read a bit out to you. Why don't you bring Glenda as well?'

Marty did not immediately reply.

With the public memory as short as it was, he was thinking, any retraction in the paper would have to appear tomorrow.

'Marty, did you hear me? Are you there?'

'Yes, I'm thinking. Hang on for a moment.'

Putting his hand over the mouthpiece of the phone, he turned to Glenda who had come out to see what had kept him in the hall. She hadn't heard the phone ring. 'It's Grace on the phone and she's in a state. Could we go over when we've eaten?'

'Of course, but what's the trouble? She was here the day before yesterday and I was thinking how well she was getting over it.'

'Something nasty in the evening paper.'

'Oh, the poor dear. Yes, of course we'll go over. You tell her, I'll put out supper and we can eat straight away. Say we'll be there in about an hour.'

'You there, Grace?'

'Yes.'

'Look, we'll both come on over after we've had supper. May be a bit later because I want to have a look at a couple of books on defamation. In the meantime don't get all up-tight about it. We'll sort it out, all right?'

'Thank you, Marty, you're a dear.' She managed a slight laugh as she added, 'And I'll try not to get all up-tight, as you put it.'

Marty had a crack at catching up with the law on defamation, and realized it wasn't too easy. It made them late so they didn't get to Grace's home much before nine.

As she led them into the sitting-room, she gave Marty the paper to read. He went slowly through it, then, as she was giving him his drink, he said, 'Grace, you didn't read me the line at the end of the paragraph. I quote ". . . but the Minister also made it plain that there was no suggestion of this in this case . . ."'

'I know, but what difference does that make? Anyone reading that paper would just say that he's covering himself, or whatever he has to do to be able to say those dreadful things. Have you read it, Glen?'

'No, we don't get it,' she said, taking the paper from Marty, who spoke to Grace. 'I think you're making too much of this, you know. What's it come down to? Three facts. The heights of the planes – we can't argue with that, can we?'

'On its own, I suppose not, no.'

'And the position of the wing – a fact which means nothing. I don't think we can argue with that, can we?'

'Well, no. Not on its own.'

'And a statistic. We can't argue with that either.'

'But it's the way the three are tied up. They might as well have said "and we think that it was all Frank Newton's fault!"'

'I think Grace is absolutely right, dear,' said Glenda. 'They shouldn't be allowed to print things in that sort of way.'

'Surely it's innuendo,' Grace said, 'or whatever it is you lawyers call it.'

'Yes, you can libel by innuendo, but I think here that the reporting of what the Minister said at the end would be seen to rob the thing of that.'

'But it doesn't, does it? The idea is there. Everyone who reads the filthy thing will come to the same conclusion, isn't that right, Glen?' Grace appealed to her friend.

'Yes, I think so. It says it in black and white.' She reached for the paper again, 'Yes, here we are. ". . . more usual for a private pilot to be at fault than a commercial pilot . . .' Anyone reading that would add "and is probably the case here . . ." Surely there is something you can do?'

Pressured by both women Marty sought refuge in his drink for a moment as he tried to remember the law on the subject. 'The law,' he said, 'is pretty clear. You can say something like this and someone can sue. Now here, and I agree with you both, it says it between the lines. And, there is probably no doubt about it, taken in isolation . . .'

'Oh Marty, for God's sake, speak English!'

He smiled at Glenda's exasperation. 'Well, to put it as simply as I can, you can upset someone, but that alone isn't enough. To sue, you've got to show it was unjustified and damaging. It's justified if it's true, or a fair comment on a matter of public interest. There's more to it than that, but here I don't think we can really do anything about it.'

Silence followed the remarks he'd made. 'Do you mean to say I've just got to swallow whatever any miserable sod of a hack reporter has to say because it's fair comment?'

'Now, Grace, dear. That's not quite fair, is it? It was said at a Press conference, and by the Accidents man. And, to be fair, it does clearly state it wasn't thought by the Minister to be the case.'

'Well, I think it's disgraceful,' Glenda said. 'It's flying the worst sort of kite – suggesting people make up their minds before anyone has anything to go on.'

'I'm afraid that's true, but I don't think we can do anything about it.'

'But,' Grace said, 'someone does know about it. The insurance company has paid Frank's insurance. Surely that means they have been into it and decided he wasn't to blame. That's right, isn't it, Marty?'

'No, Grace, it isn't. The Pacific paid out life insurance which has nothing to do with Frank's plane insurers. That's the Dominion and Commonwealth. It will be for them to decide whether they think Frank was to blame. And you must be prepared for them to come to an arrangement with whoever were the insurers for the airline, and so on, rather than let things go to Court.'

'But that means that without me having any say at all, someone may be agreeing it was Frank's fault!'

'That's right, Grace. It'll be in your policy that you give them all rights to look after the case.'

'But I won't have it. It wasn't Frank's fault, Marty, I know it wasn't!'

'I know, but remember, the investigation is still only just at the beginning. They'll probably find out exactly how it happened, and it will probably have nothing to do with Frank at all.'

'But what about that newspaper report?' Glen asked. 'Isn't

there anything at all you can do about it?'

'I could write to the paper, but I advise against it. It'll only draw attention to it. Really, I think the most sensible thing is just to forget it, and save yourself a lot of heartache, Grace.' Grace had followed Marty's advice for years. She tried to follow it now, but she couldn't forget it, nor could she forget the fact that it was possible for an insurance company to accept blame on Frank's part whatever she thought.

She slept very badly that night, and would have slept even worse if she had heard Marty's comments to Glenda on their way home.

'She'll have to come to terms with it sometime.'

'With what?'

'That it was probably something to do with Frank.'

'But, Marty dearest, we just don't know that.'

'Not now, no, but I reckon the odds on it are 80 per cent plus.'

'I don't see that. What's so special about airline people? Can't they make mistakes too?'

'Too true, but very much less likely than Frank. They're professionals. Better trained. Not doing another job as well, better instrumented and experienced, and there are two of them. One's got to remember that.'

Glenda thought about it as they drove on, then dismissed the subject with, 'Perhaps you're right, but before I beleive it, I'll want real proof.'

'Hm, me too. The trouble is, will Grace accept even that?'

'You're her lawyer, Marty, it'll be up to you to make sure she does.'

He sighed, as he replied, 'Yeah, that's what I'm afraid of, but she can be pretty stubborn.'

'Oh, I know, over little things, but they've always taken your advice before.'

'But you forget, there's no Frank now.'

'Oh, you'll see. I know her pretty well, and if it comes to it, well, we can all talk to her, and her kids are pretty bright.'

'Maybe you're right.' And then they let the subject drop.

That newspaper report, and reports in other papers, were noticed by a great many people, and brought a lot of indignant letters to the editors, one of them from a Mr Anthony Carnegie. He made the point they all did, in a thousand different ways: Since when had it been right to prejudice justice by comment based on speculation?

What didn't appear after Mr Carnegie's signature was the fact that he was the Chief Claims Officer for the Dominion and Commonwealth Insurance Company.

The next morning he'd intended to have a chat with his pure-bred American General Manager, but arrived to find a message with his secretary to go straight on in.

'Hi, Tony, park yer ass. See the paper last night, or hear the news?' His huge mass seemed to grate the words across the desk.

'Yes, I did. I've sent a letter off to the editor and I spoke to him this morning. He's going to make sure it's published. But what to do about our dearly beloved Prime Minister! Well, that's another thing. Difficult.'

'Oh sure, it's impossible without sounding like a wounded bull, but whaddaya make of it?'

'I reckon they're going to try and sew us up.'

'Yeah, that figures.' He laughed sharply as he added. 'Jesus Christ, what a stroke. A syndicated press correspondent. OK. But I don't buy some fucking local having that sort of information.'

'Nor me.'

'So it bloody stinks. But why the hell should it, Tony? That's the question. Why the hell's our cunt of a Prime Minister in there stirring up the shit?' He thought about it for a bit. 'What's the cover position?'

'I'm not sure. Everyone seems to have clammed up, which may be a trifle odd. The Government covers the Air Traffic people, but I'd imagine that'll be laid off. And Paranational are with the Merlin Mutual Ltd, and they're with Lloyds, but for the life of me, I haven't been able to find out at what level.'

'So tell me what's it all about then?'

'Don't really know. Could just be they're manoeuvring for a bit of elbow room, setting the vet up.'

'Sure. But why? It's no skin off their nose. Big claim, and it's Lloyds or whoever, so why yesterday?'

'Could be they're worried about public confidence.'

'Yeah, perhaps, but no cause for involvement. No, Tony

boy, I reckon we've a fucking fantastic situation here, if only we knew it. But what the hell could it be?'

'I don't know.'

'OK, let's kick it about a bit. Has to be politics. Why else the involvement? Now, the only thing a guy like the Prime Minister would get all steamed up about would be the thought that someone had a fucking gun on him so he's shit scared there's something for some devious guy to dig up. Right? So we've got to look for a big fuck-up somewhere. Now that as politics and not fucking insurance makes sense, huh?'

'I still think it's confidence. Let people get too worried and they'll take a train. Big stake in Paranational.'

'No way, Tony. Five minutes and the public have forgotten.'

'Well, could be a fast buck by mucking about with their re-insurance, I suppose. As I say, no one wanted to talk about it much.'

'Jesus, what a thought,' he paused, 'well, well, well, what a bloody thought, Tony.' He thought about it. 'You reckon they carried too much?' Again he paused until finally saying quietly, 'Shit, no, Tony boy, they're pretty bloody stupid, but they can't be that bloody stupid!'

'Would explain it though, wouldn't it?'

'Oh, sure. But Jesus! It would be the all-time big booboo. Christ, not even that cunt would get around it.'

'Well, they're politicians, not insurers. Might have been tempted. The sort of reinsurance premium we're talking about isn't peanuts. Lot of money out of the country every year.'

'Well, well, what a fucking thought.' Tugging gently at the lobe of his ear, he pondered on it for some time before arriving at his decision.

'Well, Tony, though there's not much percentage in knowing their problem, there's a lot in at least knowing they've got one. So let's find out. If so, we'll assume you're right and play it along like we don't know, and maybe save one hell of a lot of dough.

'OK, so I make all the noises of looking forward to a nice long lawsuit and we sit it out and see what they come up with?'

'That's right. Now has there been any approach yet?'

'No. Very cool when I first got in touch.'

'Have we got a guy in on the investigation?'

'No. I got a flat refusal. Said any claim was nothing to do

with them – Air Accidents – and he wasn't authorized for outsiders.'

'Well, well. What about the Minister? Contacted him?'

'No, I thought I'd see you about it first.'

'Fine.'

The General Manager ran his forefinger back and forward behind his right ear, disturbing the line of his heavy jowl with the movement, as he considered his first move. Then he buzzed through to his secretary. '. . . and I don't want any horse shit about him not being available. If they give you any of that crap, put them through to me.' As he waited, he chuckled, 'I just may enjoy this.' Then the secretary came through on the line. 'They say he's not there.'

'Who's they, for Chrissake?'

'I'm not sure.'

'Jesus, aren't you just too bloody fantastic. All right, put them on, but it's your bloody job to find out, so remember it, or I'll have you out of here so fucking fast your tits'll bang!' Unperturbed, she put him through.

'Who am I speaking to?'

'Minister of Transport's office here. I'm sorry, but the Minister can't be disturbed. Can I help you?'

'I asked, who the hell are you!'

'Hold on, please.'

Tony smiled as his General Manager murmured, 'For fuck's sake, these bloody people!' He was pulling at his ear hard now. He only did it when he got annoyed.

'Hello?'

'And who the hell are you?'

'There's no need to be offensive, sir.' Tony smiled as he heard it over the relay. 'As my secretary told you, I cannot disturb the Minister. But if you would care to tell me what you would like to speak to him about, I will make sure he hears it.'

'That, sonny boy,' he snarled down the phone, 'is the understatement of the bloody year! You just get off your backside and wake the guy up!' Then he did a quick switch, as he added in a mild voice: 'That is, if you people are thinking of cooperation from us.'

The man at the other end of the phone smiled. He'd heard it all before.

'Yes, I quite understand, but I have specific instructions not to interrupt him, and I'm afraid that's the position. But if you would give me your phone number I might be able to ring you back if he wishes to speak to you.'

'It's in the book.' His voice was velvety smooth, as he added, 'I shall be available here for just another ten minutes. If he hasn't phoned by then I shall be in print tonight, and you may take it that amongst other things I shall be dealing with the shit's trick of a fucking stroke he pulled yesterday. You might mention it!' And without waiting for a reply, he gently put the phone down.

It rang again seven minutes later. 'Yeah, speaking. Oh, good of you to ring, Minister.'

Anthony Carnegie couldn't help smiling at the heavy sarcasm. 'Yes, I understand you had a bit of a problem getting through. My people didn't quite understand. What did you want to talk about?'

'Well, first we're a little concerned here at the fun and games you had at your Press conference yesterday. Still, I suppose it's one way of trying to deal with a few problems.'

'What, precisely, are you suggesting?' Cold though the Minister's voice was, the quick flash of anxiety was plain.

'Someone just had to have put that reporter up to it, Minister,' the big man purred.

'Let me be clear on this. Are you saying that you consider I suggested to a reporter he ask certain questions yesterday?' But it was said with a trace of relief.

'Well, it's you guys who stand to lose if it wasn't the bloody vet's fault.'

'That's incorrect. I, as Minister of Transport, am solely concerned for this investigation to come to the correct conclusions on how the accident happened. I have no interest whatsoever in civil liability or the meeting of claims. I repeat, are you making an allegation against me of improper conduct?'

But the man's heart wasn't in it and the General Manager wondered whether it might just be that Tony Carnegie was right. Not that it really mattered, but whatever the problem, he needed to get some idea of its size.

'No, of course not, Minister. I just think you might have stepped in and stopped any discussion on liability. But now what I do want to talk about is the question of the investigation.'

'I don't think I will be able to help, but what have you in mind?' His anger was ill-concealed.

'Well, I'm quite sure that your people don't want to see this thing wind up in Court, not that it bothers us at all. But so far we've been excluded from any participation in the investigation by your Chief of Air Accidents. Now if that's going to be your attitude then no finding by any government department that places blame on our insured is going to be accepted by us. But, Minister, if we are allowed in on the act, and are satisfied it's the vet, well then, we're well able to deal with any claim.' He wondered whether the Minister's problem was really so small as to enable him to say stuff it . . .

'I see. You realize that the office of the Chief Investigator of Air Accidents has no interest at all in apportioning blame. Its report merely sets out the facts of its findings.'

'Sure, that's fine. But you'll agree it would be in the public interest for fair play not merely to be done but be seen to be done, and what better way of satisfying the people than to include the one company that'd like to protect the vet? Stop a lot of criticism and maybe one hell of a court hearing, whereas if, and I repeat if, it became known that your people had refused to let any impartial observer in on it . . .?' he let the question go unfinished.

There was a silence at the end of the phone, before the Minister replied in a quiet voice, 'Are you saying that if I refuse to let your people in on the investigation you will publish that as a fact?'

'Shit, no,' the voice quietly purred down the phone. 'Of course I wouldn't do anything like that. But just as unfortunate questions are sometimes asked, well, sometimes they have to be answered in public interest. Like yesterday, perhaps. No?'

It wasn't at all the way the Minister had wanted it to go. Refuse and it would be all over the papers the next day. And on the surface of it that was the problem. But was it? The man had said 'problems'. Could this man know about the reinsurance? But if he did, why not say something? All very worrying, he thought, as he said, 'I'm not saying that I agree to this, but if I did, then you appreciate I would have to extend the same facility to the Merlin Mutual Ltd.'

The General Manager smiled to himself as he decided to jack it up a bit more to see whether the problem was big enough to eclipse a Minister's dignity.

'Sure, of course, Minister. I fully appreciate that and it would be only fair, in a case like this if, perhaps, just for this one time, one government department was allowed to know what another was doing? No, I'd have no objection to that.'

Fascinated, Tony grinned as he imagined the Minister's reaction at the other end. The Minister struggled with himself not to react in his uncertainty, and lost, or partially lost, as he replied, 'That's a grossly offensive remark. You know very well that the Merlin Mutual Ltd are an autonomous body, and outside the Government.'

'Of course, it's just the Government's money involved. I do apologize, Minister. But whaddaya say? Are we in or not?'

'I will consider your request, and you will be contacted with my decision,' the Minister said, with icy formality.

'That's just fine, Minister. Anyway, I thought you would like to talk about it. Now, I'm off somewhere tomorrow so perhaps you will have reached your decision by three this afternoon?'

Though seething, the Minister well knew he was trapped. News by three would catch the latest editions. As coldly as he could, he said, 'I give you no undertaking on that at all. And I would make it plain that the Government would take the gravest view of any record of this conversation being made public.' And he replaced the phone.

The General Manager's whole vastness shook as he laughed while putting down the phone. He had stopped pulling his ear a long time ago. Now he just gently stroked it again, and as his jowl bobbed in satisfaction, he said, 'Now, Tony boy, who's the best guy to deal with this? He'll have to be ready to be breathing down this Accident guy's neck by four today.'

Tony had been thinking it out. 'I think we should put in a loss adjuster. That way we get the credibility of employing someone independent. Important if it goes to a fight.'

'OK, leave it to you. But I want a report on this desk, Tony, twice a day, even if it just says "nothing fucking new", OK?'

'All right, but I thought you said you'd be away?'

The General Manager laughed as he said, 'Jesus! Go on, fuck off!'

The Minister of Transport saw the Prime Minister twenty minutes after the phone call. And the Prime Minister became very, very angry as he listened.

Christopher Silaman sat back and waited for the decision. It didn't come straight away. As he calmed down, the Prime Minister suddenly barked a laugh. 'Well, Chris. No, he doesn't know we've got any real trouble, though it strikes me that after the way you've handled him on the phone he might suspect we're a touch worried about something.' He paused, then smiled as he added, 'But one day I must meet this man!'

'Why?' Silaman asked, puzzled at the Prime Minister's reaction.

'Because one day we might use him.'

'He just struck me as offensive.'

'Oh no. He's a great deal more than that, which leads me to the problem he did raise, as opposed to the one which we must hope you imagined. Tell me, Chris. Why do you think he wants to have someone involved in the investigation?'

'Because he thinks one government department will whitewash another.'

'Oh, yes, that's part of it, but it goes a great deal further than that.'

'In what way?'

'With the Government involved, but not knowing we've got a problem which dictates settlement in the end, he knows two things, Christopher. One, that any report made public is an edited version of the findings of the Investigator. So, yes, he's worried about a whitewash and suppression. But, more important, if it came to Court – and we must appear at all times to be prepared to let that happen – then, to all intents and purposes, our brief to counsel would be the original, unexpurgated report from the office of Air Accidents. In that event he's afraid that he won't be able to get at our records because we'd say that the report was not only prepared as a basis for public record, but as a basis for the Government's case. And that anything we didn't choose to publish would remain privileged on the latter grounds. This way, he makes sure he knows all we do, which is really rather astute of him, I think. But what's to do, Chris, what's to do?' he murmured to himself.

'But as you've said, it won't get to litigation.'

'You know that and I know that, and so do a few of our colleagues, but never, never must it get further than that. Right the way through this, we have got to appear to have no problem at all, be prepared to let it go to Court, and only settle on the basis of a sensible settlement reflecting liability. And we've just got to hope it works out like that.'

'But what if it doesn't?'

'Oh, if it looks like going wrong we'll just have to think again, won't we?'

'But surely, knowing what we do, the lesser of the two evils would be to keep him out of the investigation?'

'My dear Christopher, as you said at your Press conference, and I quote the unfortunate remark, "we don't believe in keeping the public in the dark about the steps being taken". Hmmmm, very unfortunate remark that, Chris. He'd have a ball, wouldn't he? Your remark one day, and the next the exclusion of those who represent the one person in the mess who can be blamed but isn't anything to do with us. Just imagine it!'

The silence that followed was only broken twice by the Prime Minister. First, he murmured, 'What a very unfortunate state of affairs you have brought about,' then, 'pity.'

Christopher Silaman felt it was a very unfair situation. But there was nothing he could do about it. Fleetingly, he wished he'd got out before the Press conference, when his hands were still clean, but no use crying over spilt milk now.

Finally, the Prime Minister came out of his reverie. 'There's nothing for it, Chris. We'll have to let him in. But now I want you to do a bit more along the lines we discussed. I want the pace stepped up. Weller mustn't have time to brood, so push it along. Secondly, discourage the personal investigation side of it. Everyone has problems, but add them up and it may begin to look difficult, and we don't want that with the aircrew. Get it dealt with as though it was a small mishap. You can sell it to Weller on the basis that he mustn't allow it to get out of perspective and become a witch hunt, OK?'

'Yes, but I don't see really what that'll achieve. If we go light on the aircrew, how can we go any heavier on the vet?'

'We won't need to, Chris.'

'Well you know best, so I'll have this fellow told he can send someone along.'

'No you won't Chris. You'll ring him, and be very nice and helpful. Also, you will mention, in whatever way you like, that the decision has been yours and yours alone. Further, I would like to have the tape of this morning's chat you had with him, and any others recording conversations in the future with him.'

'But there isn't a tape.'

'Good God above! What a man you are, my dear Chris! Surely you realize that whenever someone in any position gets in touch with you and you can't avoid it, especially when he gets you to phone with a threat, that you make certain it's taped?' The Prime Minister looked at his Minister of Transport with wide eyes. 'You know,' he added, 'the sooner you wake up to what politics is all about, the better. This "for the people, by the people" nonsense is all good stuff to a herd listening with rapt expressions as we pour it in, but, as hard fact, we fight to govern. Start learning to use some of the tools of the trade, Chris, and for heaven's sake, before it's too late. Just read the transcript made of the Press conference. I have. You know, you made a rare old balls up of it, though not as big a balls up as today!'

The light flashed on his desk. 'OK, that's it. Away you go.'

Christopher Silaman walked down the corridor away from the Prime Minister's office offended, hurt and angry. Oh God, he thought. What a mess!

Chapter Twelve

The Press conference over, Graham Weller retired to obscurity again. If he'd said 'no comment' once in a week, he'd said it a dozen times.

The Minister spoke about the accident when it seemed appropriate, but he said nothing really new. Yet somehow those who heard felt ever more clearly that the vet was to blame.

The work went remorselessly on. The Chief Investigator of Air Accidents saw the Minister again several times. The withdrawal of the policemen who had been working for him hadn't helped, and he hadn't been particularly impressed with the idea of insurance company people becoming involved. In fact, he'd protested strongly, but in vain. And so he had learned to live with them. And each time he spoke with the Minister he felt pressure, until he too began to wonder whether there wasn't a danger of getting this particular accident out of perspective, maybe too much time could be spent on it. At first he'd just listened to the crap about the 'ears and eyes of the world on a small nation, watching how efficiently it was all being dealt with', and 'speed was efficiency wasn't it?' and all the rest of it. At first he ignored it but later it began to cast a shadow over his performance. It was the little 'by the way' things said by the Minister, which led him to think that in some way the Minister was shielding him. Was he being too cautious, too slow? So the pressure began to have an effect.

He found that of the insurance people, the Merlin Mutual Ltd more or less left him alone, and he didn't involve them. But the loss adjuster sent by the Dominion was another matter, a man called Mark Simpson of Stanley & Partners. A quiet, intelligent, mild man. Despite himself and despite the fact that the man was there to spy, Graham Weller found himself liking him.

As the investigation went on, a pattern emerged which suited the Chief Investigator very well. Mark would leave whoever he was with from the team at about mid-afternoon and come into the office for tea. Over tea Graham would let him know how the rest of the work was going. After that, Mark would suggest – always with a slight diffidence which never failed to strike the right chord in the Chief Investigator's pride – that he would rather like to have a look at this or that matter the next day. This way, the Chief Investigator reckoned he knew where the loss adjuster was all the time. The fact that quite often the loss adjuster was somewhere else for part of the next day didn't get to the Chief Investigator often. But even when it did he quite understood that the loss adjuster had one or two other matters to consider.

As the days went by, Mark Simpson familiarized himself with the various parts of the investigation. When he had first arrived, the tapes covering the Air Traffic Control from Nandi, through Auckland, and down to Wellington, were still being dealt with by the typists. Normally, they would have been listened to and only a cock-up noted. But Graham Weller had been determined in this case to have a complete record. So typists patiently typed from three large reels of twenty-five-track tape, and everything remotely relevant to the two flights was set down for reading. It was a hard, long job for the Air

Traffic specialist to dig out what was relevant, before instructing the girls to type the brief interchanges between the ground and the aircraft. Satisfied he couldn't see anything to criticize, Mark Simpson left them to it.

He joined the Cessna team for a morning. Its work was impressive. The history was pretty well complete. A new plane bought by the vet three months and two days before the accident. He browsed through the airworthiness data and servicing information, and made a note to be down there when one of the team had his chat with the radio mechanic who'd carried out Frank Newton's radio repair at Masterton on the afternoon of the accident. He noted a copy of the man's time sheet. He'd started at 1.30 and finished at 4. He would have been the last man to have seen the vet before he took off. The DC8 was a bigger job. Mark didn't involve himself in it, beyond noting the name of the ground engineer who'd okayed the aircraft. Someone else to see.

Two weeks after he'd first appeared in the Chief Investigator's office, he came in as he often did, at about four. 'Is he in?' he asked the pretty Oriental receptionist. It was a ritual and, as usual, she smiled as she said she would find out. The protocol amused him. Always he was able to listen from reception as she asked the Chief whether he was in. Today, she came out, as usual, with the nice smile and told him that the Chief Investigator wouldn't keep him waiting long. Then she went back to her work. A minute later, as usual, she looked up and told him he could go in, which triggered his smile of thanks, and for about the tenth time he inwardly complimented her on her telepathic powers. But maybe there was a little light on her desk that he couldn't see. It intrigued him.

'G'day, my friend. Tea?'

'Please.'

'Well, how d'you reckon it's going then?' the Chief Investigator asked.

'I am very impressed. I should think you'll have all that you want by the end of the next week or so, won't you?'

'Yeah, perhaps. What were you looking at today?'

'We saw the bowser chap down at the airport. Apparently there was a slight discrepancy between fuel loaded and fuel shown on board.'

'Oh yes, but I don't think it'll take us anywhere. From the

evidence of the eye witnesses, fuel was pouring out of the thing when it hit.'

'Yes, but it's interesting me to see the detail you go into.'

The Chief looked happy as he poured the tea. 'Sugar?'

'No thanks.' The Chief Investigator never remembered. 'Anything new?' Mark Simpson asked.

'Well, let's see.' He shuffled some papers on his desk. 'This might interest you.' He handed a sheaf of documents over. 'Medical records of the crew on the 8,' he added by way of amplification.

'Anything to note?' Mark asked.

'I don't think so. You'll see that the Captain, Standard, had had his medical about a week before the accident, and was as fit as they come. The co-pilot, Sam Meadows, was coming up for his, but his past health record was fine.'

'Could I have copies of these?'

'OK. I'll get them done now for you.'

'Thanks.'

He left Mark leafing through his portfolio, comfortable in his chair across the desk. But the moment he was out of the room, Mark came swiftly to his feet and in a couple of strides was around the desk. Once there, he wasted no time.

As Graham re-entered, Mark glanced up from the portfolio, then disturbed himself further in reaching for his tea. 'She'll have them ready in a moment,' Graham said as he sat down. Casually, Mark looked up from the papers again, but his eyes watched the Chief of Air Accidents like a hawk as, equally casually, he asked, 'Tell me, it's been some time since I looked in on your guy working on the air traffic side. How's it going?'

'We've got the preliminaries all finished now, though they've got to be checked out again. But something does seem to have come up.'

'Yes.'

'Do you know what a QNH is?'

'Atmospheric pressure at sea level?'

'Right. And do you know its importance?'

'I think so. The aircrew set their altimeter to it when ascending through 11,000 feet or descending below 13,000. Higher and it's the international setting of 1013 millibars.'

'Right. Now, usually when an aircraft first contacts Airways the Controller gives a QNH. This time he didn't.'

'Important?'

'No. It's a frill. The thing the pilot takes it from is the ATIS.'

The loss adjuster nodded. Glancing down he shuffled through the papers before him. 'Yes, here we are. The pilot of the 8 said: "We have copied weather Mike".'

Though he appeared casual, and sounded it, Mark continued to watch for reaction as he enquired, 'Nothing else?' He waited to see whether the Chief Investigator would take the way out, and breathed a mental sigh of relief when he didn't.

'No. I was coming to the coincidence. Arrivals missed it out as well. For one reason or another it is sometimes omitted, but not usually by two people to the same aircraft.'

'What about the ATIS? Couldn't it give the wrong information?'

'Impossible. And if it had gone crook he wouldn't have said: "We have copied Mike". In fact it was serviced that afternoon and was fine. Of course, we've checked that Mike was current at the time, which it was, and we've checked the ATIS records kept by the Coordinator in the Tower and Mike was correct.'

'So it doesn't get us anywhere.'

'No, 'fraid not. But I'll let you know if anything further turns up on it.'

'Thanks,' said Mark. 'Anything else?'

'Apart from that, nothing,' replied Weller.

'Yet one of the planes, or both, just had to be at the wrong height, as I understand it.'

'Quite. One that is. But both, no. Too improbable.'

'What do you think then?'

'It's beginning to look like no attributable cause,' said Weller.

'And that's tantamount to saying that it was the vet?' The loss adjuster's conclusion hung in the air.

The Chief Investigator shrugged uncomfortably. 'That's for someone else to say, not me.'

'Will you be making any comment in your report on the vet?'

The Chief again looked uncomfortable, then he shrugged again as he said, 'I think I shall have to state, as a fact, that the vet was inexperienced in the aircraft he was flying. To that

I may have to add anything else that turns up. Anyway, I'll know soon. They're working on him now.'

'What sort of things?' Mark asked.

'Oh, we look at health. Suicide. Not that I think we've ever said so. And anything else. You know the sort of thing, drugs, drink, lack of sleep, any big problems worrying him.'

'One of your team will go over and see a few people about him?'

'Doing it now.'

'And the aircrew?'

'We have a look at them too. Nose around a bit, have a word with their medical and personnel people. Try and find out if there's any writing between the lines. Don't worry, we'll look.' He smiled as he added, 'And if you want to go along, you're welcome.'

'Kind of you, but no. I'll be away for a few days now. Got a few things to do.'

'Right, but if anything breaks, you'll presumably want to hear about it, so why not leave your number with the girl.'

'I will.' Rising now, Mark said, 'Well, see you soon.'

'All right'. Without rising the Chief Investigator raised his hand in brief goodbye as the papers on his desk claimed his attention.

As Mark left the office he gave the girl his Auckland office number. He didn't want it to be known that he wasn't going far from Wellington, and they could always relay messages to him. With a smile to her, he left.

Grace let the two of them in, and led them to the sitting-room. As they entered, they saw the middle-aged, rather tired, rather heavy, short solicitor rise to his feet. She introduced them. 'Marty, these are the two gentlemen from the Air Accidents people. This, gentlemen, is my solicitor, Mr Martin Chalmers, senior partner in Sneel, Burton and Chalmers.'

While they shook hands and Marty made sure he had the names right, she poured coffee. 'Do you both take sugar?' They nodded.

'I asked my solicitor to be here because he advised me he should be. Something to do with liability I think. But I want to be very clear to you both that I know my husband wasn't to blame. He was a very good pilot . . .'

'Now, Grace dear. I think it's better if you just let these

gentlemen ask their questions. If, for legal reasons, I don't think you should answer then I'll say so, right?'

The senior of the two men seemed slightly offended by the presence of the solicitor, as he said, 'Mrs Newton, I'm a little surprised to see your solicitor here. Very happy, of course, but I must point out that we are nothing to do with liability. We are inspectors from the Department of Air Accidents.'

'Correct me if I'm wrong,' the solicitor said, 'but your findings could be used by parties to an action?'

'I really don't know anything about that side of it, Mr Chalmers. You would have to contact the Chief Investigator.'

'I see. Still, since you have no objection, I think I'll stay.'

'Of course.' Then turning to the widow the senior man continued, 'Our reason for being here is to enquire into anything which we feel may have had anything to do with the accident, as I mentioned over the phone. Now could we start with your husband's health? We've already seen his doctor, of course.'

'Are you really allowed to go snooping behind my back?' asked Grace. Then turning to Marty, she said, 'Is that really right? Can they just snoop as much as they like without telling anyone?' He nodded.

Turning back to the inspector, she sighed and said, 'Well, if that's so, what can I tell you that you don't already know? I suppose you'll say you want to know when we last made love?' There was a trace of scorn and anger in her voice.

'Well, if you told us, it wouldn't become public knowledge and it might help us in our assessment.'

Incredulously, she raised her eyebrows. 'Are you serious?'

'Perfectly serious, Mrs Newton. Look at it from our point of view. If a man of your husband's age, er, didn't make love to his charming wife sometimes, we might wonder about his health.'

She looked at him, then laughed. 'Well, if you must know, we made love at lunch-time on the day he died, and,' she added defiantly, 'and, it was lovely and I shall always remember . . .' she sniffed and two bright tears sparkled in the corners of her eyes.

'Please don't upset yourself, Mrs Newton. We do understand,' he said soothingly.

'I wonder whether you do. How can you understand?'

'People, good people, are killed every year in air accidents.

We have to talk about them.'

'Why can't you just leave people like me alone?'

'Because if we did we might never understand how an accident happened. And it is by understanding that we can slowly but surely do our bit to prevent others happening. That's really what it's all about.'

By now she had regained her composure. And, not having thought before about the accident investigation as anything to do with safety, she pondered this for a moment. 'Is that really true?'

'Yes. Whenever anything comes to light which may be a warning to others we do our best to make sure people know about it.'

'His health was good. Very good, for a man of his age.'

'What does that mean "for his age"?' He smiled encouragingly as he asked.

'Nothing really. He wore glasses for reading.' She laughed as she added, 'In fact, the night before it happened I took them off him. He'd gone to sleep with them on.'

'Grace, I think it would be better if you quite simply answered the questions asked.' Her solicitor's voice was firm, and she looked abashed. 'What did I say?'

'Nothing, my dear,' he sighed, 'nothing, but, to coin a phrase . . .' then he thought better of it, so substituted: 'we don't want to be here all day. These two gentlemen, no doubt, have a lot to do.'

'Not to worry, Mr Chalmers.' It was a murmured prelude to the next question, which Marty knew would inevitably follow.

'What time did he get to sleep that night?'

'It must have been about midnight.'

'Was that usual?'

'Yes.'

'What time do you usually get up?'

'7.45 most days.'

'And on that morning?'

'I got up then, but Frank had had to go out.'

The questions went on for just under an hour. When they'd gone, Marty fully opened the door to the dining-room and his secretary, putting her pad away, came out.

From Bill Hulman, the inspectors discovered that Frank

Newton had been called out at a little before six on the morning of the fatal day.

As the Chief Investigator was going over the notes taken by the more junior of the two inspectors who had called on Mrs Newton, Mark Simpson was in Marty Chalmers' office. He had read the transcript of the conversation and the statement which Marty had taken from Grace Newton after the two men had gone. The solicitor had also given the loss adjuster his own statement, and one from Bill Hulman and Trevor Johnson, another client Frank had seen on that last morning.

Directly Mark Simpson had been retained by the Dominion he'd sought permission from the company to deal on a full disclosure basis with the widow's solicitor. It looked as though it had been a wise move.

The next day, Mark returned to his hotel to find a message from the Chief Investigator, via Auckland, to ring him. As he held the phone, waiting for an answer, he rather thought he knew what Graham Weller had to say to him.

'Office of Air Accidents Investigation.'

'Is he in?' There was a pause as the girl matched the face to the question. Then he heard her chuckle. 'Yes, hold on.'

He heard himself being put through then the Chief's voice on the line.

'G'day Mark. Tried to get you earlier. I sent a couple of my people to see Mrs Newton. He was a tired man, Mark.'

'Really? What makes you say that?'

'We've discovered he fell asleep with his glasses on the night before, probably a bit after midnight . . .'

'Hardly significant I would have thought,' Mark interrupted.

'On its own, no, but also, he was dragged out of bed at ten to six the next morning.'

'What an emotive word "dragged" is,' Mark murmured.

'What's that?'

'Nothing, Graham. So that's it, is it?'

'Yes.'

'Will you mention it?'

'I think I must.'

'I see. Well, thanks for letting me know. By the way, anything on the aircrew?'

'No, not really. The Captain wasn't living at his flat, though, but with one of the hostesses on the flight. Jenny Carol.'

'Perhaps he was tired too. Same hotel in Nandi?'

'Too experienced. And anyway, he'd have had a long, lazy morning. They didn't check out until midday.'

'How do you know that?'

'When one of my people went to Nandi to check and get the tapes he called in at the hotel. They all checked out together. And from this end we had a look at the bills sent to the airline. He had been charged for breakfast in his room.'

'I see. So that's closed?'

'Don't you think it should be?'

'You're the expert. I just wanted to know if you had finished with the *personae dramatis,* as it were.'

'Yes.'

'Where did you get the bit about the Captain and the girl?'

'A mate of his in the airline office.'

'Could you give me that address?' As Mark wrote it down he recollected the building along the terrace. 'Thanks.'

'OK. Be seein' you.'

Mark Simpson thought it over, and decided to stroll up to the flats. Bates was at his desk. When asked if he remembered Captain Standard and Jenny Carol he said he did. 'And a very nice couple they were too, sir. The wife and I were very much upset when we heard of the terrible thing. Ah, to be sure, here's the old darlin' herself.' Turning to the approaching woman, he said, 'I was just tellin' this gentleman here how upset we were when we heard about the Captain and Miss Carol.'

The pasty-faced, ill-kempt dumpling of a woman had a gleam in her eyes for a fleeting second. She hadn't liked Miss Carol any better than she liked any of the young women who she suspected her fool of a husband dangled after. 'To be sure, we were sorry, but we hardly knew them.' She was as Irish as her husband. 'And I don't know what morals are coming to. Living openly together like that!'

Mark thanked them and left. Perhaps he wouldn't have been in such a hurry, but for the strong waft of BO the woman carried as her ring of confidence through life. His next call was down to the airport. He was there for an hour and a half.

He turned up at the office of the Chief Investigator of Air Accidents as expected. It had been a long haul for them all. The accident was now just over two months ago. Together in the Chief's office, they had been talking for over an hour.

'I think, Mark, that just about wraps it up from our point of view.' Graham was leaning back in his chair. 'And by Christ, I hope we never have another like it.'

'No, one hopes not,' Mark commented.

'I reckon we've done the best part of six months' work in as many weeks. We've had some help, certainly, but my guys have never worked their tails off like this before.'

'Why the rush?'

'Political pressure Mark, political pressure. Silly bastards have no idea about what's involved, just scream for answers.'

'Still, you've nearly finished now?'

'Not really. All I've got so far are the facts, hundreds of them. And even now I'm not sure that I've really got all I should have, but what can I do? Now comes the longest part. Getting it all down in a final report.'

'I see, but what it all comes down to are a few observations: inexperience and possible fatigue on the part of the vet, is that right?'

'Yep, that's about it.'

'Aircrew sound?'

'Yes.'

'Comment on Air Traffic Control mentioning two omissions on QNH with the rider that you mention it as a guide to future procedure, but take the view that neither could have contributed to this accident?'

'That's right. But I rather think the point on Air Traffic Control won't get past the Minister. As you know, he edits my report if he considers it in the public interest to do so, or some such crap.'

Mark pondered for a moment as he reviewed the investigation. But as nothing more occurred to him, he said, 'Yes, yes, I see, well, I'll be away back to Auckland, Graham. And thanks for your help. It's been a very interesting few weeks.'

'Yeah, but I sure could have done without them!'

As Graham showed Mark out of his office for the last time he wished him well and they shook hands. While walking back into his office, the thought suddenly crossed his mind that not once had Mark volunteered anything. But he smiled to himself as the thought followed that it was hardly surprising in such a specialized field as air accidents. Hardly in the line of run-of-the-mill loss adjusting. Mark for his part, was fairly satisfied with the outcome of the assignment. His report was all but finished: a few lines to add tomorrow and it could go to the insurance company. He wished for a fleeting second that he was part of that company. He rather thought the real fun was just about to start.

Chapter Thirteen

'Right, gentlemen, I think we're all here. Perhaps we can get on.'

And in answer to the Prime Minister's remark the two little groups of men separated out and began to take their seats around the Cabinet table. It was the first time the Chairman of Merlin Mutual Ltd had been in the room. And it was the first time that Graham Weller, the Chief Investigator of Air Accidents, had found himself in the company of Ministers and a Prime Minister at one and the same time. The Solicitor General, on the other hand – a man in the strange position of being of the Government, but not elected, for as the legal representative of the Government, he was an appointee – had sat in the room often in the past, and with many Ministers of other administrations.

They sat in order of precedence. To the Prime Minister's right sat the Attorney General, a defunct lawyer turned politician, and beside him sat the Chairman of Merlin Mutual. To the Prime Minister's left was the Minister of Transport. Next to him was the Solicitor General, and then the Chief Investigator of Air Accidents.

'Now,' the Prime Minister began, 'the purpose of this meeting is to consider what is the correct preliminary view to take. But for that we've got to know the facts we have to deal with, so I've invited our Chief Investigator here to attend so he can go through them with us. Perhaps you would begin, Weller.'

Graham arranged his notes in front of him, gave his customary dry cough, and began. He ran through the salient points of the constituent parts of the several separate reports which would eventually become incorporated into his final report. And as he spoke the others present made notes.

'In conclusion, gentlemen, it really comes down to this, and these are amongst the points I shall incorporate in my final report which, you will appreciate, is still some time away. However, I give them to you now, because I have been directed to do so. It is not something, I may add, that I like to do.' Getting no response to the little protest at the irregularity of it all, he carried on. 'I preface what I have to say by stating that I draw no conclusions from these comments, that being a matter outside my province. I merely state facts as facts.

'The aircraft involved. The Cessna, a relatively new plane, well maintained, the sole doubt on fitness raised during the investigation was one concerning the radio. It had failed two days before February 8th, the day of the accident, but had been repaired that day. However, investigation with the Communications Technician concerned has satisfied me that at the time of the accident it would probably have been functioning properly. This is borne out by the fact that it was used in the air by the pilot, who made two transmissions, the last of which was timed at 16.35, some ten and a half minutes before the accident. My conclusion therefore is that at the time of the accident, the Cessna was airworthy in all respects.'

'Before you leave the Cessna, can you tell me whether or not there is any evidence to show that the pilot had done his pre-flight checks?' The Solicitor General's voice was quiet; even mild, but had the unmistakable timbre and resonance of a voice used as a weapon in the arena of the courts. Inflection gave it an edge.

'Yes,' Graham answered. 'Three sources of evidence. The Comms Technician saw him doing his external before he went to the clubhouse to file his flight plan. He saw him again holding at the beginning of take-off for a period of time in which he was either daydreaming or doing his checks, and from other members of the flying club, I accept that it would have been for the latter purpose. And finally, he was five minutes later on take-off than at first notified. Again, it would point to care on his part.'

'Thank you.'

'Now to the DC8. We did not manage to recover in-flight records, but we know there was a slight fuel reading intake discrepancy and one engine was working at a trifle below optimum performance, but in both respects, well within the acceptable operating parameters for the aircraft . . .'

'I'm sorry to interrupt again, but would it not have been

possible for that engine to have failed and, as a result, the DC8 lost height?'

'No. In the first place, had one engine been out the plane would have still been quite safe, and in the second, the engine I have in mind was the starboard outer. It had shown rather more vibration than it perhaps should have done. We recovered that engine and I can state categorically that its performance was well within working parameters and could not have contributed to the accident. The only other defect was slightly excessive fuel usage by one of the port engines. But again it is irrelevant.'

'Hmmm. I see. Thank you.'

'In the result, my report will contain no adverse comment on either aircraft.'

'But you will be mentioning these points?' the Minister of Transport queried.

'As facts, yes.'

'You will also add the rider, I hope, that neither has any bearing on the causation of the accident,' the Prime Minister enquired, having decided the time had come to start moving things in the desired direction, the meeting being merely a cover.

'Well, er . . . my intention had been to avoid . . .'

'Mr Weller, you are an expert. I appreciate your natural concern to avoid passing any sort of judgment which may open the way to involvement in any possible litigation. But, perhaps I can make it plain to you that, in this case, if litigation arises, you will most certainly be involved. You will therefore do rather more in your report than merely state the facts, as you have put it. You will draw conclusions, is that perfectly understood?'

Silence followed the remark by the Prime Minister, as Graham Weller tried to see a way out of it. Off the cuff, *tête-à-tête* speculation on an informal basis was a long way from this sort of thing.

'I don't think you quite appreciate the position, Chief Investigator,' the Prime Minister added. 'In the event of a case, you, sir, will be the expert witness for the Government. And with that in mind, your report will be rendered on the basis that it will be for discreet governmental use. It will be upon your report that we consider liability, we and the Merlin Mutual Ltd together, though of course, it will also be published by the Minister in its expurgated form. Do I make myself plain?'

Angry now at the abuse of his impartial role of independent investigator, a role he had carefully preserved by avoiding opinions on liability, Graham decided to speak his mind.

'To be blunt, Prime Minister, yes, I fully realize my position. You, with respect, do not. You wish to abuse it. My job isn't to give opinions on liability, but to state facts. If opinions are required for a case, those should properly come from experts who spend their time in court, or are prepared to. For my office to be seen to adopt partiality and become the expert for this or any other Government would destroy the years of work I and my colleagues have put in to establish an unimpeachable record of acting impartially for the benefit of the public. I do not intend to become some sort of pawn in a political game.'

This raised eyebrows around the table and, as Graham Weller looked at the Prime Minister, he felt unease at the crocodile smile.

'My dear Mr Weller! Oh, dear, oh, dear. What shall we do?' The Prime Minister pondered for a moment, before continuing, and as he did so there was almost an audible sigh of relief from the others round the table.

'Would you agree with me that you are a public servant?'

'Of course.'

'And your duty is one of serving the Government of the day?'

'It is a duty, but I don't regard it as so high a duty as my service in the public interest; though I would hope that both interests are served synonymously.'

'And if there was a conflict, in your mind, well then, I suppose you'd resign?'

'It has never arisen.'

'But you think that it does arise if you set out your independent expert opinion, as opposed to confining yourself to fact alone. Is that correct?'

Graham considered it, and realizing he was getting into an untenable position, tried to avoid it by saying, 'But it is not my job to act in that capacity.'

'Perhaps in the past it hasn't been. But to be asked to do it, in what way can that possibly prejudice your position of integrity with the public? Indeed, in what way can it lead to any sort of conclusion that in giving your opinion, you are, to use your misguided phrase, a pawn in a political game? Has anyone suggested for a moment that you suppress your views, or express them to suit the Government? Well, have they?'

'No, Prime Minister, no.'

'Quite. Take it a stage further. You wish to avoid conclusions in your report. Tell me, in what way would the setting down of the conclusions on an accident by the best qualified men in the field in this country be contrary to the public interest?'

And the realization that there was no answer to this led to Graham's answer of 'No way, I suppose.'

'So it comes down to this. In a nutshell, your real objection to drawing conclusions is because you really don't wish to open the door to the testing of your expertise in court?' He paused, then continuing in his silky voice, he gave the only way out.

'Or, perhaps, what you have in mind is that if you draw no conclusions, then you, as a public servant can't embarrass the Government.'

And Graham took it. It was the only way. 'It is, of course, Prime Minister, no part of our job to embarrass or absolve the Government.'

'Well, in this case, my dear Mr Weller, you will oblige me by letting me take the chance of embarrassment to the Government, and let us have your expert conclusions.'

Trapped, the Chief Investigator had to agree, but shuddered at the thought that his conclusions would appear in the published report, so he said, 'But, Prime Minister, I do think that any conclusions I draw really shouldn't be for general publication. I am sure you'll agree?'

The Prime Minister smiled, as he replied, 'Oh, yes, of course, in principle I agree, but you will have to let the Minister of Transport be the judge of that. But don't worry, I am quite sure he fully realizes the importance of maintaining your reputation for impartiality with the public. Now, perhaps, we can get on.

'Now you say both planes were OK, which conveniently, Mr Weller, is a fact which leads to a conclusion you can put forward with every confidence in the knowledge that it is most unlikely that anyone will wish to challenge it.'

A ripple of laughter went round the table, and the Chief

Investigator had enough grace to smile wryly. 'Yes, the planes are out. And out, too, are all pre-flight procedures. Which leaves me with Air Traffic Control and crew.' And he gave his findings.

'And your conclusions?'

In silence, they waited as he swallowed the bitter pill, but it was too much all at once, so he temporized with, 'I just don't know what caused this accident.'

'I accept that, but we must go further, Mr Weller, and look at probabilities. Is it probable that it was an act of God? I would classify a freak, unforeseeable weather condition as such.'

'No. One of the pilots would have had to have flown at the wrong height.'

'And Air Traffic can be shown, at worst, to have omitted a QNH direction which, in your mind, would be irrelevant for the reason that aircrew don't rely on it, but on the ATIS, which you are satisfied was transmitting weather Mike properly?'

'Yes.'

'So, to your conclusion, Mr Weller, as a matter of probability . . .' Silence fell again. 'We are waiting for it, sir.' The Prime Minister's voice was almost a purr. Weller couldn't back out now.

With obvious reluctance he finally said, 'If, as I apparently must, I have to give it, well, then, I conclude that in all probability this accident occurred because the vet failed to keep to his prescribed height.' And he felt sick at the pronouncement, and at those present for forcing him to say it.

'Thank you, Chief Investigator. Believe me, I appreciate how much you have disliked departing from your usual practice. But there it is. In this case, I assure you it's necessary. You will, of course, press on now to complete your full report, and I need hardly mention to a man of your experience that any comment from you to the media could cause grave embarrassment.'

'Prime Minister . . .' But the upheld hand silenced him, and the Prime Minister's laugh interposed before he said, 'Quite, and thank you Chief Investigator. That, I think, concludes your part here today. Does anyone have any questions of this gentleman before he goes?'

Murmurs of no and heads shaken answered him, so, with a

final dismissive smile from the Prime Minister, the Chief Investigator left.

As Graham left the building, those still with the Prime Minister had coffee and talked among themselves. 'That went well, I think.' The Prime Minister had drawn his Attorney General to one side.

'Yes, very well. Felt a bit sorry for him though.'

'Yes, but we would never have got him to agree to commit himself to paper otherwise.'

'No. Quite. Anyway, we had to get it, with old whatsisname here.' He nodded in the direction of the Chairman of the Merlin Mutual Ltd.

Then the Prime Minister suggested that they should get on. The next act of the charade was for the benefit of the Chairman of the Merlin Mutual Ltd.

'The question now is, what line do we take? First, as a matter of law as opposed to policy we had better hear from the Solicitor General. What views, Clive?'

'Off the cuff, and on an all or nothing basis, I'd say a judge would find it a trifle hard to arrive at any conclusion, on the balance of probability, other than the vet. What do you think, Stan?'

The Prime Minister was happy to let it pass. The Attorney General, a large thick-set man with a heavy, grey face and thick, grey, wavy hair, steepled his fingers and putting his elbows on the table, rested his chin on his thumbs and massaged the tip of his nose with his forefingers. Eyebrows raised, he stared across the room. Then he drew a breath, sighed, and leaned back in his chair before he spoke.

'Yep. Maybe. But it worries me. I think there's a risk here, and a substantial one. Here we have a demonstrable and inexplicable failure on the part of two Controllers. And there's an accident. Weller says no blame, the aircrew rely on the ATIS. They hear the ATIS. A single transmission, and perhaps a mistake. Couple with that the silence of the Controllers on the one point of information by which a pilot sets his altimeter, and if I were for the vet I'd go for pilot error: static over the air. I'd get tapes and show how difficult it is to hear up there sometimes, and I'd work on the coincidence. To that I'd add a rundown of the Cessna's flight: no error from the ATC people in that.' He shrugged his shoulders and threw it back to the Government's lawyer with 'No, Clive?'

'Hmmm. Put like that, yes. However good a case, there's always a risk the judge won't like it and we'd be fooling ourselves if we took the view that we just couldn't lose. And even if we did, but won on appeal, it wouldn't do you gentlemen a great deal of good. Lose a few votes, I should think.'

'So the view you two would urge upon the Government would be to settle rather than take a strong line and to deny any liability outright and shoulder it on to the Dominion?' The Prime Minister's voice was speculative as he took another metaphorical move towards Merlin Mutual Ltd – in check. Then he turned to the Chairman of Merlin Mutual.

'And your view?'

'I don't think I can commit myself at this moment, Prime Minister.'

'No, I s'pose not.' Then briskly, he addressed them all. 'OK, you chaps sort it out between you. Clive, you'd better be ready to have a word with the Merlin Mutual people when our friend here and his people have chewed it over, and we'll meet next week to take it from there. But I confess that though I don't like it, it appears to me that we may well be wise to have a settlement in mind.'

The General Manager of the Dominion read the report of the loss adjuster and smiled. Then he rang for his Chief Claims Officer.

'Hi Tony. Park your ass. Simpson's a bright guy.'

'Yes, not bad.'

'You bet your sweet life he's not bad! But what's the score with the prick I spoke to? Have they been in touch?'

'No. I dare say they're considering the line to take. Do you want me to set the ball rolling?'

'Shit, no! Sit back and wait, but when they come through let me know. It's one meeting I'll enjoy.' As he said it, the jowl responded to the treatment of pleasure as he massaged the fat behind his ear. 'Yep, it ought to be a ball. OK, scram. I've things to do.'

He was still chuckling as the door closed behind Anthony Carnegie. Then he sat and thought about it for a few moments. Better than he'd hoped for. With a bit of luck, they'd get out of it for one hell of a sight less than he'd prepared his Board for.

Chapter Fourteen

'Well, what do you recommend?' The Prime Minister's voice was brisk. This time the Chief Investigator of Air Accidents was absent.

The Attorney General replied for all of them – not that the Minister of Transport had been engaged in the to-ings and fro-ings between the lawyers and the insurers during the week.

'Walter, here,' he nodded to the Chairman of the Merlin Mutual Ltd, 'has authority from his Board to go for acceptance on the part of Paranational of 10 per cent of the total claim. Tentatively, we consider that to be a reasonable figure. Air Traffic Control? Well, we reckon that if the Government will go to, say, another 10 per cent, it ought to be reasonably attractive to the Dominion, and we take the view that, paid on an *ex gratia* basis, it satisfies the risk of litigation.'

'You agree with that?'

'Yeeeesss . . .' the Solicitor General drew the word out speculatively.

'Yes, but what?' The Prime Minister hoped the Attorney General had done a good job on the man.

'My advice would be that if you can avoid litigation for a small percentage on this one, it would be wise to do so.' He stressed the word 'can'. 'Of course, you might escape scot free.'

The Prime Minister smiled to himself. With luck they'd come up with a figure the Dominion couldn't refuse, and all above board too. All good stuff.

'But we must consider risk. A good team for the Dominion, and I think they could very well get a case on its feet. Failure of your Air Traffic Control people to give the QNH. Compounded by a simple mistake, a mishearing of the ATIS, and you've got a credible cause of the accident. Certainly, we would rely on statistics, inexperience and tiredness on the part of the vet. But on inexperience, you know, though he may not have known the Cessna that well, he'd been flying for years. If I was on the other side, I would draw the parallel between him and the commercial pilot doing a conversion course. In my opinion, and I have given it some thought since we last met, he'd flown more than enough to base competence on. And finally, and this is important, there is nothing which we can produce to show anyone put a foot wrong on his flight. In the result, I'm not sure I'd put the risk as low as 20 per cent. I think you could lose.'

Eventually, the silence that followed his analysis was broken by the Prime Minister. 'So, you think the view expressed by the Attorney General is sound, but over-optimistic. And it would be in our best interests to go higher than 20 per cent. But how much higher?'

'I would suggest that you have it in mind to go to 30 per cent or so.'

'But, tell me, isn't even 20 per cent as good as a tacit admission of liability?'

'No. It's merely a realistic facing of the fact that, in this one, liability isn't clear-cut and you're in a risk situation, apart from the fact that even the best case carries risk. Any settlement would, of course, be offered on an *ex gratia* and without prejudice basis.'

Again they pondered it.

'Anything to add to that?' The Prime Minister turned to the Attorney General.

'30 per cent would be high but not excessively so on the way the Solicitor General puts it.'

'And you?' He turned to the Chairman of Merlin Mutual Ltd.

'I have authority to agree to a 10 per cent risk contribution. More, and I would have to go back to my Board. But, well, I can say that if we were asked to carry 12½ per cent, they'd probably agree – reluctantly.' He smiled.

'Why not fifty-fifty with the Government 15 per cent?'

'We take the view that the aircrew could not possibly be found liable but if, and I repeat if, the accident was as a result of a mistake on the flight deck of the DC8 in mishearing the only QNH given, then that error would have been corrected if there had not been a failure on the part of not just one of the Controllers, but two. So in that event, if we had to split liability the greater share would rest with them. But, having heard the Solicitor General here, I am prepared to suggest to my Board that in recognition of the faint possibility that the aircrew did mishear the ATIS, perhaps because of static, then there may be a slim case for saying they should have asked for a check. Except, if they did mishear, then it would have been more than probable they would have taken in the ATIS transmission again.' He paused as he considered where that got him. Then, satisfied, he added: 'No, I would recommend an extra 2½ per cent, but you can call it a goodwill gesture, Prime Minister, nothing more.'

The Prime Minister was well pleased. The Attorney General steepled his fingers and, his chin supported on the balls of his thumbs, massaged the tip of his nose and stared across the room. He was wondering whether it had been such a wise move to appoint Walter Andrews Chairman of Merlin Mutual. The Solicitor General merely nodded. Objectively, he was inclined to agree with the Chairman. If the aircrew were found to blame, that couldn't be disassociated from Air Traffic. The Minister of Transport, fascinated by it, wondered why he was there. Coming out of his reverie, the Prime Minister grimaced and ran his hands back over the little hair he had left, sticking it back hard to his scalp.

'I see. Well, Walter, I think that makes your position clear. Can I take it that you are happy for us to deal with the Dominion on your behalf?'

'I would like my General Manager to be present at any meeting and of course I would want to be kept fully informed, but yes, that's OK by me.'

'Right. I think that wraps it up with you, Walter, for the time being. We will carry on now without you, and when we've arrived at our final view we'll be in touch. You'll understand that it's largely a political problem now.'

The meeting went on for another hour.

The intercom on Anthony Carnegie's desk came to life. He flicked the switch up. 'Yep?' 'Get your ass in here.' And the circuit was cut. Sometimes it annoyed him, but more usually the General Manager's approach to communication amused him. As he entered the General Manager's office, he noticed the gentle stroking of behind the ear. Suddenly it struck him as very funny.

'What's so funny?'

'Nothing, just something I thought about. You wanted my "ass" here? Well, sir, here it is.'

'Yeah, I've had the Attorney guy on the phone. They want

to kick the ball around.'

'How nice. Just what we wanted.'

'Sure. Ten the day after tomorrow, OK?'

'Yes.'

'Right, get jacked up. I'll want a complete file and we can talk on the way.' Anthony had got to the door when the 'Hold it!' stopped him. 'Yes?'

'How many letters have we had?'

'Last count was two hundred and seventeen intimations of claims against us.'

'Anything specific?'

'No, all the same thing. "We will be in touch again when our client's claim has been formulated", that sort of thing. I've put out the standard reply denying liability.'

'Might find out how many the other guys have had.'

'Yes, I've had a go at that. Merlin was a bit reluctant, but it appears they've had a few more, and the Attorney General's office refused to comment.'

'Yeah – which means a sackful.'

'Probably.'

'OK Tony.'

Grace was out when Bill Hulman phoned the first time: at the guild, she explained later, when they eventually spoke at 4.30.

'Grace, it kinda struck me you must be a little lonely . . . well, what I mean ter say is, we're old friends, and I kinda thought it might be nice, if you wanted to, er, would you come and have a meal sometime? We could talk a bit, er, anyway, that's what I wanted to say.' Nervously, he waited for her reply.

It took her by surprise. She thought about it for a moment and the thought struck her that she had always rather liked Bill. Why shouldn't she see him? The last thing in the world Frank would have wanted would have been for her to live in seclusion.

'Why, Bill! That's nice of you. Yes, I'd like that very much.'

'Are you free this evening? Just say if it's still, er, the wrong time, or anything. Any time, Grace, to suit you. Just you say.'

Graham would want supper, she thought, but she could do a casserole and leave it for him. He wouldn't mind. Perhaps he'd get Helen over.

'That would be lovely Bill. Thank you. What time would you like me to come on over?'

'I'll be coming by your place at about seven. Could I pick you up?'

'Hmmm. Look forward to it. See you then.'

'Yeah, 'bye Grace.'

She smiled to herself as she put the phone down, but was pleased at the transparency of the lie. She knew very well that there was no possible reason for Bill to be passing her door then, or ever. But it was rather nice.

'Mum! What's all this?'

It was 6.45 and Graham had just got in and, on going into the sitting-room for a drink, was amazed. Grace looked really beautiful.

'Bill Hulman's coming for me. Taking me out.' Then, with a trace of defensive anxiety in her voice, she continued, 'You don't mind, dear, do you?'

He laughed. 'Don't be silly. Dad would have been all for it, you know that.'

Relieved, she asked, 'How do I look?'

'Great! Just great. Would you like a freshener in that?'

She held the glass out to him. 'Gin and tonic.'

'Do you like Bill?'

'Hmmm. He's rather nice. Surprised me, you know.'

'What?'

'Him ringing.' She chuckled. 'But, between us, he's always rather fancied me, but not so you'd really notice. He's so shy about that sort of thing. His wife, I don't remember her awfully well. There was an accident in the early days up there, something to do with a tractor, and Bill . . . yes, he was in some way involved I seem to remember. But after that, he never seemed to . . . oh, I don't know, he seemed to lose interest in everything except the farm and horses.' She paused, before adding with a laugh, 'And those cows of his.'

'But I thought he and Millie were as good as married.'

'No, Millie only went to the farm about six years ago to housekeep, and he'd had two or three other housekeepers before her.'

They heard the car draw up.

Bill Hulman had been turning the idea over in his mind almost from the time his friend Frank had been killed. No one had ever known it, but he had envied Frank and Grace. Several times after the accident he had nearly said something to her, but at the last moment his courage had always failed and he'd kept silent. Somewhere he'd read that new widows often fell in love with someone who'd helped them over the tragedy. Perhaps it was that – a feeling that it would be unfair – which had kept him silent. If she came to like him, it would have to be from a position of self-contained neutrality.

Then on this day he had woken up resolved to say something to her. But when he had phoned he had felt about thirteen, nervous and unsure of himself. After her acceptance he had tried to fill the day, waiting for it to come up to six. It had been a long slow day. Millie had shooed him out of the kitchen twice, and had gone on preparing a meal which she hoped would be something rather special.

Bill had taken a great deal of trouble in getting ready. Perhaps he'd overdone it, he thought, almost wishing as he walked up to Grace's front door he hadn't taken so much trouble. But as she opened it and he saw she had taken it seriously enough herself to dress up, he was very pleased. 'Ready Grace?' He didn't want to go in and have a drink with Graham, not this evening. And Grace understood.

'Remember, dear,' she called out behind her, 'get the casserole out in half an hour: there's enough for both of you.'

'OK Mum, and have a good time. And say hello to Bill for me.'

As they walked to the car she said, 'He's got a girl, Helen Fielding. Do you know the Fieldings, Bill? He's a dentist in town.'

'Didn't know he had a daughter.'

'Oh yes. Two boys and a girl. She's a super kid. I think . . .' It broke the layer of slight awkwardness.

Anthony Carnegie and his General Manager were the last to arrive. The room was full of quiet conversation as they entered; it died as they were introduced by the Attorney General to the others. Introductions complete, they took their seats, the Attorney General taking the chair.

'Now, I think to begin with we should agree on what we are here to discuss. First, I think, we should look at the evidence in this case and see if we can't work towards an agreement and so avoid long drawn-out proceedings. Now, if mutually acceptable terms can be agreed for the settlement of the many claims, and prevent them from going to Court, it would be to everyone's advantage, and would save endless misery and hardship for the many sufferers, and we have to think of them. And that, really, is the Government's main interest. The Dominion hasn't been in on our earlier discussions. But having had someone involved with the investigation, perhaps that is their view as well?'

He looked at the fat man.

'Sure. Who wants a case? So go on, what's on your mind?'

'If we can agree . . .'

That fat man cut in, 'Can we skip the crap? As I see it, it's simple. We put views and agree, or we don't. If we do, you guys have a ball on TV, "Aren't we just the greatest?" Not that I'd mind that, if your solicitor takes the weight of the admin in getting the claims dealt with.'

'Well, I wouldn't have put it quite like that, but in substance, yes,' the Attorney General said, a trifle stiffly.

'OK. What's your proposition?'

'Ah, er . . .' It was going much too quickly for the Attorney General. 'I think we ought to agree the premises on which we base any proposition first.'

'I'd rather hear the deal first. Who knows, we might agree and save a hell of a lot of gas. If the deal's right, who cares what who thinks as to why. So, let's have it, straight, sharp and so a simple fucker like myself can understand it.'

The Attorney General shrugged. 'All right, if you insist. The Government and Merlin Mutual Ltd take the view that there is no liability on the part of either the aircrew or Air Traffic Services. However, all cases have a small risk element. In recognition of this, we take the view that if we jointly make a contribution of 10 per cent it would not be ungenerous to the Dominion.'

'Crap.' The word was like a pistol shot.

'I beg your pardon!'

'Sure, you sure should. The word I used was "crap". Personally I prefer it, but if you prefer it, "shit". The deal's sixty-forty. Or no deal.'

'Sixty-forty! You must be out of your mind. How could you possibly justify that? Do you seriously propose that the Government and Merlin Mutual Ltd bear 40 per cent of the claims?' The Attorney General's voice was scandalized.

'No. You take the heavy slice.'

No one could think of anything to say for a moment until the Solicitor General came to the rescue.

'On what basis do you arrive at that extraordinary split?'

'Let's get at it another way,' the fat man countered. 'You shoot the shit on the vet first and we'll think about that. You reckon a judge would jump on him. Now just you tell me why.'

'Very well. He was inexperienced for the aircraft he was flying. He . . .'

'Bit by bit, I think. Inexperienced, eh?' Turning to his Chief Claims Officer, he said, 'Hand the bumph round, Tony, there's a good lad.'

Quietly, Anthony Carnegie got up and laid a small dossier in front of each of the men round the table. Two for the Merlin Mutual people, and one each for the Solicitor General, the Attorney General, and finally the Minister of Transport. Silence fell as they read, broken only occasionally by the sound of a pencil on paper and the rustle of turning pages.

The fat man sat back and stroked behind his ear. As the last dossier was finished and came to rest in front of the last reader, he spoke.

'The evidence: eight statements from people we'd call, and who don't agree with you. No, sir, this guy was bloody careful, sensible and as cautious as a virgin. And where many guys would have just pushed on through the cloud he asked for radar assistance. He was meticulous. Read the transcripts of everything he said to your people that afternoon. He was a guy who delayed his flight to make sure he hadn't got a crook radio. Inexperience, my ass! What's your next point?' And he fixed his eye on the Solicitor General.

'We have reason to believe he was probably overtired.'

'Why?'

The Solicitor General went through the evidence of the vet falling asleep that night with his glasses on and the early call.

'Is that it?'

'Yes.'

'Well, I've got news for you. We've been through his call book. Item one, three days out of seven for the preceding three months he had night calls; and, item two, that was a bloody sight less than he'd been used to for years. The guy was used to six hours' sleep. So, what's special about that?

Falls asleep with his glasses on. Jesus! What a hell of a thing! That guy made a habit of it. His way of going to sleep, probably. Did you ask his wife how often he did it?'

The Solicitor felt he was on shifting sands. There was no mention of that question to the wife.

'We have carried out our investigation. The next point, sir, is one which I don't think you will be able to, er, comment on. As a matter of probability – and the Courts decide on that – it is more likely for a private pilot to have made a mistake than the crew of a commercial flight.'

'Sure, so we chip in 40 per cent.'

'But, my dear sir, 40 per cent hardly recognizes a higher likelihood of blame, which, in this case, we consider falls substantially on your insured. If, which it isn't, the probability of fault was evenly matched, then it would be fifty-fifty. No?'

'Yeah, but we haven't finished yet, have we? What about the mistakes with the Air Traffic people?'

'Our expert evidence is clear. Yes, there were two points in transmission when sometimes a QNH might have been given. They weren't in this case. But it is not mandatory, merely a frill, something done on the Controller's inclination. The ATIS is the definitive information, and as you know, it had been copied by the aircrew. No, I think that's a non-starter.'

'Sure, by itself, you just may be right. But for it to have no importance you'd have to satisfy a judge that the crew had got the ATIS copy right. Wrong, and you're up the Khyber without a whatever – right? And had the Air Traffic boys made what my guys would call "the normal transmission", then any error in copying the ATIS would have been looked after, right or wrong?'

'Possibly, but we have no reason to believe that there was any likelihood of crew error.'

The fat man was enjoying himself immensely. 'Do you think a judge would be impressed by, say, a crew of guys with personal problems, or tired, or ill, or if it were shown the two guys up front hated each other's guts?'

'Yes, of course, but there is no evidence of this.'

'But, if there were – I am, of course, just kicking the ball around – then just like you say for the vet, the poor sod was tired, so it would cut back, wouldn't it?'

'If such a suggestion could be substantiated, well yes. But really, this is hardly the point, is it?'

‘Well, there we disagree.’ Said quietly, he let it ride the air for a bit, watching consternation flicker across the faces round the table. His finger worked the fat behind his ear with hard, sustained vigour, and he watched and waited, savouring the moment. The faces watched him intently, all waiting for him to amplify the enigmatic remark. But he decided to wait until one of them couldn’t stand it any longer. Ultimately it was the man across the table, the Chairman of Merlin Mutual Ltd, the company which carried the can for the airline, who broke the silence. ‘I advise care, sir, in amplifying that remark.’

‘Yeah, a fucksight more care than your guys have taken. Tell me, how many of your guys knew the pilot’s dad died the day before the accident? Would that make for concentration on the job?’

Appalled that it might be true and had been missed, the Attorney General shot forward in his seat. ‘Is that a fact, a certain fact?’ he asked.

‘Tony, give them the statement from the guy at the airport.’

And they read it carefully. Mark Simpson had taken care with it. Nothing the man had seen or heard had been left out. It even mentioned the doubt he had felt as to whether he should have taken the serious step of setting the machinery in motion to ground Captain Harry Standard.

The Attorney General looked up, his face very grave and, looking at the fat man and Anthony Carnegie, he said, ‘Gentlemen, I wonder whether you would be so kind as to leave us for five minutes. I am sure they will have a cup of coffee for you outside.’

Five minutes stretched to twenty, to thirty, and it wasn’t until three-quarters of an hour later that the doors opened again. The General Manager had been content to wait, having no intention of leaving now that they were so plainly rattled. During that time, the Prime Minister had been contacted for a long private conversation with his Attorney General, also the Chief Investigator of Air Accidents, the manager at the airport, and a few Board members of Merlin Mutual Ltd. Their conclusion was summed up by the Attorney General, as the fat man and his Chief Claims Officer drank their third cup of coffee outside the room. ‘. . . In conclusion, I think we’re in trouble. If the Captain was flying the leg with that sort of weight on his mind, well, he could have let his mind wander and so made a mistake. But whatever the truth, it must not get out. A Captain allowed to fly with that on his mind, Air Traffic omissions, the result would be disastrous! The public must not know. That is the Prime Minister's directive.

'Now, plainly, what we have learned places a very different light on the whole thing, and I think now we should see whether or not we can settle with the Dominion with them carrying 50 per cent of the claim, and split the balance between us 25 per cent apiece. Is that agreed?'

'Hardly agreed. You're talking about a great deal of money.' The Chairman of Merlin Mutual Ltd paused. 'Yes, a very great deal of money. And I for one am not prepared to be bulldozed into this without rather more thought, and I will not be making any recommendation to my Board until we have had the benefit of our own people looking into this a bit more thoroughly than seems to have been the case so far. I'm not so much concerned with the facts. I accept what that bull of a man has produced. But now I think I will look for further independent opinion on the interpretation to be placed on the Air Traffic Control omission, in fact on all the facts. And I am bound to say that my Board won't act in the absence of legal opinion which supports the Attorney General's view.'

'So are you saying we can do nothing now, say nothing to the Dominion?'

'You cannot count us in for 25 per cent, if that's what you want to do.'

'I see. Well, in that case, gentlemen, and having heard the Prime Minister's view, I am prepared to offer the Dominion a third – at this point in time, 20 per cent to be borne by the Government, and I dare say you,' and he looked at the Chairman, 'would go to 13 per cent now?'

'If it helps, yes, I'll go the extra ½ per cent now.'

'Get them back in, will you?'

The Minister of Transport, nearest the door, went out.

'One hell of a long five minutes!' the General Manager observed affably as he took his seat.

'A lot of money at stake,' observed the Attorney General, who was finding the Prime Minister's directive very difficult in the presence of the Merlin Mutual people and the Solicitor General. 'But we have considered your proposal with the greatest care, and I feel it right to say that your comments have caused us concern. However, we continue to take the view that if it came to Court proceedings the probability is that the vet would be found at fault. Nevertheless, we are prepared to revise our without-prejudice offer to settle to one-third being borne by the Government and Merlin Mutual jointly.'

Rising from his seat, the General Manager nodded around the table and started to gather his papers together. 'Ready, Tony? I think we've wasted enough of these gentlemen's time. G'day all.'

'Wait one moment, please. We must have time to consider . . .'

'All the time you want, you asked for this meeting, not me. I dare say a few writs will start flying around soon. I don't mind. We'll pay 40 per cent into Court and it's my guess that'll be enough to see you carrying the costs. No skin off my nose.'

'Would you be prepared to consider, if offered – which I am not doing – 40 per cent from us?'

'No. Sixty-forty or we all go off to battle. G'day to you all again.'

As the chauffeur eased the car out of the space and into the noonday traffic, the General Manager chuckled. 'Oh, Tony, did you just see those stiffs' faces! Shit, that was good. Best fun I've had in years.' And he shook with laughter. Later, when he'd finished enjoying it to the full in deep, cavernous, rumblings which shook the whole of his vast frame, he said, 'You know, they'll fall about for as long as we let them, but in the end, they'll come across. Problem is, when? I think, Tony lad, that you'd better give it five days then tell the Attorney we've had a writ and what's the score. Do we join him and Paranational as co's with us, or what? That'll frighten the shit out of them, and then I reckon they'll offer 55 per cent in three days!'

'At 50 per cent the guy would be struggling. Might even be 45 per cent.'

'Betcha a hundred bucks it's 55. Jesus! Did you see them? The Merlin Mutual guy was pure insurance; and the Solicitor looked like he had crazy clients, but the Attorney! He looked like he'd been caught fucking in public! They're hiding something, Tony boy, and unless I'm very much mistaken, they're prepared to buy their way out.'

'Oh I know, but even so, they can only go so far. Still, OK, you're on.'

'Christ! It's like taking candy from a baby, but if I win, I s'pose you'll be round licking my ass for a raise! And you know what? If we get out of this at even 50 per cent, I reckon you might just have earned it!'

They drove on in silence, punctuated once by a murmured 'For fuck's sake, I wouldn't give one of 'em house room!'

'Would you settle for 30?' asked Tony.

'Jeez. If they hadn't got some smelly washing we'd be happy at 20, and then I'd reckon we'd have done bloody well. Still, that's their problem, silly buggers.'

'It's all very well, but what I don't see is how they're going to shell out more than they might without a lot of people asking a lot of questions. If so, then they're blown anyway. Someone's bound to start digging, then it'll just be a matter of time.'

'You'll see, laddie, you'll see, come the day our beloved Prime Minister wraps it up. Till then, you figure it out.'

And he chuckled again.

Chapter Fifteen

It was three days later that Anthony Carnegie wandered into his manager's office with the good news. 'Well, I reckon I'll owe you a hundred bucks by lunch-time tomorrow.'

'Why?'

'Our friends, or, to be precise, the Attorney General's office, have been in touch asking whether we could find it convenient to go and see him at two tomorrow. Can you make it, or would you rather I went alone?'

'Shit, and miss the coup dee grass?'

'I'm not sure that is quite how one is meant to pronounce it,' Anthony murmured.

'Yeah, so they tell me. But you can bet your sweet asshole it's convenient. And of course we'll be there on time. Arrange the car for five past two. Now fuck off.'

Their first evening together had been quiet, and Millie's meal very nice. But Grace reckoned the girl couldn't really cook as well as she could. In a way the evening had been a relief, but as it progressed she wasn't sure in what way.

But later, in bed, the truth had found its way to the surface. Immediately it became recognizable, she had thrust it back but it wouldn't remain in her subconscious, it kept bobbing up. So, unable to escape them, she began to take cautious notice of the thoughts which, unbidden, rose in her mind. And she came to admit to herself that, yes, she had been scared that no one would want to court her at her age, and yes, if she was honest, the time would come when she would begin to miss love in her life. Only middle-aged, perhaps a little over in some people's book, she realized she still had a long time to go. It had been a lovely evening, and she had been touched by a side of Bill Hulman she wouldn't have known existed in the scruffy, albeit rich, farmer. At heart, he was a romantic. And just before sleep claimed her she smiled, before drifting off with the image in her mind of him, rather shamefacedly, lighting the candles with the muttered comment, 'Er, I don't like hard light much, that is, er, if you don't mind?' She hadn't.

The meeting between the Prime Minister, the Attorney General and the Chairman of Merlin Mutual Ltd was scheduled for ten in the morning. But ten came and went and the two were kept waiting as the Prime Minister's prior appointment overshot its allotted time. At five past, they were joined by the Solicitor General. As the Government lawyer he had also been asked to attend.

Worried by the delay, the tall man at the desk in the anteroom leading to the Prime Minister's suite discreetly flashed the Prime Minister. The light went on and he picked up the phone. 'Yes, Prime Minister. You do remember you have an appointment.'

'Yes, I understand . . . Yes, Prime Minister.' He carefully replaced the phone. As he came towards them, they turned to him expectantly and, in the case of the Attorney General, also with a trace of annoyance. Ten was always ten in his book, and he liked it to be so in everyone else's as well, Prime Minister or not.

'Well?' he asked with a trace of asperity.

'The Prime Minister asked me to apologize and say he will

be a few minutes yet. Could I arrange coffee for anyone?' They had coffee and speculated on what crisis was keeping the PM.

Behind the heavy doors the Prime Minister was speaking to the Minister of Transport.

'Yes, Christopher, you have made some very serious mistakes: the Press conference, the investigation, and the phone call, which now, I think, must have told this man we've got a problem.' He paused to let the gravity of it all sink in before continuing, even more portentously, 'and I may say that I'll be considering your future when all this has blown over. Now please leave, but before you do, I want you to remember. Your mistakes are on record in one way or another.'

Silaman cut in: 'But Prime Minister, throughout I have acted . . .'

'On your own initiative, Christopher, on your own initiative.'

'But that just isn't true! You have instructed me throughout.'

'Oh, hardly accurate, I think. Certainly I may have given the odd word of encouragement,' the Prime Minister purred, 'even advice, but I mean, how will it look? You're the Minister responsible for an investigation which has been proved to be at best, bad; I am the Prime Minister, not someone who is expected to know the affairs of the Ministry of Transport intimately. Why do I have Ministers, if not to look after things for me? I think that is the view the public would accept, and you, my dear Christopher, have, to coin a phrase, made a balls up. However, all is not yet lost, so don't fret. But, in the event of things becoming public,' he paused, 'well,' and he paused again, 'I am sure I can rely on you to accept the responsibility of a Minister?' Again he paused. 'But if you have to, it won't be the end of the world, you know. No doubt after a short period in the wilderness we'll find another job for you; not Transport, perhaps, but something. But if I have to, er, sack you it would be a different story. I would find it virtually impossible to help you further. You must understand that.'

A great many things rose in Christopher Silaman's mind, but were left unsaid as the futility of any argument hit him. 'What do you want me to do?' His voice in defeat was flat.

'Do?' The Prime Minister leaned back in his chair. 'Nothing, just carry on. As I say, I might be able to get round all this, at a cost,' he added grimly. 'And if so, so be it. We must retain power, but,' he sighed as though it weighed heavily with him, 'since you ask, the best thing to do would be to let me have an undated letter of resignation. I have something here which covers everything. I'd like you to sign it now.' It was said with velvet smoothness, before silence fell between them as the Minister read it. Then the scratch of his pen was heard.

Rising, the Prime Minister took his Minister of Transport by the elbow. 'Don't worry, Chris. With a modicum of luck I'll never need to date it.' At the door the Prime Minister added, 'Nothing further, is there, Chris, just at the moment?' Had he not been given the opening, it is unlikely that Christopher Silaman would have said anything. But as he stood just inside the door the reality hit him. Anger flashed through him. And with it, caution thrown to the winds, he heard himself sign his own political death warrant.

'No, not quite all. The whole fucking issue stinks! You make a disastrous error of judgment on the extent to which the State will be its own insurer; and another on Airline Insurance. Then you consider anything justifiable which will prevent those mistakes becoming public. God! The whole thing stinks! But oh no, nothing is too dirty, is it? With you the end will always justify the means. You fix a Press conference, go much further than was justified on television . . . Compromise and abuse Weller and use me. By God! It stinks!'

'Oh dear, oh dear. Well, go on. You'd better finish now I s'pose and get it all off your chest.'

'Yes, I intend to. When forced to open the investigation to the Dominion you make sure it's a whitewash. But when it goes wrong, what do you do? Blame Weller, as though it was his fault, poor bastard. And it doesn't end there, does it? You line me up in case it all goes wrong. And you're prepared to shell out millions from the taxpayers' pocket just to keep your job. Nothing is too much, is it? Anything's OK providing it keeps your mistakes and your lack of integrity from the public. Oh Jesus! The whole bloody fucking business stinks!'

'Hmmm, how splendidly eloquent.' The PM's voice carried the merest trace of tolerant amusement. 'Of course, my dear man, it stinks! But I am the leader of the Government and I can assure you that I intend to retain that leadership because I make a damn sight better job of it than anyone else. We all enjoy power, you, my dear Christopher, included. Anyway, all that's irrelevant, because the alternative to us would be a national disaster. But no matter. What we must think about is you. Now, you have a choice, my dear Chris. One: get out now. I shall sack you today. The discovery of the death of the DC8 Captain's father is enough. Or two: you can stay in your job and just pray that I sort it out without any fuss. But I will hold your resignation, for if a fuss arises, you can be sure that my role will be that of victim of a failure on your part.'

He looked at his Minister of Transport and saw his unhappiness but felt very little compassion. Nevertheless he said, 'Chris, I like you. I think you are an able man. I even have sympathy for your views. But my dear man, if you are going to be a politician you really must learn the facts of life. What if it does cost fifty million bucks to retain power? In the context of the money that comes and goes it really isn't the end of the world. And which is the better alternative. To admit the error and lose the public and let our half-baked opponents in to ruin the country? Or keep their confidence and pursue our policies?'

'But it's not really that,' said Christopher. 'The error in insurance didn't matter: it's the tactics you seem to think justifiable.'

'Yes, but you really must understand that once we have decided on our course of action we have to follow it through and win out, or lose credibility completely. You don't want to have to go back to a piddling little chain of markets, now do you?'

'I s'pose not.'

'Quite. No more than I would want to go back to the fearfully boring business I was in. So be a sensible chap. Accept politics for what it is. Realize you have to fight to retain power sometimes, and make up your mind to do the best job you can while accepting the limitations of the game. It's all in the best interests of the public in the long run, you know.'

And Christopher Silaman realized he had no real choice. If sacked, even his days on the back bench would be numbered. 'All right, I'll go on.' But it was said with the reluctance of a choice between two evils.

'That's splendid, for you know we really do need chaps like you. But now we must work on this and get shot of the problem on the best terms we can.'

'Yes, but what about Weller?'

'I don't think we need to worry too much about him. If the thing becomes public, well, he's shown up as inefficient.'

'I see. And what about the Dominion or the Merlin Mutual? Surely one of them is bound to say something?'

'No. The Merlin people wouldn't dare and the Dominion are more interested in money. Anyway, that about wraps it up. But in future I do not want to be called to the phone to be told that our thinking has been way out. Nor do I like being forced into taking important snap decisions. But there we are. In fact, there is a bright side to all this, you know. We can up our contribution without it looking odd. That'll get rid of the Dominion, which just leaves us with burying it good and deep. And I don't think that'll be too difficult.'

Fully committed again now, the Minister of Transport couldn't think of anything to say except: 'Well, I sincerely hope you're right.'

As he opened the door the Prime Minister smiled and said, 'Don't worry.' Then, seeing those who were waiting outside, he said, 'Ah, there you are. Sorry to keep you. Come along in and bring your cups with you if you like.' As they trooped in past him he nodded to the tall man, who picked up the phone to arrange another pot of coffee and a cup for the PM.

'Now, gentlemen, the position as I have understood it is that the Dominion people had a few nasty surprises for us. The vet, they say, wouldn't have been unduly tired. The Captain of the DC8 was a worried man. And finally, they make the point that two Controllers made the same mistake on the one vital thing which relates to altitude. So, they say, take these things together and you have your crash – right?'

'Yes, more or less,' the Attorney General replied.

'And on that they propose that together we should pay out a substantial share of the claim?'

'Yes.'

'OK. First,' and he turned to the Solicitor General, 'what are your views now on liability?'

'I don't think the position has altered that much. If a judge accepts that "we have copied weather Mike" means no more nor less than that, you're home and dry. If so, the fact of the father's death is irrelevant. Against that you still have the same position on the vet. True, a judge may discount tiredness, but he still has to decide on probability. However, I concede the risk is made greater. But how much greater is difficult to say. Really, it all boils down to what you are prepared to pay.'

'Thank you. Most interesting. Well now, we don't want to take up your time, so unless you can help further the Attorney General will be in contact when we've reached our decision.'

They waited for the Solicitor General to leave before continuing. The Prime Minister drained his coffee, then, having replaced the cup carefully, turned to the Chairman of Merlin Mutual Ltd.

'Now, Walter. Let's have the view of your Board.'

'Well, I confess we have been advised rather differently from the Solicitor General. Our advice has been that a judge may find it difficult, not to put a fine point on it, very difficult, to ignore the coincidence of failure on the part of the two Controllers. But that's your problem. Ours is raised by the further advice which I frankly expose to you. In brief, our counsel takes the view that a judge could decide that if there was a mix-up, perhaps a mis-hearing of the ATIS, then the aircrew should have been more careful. At least, he doesn't put it quite in those terms, but he does say that there would be evidence sufficient, given the ATC omissions and if he finds as fact only a single ATIS transmission, on which to base an unimpeachable finding of fault against the airline and the Air Traffic Services.'

He leaned back in his chair as they waited for him to continue. He was deciding not to add the final part of his counsel's opinion, that in the event of such a finding by a judge it was quite on the cards that he would hold the aircrew more blameworthy than the Air Traffic people. 'In the result,' he concluded, 'and to avoid the possibility of being found against entirely to the exclusion of the vet, I have been empowered to offer a contribution of 20 per cent.'

The Prime Minister looked at him. He'd known Walter Andrews for years. 'I see. Well, we don't want to muck about any more, Walter. I think the Government will go to 20 per cent. And that leaves us 20 per cent short of what we are led to believe the Dominion will settle for. Anyway, we're seeing them this afternoon, but frankly, I don't think we'll be able to settle at 40 per cent, and if not, then I take it you are happy for the thing to go to Court?'

It was his last move in the game. Walter Andrews felt uncomfortable. He suspected he was having his bluff called, but the problem with the Prime Minister was that it was very, very hard to be sure. He turned it over in his mind. He remembered the fat man from the Dominion, a hard man, not likely to move very far from the 60 per cent. If so, then with 20 per cent from the Merlin, that left the Government with 40 per cent. And he could think of no reason why they should pay out anything like that.

As though reading his mind, the Prime Minister laughed and said, 'It doesn't add up, does it, Walter? Believe me when I say it is most unlikely that we will go higher than you. At best, we might be persuaded to match your offer of 20 per cent each. It's up to you. If it wasn't the vet, Walter, then a judge might well say it's more aircrew fault than ground services if they got the ATIS wrong. Well . . .?' He let it hang in the air.

'You say you'll match our offer. What's your highest figure?'

'That will depend on you. What can you go to? 25 per cent?'

The Chairman of Merlin Mutual rubbed the back of his neck.

'Say no more, Walter, I see the signs. OK?'

The Chairman nodded briefly.

The Prime Minister nodded to the Attorney General, who wrote the figure 25 per cent in figures and words into the document before him. Then, having initialled it, he passed it over to the Chairman to read and sign.

Halfway through reading it, the Chairman looked up.

'Why the objection to the public knowing the settlement figures?' The document dealt with it specifically.

Smoothly, the Prime Minister replied, 'We think, Walter, that it would hardly be in the public interest to know that despite all denials of fault on the part of the Airline and the Air Traffic people, we had decided to make such a substantial contribution. It could do the Airline a lot of harm, confidence and so on, you know the sort of thing.'

Having read the rest of the document the Chairman signed, and as he did so, noticed that he was not merely binding himself to secrecy, but also his employees. 'I'm a bit concerned here, about there being no leak from my people.'

Leaning forward, the Prime Minister fixed him with his eye as he replied, 'If, Walter, they value their jobs, then I dare say they will observe the rules, don't you think? After all, we are your majority shareholders. If 25 per cent got out,' he raised his hands and shrugged, 'who knows . . .?'

He let it hang in the air as the Chairman appreciated the position. Certainly, if it came to it, he wouldn't be able to shelter behind the fact that his hand had been forced by his majority shareholder. For once he and his Board had suffered no interference. Suddenly he saw why. Despite himself, the neatness of it made him smile. Again it was as though the Prime Minister read his mind, as he murmured, 'Autonomy has its drawbacks, doesn't it Walter?' Then more clearly, he said, 'Anyway, thank you Walter. We would like to discuss this further at a Cabinet sub-committee, and I'll phone you after we've seen the Dominion people this afternoon.'

'Are you going to see them?' the Chairman asked in surprise.

'No, no, not personally.'

As the door closed behind the Chairman of Merlin Mutual Ltd, the Prime Minister and his Attorney General smiled at each other. But it brought no relief to the grimness of Christopher's face.

'He's going to be awfully upset when he finds out we're not going fifty-fifty with him – that is, if we don't,' the Attorney General said.

'Hmmm, but I think I did make it quite clear that we were not committed to that. I think I said "at best we might be persuaded to match your offer" and I did confine parity to 20 per cent each, did I not?'

'Yes.'

The Prime Minister nodded in satisfaction before turning to his silent Minister of Transport. 'I wanted you in on this, Chris, to make it a strong committee and, of course, because basically it's your department's baby. Now the question we have to decide is just how far do we go to meet the Dominion? The meeting is set up, isn't it?'

The committee broke up just ten minutes later, with luck to be adjourned *sine die*.

The two insurance men left at five past two for the two o'clock meeting. 'I don't think you know . . .' began the

Attorney General. 'Yeah, we met at the last meeting,' the fat man said.

Christopher Silaman acknowledged the two men from the Dominion as he took his seat beside the Attorney General. A clock somewhere chimed the quarter hour. The fat man ignored it and the two Government men felt the frustration attendant upon knowing a social solecism has been committed but not acknowledged by the offender, and as such, it was inappropriate and belittling to mention it.

The General Manager enjoyed not mentioning or apologizing for his lateness – his version of the psychological oneupmanship trick of the salesman who will ask for coffee if tea is offered. 'OK. What's the deal you guys have in mind?'

The Attorney General forced a mirthless laugh, which lingered for a moment. 'Yeah, me too,' the fat man commented, underlining the futility of tactics.

'Yes, well,' the Attorney General began, 'to put it bluntly, we find that we just cannot bring ourselves to see things in quite the same light as you.' He thought the fat man was going to interject, so he hurried on, 'But we do accept that our earlier thinking may have been a little bit out . . .' Seeing the fat man's look, he amended, 'Well, perhaps a trifle more than a little. Not surprising, I think, when you appreciate quite how disturbing it was to find that you had information which our people had missed; information that was as disturbing in its nature as it was disquieting to discover that it was as readily available to our people as it was to yours, but ours missed it. Be that as it may, we have now revised our view . . .'

'Look, I've a bloody busy insurance company to run. Just tell me what you want me to agree to.' The General Manager cut the Attorney General short, and Christopher wondered how one deals with a man who so totally disregards all the niceties of respect due to a Minister of the Crown.

'Well, we had in mind something like bearing one-third. Now, before you . . .'

The fat man cut in again before he could continue. 'Before nothing, sir. If that's it I go and you guys get joined as co-defendants. Is that it, or are we still playing games?'

'Well, you know perfectly well that your figure of 60 per cent is totally unrealistic.'

'Really?' he said in surprise. 'How unrealistic?'

'Well, if you take the statistics . . .'

'Stuff statistics! By percentage, just how unrealistic?'

'At best, we couldn't see our way to any more than, at the most, 45 per cent.'

'That's what I wanted to hear. That's your best offer, is it?'

The Attorney General felt pleased that it had been so simple. It wasn't bad, with the Merlin Mutual carrying 25 per cent which they could just about do with a medium-term loan. 'Yes.'

'Right. Thank you, gentlemen.' The fat man was rising. Consternation showed itself on the face of the Attorney General. He had expected to get down to the nitty gritty.

'Why? Where are you going?'

'You said 45 per cent was tops and I'm not interested. It's as simple as that, so you'll be hearing from our lawyers tomorrow or the day after.' He was picking up his papers and had opened his briefcase before the Attorney General recovered enough to speak up.

'Please! Will you please sit down. I'm sure we can talk this thing out.'

The fat man stood and looked at him for a moment, shook his head, and laughed before he spoke. 'Jesus! You people! Right, one last try and I mean one last try. No agreement this time, and that's it. Finito.'

Anthony noted mentally to mention to the General Manager that the second 'i' was said as an 'e', and smiled to himself, which was unfortunate. The Attorney General saw it and anger boiled up in him. 'This is no laughing matter,' he snapped.

'Yeah, I'd go along with that. So who's laughing? What's your final offer? I'll say yes or no. And from the way you people conduct business – shit, I feel like saying no just for the hell of it!'

The Attorney General heard the finality in the fat man's tone of voice and hesitated. Of course it was bluff, in so far as the man had asked for 60 per cent. But he felt, quite instinctively, that if the fat man left the room now, it would cost more to settle later. He was equally sure, however, that here and now he was prepared to settle for less. But how much? How much? What was the lowest figure? Would he accept 50 per cent? Would he or wouldn't he? The question went round in his mind, and he well knew he had several million dollars to win or lose in the next minute.

The silence was broken by the fat man. 'OK. Time for cards on the table. You won't tell me, so I'll make it a one-bid session. All I want is a straight answer here and now. I assume you have the authority?'

The Attorney General nodded.

'I'll accept 55 per cent, take it, sir, or leave it. I sit down again, or we go. So what's it to be?'

The Attorney General looked at him. Then almost casually said: 'Yes. But subject to conditions.'

'Yeah, I expected that. No noise. Is that what you have in mind?'

'You are to agree that under no circumstances will you make the percentage split known, and further, you are not to reveal the sum you finally pay out in the absence of written governmental approval from the holder of my office. You are not to comment on the payout or liability, or the handling of this claim, or comment on any Government statement. You are to permit the Government to appear to have had nothing to do with this claim except that you will have asked the Government for its physical assistance in dealing with it. In effect, all claims will appear to be settled by your company, but the Government will appear to be lending you staff and expertise. And finally, the settlement is wholly binding on all parties. Would that be agreeable to you?'

'Sure, if it can be done. I s'pose even if we had to disclose the payment it wouldn't tell anyone anything. Any worries, Tony?'

'I think there will be problems but I think we should be able to get over them with, er, the help of the Government.' Then he thought of a snag. 'But under these terms, the widow gets 55 per cent. How will you explain that to her and keep her lawyers quiet?'

'I think you can leave that to us,' replied the Attorney General. 'Now, if you would just sign the agreement, we can get on.'

It was four-thirty when they left. In the car the General Manager continually stroked his jowl into vigorous movement, and accepted Tony's cheque with a laugh. 'Thanks, laddy. I reckon I'll have it framed to remember the day when I saw real live politics at work. Christ, what those guys will do to stop our public from knowing what's not good news! Still, what the hell. It's a spit in the ocean compared with

Watergate, but oh Jesus!' he chuckled again.

'I was interested in the conditions.'

'Yeah, but Jesus! What a hell of a price to pay, eh?' He chuckled again and his jowls bobbed in satisfaction.

Chapter Sixteen

'And tonight, after the news, we have a change in our advertised programme. To replace "Where Are They Now?" the Prime Minister will be addressing the nation, so stay tuned. In the meantime, relax and live a bit with an old favourite.' As the signature tune took over, Bill turned to Grace.

'Want to see this, Grace?'

'Not particularly, but I must hear the Prime Minister. It may be about the crash.'

'Yes, of course. But how about a bit of music till then?'

It was 8.30. They had eaten and the Prime Minister wasn't scheduled till 10. 'Hmmm. Be nice.' Turning the TV off, Bill went and put on Oscar Peterson's 'Girl Talk' and left the lights low. Then he joined her on the sofa. It was just one more evening to add to the many they had spent together.

'That's nice,' she said, as the trio's music throbbed quietly in the room. 'What is it?' He started to explain what he was thinking about. She listened with attention. Then he fell silent. All the lights were green. 'Grace, would you like to dance?' She laughed as she got up. 'Oh, Bill dear. What an old fool you are. I thought you . . . Oh, well, it doesn't matter. Come on.' They swayed in time to the music. And he felt an excitement which took him back years. Then sensuality struck him hard and mortified him as, before he could stop it, he felt himself begin to harden as he pressed against her. He drew back, but then almost in confusion, he yielded to her pressure as she drew him back into contact.

She had felt it begin to happen and it had brought a little thrill to her. It was more than she wanted at the moment but, in feeling it, she was suddenly aware that she was glad, and knew the time would come. So she brought him back to her. As she did so, she whispered, 'Oh, Bill. Dearest Bill, it's lovely to know you don't just want me as a nice old lady companion.

But you must give me a little time. For now, though, I'd like a kiss.' Gently, tenderly, but with just a promise of more, they kissed and danced. And he liked her caressing the back of his neck.

'And now we have the Prime Minister.' The screen was filled with the picture of the well-known face on which a member of the Opposition had capitalized during the last election with the comment 'Would you buy a used car from him?' But there was a little more point in the comeback, 'I don't know about cars, but my wife, for sure, wouldn't buy hairpins from that guy.' The pause at the rally where the remark was made had been filled with laughter, which had redoubled when 'Cos one thing's for sure, if she did she'd know they were bent' had been added.

The camera panned back to show the heavy desk at which the Prime Minister sat, hands resting lightly on it. He had a good repertoire of little tricks for putting things over. 'Good evening.' He leaned forward to take his weight on his elbows and to establish the intimacy he wanted with his viewers and, on cue, the camera edged in to the top of the desk to cover hands and face. With ease and balance established, he was ready to begin.

'Tonight, I want to talk about the terrible air crash we all suffered a while back. You may remember that at his Press conference, the Minister of Transport made it plain that we in Government placed a high priority on finding out the facts and a high priority on letting you . . .' he paused to make the point, '. . . the public, know how it was going along. But equally important, and to many of even greater importance, was to re-establish people's lives as quickly as possible. We in Government have been acutely aware of the suffering borne by those who were made homeless by this disaster, and of course, those poor people who lost loved ones.

'From the beginning, the Government realized the danger of this thing becoming a long drawn-out affair and had this been so it would have been a heartbreaking time of uncertainty for many. And so we decided, in Cabinet, that if we could avoid that possibility we would do so. And in taking this view we felt confident that we were expressing your will.'

Again he paused, and smiled, before continuing, 'I am pleased to say, our efforts have been successful. Today an agreement was reached between the insurance companies concerned, and I think they would both agree this would not have been reached without intervention by the Government.

'And your Government has gone further than merely to bring the parties together. We intend to make available to the major insurance company involved all the necessary staff needed to ensure that claims are handled quickly and with the minimum of delay. I am told that already a full list of those with claims in this tragic matter has been compiled. And I am told that all will be contacted within the space of the next few days. It was a terrible disaster but, in so far as it has been humanly possible, we will lessen its effects as much as possible.'

He leaned back in his chair. 'All claims will be met generously and in full. Now I know many people have been asking the question: how could this accident have happened? It's a question that, I confess, has troubled me deeply, for to know the answer to that would ensure that its like would never trouble us again. But I must be frank with you. We do not know, and we will never know. We can speculate, yes, but,' and he smiled disarmingly, 'speculation is a pointless exercise to you and I, the laymen. But expert analysis is not speculation, and you may rest assured that all the things that could have played a part in this accident have been identified, examined, and will be the subject of further scrutiny with the object of bringing in changes in procedure to eliminate any such weaknesses.

'An an example of what I am told the experts have in mind is something called air separation. This, we know, must have been at fault here, or the two aircraft could not have met in mid air. What we do not know is the reason for its failure, and that is what we will never know. But to safeguard against another failure, we will ensure that the vexing problem of air separation between aircraft is reviewed.'

Now, in winding up, he leaned forward again. 'But, for the record, I say this. We, in this country, had, at the time of this terrible event, the highest safety record in the world. We have the finest people at work safeguarding our air travel. This accident was a freak, and its like will, please God, not darken our lives again. But, having happened this once, we in Government have worked to lighten the aftermath. I have been happy to be able to tell you of our success in this tonight. And I take this opportunity of thanking all those who have worked so selflessly to achieve this result. Without them, well . . .' he shook his head, spreading his hands. 'Our efforts to alleviate the misery and horror of this accident, both here and abroad, depended for success on those who serve your Government, and they have done a fine job.

'Finally, and publicly, I commend the insurance companies, who have demonstrated that humanity and big business can go hand in hand, and who have allowed their hands to be joined across the table by Ministers, your Ministers, who dedicated themselves to this difficult task.' Then he said, 'Good night to you all,' relaxed, smiled gravely, and faded from the screen.

'What does it mean, Bill?' The confusion was sharp in Grace's voice.

'I don't think I under . . .', he began, but broke off as the announcer, now back on the screen, began to speak. 'Now we have a special programme on the Prime Minister's address. In the studio talking to Ian McCrea we have two prominent lawyers and a director of a major insurance company. Ian McCrea.'

'Good evening. We have just heard the Prime Minister, and for a first comment I turn to James Partridge, QC. Tell me Mr Partridge, the Prime Minister said we would never know the cause of this accident. But claims are to be met. What does this mean?'

The lawyer, in his fifties, grey-haired, and with a long face lined with the cares of others borne over many years, coughed gently.

'It means a settlement of some kind has been reached between those who could have been parties to an action.'

'What sort of settlement do you think would be on the cards?'

'I don't know the facts, and I confess I don't know which insurance company he was referring to. But if one takes the constituent parts of the problem, I should imagine that here we would be thinking about the pilot of the light aircraft . . .'

'The vet, Frank Newton,' McCrea interposed. The lawyer nodded before continuing, '. . . and the aircrew of the DC8 involved, perhaps just those two elements.'

'Would you agree with that, Mr Prescott?'

Younger, pinkly round and not tall, the man tipped for one

of the next appointments to the bench looked gravely at his hands resting clasped around the knee of his crossed legs. At the bottom of the screen appeared 'John Prescott, QC'. He looked up. 'In the main, yes. Yes, I think that's correct. Plainly some sort of settlement has been reached. Clearly in such a case one would consider the possibilities of findings by a judge, were it to go to him, which must have been a possibility here. Then, having assessed what the potential parties to the possible action faced as a risk of a finding against their insured, a compromise has been reached. However, I would add to the list of possible litigants the people on the ground. If an Air Traffic Controller gave the wrong information he could be liable. And since he is the servant or agent of the Government, then the Government could be involved.'

'As a defendant?'

'Yes.'

'But it appeared from what the Prime Minister said that the role of the Government has been that of conciliator between rival insurance companies. Would you comment on that Mr Partridge?' He directed the question.

'I tend to agree with my friend here. The Air Traffic Service could certainly be a party. But to return to the point you make, yes, it does seem that what the Prime Minister was saying was that two insurance companies have been involved and one has emerged with the major portion of the settlement to bear. His words were, if I recollect correctly "the major insurance company involved". Now, despite the Prime Minister's words on the point, it is inevitable that people will speculate. So perhaps at least we can ensure that it is informed speculation. Yes, from this we can go some way to discovering what the settlement was, I think.'

'In what way?'

'To do that, I would need to know the insurance position.'

'Can you help there, Mr Mankowitz?' The General Manager of the Republic and Capital smiled. An actuary, he looked more of an academic than a general manager, thin and balding, with large glasses. But the voice of Gerard Mankowitz sounded as if it came from a much bigger entity. 'Yes, I don't see why not? Anyone who wanted to could find out easily enough. Merlin Mutual Ltd stand more or less behind Paranational, and the Dominion . . . that is, the Dominion and Commonwealth, behind the vet.'

'Mr Prescott, would you agree that, with this information, one could arrive at a fair idea of the position?'

Aware that he must tread carefully, and not upset too many people who trod the corridors of power if he wasn't to jeopardize his chances for the bench, Mr Prescott said, 'You know, I am inclined to agree with the Prime Minister. I don't think that this sort of speculation is particularly fruitful.'

'But it's a fact, isn't it, that people will speculate? Given that state of affairs, wouldn't you agree with Mr Partridge here that it is better that it should be informed?'

'I take your point, but,' he said with a smile, 'I am not enamoured of the art of speculation. So perhaps you had better address your questions to my friend here, if you must pursue a line which the Prime Minister has said he plainly deplores.'

'I see, thank you. Well, Mr Partridge, what do you think?'

'With respect to my friend, I don't agree with him or the Prime Minister. People will speculate, and they needn't – or needn't on the overall picture. But, can you tell me, Mankowitz, have you heard who the euphemistically referred to "major" insurance company is?'

'I rather think you will find it's the Dominion.'

'I see. The view has been taken that the vet was probably to blame, but not entirely, for with another company involved, clearly someone has taken an accepted view that the aircrew weren't wholly blameless.'

'Could you suggest in what way to blame – either of them?' McCrea pressed.

'Not really, but I suppose it's commonsense. I would assume that the view was that the vet went too high, and the aircrew have been apportioned some of the blame for simply not seeing him.'

'And you, Mr Prescott?'

'I think I have made my position perfectly clear. I am not prepared to enter into this sort of discussion. And that my learned friend has seen fit to do so, appals me.'

'My friend is, I fear, being rather more than a little naive.' The remark was a whiplash from the older lawyer. Having been passed over for a judgeship, and perhaps not so concerned about his image, the result was that he had a very good one.

'Now, gentlemen, please. Can we turn to the speed of this

settlement?' McCrea turned to the General Manager.

'If we accept the Prime Minister at face value, and we have no reason not to, he and his Government have done a fantastic job. Magnificent.'

The camera then panned back to take them all in before spotting in a close-up on Ian McCrea, who wrapped it up by saying, 'Well, that's all we have time for. In a word, it appears that our Prime Minister's achievement has been magnificent and though we may never know to what extent blame has been laid on the unfortunate vet, Frank Newton, or to what extent the aircrew were to blame for not seeing him, none the less the picture has become clearer . . .' He paused. Personal feelings were to be avoided by people in his position, but he felt a touch of pity for the vet's widow. So, unusually for him, he added, 'But, as the Prime Minister indicated, perhaps it is best not to speculate further. And our sympathy must go now, before the clarity of this disaster is lost in the passage of time, not just to those who lost homes or families, or even to those who lost their lives on the ground or in the DC8, but also to Frank Newton's widow. We must remember that none of us are incapable of making a simple mistake, and the enormity of the consequences can make it no more than that – that is, if indeed it was a mistake on Frank Newton's part.'

His summation complete, he turned to the panel. 'Thank you for being with me, gentlemen.' Then, in final grave close-up, he said, 'Good night.'

The video recording over, the Prime Minister switched off the set and, turning to his wife, said, 'Well Julia, how did that strike you?'

She looked up from her knitting. 'Oh I don't know. Should it have struck me particularly?'

'I just wondered.'

'Don't be silly, dear. As always, a masterly and thoroughly convincing performance. Was it meant to be any different from any of the others?'

'Bit more important, otherwise not.'

'Well, it was very good.' As she went back to her knitting the phone rang. The Prime Minister received the congratulations of his Attorney General calmly, though he was in fact immensely pleased. 'Yes, I think we're out of deep water now. Heavy casualties, of course, even thought we'd lost our queen once or twice. Still, all over bar the shouting now, and thanks for your help. Invaluable.'

Twice more that evening he was disturbed in his study by the phone. Then the affair began to recede in his mind: just one of the little political annoyances, soon to be forgotten. But he did spare a thought for the luck of it happening early in the life of his Government. Even if anything went wrong, it would all be too long dead to provide any political ammunition for the Opposition at an election. As he reflected on it, he smiled to himself. In a way, he thought, it had all been quite a good thing. Certainly, the public's conception of the Government's handling of it must reflect a good deal of credit on him. Yes, he thought. It had all turned out rather well. Then he dismissed it from his mind. There were other things to deal with.

'Come along in, Grace.' Marty, standing before her in his waiting-room, smiled down at her, but felt trouble in the air as she looked back at him, her face pinched with anxiety, yet firm in resolve, an implacable glint in her eyes. She followed him into his office.

The man in the dark blue suit, dark-haired, tall, and big but sparely built, rose as she entered. Their eyes met and he felt the chill of her feelings as his eyes crinkled into a smile which was often taken for one of intimate warmth, sympathy and understanding. Her hostility didn't worry him. It was because of his impregnable charm that this man from the Attorney General's office was the natural for such assignments as this. He walked across the room towards her, the smile in place, his hand outstretched to begin the business of closing the gulf between them. 'Hello, Mrs Newton. I'm Sinclair Tichfield and I'd like you to call me Sinclair. And may I call you Grace?'

'I don't really mind what you call me, but I would prefer to be called by my surname. I don't know you.'

The little rebuff made no dent on the man as he replied smoothly, 'I quite understand. I just thought you might prefer it, but I would like you to understand that I have come to see Marty here, and now you, to do all that I possibly can to help. My office, as you probably know, has been set up to do all we can to deal with the claims of all those poor, unfortunate people like yourself who have suffered. It's not been possible to see many of the others, of course, but in your case, well, I thought that I would like to deal with the settlement side of Frank's death with you personally. I wanted to meet you and see if you have any special worries which I might be able to help iron out.'

He paused, the time reached when it was necessary to start her talking, the only way to squeeze the hostility out of her. She turned to her solicitor. 'Do I have to talk to him? You said nothing to me over the phone about anyone else being here.'

'I think you should, my dear. Sinclair and I have had a talk and I think you should hear what he has to say. Then, if necessary, we can have a little chat about it afterwards, all right?'

'If you say so.' Equally coldly, she turned to the man. 'What do you want to say to me?'

'Well, Grace, the position is this. I have come with authority to settle your claim today. So first perhaps we should see how you and Marty look at the whole thing.'

'Why are you offering me money? You've blamed Frank and I thought that people didn't give money to someone if it was their fault.'

'Yes. In a way, that's correct. But here, no one has, as you put it, been blamed. That's something which happens in a court and this isn't happening there.'

'But the insurance company he was insured with is meeting the claim, isn't it?'

'Yes. That's largely true, but they aren't saying Frank was to blame. In fact, every settlement is being made on the clearest possible basis of avoiding that. In lawyers' terms, each is made without prejudice and on an *ex gratia* basis, and I am sure Marty has explained what that means.'

'I don't care about the niceties of your law. The fact is that the people Frank was insured with are paying out money, and they wouldn't be doing that if they didn't think they had to, and that means they think Frank was to blame. Whatever you say about it, everyone knows that. So everyone thinks that Frank was to blame.' It was said without passion, a cold statement of fact. And the man thought about it, and the best way to get round the problem this woman presented.

'I understand Grace, I really do, and I know, we all know, how you feel. But what could we do? The people who have to meet the claims aren't able to be guided, all the time, by personal feelings. You must see that. They've had to look at it as a risk in Court, and come to a decision on what they feel could be the result. You could be right. Maybe it wasn't Frank's fault, but look at it this way. How can anyone be sure it wasn't Frank? No one, not even you, I think, can be sure of that. So the insurance company has to have that in mind. Now, what do they do? They have to do what good businessmen should do in looking after the interests of the thousands who have trusted them with their money. Do they risk the enormous cost of a case which they feel, even doing the best they can, would stand a fair chance of being lost, if not completely, then largely so? Or do they arrive at the most sensible estimate of what they think may be the end result in Court and cut their losses?'

'I am not interested in what they do to cut their losses.'

'Well, let's look at it from a personal point of view. Say I said to you, Grace, that all you had in the world was a hundred bucks, and the position crops up where you are given a choice. Either you pay out fifty bucks, or throw a dice, and if you score less than four out of your possible six you're going to lose the whole of your hundred. The choice: pay fifty and at least you keep fifty, or risk the lot with a two-thirds chance of losing. You know as well as I do that you wouldn't hesitate. You'd pay the fifty bucks and avoid the risk. Insurance companies face those sorts of decision all the time. And if, in this case, they fought and proved Frank's innocence they would still have a very big bill to pay, which, one way or another, would not be covered by the costs awarded to them. So you see, it's a big problem, isn't it?'

'For you, yes. But I am not you or an insurance company. I am Mrs Frank Newton, and my husband has been blamed for a terrible thing which, I know, he didn't have anything to do with.'

With a great deal of sympathy in his voice, he said quietly, 'Now Grace, you can't know that, can you?'

'I knew Frank. He just couldn't have made that sort of mistake.'

'We don't say he did, Grace. Only that if a judge had to decide . . . well then, we think he would probably be forced to say he did.'

'I don't care, and I don't believe it. It wasn't Frank's mistake, and I think it was wrong for anyone to accept that it was.'

He decided to change tack. 'There is something else I want you to think about too, Grace. Other people. Many, many people have suffered. Can you really say that you would have preferred for them to go on suffering for perhaps three or even four years, having to wait all that time for their compensation? But now all those people will receive their compensation within a few weeks. What would you have done? Fought to clear Frank and made other people suffer for a long time, or, if you had the power to ease their suffering, wouldn't that have been what you'd have done?'

Marty raised his eyebrows and was about to speak, but decided to hold his peace in Grace's interest. And the man sat back as she thought about it, thankful that she was no lawyer and knew nothing about payments on account being ordered by judges in cases where it was solely a matter of who was to pay and not whether anyone was going to pay. At last she replied, 'From your point of view, I s'pose you're right. But it doesn't change my mind at all. To me, Frank has been wrongly blamed.' The man made as though he was going to chip in, but she silenced the interruption with her hand, as she added, 'I know all about the without . . . without prejudice thing, but it doesn't make any difference to what people think.'

Feeling he was getting somewhere at last, the man moved in quickly to close the deal. 'So what it comes down to is really this, isn't it? You agree we were right to do all we could to prevent people from having to suffer longer than they absolutely had to. But you don't approve of what was necessary for this to be done. That I can understand,' he paused, 'but I admire you, admire you a great deal, for understanding the problem and agreeing that overall, given it as a personal choice, you would have chosen to act as we have done for the better good of all the sufferers, rather than to satisfy your own need to clear Frank. It's a sacrifice everyone would admire. I think that's right, Marty, don't you?'

The solicitor nodded gravely, as he replied, 'Yes, yes I do.'

And Sinclair Tichfield watched her to see if she'd swallow it. Too weary to argue, she said nothing, which the man took as that obstacle overcome. 'Now,' he continued, 'it does go both ways. You, along with everyone else, will benefit in so far as you too don't have to go on in doubt about a settlement.

Now Marty and I have thought about this very carefully. We have, or at least Marty has, been in touch with Frank's accountant, and I know what Frank was pulling in. We have discussed, as we've had to as lawyers, the prospects of how long we think Frank would have expected to work. He was very fit, enjoyed his work, and would have gone on for a long time. And we haven't ignored inflation. And, of course, we have considered the value of the Cessna. So all in all, Grace, I think we have done pretty well and not overlooked anything. What do you think Marty?'

'To put it bluntly, Grace, you wouldn't do any better, and probably not as well from a judge, even if he found one hundred per cent for you, with no blame on Frank at all. So my advice is to accept this offer.'

They both waited for her reaction, but were disappointed with her quiet 'I see' when it came.

'Aren't you interested in the amount, Grace?' Marty asked.

'Not particularly,' she replied, then added, 'Whatever it is, it's only money. It doesn't bring Frank back. And it doesn't clear him.' She paused as a new thought went through her mind, and as it cleared, she continued, 'In fact, I don't want your money. If I take it, I will be accepting blame for Frank.'

'But that's not true, Grace. You would accept it on the basis that it was an *ex gratia* payment, liability not decided. It would be neutral.'

'To you, a lawyer, Marty, maybe.'

'To—to everyone, Grace. But apart from that, you've got others to consider. This money would not only be money you could use, if you wanted to, you could do a lot for Maggie. She'll want to stop work when she has a baby. Henry has three children, remember. A lump sum for them in trust would be a fine thing. And Graham, well, when he gets married he'd be pretty grateful for help with a house. So it's not just you who is affected, Grace. It's the family. And, Grace dear, you must remember I knew Frank. We were close and I know that if he were here he'd say take it. Now you know that, as well as I do, don't you Grace? He would, wouldn't he?'

She pictured Frank here in this office, listening to this conversation, and knew Marty was right. Frank, unselfish Frank, wouldn't have hesitated if he could have done anything for her and the kids, and now of course the grandchildren. But deep inside she felt the betrayal of it. Whatever they said, if she took the money it would be a betrayal, an acceptance of guilt for this terrible thing. And she wondered how she could decide. 'I don't know, I just don't know,' she said. Then, suddenly from nowhere an idea formed in her mind, and she asked how much the sum offered was.

'We have rounded it up to $135,000.' The man said it quietly, for that amount of money spoke for itself.

'I see.' But she didn't seem particularly impressed as she went on: 'Marty, I want to talk to you alone now about this.'

The man rose, the battle won, and, smiling, he said, 'I'd like to get this cleared up today, Marty, so I'll leave the acceptance form with you and wait, if I may?' Marty nodded as he showed him out.

'It's a good settlement, Grace.'

'Yes, but I want to know something. What does it really mean if I do? I mean . . . what I want to know is, could I take the money and then take it to court myself? You see, I appreciate what this amount of money would mean to the family, but I was thinking that I could use some of it to fight with and the rest could go to them. Could I do that?'

Marty sighed. 'No. No you couldn't. In the first place I won't have you chasing what I am afraid, my dear, is a will-o-the-wisp case through the Courts. I owe that to Frank. And secondly, if you take the money you have to sign a release which, in effect, agrees that you accept the money in return for relinquishing all claims you may or may not have.'

She pondered for a few minutes, before she spoke again. 'Tell me. If I don't take the money, I could sue for damages then, couldn't I?'

'My dear girl, for God's sake, be reasonable. Why should you sue for what has already been offered to you?'

'Oh, it wouldn't be for the money, Marty, but to get a judge to say that it should be paid by the Government or whoever, but not the company who Frank was with.'

'And have you any idea of the risks that involves? Look, OK, let's for one moment accept that you refuse the money and sue. In my view, you would lose, Grace. I am sorry to have to say it, but I am bound to. And if you lost, as I am sure you would, then you not only lose the $135,000 which only requires your signature on this form to be yours, but also you would face a very, very big costs bill, a huge bill!'

'How much, Marty?'

'God preserve us! If you must know, I think you'd be lucky to get out of that sort of case at anything less than a hundred thousand.'

'I see.' And she was perfectly calm as she said it.

'OK, now be a good girl and sign this thing, all right?'

'Give it to me.'

He passed it across the desk. She looked at it, then very deliberately picked it up and tore it slowly in half. Then, looking at her solicitor and old friend, said, 'Frank and I weren't badly off, and I have just received $100,000 from his insurance company covering his death. I am going to use that money, Marty, to clear his name. I don't know how yet. I must think about that, but at this moment I am not going to sign anything which makes it impossible.'

It was all said with icy calm. Quite when it had all become clear in her mind she wasn't sure, but from the mists of confusion created by the inducements put before her had emerged the clear picture that she was being bought off, was even being offered more money than she would have been if they were offering honestly and laying part of the blame on Frank. And she had seen more than the picture of Frank in that office, as it were, telling her to take the money; she had seen the Frank she knew, and the Frank she knew didn't make careless mistakes. Finally, it had become very clear to her that she could never live comfortably with herself in the future were she to take money as a bribe to let the world think, and go on thinking, that it was his fault.

'Grace, my dear! What can I say? It's . . . it's bloody pigheaded, pointless lunacy, and I just will not let you be so incredibly blind and stupid and, my dear, selfish. Frank's dead, and blame or no blame, it really doesn't matter to him. And you know, he wouldn't have wanted you to think like this, now would he?'

'You would refuse to act for me, Marty?'

'Yes, Grace, I would, and so would every lawyer you approached. No one would sanction a course of action which can do nothing, and I repeat, nothing but lose you a great deal of money and see you saddled with costs. You just can't do it. The whole thing would be completely pointless.'

He put his face in his hands and pressed hard for a moment, and wished to God that he had realized quite how difficult Grace was going to be. But even so, this was a bloody sight worse than he could possibly have anticipated. Then he thought of Glenda. Perhaps she could help. And, of course, he'd better get in touch with Henry.

'Look, Grace dear, I think that the best thing to do is for you to leave this for the moment and go home and think about it. We can have another chat next week. In fact, tell you what, how about coming over to us for the evening next Wednesday? We can talk about it then, OK?'

'I shan't change my mind, Marty, but yes, if you'd like me to I'll come over on Wednesday, because whatever I do, I don't want to lose your friendship over this.' Her voice softened. 'And it's nice of you to take so much trouble.'

'It's what friends are for, my dear. And I'll go all the way on this one to stop you behaving like a lunatic. Anyway, off you go now. I'll deal with the guy outside and we'll talk again next week.'

As he showed her out, he was trying to remember whether he had Henry's number. With a curt nod, she passed the man in the reception room and left.

'I'm sorry,' said Marty to Sinclair Tichfield, 'it's all been a shock to her. What worries her is that taking the money is an admission to herself that it could have been Frank's fault.'

'What's the position then, and in particular, what's this?' He held up the torn paper.

'Oh, nothing really. She got all up-tight when she realized that in signing it she was relinquishing all rights. But don't worry, give her time to get used to it and she'll sign.'

'For her sake, I hope you're right. The last thing in the world we want is to face her in Court and see her fail, which obviously would be what would happen. That would be a tragedy. And really, you know, but for the Prime Minister's personal concern for her, we wouldn't be making this sort of offer at all.'

He paused to review it all for a moment, before he added, 'I'm not sure we made that sufficiently clear to her. Perhaps if she realizes she is receiving payment in full she will realize that she is only doing what she'd do if he wasn't to blame at all. It's no admission on her part. I wonder whether when you see her again you would make that and the PM's personal concern plain to her, Marty?'

'Yes, I will. But don't worry, she'll come round.' And they parted.

PART THREE

Chapter Seventeen

'May it please your Honour.' And a silence in which one could have heard the dropping of a pin settled on the Court. The judge, in black, sober robes, smiled courteously from beneath his wig at the members of the Bar as the play began. The actors, shorn of individuality by their lawyers' dress, could express their personality only by voices and gestures. Even their faces were distorted into caricatures by the encircling wigs. This dehumanization emphasized the clinical nature of the business: the presentation of fact, its dissection, and the ultimate determination of truth, in so far as it lay in man's power to discover the truth.

'And members of the jury.' Their role had begun. The twelve ordinary men and women forgot the little things which had caught their attention: the members of the Bar in two ranks, with solicitors behind, the ringing tone of the usher, the quiet, dignified entry of the judge. They forgot the strangeness of it all and focused their attention on the voice and presence of the barrister now on his feet. Twelve men and women who were to use their commonsense to give the judgment of the community. In contrast to the legal people, they looked exactly what they were: just twelve ordinary men and women, dressed as a cross-section of the community would dress for a christening or similar event. Their role: to sit, be silent, listen to the evidence, be reminded of it, be told the law, and only then give judgment as they saw fit.

In this case, if the judge found for the vet in part or whole on the personal injuries issue, it would be for them to decide whether or not the vet had indeed been blamed, or been blamed too much. A Press conference, Ministerial comments and Prime Ministerial broadcasts, reports in the papers, coverage by radio and television – all these needed interpreting. But then came a more difficult question. Was the criticism justified? Had the vet been unjustifiably blamed? Or had it all merely been fair comment on a matter of public interest? If not, then had what had been said damaged the reputation of the vet? And if so, then and only then would they have to consider money. But what would be the right sum to wipe the slate clean, as clean as it should be? Then finally came the last question, one of censure. Could the action that had been taken be considered an abuse of governmental power? Was it a case for the punishment of exemplary damages or not? And if so how much was required to punish a Government?

But the questions were important far beyond the reach of the Court alone. Apart from the Government there were many others who could have been on trial for libel and slander. The media were watching and waiting, wondering if they too might be finally paying large damages to the widow on the aftermath of judgment.

As he prepared to open the case for the plaintiff, Reginald Carter, QC, drew a quiet breath to calm the nervousness which still attended the opening of all the major cases that came his way; had he lost this nervousness he would have been on a lower pinnacle in his profession. As he hitched his gown around him and arranged his notes for the opening on the small lectern before him, the judge looked down at him and thanked God that in this case he wouldn't have to suffer fools gladly. Reggie, a tall imposing man, had, he considered, an excellent mind.

While the judge waited for the silk to begin his opening, his mind went back to the pleadings. Instinctively, his eyes sought the woman who had brought it all about. As his eyes rested for a second on her face, she glanced at him. Their gaze held for a time. Dispassionately, he weighed her up and wondered why she couldn't have accepted the overwhelming verdict of the past; learned to live with it, and so come with the passage of time to avoid remembrance. All so very sad, he thought to himself, when one realized that but for this case, to say 'Frank Newton' to the man in the street would merely be met by a puzzled 'Who?' Surely it would have been much better than this. Was it loyalty, or was it all merely *amour-propre* which had prompted her? he wondered.

The Solicitor General, representing the Government, one of the parties against whom Mrs Grace Hulman had brought the proceedings, sat comfortably back in his chair. Before him his brief was scattered about in an orderly chaos of paper around a virginal white note-pad. He played with his gold pencil and looked at the judge: a good man on personal injuries work who had had a good practice before his appointment. Sensible of the Chief Justice to put it in his list.

The case didn't worry the Solicitor General overmuch. Certainly he foresaw a finding of fact against him – some minor irregularities in Air Traffic Control procedures – but nothing to support fault. And equally, no fault on the crew of the DC8; perhaps suspicion, but probability needed more than that as proof to support a finding on liability. And if he was right, well then, all this bloody nonsense about defamation would simply fall to the ground and the jury be left with no job, their time wasted in a non-event. But better that than the possibility of two trials – liability for a judge alone, to be followed by a jury on defamation.

He smiled to himself as he thought how very different the judge looked on the Bench: much more desiccated on the Bench than in real life. A long, lined grey face, a face which to men in the dock had often seemed to carry a trace of malevolence. Attributable, perhaps, to the deep line which cut down from the side of his mouth, an ineradicable part of him now, though in youth that line had come from a conscious effort to gain gravity and authority beyond his years.

Grace sat nervously beside her solicitor, shrinking inside and suffering the intimidation of the hour before they had entered Court.

Attention caught and held, Reginald Carter felt the moment had arrived. So in answer to the judge's nod, he began, his voice calm and well-measured. 'In this case,' he cleared his throat quietly, 'I appear for the plaintiff with my learned friend Mr Jeremy Patterson. My learned friend the Solicitor General appears for the Attorney General, and with him he has Miss Mary Standhope. And my learned friend Mr John Prescott, with Mr Stephen Isles, appears for the second defendants.

'The plaintiff claims under several heads of damage in this case. Her first is in respect of the death of her husband and consequential loss and is brought against Air Traffic Services and Paranational. Now that is a matter for his Honour to consider. Should he, in his judgment, find against the plaintiff, then that is an end of the whole case. The vet was rightly blamed. However, if he finds at all for my client on liability, then we will enter the second part of this trial, the defamation claim against the Government. It will then fall to you, members of the jury, to consider, first, was Frank Newton wrongly blamed, and if so, to what extent? What damage in money terms did his high standing and reputation in the community suffer? Then you will have to consider whether or not what the Government did was done in such wrongful concealment of fact as to be an abuse of its power. If so, then you will decide what sum in damages should be awarded as a sufficient mark of your disapproval of that abuse; a matter which is, to all intents and purposes, a matter of punishment. I will deal with all this in greater detail later. Now, however, I will begin to outline the plaintiff's case.

'This case arises out of the air disaster which, no doubt your Honour will recall, occurred to the north of Titahi Bay on February 8th, now nearly two years ago. It was a collision between a Cessna 172 and the second defendants' Nandi to Wellington DC8. The plaintiff's husband at that time was the pilot of the smaller of the two aircraft. He, with some one hundred and sixty people, including the aircrew of the DC8, lost their lives. Following that disaster, an investigation into its cause was begun.' He paused to give point to what he intended to say.

'And it was during the time of that investigation, when no one knew the cause, that much of what the plaintiff now complains about occurred. Several things happened. A Ministerial Press conference was called. And it was then that the finger of blame was first pointed publicly at her husband. It was followed by a broadcast by the Prime Minister in which he chose to confirm that finger of blame. And later, on many occasions, no opportunity was missed by the Government to strengthen public opinion that her husband was to blame. And yet all was done in the absence of a single shred of concrete, clear evidence.

'Finally, the Prime Minister appeared on television, and, it is my submission that at that time, though he avoided outright damnation of the unfortunate Frank Newton, nevertheless by the time he had finished what he had to say, there would not have been a reasonable man, woman or child left in the land, or beyond, who would have been left with the slightest doubt that this appalling disaster had been rightfully laid at Frank Newton's door.

'And this was wilfully wrong. It was done, this assassination, in the absence of any clear proof. But it went further than that. It was done in the concealment from the public of material facts discovered during the investigation. There was never any mention of an oppressive problem carried by the Captain of the DC8, one which could well have led to a lapse in concentration. And there was never any mention of omission on the part of Air Traffic Services in their ground-to-air procedures, omissions in transmission of what is referred to as the QNH, letters which live on from the last World War.' He paused and shifted his weight. 'QNH. In essence, a QNH reading is that of atmospheric pressure at sea level. Its purpose – vital to any aircraft descending below 11,000 feet – is to recalibrate the altimeter on the flight deck of the descending aircraft. For the purpose of this case you can take it that above that height all altimeters are calibrated to the international artificial standard setting of 1013 millibars.

'Now, why is it vital for all aircraft descending below 13,000 feet to have altimeters set to the actual atmospheric pressure of the day, and not the high-level cruising standard QNH of 1013? In a word, real height: for every one millibar added in calibration of the altimeter, that altimeter will register an extra height of 30 feet. To give an example, let us assume an aircraft has been cruising at 25,000 feet. Its altimeter will show 25,000 feet with a setting of 1013 millibars. And let us suppose that the actual pressure at sea level is 980 millibars – an area of low pressure is how the weather people on TV would describe it. But say that aircraft does not reset its altimeter to 980, but lets it remain at 1013 throughout its descent for a landing. Well, then it will probably crash. Why? Because there is a difference between the actual and artificial QNH, a difference of 30 millibars between the 1013 by which the altimeter is calibrated and the 980 by which it should be calibrated. 30 millibars, each one meaning an error of 30 feet, gives an error of 900 feet. In those terms, an altimeter calibrated to 1013 in an area of actual pressure of 980 will still read 900 feet above the ground as the aircraft crashes into it. So it is vital that all aircraft carry altimeters calibrated to the same and correct QNH reading.' He moved a piece of paper in front of him before continuing, and when he did, his voice was very mild.

'And in this case, the omissions of the Air Traffic Controllers were to leave out the descent QNH!' He paused again for effect, then continued in a stronger voice.

'This accident occurred below 13,000 feet. It occurred at either 3000 feet, which was the cleared height of the Cessna 172, or,' again he paused, 'at 4000 feet, the cleared height of the DC8, and we must ask ourselves, as a matter of probability, and his Honour will have to decide it, at which height did this appalling accident take place? I say probability, for there is no concrete proof. Yet in this case the plaintiff claims damages, for she says that, as a matter of near certainty, let alone probability, the height at which this accident occurred was 3000 feet, the height at which her husband was properly flying. She says that there was indeed a QNH error and it had to be in the order of 33 millibars. She says that one cannot overlook the facts, as the Government chose to do.

'On the one hand she presents her husband, a careful, methodical man, well used to and experienced in flying, someone who, as your Honour will see, took his customary care, was fit and well, and appreciated what he was about in entering cloud. And we will demonstrate that he at least received a QNH dictation – several. First from the meteorological office when he was on the phone with pen and paper for notes, and then again immediately after he took off. But that is not the end of it, for yet again, for the third time, he was given a QNH, his second in flight. He was only in the air for just twenty-six minutes. And it required no change during that time.

'Indeed,' he continued, 'it is perhaps apposite at this point to deal with that specifically, so your Honour and the members of the jury will have it in mind throughout the course of this trial.' He picked up a sheet of paper from his lectern. 'I read from the transcript of the first airborne transmission from the Cessna, made moments after take-off. It was then that the Flight Information Officer at the Wellington Centre said this: "Echo Lima Sierra" – that was the Cessna's call sign,' he interposed, looking up. '"Roger – Wellington area QNH 1018 millibars".' Again he looked up. 'Can we be sure he heard that? It is a fundamental question of vital importance that we have to satisfy ourselves on if the plaintiff is to succeed in this case. And on that, I am happy to say yes, he heard it, for he said "Echo Lima Sierra", so we know it was Frank Newton speaking. Then he said this: "Roger – 1018 millibars".'

He paused again, before continuing. 'There can be no doubt about that. And, you may think, the fact that he didn't just stop at "Roger" but went on to quote a reading back, and so open the way to correction, shows that he fully appreciated the importance of the reading and, of course, its purpose. And then, without further incident, he flies on to oblivion.' He let it hang in the air. 'Yes, oblivion. But not before seeking radar assistance. Not mandatory, but he was a careful man. And not before it was finally said to him by a further Controller, "Check QNH 1018."' Someone at the back of the Court coughed, but it died and it was as though the words still lingered on in the lengthy silence. Then, to drive it home, Carter murmured again, 'Check – 1018 millibars' – and no doubt he checked.

'But what of the DC8? They would have been given a QNH and we do know that they heard what is called an ATIS. But whether correctly or incorrectly we will never know. What we do know is this. In the first place, unlike the Cessna, the DC8 was required to make an in-flight change in the calibration of its altimeter on descent through 11,000 feet. Now, was this done by a disturbed captain, a man who at best would have his father's death on his mind?

'We will never know, for, unfortunately, the tapes don't permit one to distinguish between the Captain and his co-pilot, so it is a fifty-fifty chance it was the unhappy man. But even if it wasn't him, but his co-pilot, and his co-pilot made a mistake, well then, you may think there would have been a fair chance of his troubled captain failing to check his co-pilot. In either event we have the seeds of a disaster. One man and a mistake, a disastrous mistake, unchecked by the ground staff in their omissions.

'Now, what is this ATIS, this thing relied upon by the air-crew? A simple one point message as to the vet? No. It gives a thirty-five second transmission of seventeen information items. How easy to make a single mistake in hearing all that, you may think.

'But of course, you will remember that Frank Newton checked his QNH back. You will remember he said quite clearly "Roger – QNH 1018 millibars" so, of course, you would think, would you not, that the DC8 would have checked its QNH back. But there was no check back . . .'

He was cut short by the swift rise to his feet of John Prescott, QC. 'I really must protest, I really must. Not only has this opening been as emotive as it could possibly be, but when my learned friend seeks to mislead the Court, then has come the time to stop it. Most certainly there was a check back, and that should be made plain. Indeed, it is scandalous that my learned friend should seek to mislead the Court in opening!'

'Oh dear, oh dear,' Reginald Carter said. 'Your Honour, I am so very sorry to have upset my learned friend, but if he hadn't been so fearfully eager to put his case – almost the whole of it, one might say – he would have heard me mention what he, I think, will suggest was a check, though I wouldn't, and neither I dare say will your Honour, let alone the jury . . .'

'Enough, Mr Carter.' The judge's voice was very dry as he turned his attention to Prescott. 'Mr Prescott, I think we must bear with an emotive opening for the benefit of the jury. But one which, I confess, I am finding a trifle tedious in its repetition. But don't concern yourself. I dare say I will be able to see the trees for Mr Carter's wood.'

Prescott's 'If it pleases your Honour' was almost inaudible as he subsided. Having made his point, he wished he hadn't as he realized, far too late, that he would have been a great deal wiser to have held his tongue. His conviction was confirmed as Carter started to speak again.

'Yes, I am much obliged to my learned friend. He calls it a check. Well, I won't comment on it now, but his case, which turns on five words in which the "QNH" doesn't . . .'

'Your Honour, this really is too much. I . . .'

The judge cut him off gently. 'I am inclined to agree with you, Mr Prescott.' He coughed quietly to himself. Then, when he was ready, he looked up from the Bench and down at Carter. 'Enough is enough, Mr Carter. Mr Prescott will no doubt put his case when the time comes. Meanwhile, pursue your own.'

Unabashed, Carter continued. 'Certainly, your Honour, I am obliged. Now where was I?' The judge was about to tell him, but then avoided the little trap of an advocate gaining the judicial weight for what might be a bad point. Aware of it, Carter was left to remind himself. 'Oh yes. The DC8. In a nutshell, what my learned friend will be forced to rely on is no more than, and I quote "We have copied weather Mike".'

He paused and looked across at the jury. 'Does that tell us that the DC8 had the correct QNH? No, indeed it doesn't. For unlike the vet, who repeated the QNH correctly, it mentions it not at all. But it goes further. For the Air Traffic Service compounded the error. Air Traffic Controllers, two of them, would usually have given a QNH, but for some inexplicable reason, on this day, to this single aircraft, they didn't – and there was a crash.' He took his time, before adding, 'No, they didn't give the one piece of information which was vital for the calibration of the altimeter. And there was a crash. That crash occurred because one of the planes was at the wrong height.' He rested on his lectern and let silence fall.

Then, drawing himself to his full height, he said, 'And so we have it. On the one hand, a faultless flight by a private pilot, and on the other, a captain who was disturbed, at best, and a failure on the part of the Air Traffic Services. And the private pilot, the little man, was held to blame. This vet was not to blame. That is the plaintiff's contention, and one which will, I venture to suggest, find support here in this Court.'

He gathered his papers together, then turned to the jury. 'So far I have more or less been engaged with his Honour, for this case is, first, one in which he will find on liability. But after that, should he find the vet not to blame or less to blame than you would think was the case which was publicly made out by the media, Government, and the rest of them, well, then the case enters your sphere. His Honour will deal with the law at a later stage and, indeed, as I deal with it now he will correct me if I am, in his opinion, wrong.

'But first, I must tell you that you are only concerned in this case as to whether it has been the Government who has defamed this man . . .'

Now it was underway, Grace's attention wandered, and her mind went back to that time when she realized Marty wouldn't help. She glanced to her left and watched the man whom she had come to trust implicitly. Quiet, middle-aged, iron-grey-haired, slightly built, and always courteous, she remembered the first time she had seen him. His grey eyes, cool and calm, and yet somehow penetrating, had made her feel from the outset that she had found what she needed. She remembered how nervous she had been as she had entered the cool, large lobby of the multi-storey block which housed his firm of solicitors and barristers, the ride up in the lift to the tenth floor, the smiling receptionist sitting at her desk in the book-lined hall from which two corridors ran to give access, over lush russet carpet, to doors through one of which she would shortly pass. To what, she had wondered. Polite rejection yet again? And so home in final defeat? Twice she had been told by solicitors that they really thought the only advice they could give was the same as Marty's. So, as she had made the appointment to see Charles Gray of Gray, MacKinnock, Lampson & Co, she had decided it would be the last attempt. Another refusal and she would sign the form and give the money to the children – and be infinitely miserable.

She remembered his first words to her. 'Grace Newton, have you come to see me about your husband?'

The name connection had surprised her, but she had forgotten the rest of it, except that, unlike Marty and unlike the others, he hadn't treated her as an errant child to be gently forced back into line, but had listened carefully to her and, as she had talked, had made notes and asked the odd question. Then, when she had talked to a standstill, he had gone over the ground, as the others had. But with a difference: not to ram it down her throat and use it to turn her away from a case without hope, but to make sure she realized the full implications of all that she proposed. Had she heard the conversation tape, it would all have come back to her with crystal clarity.

'Even with all that against you, you want to go on?'

'Yes. I don't think you have told me anything I didn't know. I've thought about it, and of course, I've thought about giving up. In fact, if you turn me down, then I will. Not because I think I should, but because I just can't fight the whole world any longer.'

'You do realize that you face about a ninety per cent chance of failing?'

Wearily, she replied, 'Yes.' Her flat answer had led him to meditate before he continued, 'Tell you what, I won't promise now that I will undertake all that you want for you must see that I have a duty to do the best I can for you, not merely to take your money to keep you happy.' He laughed. 'No, that isn't a duty, but you know what I mean. Though I dare say there are some who'd be delighted to take your money.'

She nodded, aware that it was true, and for that reason she had taken enormous trouble in the selection of the only three solicitors she had decided to approach.

'Anyway,' he interrupted her thoughts, 'at the moment we have nothing to go on. And if it doesn't get any better than that, then I am afraid that is the end of it, at least as far as I can concern myself. But I'll look into it. Though I warn you that even that won't be cheap, but if you would like me to I will willingly do so.'

'I'd be very grateful, but why you, and not my own solicitor or the others?'

He thought about it, then decided to tell her. 'Three things. One, like everyone else, I saw the send-up on TV and the rest of it, and I don't like trial by misguided opinion, and I'd like to see whether that opinion was misguided. Governments aren't unknown to do things in the great cause of self-interest. Two, I never knew Frank, but it just so happens that one of my partners had a bit to do with him in flying. The other day he said to me: "It's just unbelievable. Frank Newton wasn't the sort of guy to get his altitude wrong, cloud or no cloud." And three, I admire you for your loyalty, however misguided it may be, and I think that someone else should check it out. At least then you might one day be able to reconcile yourself to the probable truth.'

'That, ladies and gentlemen of the jury, is the law. But from the outset, I want you to have three things in mind, and to keep them in mind throughout the case. One, the Government . . .'

The Solicitor General was on his feet and his interruption cut across Carter's flow like a knife. 'Your Honour, I think I know what my learned friend is about to say, and I have instructions on the point which lead me to this interruption. If I may I would be obliged if I could address your Honour in camera.'

'Very unusual, but if you feel you must, then so be it. Usher, clear the Court please.'

As the doors to the Court closed for the closed session, the judge nodded to the Solicitor General to begin.

'Your Honour, I think you know what I have to say. My learned friend has mentioned that certain facts were not made public: the death of the father, the Air Traffic Control business and, of course, I cannot avoid their admission on the question of liability and, to a certain extent, as background fact to his defamation action.

'However, my learned friend was proposing to do a great deal more and use them in an attempt to discredit the Government. In the national interest, I would ask your Honour to give a direction that that must not be pursued. It is one thing to allege that facts that may have affected liability were omitted from a report in the public interest – an error of judgment at worst – which has nothing to do with liability, though, of course, defamation can flow from that. No, I have no objection to that. But it is quite another to say that omissions were deliberately used by the Government to protect itself and to mislead the public as a deliberate policy of deceit.'

'Yes. And what do you say, Mr Carter?'

'Apart from liability and defamation by mistake or error of judgment, as it were, to which my friend raises no objection, this case concerns deliberate defamation. It is a live issue against the Government, which can hardly hope to shield behind its definition of public interest.'

The judge considered for a moment before saying quietly, 'Yes, but I anticipate that the Solicitor General would reply to that by saying you must have regard for the national interest; that your case could adequately, and should properly only be pursued on the basis that the remarks and conclusions which came from the defendants, and which you allege defame, are only defamatory in the event of my finding that the plaintiff's husband was not to blame or *de minimis,* which, if so, should be construed as an error of judgment on the part of the Government in their assessment. Still defamation, of course, because you would say that the evidence was there to be seen and they should have seen it and had they properly appreciated it they should have taken care not to present a misleading picture to the public.'

'Partly, your Honour, but it goes further. My case, which is well-founded, lies in the knowingly wrongful, and plainly wrongful, heaping of the blame on that unfortunate man's head, and to do that, the Government had to abuse its position of trust to conceal facts it well knew, and which, if acknowledged, would have defeated all possibility of heaping the blame on him. That goes to damage, and if the jury took the view that the Government deliberately concealed facts for that purpose, they would be entitled to take it into account in considering damages. It's a separate head of damage, and a very large sum could be awarded under it as a completely separate entity to what I'll term the simple defamation. To shut the door on that places the Government above the law.'

'And what do you say to that?'

'I think . . .' The argument on exclusion continued for twenty minutes. Then the judge gave his ruling. 'The Solicitor General objects to Mr Carter pursuing that part of his case which goes to the issue of whether the action of the Government was discreditable, in the sense of concealment of facts being an abuse of its power. He does so on the basis that for a Government to have been shown to have done that would be contrary to the public interest. Mr Carter does not share that view and urges upon me the proposition that to accept that view would be to place the Government above the law, and beyond the reach of justice at the hands of the ordinary man.

'In his submission, the Solicitor General expresses the view, with eloquence, that the plaintiff should pursue defamation on the basis that if defamation there was, then it arose from merely a misguided appraisal of what was material to the accident – that is, if I find the Captain's state of mind material and/or if I find the Air Traffic Control omissions material and attach any degree of liability to these two matters.

'But Mr Carter counters by saying that in all the circumstances this is a case in which the Government as, no doubt, to a limited extent, insurers for the Air Traffic Service, had a vested interest. And perhaps because of that, we have here something a great deal more sinister than a mere mistake. He postulates as a matter for the jury a deliberate covering up which facilitated and was necessary for the wrongful heaping of blame on to the vet. He says that goes to damage under a separate head of damage and should be a matter for the jury, if he succeeds on liability.

'I am not unmindful of the demands of the public interest. But I am bound to point out that this is a Court in which justice must not only be done, but must be seen to be done. Further, I take the view that, though I do not necessarily accept Mr Carter's contention, nevertheless it is a view which would be open to the jury to accept. Should they do so, then it renders the defamation, if defamation there was, a great deal more serious than might be the case. Damages may be small, if awarded at all, on the basis of mere mistake and bad judgment leading to a failure to exercise their duty of care in respect of this vet's reputation. But it goes further. For exemplary damages, over and above damages for defamation, are at issue. And, should the jury take the view that here it has a deliberate perversion of fact by the Government, to shield itself in the public eye, and that shield was forged in defamation of an innocent man, this being the purpose of the exercise, then a substantial element of damages could well reflect that. In my view, the plaintiff cannot be excluded from this element of the case, and she may proceed.

'I add this. If this or any other Government behaves discreditably in seeking to further its own ends, and is found out – not that I express any view one way or another as to whether that is or is not the case here – then it will not find sanctuary in any Court of mine, and in that I am speaking for my brothers on the Bench.'

'Your Honour, I seek leave to take this matter to the Court of Appeal.'

'No. If you wish to pursue it further you will have to make out a case for leave to appeal to that Court. Your application is refused.'

The Solicitor General and the Attorney General had considered this before the case. To push it that far would start too many questions. So with a shrug of his shoulders the Solicitor General said, 'Very well, your Honour. I shall not pursue the matter further.'

'I think you're wise not to,' the judge said. Then he added, 'Now we had better get on, but before people come back I mention that I would like to see leading counsel in my Chambers when we adjourn for lunch.'

Intrigued, the jury paid yet greater attention, and reporters with pens at the ready waited for news of what had been of such importance for the Court to be cleared. But they waited in vain, for Carter, on his feet again, broke the silence as though there had been no interruption.

'You will remember that when my learned friend discovered that he had something to say to his Honour in private I had got to the point where I was asking you to bear three points in mind, and to keep them in mind throughout this action. Each, you may think, and come to think more firmly as we progress, is a matter of very real importance. One, the Government had a vested interest in blaming the vet, for you see, ladies and gentlemen of the jury, it just so happens that the Government was, to all intents and purposes, an insurance company standing to have to pay out if any blame for that terrible accident could come to rest with any of their servants or agents, which Air Traffic Controllers certainly were.

'So remember, and remember well. It was not as the Prime Minister would have had us believe when he made his well-remembered broadcast, that the Government was full of good chaps bringing about, to use his phrase, the position of, I quote, "letting their hands be joined across the table" as though liability were nothing to do with them. Remember well that never, for one second, could one have devined from anything said that the Government had any interest other than altruistic.' He shook his head. 'But such is not, I fear, the case. So, one, the Government was to some extent an insurer, and concealed this interest. I don't suggest that their interest would have been high in percentage terms, for no doubt the Government would have laid off all but perhaps the first 10 per cent, but in a claim of this magnitude, 10 per cent could represent millions of dollars. So they concealed that interest.

'Two, the Government was carrying out the investigation, and what was made public was only what suited the Government. It was in their power to do this.

'And three – and mark it well – did they conceal anything or not? The answer is yes. They concealed vital information which, had it been made public, would have prevented their perfidy in blaming the one man who could say nothing . . .' Now his voice commanded greater attention. 'No, he could say nothing, for they blamed a dead man, and used concealment to do so. They concealed their role as part insurer; they concealed the fact of a mistake on the part of a Controller; they concealed the fact that another mistake was made by another Controller; they concealed the fact that each made the same mistake; they concealed the fact that this mistake was the omission of the one piece of information needed to calibrate the altimeter as the DC8 descended . . .' and his voice suddenly dropped, 'and they concealed the fact that the man in command of that DC8 was troubled, was a man who had no right to be flying.' Then he paused and the silence seemed to tighten and stretch, before he added, almost conversationally, 'And perhaps they concealed more as the evidence may come to show. And in the light of it, all you will be asked by me to consider is what sum in damages you should award – a little, for a mere error of judgment; or something to recognize as pernicious a piece of treachery as has ever been perpetrated on a gullible, believing, innocent public, and on an innocent man.

'You deal, ladies and gentlemen of the jury, with a situation – and it is grave – in which the Prime Minister and others in his administration have lent themselves to perversion of the truth. And that raises a question I am not going to attempt to answer here. Why haven't they emerged as honest insurers, why have they concealed, why were they prepared to go to such lengths to mislead you and the world? I dare say we will have the answer one day, but I am not privy to their business or their thoughts. Indeed, it may have been simply to avoid liability, who knows, but it matters not, for the mere fact is enough, and I am not going to permit my client to become a crusader. She is simply here to present her case and find justice at the hands of his Honour and yourselves.' He paused and rested awhile on the lectern, then collected himself for the next phase. The ground had been prepared and now the time had come to seed it.

'Now, to turn to the evidence which I shall be calling. First . . .'

Grace's mind flicked back to the second meeting with Charles Grey. Even more nervously than before she had smiled her anxiety at the receptionist and waited. As she waited she had been tormented by the thought that face to face he would say to her that he was sorry, but there was absolutely nothing he could do. But it hadn't been like that. He had smiled encouragingly at her and quickly come to the point.

'Ah, Grace Newton, just the girl I wanted to see. I don't know whether we'll ever have a case, but I will tell you there is one hell of a lot more to this than meets the public eye; enough, in any event, to justify going a little further.'

'Why, what's happened?' she had asked.

'Something just a trifle strange. You remember mentioning to me that you saw a man from the insurance company?' She had nodded. 'Well, I rang them up and directly I mentioned your name I was whistled straight through to the General Manager, very much to my surprise, I may say. Now, listen to this!' He switched on the tape deck and she heard the recorded sound of the ringing of a telephone. 'Good morning, Dominion and Commonwealth. Can I help you?'

'Yes. I would like to speak to someone about the claims being made arising from the DC8 disaster.'

'Is this a general enquiry or specifically about one of the claims?'

'I act for a Mrs Newton.'

'Did you say Newton? Grace Newton?'

'Yes.'

'Please hold, sir. I am putting you through.'

'To whom?' he'd asked, but there was no reply. Then the next connection was made.

'Hi, who the hell are you?'

'I might ask you the same question.'

'You first, fella, it's your enquiry.'

'Charles Gray of Gray, MacKinnock, Lampson and Co.'

'Jesus! Thank Christ for that. I thought maybe you were the tit she was with a while back. I think that guy still uses a catapult and bullshit as shot. You, I know of. Me, I'm the General Manager here. Now tell me, is this girl still trying to lay it on the line?'

'If you mean what I think you mean, yes. She isn't going to let it go. At least, not yet.'

'Good. Now I want to know this, Gray. If I did happen to say anything, would I be able to count on it as being recorded, but erased after Grace Newton has heard it? No, shit no. That's bloody stupid. Look, let's go further than that. I would like you to act for me. I am considering litigation and I want you to take me on as a client on a retainer of a hundred bucks.'

'Yes, I think I see what you have in mind. You want to talk as client to solicitor in the preparation of a case, and so with privilege. Is that correct?'

'Yeah, you got it in one, buddy.'

'First, I'd need to know what litigation you have in mind. You can't just claim privilege with no good reason; rules and so on, you know?'

'Yeah. Look, someone some time ago called me offensive in

the hearing of others. I might like to do something about that some time.'

'I see. Well, I confess I don't like to lend myself to evasive legal games of a rather dubious nature, but if you give me your assurance that your wish is to explore the possibility of legal action against someone who, *prima facie,* without justification, slandered you, then I would accept you as a client. Then anything you said to me in connection with the preparation of that case would be privileged and go no further than myself. Unless, of course, you wanted it to.'

'Yeah, but I've got a problem. Whether or not I've got a case may turn, in your sort of language, on what happens in another case. You see, Gray, I alleged that our Minister of Transport had rigged a Press conference, and he called me offensive. Now, as I see it, if he did rig it, then it was slanderous to call me offensive, but if not, then I s'pose it's OK. But to a man in my position to be called offensive by someone in his position is bad news, no?'

'Pretty thin, I would have thought, but if it was heard by the right people, yes, it could be said to be harmful to the reputation of someone in your position – just. Anyway, I think it would be enough for me to justify a client and solicitor relationship.' As he finished he chuckled. 'But what follows now, sir?'

'Well, I don't want to get all involved in big costs to prove this guy rigged the conference, but if this other action succeeds it would open the way for me to go ahead and cost bugger all. Do you understand what I say?'

'I'm beginning to get the drift of it, but do go on.'

'Yeah, so I'd like you to act for me, but bearing in mind that if this other action goes anywhere it'll help me, I'd like your client to accept something to help with her expenses in return for anything she digs up which helps me sue this guy. Whaddaya think?'

'Not unheard of. What figure would you have in mind?'

'Well, I reckon that it would pay me to meet, oh, say a third of her costs.'

'Very generous of you. But, yes, it may save you quite a lot of money if she won.'

'Yeah, but even if she bloody loses I'm still OK. If I fought and lost it would cost me a hell of a lot more than a third of her costs.'

'Yes, perhaps so. You will be writing to me on this, will you?'

'Yeah, I'll be writing.'

'Good. And in that case if I have your instructions to this effect by the time I see the plaintiff in the other action I will take her instructions. But have you considered that she may not pursue things as far as you would need for use in your, er, case?'

'Yeah, and if she don't, then I've only lost a third of the money it would have cost me to get to the same point, right?'

'It's one way of looking at it. But can you give me, er, what shall we call it at this stage . . . any further instructions?'

'Because I put pen to paper for a purpose I can't disclose, no. Nor can any of the servants or agents of this company. But that raises a question. Would a loss adjuster I used called Mark Simpson of Stanley and Partners be a servant or agent of the company?'

'I fear so,' the solicitor replied.

'Pity. But not your client's former solicitor?'

'No.'

'Well, well. I wonder whether that piece of paper would apply in keeping secret information given to your client's former solicitor before it was signed? Still, some guys are here to shoot some crap so that's it. And about my case, we must get together some time.' As the solicitor was saying goodbye the line cut dead.

Grace looked bewildered as she asked, 'What does it all mean?'

He laughed. 'Our friend has agreed his settlement bearing a part of the liability on behalf of Frank under an agreement of non-disclosure of anything to do with it. In the result, when the Chief Investigator of Air Accidents' report becomes public that is all that will become public. And our friend, deviously but not in breach of that agreement, is telling us that there will be omissions in it. And further, that we can find out a little bit more from Marty Chalmers, who is not covered by the agreement and who had information given to him before it was made.'

'But why didn't he give me that information?'

'I dare say he didn't think it would be in your interests to have it. Don't be annoyed, he was only doing the best he could for you, as he saw it.'

'And why does this man want to give me money?'

'You heard. He thinks he has a case, which you might win for him. And if you are prepared to let me use anything to help, it saves him money.' He looked blandly at her.

'Oh come on. I am not as stupid as that.'

He smiled again as he said, 'Pity, really. But I suppose it was inevitable. OK, what it comes down to is that you won't take their money because it would shut you up for good. His company has obviously reached a very good settlement and he doesn't want to blow it. But through you, he can have his cake and eat it. So he is saying "go on and do what I can't, and good luck to you", and to give his encouragement a little point he offers to help out with the bill. In effect, Grace Newton, though he doesn't say you have a case, he does say there is something for us to find which would help it.'

'But I can't take his money?'

'Why not? No strings, and who are you or even I to decide he has no case in slander? Who knows?'

'Absolute nonsense! What would his damages be, anyway?'

'I should think he'd get at least a cent,' he laughed as he said it, 'but principles don't count costs, as you well know. A lot of people waste a lot of money on what someone else thinks is, as you so neatly put it, "absolute nonsense". After all, every fight has a loser who thought he would win until he lost.'

'But would it be right to take it?'

'I have already accepted on your behalf, and you will just have to be guided by me, your lawyer, won't you? And yes, it is all right. Yours is a cause to which someone has donated money. There are lots of them. And here it goes further because, who knows? He might well be buying, quite properly, research which he could use in a case of his own, and a good deal more cheaply than if he undertook it himself.'

Still reluctant, she said, 'But you know very well he wouldn't bother.'

'He didn't say that, or even imply it. Lord, you would be amazed at some of the cases I am asked to deal with – anything where *amour-propre* is concerned. And just think how denting to the pride it must be for a senior commercialist to suffer being called offensive by a Minister of the Crown?'

She couldn't help laughing at his mock seriousness, as she was persuaded. 'OK, and thank him for me.'

'I have.'

'Well, when do you get in touch with Marty Chalmers?'

'We spoke, a shade reluctantly on his part, this morning.'

'And?'

'It appears that the Captain of the DC8 had a father who had died forty-eight hours or so before the flight, and he had been badly cut up about it. And it appears that there is some question of an irregularity in some of the Air Traffic Control procedures in connection with that flight.' He paused. 'So that, and the phone call, changed my mind. In fact I had been going to say to you today that I was sorry but you would have to learn to live with it. But now, what's it to be? Do we risk an expensive mare's nest and greater disappointment, or forget it?'

The silence was very short before she said with quiet determination, 'I must know.'

'Yes, I think I agree,' he murmured in reply.

'What will you do now?' she asked. And they talked for another twenty minutes before she left.

Reginald Carter, QC, had commanded the attention of the Court for two hours and five minutes when he finally clasped his hands in front of him and, as though washing them slowly, he entered the short straight before the post marking the end of his opening.

'So there it is. In brief, the plaintiff has a case which, I venture to say, will leave his Honour with no option but to find for my client. And I trust it will be a pleasant duty for him, for it will see a case resolved which, in my submission, needs savage rectification to remedy the travesty of justice meted out on this poor woman over the past years. And there, ladies and gentlemen of the jury, you will have your part to play. You will play it well by marking the occasion with an award which, to coin a phrase, will make people sit up and listen, and hear a very different tune to that played by the Government; a state of affairs, members of the jury, which is truly terrible – terrible that such a position of trust should have been so abused. Yes, it is a terrible thing.' As he added the last few words, his voice dropped. He paused. Then with sudden power, he said finally, 'But, thank the Lord, we live in a democracy and you, the representatives of the people, have the power to assert that fact without fear or favour. And in the fulfilment of that role you will go beyond this Court, for you will be restating the rightful demands of your countrymen for unwavering integrity in government. And that, ladies and gentlemen, will be your rightful duty in this case.'

The judge, not wishing to spoil the effect of the peroration, let the silence linger on until Carter, satisfied with it, began to move again. Then he said, 'If that's a convenient point, Mr Carter?'

'Yes, I think so, your Honour.'

'Very well. We will adjourn now until 2.15. However,' and he raised his voice for all to hear, 'before I adjourn I would remind the Press of their duty. Allegations have been made today of a very serious nature, and of a type concerning which speculation could become rife. That must not happen. The facts, of course, will no doubt be reported. No comment is permissible during the course of this trial, for the facts are *sub judice.* And should this rule of law be breached, it will be in contempt of Court and that will be a matter for me. Should such a case be brought before me after this warning, then the offender will go to prison. I hope that is plainly understood, and I shall count on what I have said as having reached the ears of all concerned who are outside this Court.' And he rose and strode from the Court.

'The judge will see you now, gentlemen.' And the associate ushered them in.

'Ah. Come along in and sit down.' He gave them time to sit before continuing briskly, 'This case, you know, really shouldn't go any further. It'll be very damaging, very costly, and I rather think we will end up with a compromise. So what about it. Can't you chaps get your heads together and settle, eh?'

The Solicitor General nodded his head. 'I think I can say for all of us, judge, that we've tried.'

'Yes, I'm sure you have.'

'But, I am sure you will appreciate the problems, judge,' John Prescott added.

'Oh, I appreciate it won't be easy. But Carter, can't you do something? Your client must surely realize the danger she stands in? I am not expressing any opinion, of course, but it must be clear that her chances are, well, if not totally remote, not far from it. I don't want to have to find against her, but if I do it'll be a tragedy, won't it?'

'I am not unmindful of that, judge,' Carter replied cautiously, 'and neither, I may add, is she.'

'I see. And you two. Every case has its risks, and here, perhaps, a great deal heavier than an outside chance. Can't you talk to your people and do something?'

'I am sure you realize we've all had it in mind. The best I can say is yes, I will try,' replied the Solicitor General.

'And you, Prescott? Your airline must face a risk too. Higher, perhaps, than the Air Traffic people.'

'I can't comment, judge. But I take the point.'

'Good. Anyway, I thought I would have a word with you all, for really, this isn't going to do any good in the long run, is it? Well, thank you for coming in, and I very much hope that after lunch you'll be able to tell me it's settled. I am sure, quite sure, it would be best, right?' And he nodded to them as they trooped out.

If only he knew the problems. It was a thought common to them all, as they went off to talk, yet again, to their clients.

Chapter Eighteen

'All right, Gray?' Carter's voice outside the court-room was quite different: quiet, precise, and devoid of dramatic intonation. The question was simply a greeting not calling for an answer, for he knew when an opening had gone well. And knowing this, the solicitor merely nodded as the QC gave the Hulmans the benefit of his serious but calm and confident smile.

'Right,' he continued. 'I think we ought to go off somewhere and have a little chat. Let's go in there.' And they followed his billowing robes across the wide corridor to a door on the opposite side. As they walked, Grace thought again how different these people all looked without wigs. Carter's, she noticed, now looked like a dead grey cat swinging nonchalantly from his hand.

'Well now. What I have to deal with isn't uncommon, so don't worry about it. The judge wants this case to be settled. What it comes down to is this. He is afraid that, although we may well hit at the credibility of the Government and satisfy him about the Air Traffic business and the Captain and all the rest of it, nevertheless, it won't be enough. And what he would really like to do is avoid having to find against you.'

'But how can he say that? He hasn't heard the evidence yet. How can he say something like that, especially after your speech this morning? I was watching the jury, and I know they . . . well,' she searched for the word '. . . sympathized, I suppose.'

'Yes, Grace,' Charles Gray said. 'But as we've known all along, sympathy won't win it for us. If he finds against us on liability, we are sunk. It's a fact we can't avoid. The fact that there was deceit on the part of the Government; even that they blamed Frank publicly for the wrong reasons; none of it's enough, if it still turns out to be true.'

'Can I say something?' Bill Hulman coughed as he gathered his thoughts. 'We've known this for a long time, haven't we, Grace?'

She nodded her head as he continued, 'So we're not backing down now because a judge, before he's even heard the evidence, wants to stop it, and stop it, I reckon, so's to save the necks of the bastards.'

'Anyway, be that as it may,' Carter said, 'he had us all in to see if we could do something about it. So there we are.'

'But isn't it wrong for a judge to say what he thinks like this? I mean, here he is, right at the beginning, doing what he should keep till the end. How can we expect a fair hearing now? He'll never say he's changed his mind.' The anxiety in Grace's voice was clear.

The silk shook his head and smiled as he wondered how best to put it. 'No. You needn't worry about that. All he is doing is expressing the doubt we have all had. But it's not a decision, just a tentative first view on risks after seeing the pleadings and having heard the opening. So he's said, "All of you think again. Do you really want to go through with this, or wouldn't it be better for everyone concerned if you settled your differences out of Court?" And of course he's right, if it were possible. Still, what I want from you now is instructions. I merely advise. It's for you to decide. Do you want me to make a fresh approach to the other sides?'

'When you were in with the judge,' said the solicitor, 'I told Grace and Bill what it was all about and they have decided that we stand firm. Either they agree to pay full damages in respect of Frank's death and agree to the prepared statement being read out in Court, in which case we will forget the defamation, or we go on.' Turning to the Hulmans, he continued: 'But before we actually finalize that with Mr Carter, have you heard anything from him which makes you want to change your minds?'

'No.' Grace's voice was firm. Bill merely nodded his agreement.

Carter nodded, as he said, 'OK, but as I've said before, don't count on victory. But having said that, you may rely on me to go all out for you, hmmm?' And with a smile and a nod he left them to go back to the robing-room.

As the Hulmans went with their solicitor, Charles Gray, for lunch, the Solicitor General joined Carter in the robing-room. 'Oh hello, Reggie. Look, I haven't had a word yet with John, but it may be that we'll have something to say when I do. Will you be here?'

'Yes, anytime,' Carter answered as he looked up from the papers of another case spread out on the robing-room table in front of him. Habitually he worked during lunch hours. He was disturbed again as the other silk entered. 'Ah, there you are, John. Let's go and have a chat?' Carter didn't disturb himself as the other two men left the room. He was hardly visible behind the cloud of smoke from his pipe.

In the Conference Room next door, the Solicitor General lit a cigarette and, staring out of the window, took a long draw on it. John Prescott sat down and started to read a note he had with him, but looked up: 'Well, Clive, what do you think?'

'Hmmmm?' Two angry drivers outside had caught his attention. 'What do I think?' He considered the question as he repeated it then replied, 'I think this thing is going to cause an awful lot of trouble. I dare say we'll win, but it'll do untold damage to my people.' He pulled meditatively on his cigarette again.

'So, what's the position? Has Carter come up with anything?'

'He'll be there when we want to talk, but I thought we had better see what we think first. What do your people say now?'

'Oh, I've had a crack at them but they still take the view that it's your problem. Perhaps a few harsh words to say about aircrew, but I don't for a moment think he'll find against them.'

'Hmm, perhaps.' He paused as he went over it again in his mind. 'But, if he really stuck his neck out you know, then it's just possible he could go overboard. If he could find for this woman I think he would. But still,' and he was thinking aloud, 'if he did, I have no doubt he'd be reversed on appeal. Not that that's a great deal of comfort, is it?'

'No, not for you. But, as I say, that's your problem. However, you're right: he's a plaintiff's judge, and with that in mind we've decided to help a little more.'

'What will you go to?'

'35 per cent, and that is positively our last word on it. They don't like it but they'll do it. But what about you?'

'Well,' he replied slowly, 'the problem is that there is no way I could get my people to agree to their statement. My people just will not admit publicly that they made a mistake, and even less, of course, that they wilfully concealed material evidence,' then reflectively added, 'I suppose no government would. So really that's it.'

'That's all very well on defamation, but what about liability. Can't we settle that?'

'No, I don't think so. But I'll try again with Carter. You say 35 per cent, and I've got authority now to carry 55 per cent, but I don't think she'll take it.'

'Why not? No one in their right mind would refuse 90 per cent!'

'Because my people will only offer it on the basis of a settlement on terms endorsed on counsel's brief. And that is the one thing she doesn't want. She's here to vindicate her husband in public, so I can't see her agreeing. But thanks, John. I'll go and have a word with Carter now.'

'Now just wait a minute.' There was a hint of exasperation in Prescott's voice. 'From my people's view this is bloody unsatisfactory. You say we can give her 90 per cent, which will certainly settle liability. And that's all I'm interested in. So why can't we settle that and let her go on the defamation side with you alone?'

'The two are too much tied up together. I can settle, as I say, on undisclosed terms, but it won't be what she'll agree to, so in a way the money has become secondary. You can always stop it by disassociating yourselves from me and giving her 100 per cent and admitting publicly that the whole of the blame rests on your aircrew. It's as simple as that.'

'Ha! I can just see my people agreeing to that. OK, we'll go on then, but the whole thing's bloody nonsense, and at the end of the day's play I shall certainly have something to say on costs.'

'Hmm. I rather thought you might. But we'll just have to wait and see, won't we? With a bit of luck she'll go down without trace and we won't be worrying about costs.'

The Solicitor General paused as the nature of the case struck him afresh. 'I think, you know, that it is the oddest case I have come across. We will win, probably, but the casualties, as it were, in doing so will far outweigh the victory. Still, there we are,' he added as he made his way to the door.

Carter looked up as the Solicitor General re-entered the robing-room. 'Well,' he said without preamble. 'What have you got to offer now?'

'We'll go up from $100,000 bucks to $120,000 – 90 per cent odd – on condition that you drop the defamation side and the settlement is one which is on terms endorsed on counsels' briefs.'

'No statement?'

'No. No statement.'

'In that case, we go on. Give that and you could probably keep your money. Still, there it is. But the judge won't like it.'

'No, I suppose not. Coming out for a sandwich?'

'No thanks, Clive. Better press on with this.'

'See you then.' The Solicitor General took his gown off and left the room. But Reginald Carter didn't hear as he plunged back into the problem of how to protect a minority shareholder.

Over coffee, Bill turned an anxious face to Charles Gray as he asked, 'I know we've been over and over it, but do you really think it is as bad as Mr Carter seems to think?'

'Oh, he has to be a bit cautious. Look at it from his point of view. He tells you he reckons the case is difficult. Then, if it is lost, no one can say he didn't warn you. But if you win, well then, our Mr Carter has done better than we thought he might. Better than over-optimism isn't it?'

'Yes, I suppose so.' But the worry of days, weeks, months,

the worry of nearly two years, was now becoming horrifyingly disturbing in the reality of the event. Grace looked drawn and white, and Bill also looked as though the going had been pretty tough. Both had supported the other as the case had drawn closer, but each had had their nights more and more disturbed by the thought of the enormity of what it was that Grace was undertaking. The appreciation that they, two little people, were daring to defy the Government hadn't exactly made for peace of mind.

Yet now Grace would have given up life itself rather than turn back, and Bill, in friendship, love and finally marriage, had come to carry the full weight of her burden with her. Fortunately for her, for at times she had felt the lack of strength to continue; he was a very strong man. And just now they were sharing courage by holding hands under the table.

'May it please your Honour, I'll call my first witness, the plaintiff. Mrs Grace Hulman please.' She got up, feeling terribly nervous. As she walked to the witness stand the judge sighed to himself. He had hoped it would have been settled.

'I am to take it then, am I Mr Carter, that the whole issue is still live?'

'Yes, your Honour.'

The judge nodded as he prepared to take his notes of all that struck him as relevant as the days of the trial went by. Parts of the evidence underlined in red, were to be used in his judgment on liability, or in summing up, if he found himself in a position where there were defamation issues for the jury. Not a likely thing to happen, he thought. Still, if he found himself persuaded on liability, so be it, he thought. But he didn't envy Carter his task.

The oath was administered, but had Grace been asked what she had said, she wouldn't have known. The judge, sensing the turmoil beneath her fairly calm exterior, nodded gravely to her, and in a humane attempt to help her in her isolation in the witness-box, said: 'Now, Mrs Hulman, I would like you to remember to speak clearly enough for that lady there,' he gestured to the farthest away member of the jury, 'to hear. That is very important. Also, you may find you are giving evidence for a long time. Would you like a chair?' He finished on a gentle note with a reassuring smile to her.

She managed a fairly firm, 'No thank you, sir.'

Very well, but if you change your mind, make sure you let me know.' And his concern for her and slight smile helped restore the damage to her nerves. She had vaguely dreaded the thought of actually giving evidence, but even so was wholly unprepared for the shaft of almost paralysing fright when the moment came for the long, exposed walk to the witness-box. But the judge had made her feel better, and though her heart was still pounding she found she was ready as Carter gently and slowly led her into her evidence.

To begin with, the questions covered what everyone knew: from her name, through her marriage to Frank, to just before Frank's death. And Carter was glad to see her confidence returning as she became used to the process of listening, thinking, and giving an answer.

'Now, Mrs Hulman. I would like to turn to the sort of man your husband was.' And she began to sketch Frank as a person, and the figure she had known so well in the past began to take on an identity in the minds of the jury. And because Frank looked what he was, Carter had a photograph given to the jury to see, and they saw that he had a face which seemed to support what Grace claimed for him; a man to trust, a careful man, someone you would probably like had you met him. But also something of his strength of character came through: his acceptance of hard work and thoroughness – all the things which by middle age become set in a man's face.

And Carter watched the judge, gauging the impression he was forming of Frank Newton. Good, he thought, for the judge was taking a careful note of all the plaintiff was saying and underlining part of it. But Carter was acutely aware that the judge's impression of Frank, the linchpin of the case, had to be better than good. More work on it had to be done.

'Thank you. Now I would like to turn from the question of the sort of man your husband was to the business of flying. When did he first become interested in it?'

She considered. 'I think it must have been about sixteen years ago, maybe a bit longer,' she replied.

'And what brought it about?'

'Really, the practice. Frank had been doing very well and at much the same sort of time, my present husband was becoming interested in horses; he does a lot of racing and training now. And, if I remember correctly, it was then that Frank began to find himself being asked to do that sort of specialized work, which began to mean travelling. At first he used the car, trains and airlines, but it was all very inconvenient. So he started flying lessons and got his licence and then his first plane.'

Together, they traced Frank's flying history, the types of planes he had had; and she produced the flying logs which he had kept over the years.

'And when did he get the Cessna 172?'

'About two or three months before the accident.'

'It was a new plane to him?'

'Yes.'

'And how did he set about flying this new plane? Did he, as it were, get in and learn by experience, or what?'

'Oh no. That wouldn't have been like him at all. He had a friend . . .'

'Would that be a Mr Andrew Cairns?' Carter interposed.

'Yes.'

'You were saying?'

'Yes. Well, Andrew, who's an old friend, though younger than Frank was, had a Cessna 172, so before Frank flew he went up with Andrew several times.'

'Mr Cairns will be giving evidence, your Honour, but before I leave this, Mrs Newton – I apologize, Mrs Hulman, of course – I would like you to answer this. I preface it by asking you whether you have seen the report on this accident prepared by the office of Air Accidents, the published report, that is?'

'Yes, I have seen it.'

'Good. In it the observation is made that in the opinion of the Chief Investigator of Air Accidents, and I quote, "The pilot of the Cessna 172 was relatively inexperienced in the flying of that aircraft". Would you accept that?'

But before she could answer the Solicitor General was on his feet.

'I object, your Honour. My learned friend should know better than to seek expert opinion from a layman.'

'He's right, Mr Carter. I don't think you can ask that question of this lady.'

'Very well, your Honour.' Then turning back to Grace he continued. 'Now I should like to consider with you your husband's condition as it would have been when he set out for the airstrip. Tell me, had he been overworking recently?'

'No more than usual. But he did work hard, he had always done so.'

'Harder than usual?'

'No, in fact on that day in particular his workload had been quite light.'

'And for the week, month or so, before then?'

'Much the same as always. If anything a bit less I think.'

'Did he have any worries that you were aware of? Not trivial, but anything which would have been disturbing?'

'No.'

'Tell me, were you and your husband happy together?' Her answer was only just audible but carried in the Court to all ears. It was a 'Yes' that would have brooked no argument.

Charles Gray was feeling pleased with the way it was going. Grace had settled down well and was making a very good witness.

An hour and twenty minutes after Grace Hulman had taken the stand, Reginald Carter sat down, the examination in chief of his first witness completed.

And as he sat down the Solicitor General rose quickly to his feet. 'How old was your husband, Mrs Hulman?'

'Fifty-five when the accident happened.'

'Fifty-five. I see. And how many partners did he have?'

'None.'

'None? But it was, I think, a very busy practice. That is correct, isn't it?'

'Yes, but he could handle it.'

'But it made considerable demands on him?'

'I don't think they were too great.'

'Well, let us consider that together. Was he ever called out at night?'

'Yes of course. He was a vet.'

'How many times a week would you say?'

'Oh I don't know. Maybe once or twice a week.'

'Oh come, Mrs Hulman. More than that, surely.'

'Maybe a little more,' she agreed.

'And of course there would be the more disturbing calls, wouldn't there? I have in mind calls at anything after about 4.30 or 5 in the morning which would take him from his bed, but be too late to permit him to return to it, yes?'

'Yes, occasionally.'

'More than occasionally, I think, Mrs Hulman. I understand it was something which happened quite often. Early-rising farmers discovering an animal which had become sick in the night. Wasn't that the case?'

'Sometimes.'

'Once or twice a week, perhaps?'

'Sometimes.'

'And, of course, neither you nor your husband could predict such occurrences?'

'No.'

'And so there would be no question of going to bed early in anticipation, as a business man might who had an early train to catch. That is correct, isn't it?'

'I suppose so.'

'And so there were days, weren't there Mrs Hulman, when your fifty-five-year-old husband would find himself very tired, by reason of an early call, perhaps in a run of disturbed nights?'

'Yes, sometimes he was tired. But then he would go to bed early the next night.'

'Oh yes, I appreciate that. But it would mean, would it not, that it would only be after having had to spend the whole day tired that he could remedy it by early sleep at night – the next night?'

'Yes.'

'And you say that there were times when he would go to bed early to catch up on his sleep?'

'Yes.'

'But then I suppose there were times when this would be frustrated by calls for his services during the night which, he had hoped, would have been an undisturbed early night?'

'Sometimes.'

'Enough of this, and I suppose he would become considerably overtired.'

'I don't think it ever happened quite like that.'

'I see. But let us go further. As a matter of habit, did your husband read at night?'

'Not always.'

'When not?'

'If he was tired.'

'Then he would go straight to sleep – a conscious choice?'

'Yes.'

'But if he chose to read, then he would read until he felt sleepy and then go to sleep?'

'Yes, of course.'

'So you would say your husband was quite a good personal judge as to whether he was or wasn't tired?'

'I think that's a stupid question . . .' But she got no further, for the judge coughed gently and having caught her attention, said quite gently but inflexibly, 'Mrs Hulman, I can understand your vexation, but you must let counsel ask what they want to ask, and you may rely on me to prevent questions which should not be asked. So do not comment: merely confine yourself to answering the questions, even if they do strike you as, er, a trifle silly.'

'I'm sorry, sir.'

'That is quite all right, but remember what I have said. Now go on.' And he nodded to the Solicitor General, who courteously acknowledged with an 'I'm obliged'. Then turning to Mrs Hulman, he continued. 'Now, I would like an answer to my . . . silly question, Mrs Hulman. Do you want me to repeat it?'

'No, was he a good personal judge as to his state of tiredness at night? Yes, he was.'

'And he read at night?'

'Yes, sometimes, if he wasn't too tired.'

'But Mrs Hulman, that is not quite accurate, is it? Didn't he sometimes, occasionally, pick up a book, or something he wanted to read, but then fall asleep over it? Think well, Mrs Hulman, for you are under oath. It happened, didn't it?'

Her 'Yes' was clear, but it was also clearly a reluctant answer.

'And that would suggest, Mrs Hulman, that he hadn't realized how tired he was, wouldn't it?'

'Not necessarily.'

'But yes. Necessarily so. Or are you suggesting your husband picked up his book, not to read but to sleep over?'

'No.'

'Thank you. Now when did that last happen?'

'I have no idea.'

'Really? Well perhaps I can help you. Do you remember two gentlemen from the office of the Chief Investigator of Air Accidents coming to see you?'

This jogged her memory. 'Yes. And I know what you are going to bring up. I remember now, Frank did fall asleep that night as he was reading.' And it wasn't until much later, long after the case had finished, that she really remembered that Frank hadn't been reading, but had dozed off in the quiet moments between helping her with a crossword.

'Yes Mrs Hulman. Frank did, indeed, fall asleep that night as he was reading – an overtired man. But no doubt he would have awoken refreshed for the new day, – that is, had he not been woken up on that morning, of all mornings, at 5.50. But you don't know that, do you Mrs Hulman? For usually you and Frank would not have woken until nearly two hours later, at 7.45. Is that correct?'

'Yes.'

'And so, Mrs Hulman,' he paused that all might appreciate the importance of the question. 'I think we may safely conclude that had your husband lived until the night of February 8th, then it would have been an early night, a night on which to catch up on lost sleep, no?'

'I don't know.'

He paused, the point made, and moved a sheet of paper across in front of him to refresh his mind on the other point to be handled with this witness.

'Oh yes. Now we can turn to another matter? Your husband's radio set in the Cessna. Perhaps you can help us on that. He had been to Christchurch, I think, and that was two days before the accident. Do you remember?'

'Yes.'

'At what time did he get in that evening?'

'I can't remember.'

'I see. Well, perhaps I can assist you. Now think back. He came home and was a trifle angry that the radio in his nearly new plane had broken, and he told you about it, didn't he?' It was a long shot, and as he watched her he wondered whether it would come off. And as he watched her searching her memory, he thought, no, not a chance, but it had been worth a try. Then suddenly she remembered. Frank had grumbled about it, but not having had a good day herself, she'd been impatient to tell him about it and had hardly listened to him. She'd had a row in committee with June Springer, and Frank had only been interested in his wretched radio.

'Yes, I do remember,' she replied, for she was a very truthful witness, which was something the judge noted. Almost too truthful for her own good, he thought.

'Did you eat together that evening?'

'Yes.'

'So he was back by when?'

'Maybe 6.30 or so.'

'And he was worried about his radio?'

'Yes.'

'Tell me, where did he tell you it had broken?'

'I can't remember what he said, but he mentioned about only just having got off the ground when it went.'

'Were you doing anything that evening that required his being home by any special time?'

'No, I don't think so.'

'So if he had been an hour or so later it wouldn't have mattered?'

'No. But I don't see what this is all about.'

'It is not for you to ask me questions, Mrs Hulman. But I think I will answer it on this occasion. You have told us just how very careful your husband was as a person. Yet, when in no hurry, and when still within a short distance, apparently, of Christchurch Airport his radio fails – and at a time when one would expect men capable of repairing it to be at work there – it appears that rather than turn back in the interests of safety he chose to fly the distance home with no radio. I trust that makes it crystal clear, Mrs Hulman?'

And he sat down, well pleased at the unexpected bonus which his little hunch had brought. No one in the past had thought to ask Mrs Hulman for information about the radio and since he had cleared Christchurch Departures on take-off, no one had known quite when his radio had failed. Yes, he thought to himself, it goes well, my boy, very well.

It had all passed, or appeared to have passed her counsel by without moving him in the slightest. But beneath that exterior of unconcern, Reginald Carter, QC, was wondering what the hell he could do to repair the unexpected damage: something their case could ill stand this early on.

John Prescott, QC, rose slowly and very deliberately to his feet and with wonderful effect for someone of his short but portly build. Once on his feet, he took all the time in the world to apply himself to the task of beginning his cross-examination of the woman. He had a rather fruity, pompous voice.

'Mrs Hulman. I appear for the second defendants, Paranational Airlines. And you sue them in negligence, saying that it was a fault on their part – or in this case, on the part of their crew – which brought about the accident. Tell me, have you any idea as to the amount of experience a man has to have before he is permitted to become a co-pilot on the flight deck of such an aircraft, let alone a captain? Have you any idea of the medical requirements these men have to satisfy to retain their positions as aircrew? And that, at best, none of them will be allowed to fly beyond the age of fifty-five? And . . .'

But Carter was on his feet. 'Yes Mr Carter?' the judge cut Prescott short.

'Only my learned friend's eloquence and superb delivery, which I confess held me absolutely spellbound, prevented my objection earlier, your Honour. But I fear I must interrupt to point out, in case it's slipped his mind, that now is not the time for speeches, and . . .' He stopped as the judge cut in, but though Carter was silenced not so the little burst of laughter which ran round the Court.

'Yes, he's quite right, Mr Prescott. And of course you will keep it in mind that you face a lay witness who, if one defines your, er, remarks to her as a number of questions, would not be competent to deal with any of them. Now, can we get on?'

Prescott, quite satisfied that the jury would now be beginning to draw parallels between a 55-year-old vet as a pilot and the members of the aircrew, murmured, 'I am obliged to your Honour.' The judge looked at John Prescott for a few moments, but held the rebuke he had in mind in check. Then he turned to Grace Hulman and said, 'Mrs Hulman, I want to be clear on a point. In your pleadings – I assume you are familiar with them and that you sanctioned them before your solicitor delivered them . . .' She nodded. 'Please don't nod, Mrs Hulman. It presents a great deal of difficulty to a shorthand writer who cannot hear a nod, nor do I believe there to be a symbol for a nod.' He smiled at the slight drollery.

'Yes,' she said.

'Well, in your pleadings you deny that your husband was a tired man at the time of this accident. Do you still maintain that standpoint, in view of your evidence in answer to the Solicitor General?'

She hesitated, well aware of the importance of it, and wished she could avoid an answer. But she knew that would be worse than silence. 'I think that, yes, he was perhaps a little tired, but no tireder than was often the case, and not so tired that it would affect his ability to fly with his usual skill.'

The judge nodded. Quite a cogent answer, he thought, but clearly the man was tired. 'Thank you,' he said. Then he nodded to John Prescott to continue.

'Mrs Hulman, your husband had a busy practice?'

'Yes.'

'And no partner?'

'That's correct.'

'And he was in the full vigour of an active, fit man?'

'Yes.'

'In love, one might say, with his work?'

'You could put it that way.'

'It would always come first without complaint on his part?'

Her mind went back to the trip to Wellington together, which had never taken place, and she answered 'Yes.'

'Not a man to retire early?'

'No.'

'Nor a man who would welcome anything less than full employment?'

'It depends what one considers is full employment,' she countered.

'Quite, but in ordinary terms I have in mind that it would make him restless and perhaps unhappy to suddenly find that instead of a busy day ahead he was faced with several hours of waiting before he could go to his next appointment?'

'No, he wouldn't have liked that.'

'So we may take it, may we, that your husband didn't have it in mind to enter semi-retirement when your son entered the practice. That was the intention, wasn't it?'

'Yes, but I don't see . . .'

'I think you will.' He hitched his gown around himself before addressing her again. 'Is your son a lazy man?'

'No, of course not.'

'I see. Now concerning the practice. It would appear that there wasn't any great prospect of the practice becoming very much greater in the years ahead?'

'No, except there was scope for again taking on the minor work which my husband had got rid of.'

'But that would have represented a small addition?'

'It would have been more work.'

'But not enough to be a practice, a worthwhile practice on its own?'

'No.'

'So we come to this, do we? Your husband, who had no intention of entering any form of semi-retirement, is carrying on a practice which is big but has little prospect of any appreciable growth, but into which he is to introduce his son – not a lazy man – to give, in the end result, two hard-working men enough work to do and to avoid under-employment for either of them?'

'That is one way of putting it.'

'It's the only way, isn't it?'

'I don't think so. My son would, I suppose, have generated some of his own work and I expect that my husband's reputation would have increased and he would have gone farther afield for important work, especially in racing.'

Carter had been making few notes as he listened to Prescott getting into deep water, and he thanked God that the man was making a pig's ear of what had started out as quite a good point. So easy to do.

The Solicitor General was bitterly regretting the agreement he had reached with Prescott to let him deal with the point, and wondered whether he would get out of it with anything left.

'That may have been a hope for the future, but it would have taken years to get to that point, wouldn't it? I mean, it wouldn't have been a quick, dynamic, overnight growth?'

The judge smiled quietly to himself. It was always a trifle amusing when counsel began to make a balls-up. Had it been a junior counsel, he would have helped. But men of Prescott's experience? No way.

'I agree.'

'So isn't it a fact that your husband, in anticipation of the time his son would join him, was carrying a practice which was very heavy indeed? So heavy that even when his son joined in it would still mean there was enough work for each to avoid under-employment?'

'I don't think I would accept that. When Graham came in,

I think it would have meant more that my husband would have fewer disturbed nights, would have been home more often in the evenings and for lunch, and had a few more days off, more golf at weekends, and so on.'

'And, in those circumstances, had they come about would you have said your husband was taking it easy?'

'I suppose not.'

'So it comes down to the fact, does it not Mrs Hulman, that in preparation for the advent of his son into the practice, your husband was, and had been for some time, over-employed, had been over-working. Which, when joined by his son, would have reduced to a level which other professional men would have regarded as reasonable?'

'No, I wouldn't agree that he was over-working. Working hard, yes.'

'Too hard, I suggest. So hard it was a feature of his life to be over-tired. Indeed, as we have heard, he fell asleep on the night before the accident without meaning to.' And he tried to lose her denial by the swirl of movement in sitting down and saying a loud 'Thank you, Mrs Hulman.'

But Carter was on his feet for re-examination without a pause. 'My learned friend chooses to break the encounter off on this point at this stage, Mrs Hulman, so perhaps we can go on. I can't give evidence, but in the course of the past year or two, would I be correct to say that you have come to some appreciation of the workload carried by a successful solicitor or barrister?'

'I know the hours you put in,' she replied, and there was a faint laugh in Court.

'Yes. Well, would you say your husband worked as hard?'

'No. I wouldn't have stood for it.' And this time the members of the public and Press laughed out loud and some of the jury smiled.

'Quite. So much for my learned friend's point.' It was said very dryly, and not said until there had been a silence to form an unrippled pool of concentration for it to be dropped into.

'Unless your Honour has any questions?' Carter said to the judge, who shook his head. 'I'm obliged,' he said. Then, turning back to Grace, he smiled at her as he said, 'Thank you, Mrs Hulman.' As she walked away from the witness-box she heard Carter ask for Andrew Cairns.

Middle thirties, he looked as men look who live with the

weather in all its moods. He took the oath, his voice firm, assured and lively.

'Andrew Cairns, a farmer, and someone of considerable flying experience, first in the Air Force and then for business and pleasure. Some fourteen years in all I think, is that correct?'

'Yes.'

'Well, let us first look at that experience, shall we? I believe . . .'

As Grace settled herself back in her seat Bill took her hand and gave it a slight squeeze of reassurance. 'How did it go?' she whispered. 'Good, I think.' To have told her of the hopeless feeling which had begun to eat away deep within him at times during cross-examination would have done nothing for her, so wisely he kept silent.

She felt relieved, and then exhausted, and only half heard the questions and answers which, bit by bit, built up the picture Carter wanted to build of Andrew Cairns. Flying instructor in the Air Force, keen on flying since then. And more than that, a successful farmer, a man of high standards and one who would only employ the best to deal with his problems in life, and could afford to. An intelligent, aware man, someone the jury should listen to and be affected by in their judgment.

It was a slow, deliberate process, allowing all the time necessary for those who were to sit in judgment to form an impression which would remain, and not be forgotten, a fate which can so easily overtake an early witness in a long case. And only when he was quite sure that the mere mention of Andrew Cairns in a speech or in the summing-up at the end would bring back a clear memory of the witness and his evidence, did Carter begin to ask the questions, the answers to which would be heavily relied on later.

'Now. In this case the Government were at pains to create the impression that the pilot of the Cessna was a man of inexperience. You had flown with him. And I want the Court to have the benefit of your opinion of him as a pilot?'

'He was meticulous, careful, very safety conscious, and would not have dreamed of taking any plane up unless he knew it backwards. I would have flown happily anywhere with him.'

'Did he know the Cessna?'

'Yes.'

'And how did he achieve this familiarity?'

'I took him up in mine several times.'

'And by the end of that, how would you rate him on the plane?'

'Excellent.'

'It has been said that he was tired. Perhaps you'd known him to be. Can you comment?'

'I can remember him saying occasionally over a drink in the club that he was tired.'

'After a flight with you?'

'Yes.'

'Had it affected him in any way?'

'Had he not told me I wouldn't have known. And I would like to add this. When he was up with me, he was making a greater effort than he would have if he had been less familiar with the plane. But not once did he appear to have a lapse in concentration. I suppose – just as you must – that he had trained himself to work hard and go on performing well. Certainly he never showed any strain.'

'Is the flight deck of a Cessna particularly difficult to assimilate?'

'No. And if anything, Frank Newton spent rather more time familiarizing himself than I would have thought all that necessary. He was a very careful man.'

'Thank you. Now, on something else. There is no conflict on the question of his capability as a vet. Did you use him?'

'Yes, and he was excellent.'

'Just so, but the point I should like you to consider is this. As a vet he was excellent and you as a user of vets are in a position to say this. You also fly, and are well experienced in the gauging of the ability of others in that field. How would you have rated Frank Newton?'

'Very competent.'

'Oh by the way, did anyone from the Air Accidents office come to see you to find out whether Frank Newton was or was not experienced?'

'No, they did not.'

'Thank you.'

The Solicitor General took it up where Carter had left off. 'Very competent, by what standard, Mr Cairns?'

'Private pilot standards.'

'Quite. Which are not nearly as high as those for commercial work?'

'You can have a relatively poor commercial pilot and a private pilot who is comparatively the better pilot.'

'Oh yes, but the fact remains that to hold a private pilot's licence requires infinitely less of a man in knowledge, experience, and in physical terms than to hold a commercial licence. Correct, I think?'

'Yes.'

'And good though Frank Newton may have been, you are not, I presume, seeking to equate him with a commercial pilot of the standard one would expect on the flight deck of large passenger aircraft run by an airline with one of the highest safety records in the world? Or do you indeed seek to do just that?'

And realizing the trap and destruction of credibility if he tried to go that far, Andrew Cairns answered 'No.'

'Thank you.'

'Now, I would like your opinion on another point. Please consider the following hypothetical case. You take off from Christchurch but within minutes of take-off your radio fails. It is within working hours. You are in no hurry to get home. Would you fly to Masterton in silence so that, should an emergency occur, you would not be able to be contacted, or make contact, or would you turn back to see if your radio could be fixed?'

Andrew thought about it, but nothing came to his mind with which to take the edge from it. 'I don't know the full circumstances so I can't really answer.'

'But within the circumstances I describe?'

'With only those to think about, well, I probably would have turned back.'

'I see. Thank you Mr Cairns.'

'Mr Cairns.' John Prescott's voice was soft and slow. 'In answer to my learned friend Mr Carter, you said this: "Frank spent rather more time familiarizing himself than . . ." and I stress this part of your answer "than I would have thought all that necessary". Do you remember?'

'Yes.'

'What precisely did you mean by that?'

'Just that he was a very thorough man.'

'Aren't you a thorough man?'

'Yes.'

'As thorough as Frank Newton?'

'I think so.'

'And he spent more time than you would have thought necessary, more than you would have needed to spend for the same job?'

'Maybe.'

'Was he a mentally slower man than yourself, this professional man?'

'I wouldn't have though so, not in conversation.'

'And so, not in taking ideas?'

'Probably not.'

'Tell me then, can you give us any idea why this man who you equate with yourself took longer than you would have thought necessary to do the job?'

'I can't speculate. Perhaps he was just making doubly sure of things before going on.'

'Or, I suggest, he might simply have been an over-worked man whose tired brain was a little slow. Thank you, sir.'

Back on his feet again, Carter went straight in. 'Or, as you said, Mr Cairns, he might have been spending a little more time than even you, a careful man, might, to ensure he really was fully conversant with all he needed to be?'

'Yes.'

'And in your view he was a very careful man?'

'Yes.'

'You were asked to speculate concerning a radio failure. I suppose that at best, if you had turned back . . .'

But the Solicitor General was on his feet. 'Really, your Honour! My learned friend should know better than to lead his own witness.'

'Yes, please be careful, Mr Carter.'

'Very well. Let us assume, Mr Cairns, that you have taken off a little after four o'clock. What, in your view, would have been the earliest you could have presented your aircraft to a technician to examine your radio if your return had been to Christchurch?'

'Maybe after clearance and finding out where to go, and finding the guy . . . oh, near five, I suppose.'

'And in your experience, what would the chances have been of getting anyone to do a repair job starting then?'

'Very small.'

'And if the repair was done, would you have known how long it would have taken?'

'No, of course not.'

'Or whether, even if started, it would be successfully completed that night?'

'No, and also I would have had in mind a silent return to Christchurch.'

'I see. And would you have considered these points as you flew away? Would they have affected your decision to return?'

'Yes they would. And with those things in my mind and the fact that, if seriously delayed, I may face a night flight, and without a guarantee of the repair being finished that night, I think I would have decided to continue and not return. Especially bearing in mind that from Christchurch to Masterton doesn't involve going near any main airport.'

'Thank you, that is all – unless your Honour has any questions?'

The judge shook his head. 'OK Mr Cairns. Thank you for your help.'

The judge, looking at his watch and noticing it was 4.35, said, 'Ten o'clock on Monday, I think,' and, to the usher's call to be upstanding, strode out, the first day of the trial finished.

Walking together to their adjacent offices, Carter and Gray talked it over. Their conclusion was that Frank Newton hadn't come out of it nearly as well as they had hoped he would. That he was tired would be unshakeable now. Experienced? Yes, but in comparison with pilots of a commercial airline? Not in the same league.

'What are you doing for the weekend?'

'Fishing,' the solicitor replied.

'Lord, you chaps have it easy, don't you?' the barrister said. 'I've got a solid weekend's work to do.'

'You chose it, Reggie,' Charles Gray replied.

'Sometimes I wonder why.' And they parted.

Grace and Bill spent the weekend quietly at home and weren't disturbed because, as yet, the case hadn't caused that much excitement.

Chapter Nineteen

Christopher Silaman had heard the opening.

Dear Prime Minister,
Today all of us have been reminded of the catastrophe of some two years ago, and today, in the opening of the case, mention was made of evidence which is to be called, the nature of which may well be considered to have a bearing on the cause of the accident. I cannot comment here for of course it is not for me to consider this in the context of the case. However, I am very conscious of a personal failure which, but for today, I would not have appreciated existed. I held the job of your Minister of Transport. My failure was that of the Ministry, in failing to discover all that those who represent Mrs Hulman have discovered. I take responsibility for this failure.

It is therefore with these matters in mind and the fact that it was upon a lack of complete information that you came to the personal decisions that you did at the time, and which are now questioned, that I feel compelled to offer my resignation. As you know, I had no part in the decisions made. However, it was at the Press conference which I originally held that Frank Newton first appeared to become blamed. My failure in that Press conference – suggested by yourself – weighs with me. I don't suggest, necessarily, that had we had all the information now gathered it would have made any difference to events that followed, views expressed, or political decisions taken. But it might have done, and had it done so, then it may have been that the present case would not have been brought. I know not.

Finally, I must thank you. When I first entered Government I knew little of politics and the detailed and personal interest you took was invaluable. Indeed, it led, by reason of your greater experience, to many of the early decisions affecting my portfolio, which would not have been mine in my lack of experience. I was deeply conscious of your early interest and guidance, which with your wealth of experience and appreciation of the greater political issues involved in the decisions of those early days, ensured that there was a cohesion in policy which, I fear, I could not have fully appreciated. I must thank you, too, for the interest and detailed guidance you gave following this disaster. Without it I would have had grave difficulty in discharging my duty. And it can only be with infinite regret that I find I have to write this letter now in the knowledge that, despite your interest, I have nevertheless failed you. My regret is particularly poignant in view of the fact that now, having held the job for something over two years, I feel that I have reached the stage of experience in my office where I can, as it were, be independent in my function, and be relied upon by you with confidence; a pity I was not as advanced along the political road two years ago.

Again I must thank you for your many kindnesses, and I trust that I may continue to serve you and the Party in whatever capacity it is decided I would be of most use.

Yours,
Christopher Silaman
Minister of Transport

Christopher Silaman read the letter through carefully and, happy with it, turned to the next.

Dear Sir,
Attached is my letter of resignation to the Prime Minister which, I think, speaks for itself, and which you may publish.

With best wishes,
Christopher Silaman
Minister of Transport

But he didn't ring for his confidential secretary yet. Soon, he intended to, and then she would photocopy both letters before carefully timed distribution to editors of all major papers, one in advance of the others. The original to the Prime Minister would be delivered to his office, but not before all the editors had received theirs. Not that the Prime Minister would be able to deal with the matter easily, for he was on his way to a conference in Brussels.

Before the Minister called his secretary, he wrote the following additional note by hand:

Dear Prime Minister,
Two years ago you were bloody worried that the whole miserable mess would spill over and you needed a scapegoat to cover it. You will remember you forced me to sign a letter of resignation, in which you comfortably divorced yourself from your own decisions – terribly misguided in the event – on insurance cover to be carried.

I have thought carefully about this and have decided that I am not prepared to be used in this way. For what it is worth, I think that there is now no way in which you will be able to avoid the consequences of your deceit, not merely on the decisions you took, but after the crash when I reckon you went overboard in covering the whole thing up. I think this case will show up the cover for what it was – a cheap political move to try and retain power, and done at the horrendous cost to an unknowing public.

I can't take any credit in something I went along with, and not a great deal more in resigning now, but at least I think that I have come to my senses at long last and I am buggered if I am going to go along with the whole thing any further. So I suggest you accept my resignation.

You will note that the terms of my letter don't let any chinks of light in on the cover up, as such. Having gone along with it, I think I have no option but to honour the code. However, I give you fair warning that my continued silence can only be secured if you simply accept my resignation. I think I have defused my earlier letter of resignation held by you, but if you use it, then it's war. And if you seek to discredit me with the Party or disturb my seat, then it will be bitter war.

I hope it won't come to this, and to avoid it, I am prepared to sit on the sidelines for the few remaining years you may have as leader, if somehow you get round the present problem.

Yours,
Chris

He read it through, then added a PS. 'You once said something about learning to use the tools of the trade; perhaps this is what it is all about!'

Then he leaned back in his chair to think the whole thing through again. He had slipped into Court that morning and heard Carter's opening, and now he wondered what would be the best thing to do to avoid political annihilation. Even having written the letters, he wasn't sure. Send the letters, or hold his hand and pray that the Prime Minister would come up with a political stroke that would save all their necks? If only he could be sure of that. But gnawing away at him was the fact of the earlier letter he had so foolishly signed as the price of being kept in the fold.

He stared out of the window and wished he had a crystal ball. The problem circled in his mind. If the Prime Minister acted first and the earlier letter became news, then he, Christopher Silaman, was dead. But if he sent his in now he was, perhaps, just badly wounded. But need he even be wounded? Would the PM get out of it? It would be an awful pity, he thought to himself, if in the result it transpired that the PM would not have used the earlier letter. What to do, Chris? What to do? Head in hands, he gazed sightlessly across the room. Finally he decided to think it out over the weekend, to do nothing precipitate. But it went round and round in his mind as he wondered which course to take.

'Would you like a drink, sir?'

The Prime Minister looked up at the air hostess and was struck, as he usually was these days, by pretty girls. And the thought floated into his mind that, away from his own front doorstep, thank God, he might be able to arrange a bit of fun. He looked at her more carefully and saw the girl had freckles. He liked freckles, and her Irish auburn hair made the paleness of her skin very sexy, as sexy as her long legs and beautiful figure. Not bad uniforms, he thought. And he wanted her slim firmness of youth: to forget his age, to forget the straightjacket of the position he held which had made him give up the little pad he had had in the capital when he'd come to such prominence that people would notice and remember him. And he wanted to forget a wife who was now just a terribly dreary habit, held expensively together in a shape, only to sag in bed.

'Yes.' And he smiled. She recognized it straight away. The world over, tired men who had killed life for the sake of ambition produced such smiles, lust lighting the weary eyes. Sometimes she gave them the answer they wanted and sometimes not. As she looked down at him she thought, why not? Might be something to remember, and she reckoned he was probably in pretty good shape. Just occasionally, a guy like him had something to offer, apart from a bloated belly, a tired dork and an apology for an orgasm. At least they all had one thing in common: they were all well scrubbed. So she let her eyes be held for a second longer than a hosty's eyes stayed when her answer was no, then got him a gin and tonic.

Pleased with the 'perhaps . . . probably yes', he thought about it for a few moments as he went over the schedule in front of him. And he smiled as he saw a slot available by making a few minor alterations. Yes, he reckoned, he could fit her in after about ten the next evening. Then he tore a scrap of paper off the pad he was using and wrote 'Supper ten tomorrow and stay? If so, ring me at hotel six sharp'. When she collected his empty glass the scrap of paper changed hands, and later she smiled in passing and nodded. Then he dismissed it from his mind as he returned to his papers.

He had been delayed leaving Wellington until midday, so as to be briefed on the case. He'd been a bit upset that the wretched judge had refused the Solicitor General's application, but not surprised. But the outline of some of the evidence Carter had mentioned he would be calling had been a bit of a stoner. For a long time, of course, he had realized the dangers of the case, but reckoned that if the worst came to the worst he could handle it. The past insurance cover balls-ups were well covered now, and with dear old Christopher's letter as a first line of defence, he reckoned he would be able to keep the line from being breached, though it might be a bit rough.

But if Brussels went well, he could use that to swamp the media, and he was pleased that he had had the inspiration to leak the abortion business. Pity he had had to, but it was good news value. And it had been well worth creating the bit of fuss with the Union people on relativities just now. Get everyone hot and bothered, but be easy enough to cool down when it was safe. And the nuclear and fishing business, all good stuff, and with a bit of luck there would be a little bloodshed when they arrested the next boat. Yes, he thought to himself, with all that jacked up there should be plenty to keep the Press and public occupied over the next week or so. And if that wasn't enough, then there was always the arms business to leak.

But the problem, of course, was timing. If he had to use poor Chris in this business it had to be timed to a nicety. He read the statement which the Deputy Prime Minister would give if things got too hot in his absence, and smiled at the injured innocence of a Government which was displaying the highest degree of integrity in doing its best now to make amends for the past error of one of its Ministers. There were two statements for his Deputy to use: the first dealt with an error which came about because of lack of all the information surrounding the facts of the crash; and the second was for use in the unlikely event of the case going very badly, for use if people began to think that there was something more sinister to the Government's handling of the business than merely a mistake on interpretation of incomplete fact. Yes, if it looked as though the water was going to get too deep, he thought, then there was the second line of defence. And that would be OK, he thought.

And then he turned to the photocopies of the letter he had drafted for Christopher to sign just under two years ago. With them before him he felt relieved that he had had the foresight to have it done. It was a letter which in one way was a trifle odd. It only had at most three paragraphs – one to the page and so could be composed, at the last minute, in different ways:

'Dear Prime Minister,

'Acutely aware as I am of the fact that as your Minister of Transport I have failed and misled my colleagues by reason of that failure, and aware of the gravity of this, I consider that I have no option but to relinquish my office. I do so in the sincere hope that it will make it plain, as is right, that I accept the full responsibility for my decisions and for the matters upon which I advised you and our colleagues.

'With the volume of work involved in governing a country which has a strong tradition, at least in our Party, of implementing change when it becomes necessary, and not when it is too late, and in the implementation of reforms which reflect the will of the people, no Prime Minister has any option but to rely on each of his Ministers to care for his own sphere of influence and avoid the insupportable workload it would impose on him, should we fail in this duty.' He turned to the next page.

'When first undertaking the job of Minister of Transport, I naturally reviewed expenditure. In this, as I now realize, I made a very grave mistake and substituted the ephemeral benefits of short-term gain in place of the more general policy favoured by you to contain public expenditure – a policy pursued by you not at the expense of maintaining what is necessary for the safeguarding of the framework of society, and not at the expense of placing a society of our size in any financial difficulty. In brief, I took a bad risk: one which didn't come off and which, in the result, has had disastrous consequences. In my review of the level of reinsurance cover to be placed on the international market to cover claims against those involved in the sphere of transportation and who were servants of the Government (and in this case I have in mind that Air Traffic Services), I looked only to the past. I saw an impeccable record and I weighed this against the annual insurance premium which, as money paid out of the country each year, adversely affected our balance of payments position. And I had in mind the terrible financial position which we inherited from the last Government which could only be described as the result of ineptitude and an appalling lack of responsibility.

'In the result, I saved a premium of several million dollars per annum and placed the transportation public service risk wholly with ourselves as insurers. Prior to that decision, any claim greater than ten million was met by insurers, not the Government.

'This error of judgment has cost the country dearly, and I cannot avoid the blame. And I say this with it particularly in mind that the policy I chose to follow would not, I now appreciate, have found any favour with you, but as a departmental matter, I dealt with it as I saw fit . . .'

Nodding gently to himself, the Prime Minister paused and wondered whether people would accept that he knew nothing about it, and decided that if it had to be modified, it could be done later by comment from himself when he could mention that though he knew the Minister of Transport was concerned about the cost/risk ratio he didn't know the details, had no idea he was considering making the Government its own insurer. Yes, that would do, he thought. Then he turned to the next page.

'. . . Within my sphere of influence, and as a matter upon which I could and did make my view felt, was the question of the degree of liability to be covered directly by Merlin Mutual Ltd.'

Again the Prime Minister looked up as he thought about this and the possible problem with the Opposition, who would shout 'not true'. But, he thought to himself, why not? It could always be said that he asked Christopher to consider this or, even better, that the Minister of Finance asked him, as part of the whole question of insurance, to deal with it. Well, if it came to that they might have to give it a thought, but on the face of it, it looked OK, he reflected, before returning to the letter.

'. . . In this I was concerned with profitability and noticed that the reinsurance premiums were high and were so because all but the first twenty million of any claim was to be borne on the world market, much of it with Lloyds. In looking into the risk, I noted that the highest financial element was that relating to the cover afforded to Paranational Airways. And I regret that I took the view that with such an airline, too much money was being paid out on reinsurance premium in respect of too small a risk. At my instance, this level of reinsurance was raised, with, as we now know, disastrous consequences in terms of Merlin Mutual profitability which will probably have its effect for years to come, for its debt now to the Government is large. It was a disastrous mis-judgment, and I take full responsibility for it . . .'

As he held the page in suspension, half turned for the reading of the next, the thought crossed the Prime Minister's mind that if the letter was published, someone might wonder what the hell the Merlin Mutual Board were doing. But he comforted himself with the thought that in answer to that, one might say that a Minister of the Crown would be very persuasive. And then he flicked over to the next part of the confession.

'. . . In the course of the investigation of the air crash facts were not discovered which have subsequently emerged, and for that I must, I fear, take responsibility. Normally, following a crash there is a procedure which is as slow as it is thorough. In this case, I regret that, over-persuaded as to urgency, I brought pressure to bear on the Chief Investigator of Air Accidents. I did this particularly (and I find it difficult to forgive myself for it) because I was convinced at a very early stage that the accident could only have been the fault of the pilot of the Cessna. It was a conviction born of ignorance and the arrogance of the layman, and when ostensibly supported by the opinions expressed at my Press conference, which I called prematurely, my views became set to the point of, in effect, hampering the office of Air Accidents in its search for fact. It was inexcusable, but no less inexcusable than the foisting of my views on you as matters of fact. But for this, I well know you would not have been minded to say all that you did say in public, which you said in the mistaken belief that your statements were incontrovertibly correct. I profoundly regret this . . .'

Again the Prime Minister nodded to himself. Yes, that was OK. He turned to the last page.

'. . . Therefore, for the reasons I have set out, I would be grateful if you would accept my resignation.

'Finally, I should like to end on a personal note. I have much to thank you for and I will always count it a privilege to have been permitted to serve under you. When I have come to you, as I have done occasionally for advice and support, I have always been immensely impressed by the fact that, though heavily committed, you have always made time to consider a problem and given me great help in the exercise of your experience. I merely regret that I did not have the sound sense to include the matters I mention in this letter among those I brought to you.

'It is beyond apology and it is with a very heavy heart that I find that my passing from office should be under circumstances which, I fear, must cause you distress. Again, thank you for your many kindnesses.

With best wishes,
Yours,
Christopher Silaman'

The letter read, he speculated on whether he would have to rely on it in whole or in part, and if so when? He hoped it wouldn't be necessary. He really rather liked Christopher, but all it needed now was a message to his Deputy and the letter, or those parts of it that it had become necessary to rely on, would be published. That, and suitable action by the Deputy

Prime Minister, if he wasn't back from Brussels when it broke, to swing public opinion neatly down the blind alley set for it. Pity about Chris, of course. Lost in thought, he pondered on it.

The real problem was that once he had used the letter, its usefulness was at an end. Today had inclined him to publish just the third part, but if he did, then if a more urgent need for use of the first and second parts arose, it would be dead ammunition. No one could resign twice. He was still pondering on it when the hostess disturbed him, but not before he had decided to postpone any final decision till after the weekend.

'Can I do anything for you, Prime Minister?' Diverted from his sombre train of thought, he looked up at her again, smiled quietly, and said, 'Not at the moment, thank you.'

'So, as you were leaving the club that afternoon, you are quite sure that you saw the man in the photograph, Frank Newton?'

'Quite sure.'

It was the last answer to the first examination of the first witness of the week. It was a fine Monday morning, but that seemed a long way away from the Court, where the windows collected nothing more than an occasional shaft of passing sunlight as the sole reminder to those within of the outside world.

Carter sat down and the Solicitor General rose. 'How can you be so sure, Pertwee?'

'He was the guy I saw. Like I said, if you'd known a guy you'd seen a couple of hours ago was suddenly dead, you'd remember 'im. Bring it back to mind, like. Stands to sense, don't it?'

'And what was he doing?'

'On the phone. Jist before four, wasn't it?'

'Oh, yes. But you have told my learned friend here that you saw that he had a pen and paper with him, correct?'

'Yeah, like I said.'

'Tell me, when were you first asked to recall this?'

'Aw, about a year ago. Bit less, p'raps.'

'Had the paper and pen been killed too – to engrave it on your memory?'

The judge let it ride, but decided that too much of these sort of tactics would be stopped.

'That's daft.'

'Yes, of course. So I ask you. What makes you remember the paper and pen?'

'I dunno. Just do, that's all.'

'Go back to when you made a statement first. Do you remember that?'

'Yeah.'

'You were asked if you remembered a man by the phone that day as you left the aero club at Masterton?'

'Yes.'

'You were shown a photo, and you said he was the man?'

'Yes.'

'Now think carefully. Did you volunteer that there was a man by the phone who had paper and pencil . . . was it pencil or pen, I forget?'

'I can't be sure.'

'About what?'

'Wevver I said about the pen or pencil and paper, or not.'

'And you can't say whether it was a pen or pencil either?'

'Well, no.'

'But why not? You say you saw it. What was it like?'

'I can't . . . well, I mean, it's a long time ago, isn't it?'

'Yes, indeed. And I suggest to you that if the truth be known, you don't know whether the man had a pen, pencil, or paper, or not. But that you think he did purely because it was suggested to you that he probably did have. Is that right?'

'No.'

'As you approached him, he would have had his back and left-hand side to you as he faced the phone, correct?'

'Yes.'

'And you didn't look back?'

'I don't think so.'

'You don't think so! Tell me, do you really have any clear recollection of anything more than seeing this man at the phone?'

'Well, I saw him.'

'That I accept, but can you remember which hand he held the pencil or pen in? Was he talking or writing? Where was the paper? What sort of piece of paper was it? Scrap? Pad, or what? You see the problem, Mr Pertwee. And mine is to understand how you could have seen any paper or pencil when your approach to this man on the phone was from the left and behind. Do you appreciate that problem which faces the learned judge and jury in this case?'

'Yes but I saw him.'

'But I suggest that you have no picture in your mind of a man with writing materials. But if you say you do, well, no doubt you can answer the questions I ask. Perhaps you can tell us the position of the paper. To the left or right of the phone? Can you help on that?'

Adrian Pertwee tried desperately to cast his mind back to that fleeting glance at the man on the phone who he had passed quickly with a nod on his way out of the clubhouse, his visit frustrated by the absence of the secretary. It came and went as he strove to remember. The face was there, but what else? He tried to the best of his ability, but the rest of the picture was lost and the more he tried to focus his mind on the detail, the more indistinct it all became. Finally, he had to give up and as he answered he wondered how he could have been so sure of the facts before the case had started. Maybe it was that his mind had indeed grasped at suggested fact. But now he couldn't see it, couldn't give any detail.

'No. I thought I could see it but I can't.'

'So it comes to this, Mr Pertwee, doesn't it? You are not in a position to be able to satisfy this Court that he was taking notes on paper for later reference?'

'No, s'pose not.'

'Thank you.' And John Prescott for the airline sat down.

In re-examination, Reggie Carter tried to repair the damage but the best he could do was to re-establish that though Pertwee couldn't remember details, he had had a firm impression that the man at the phone had been writing or was ready to do so. But, as the witness left, there was clear conviction in the air, felt by all in the Court, that no one would take the view that Frank Newton had in fact been taking a note. Of itself, it was not vital to the plaintiff's case, but it was undeniably another small nail in the coffin. And they were mounting up. A man so busy in his practice as to be able to look forward to taking in his son, yet not suffer underemployment as a result; a man who the night before the crash took a book to read, but fell asleep instead and was woken very early the next day; a man who was intelligent, yet for unexplained reasons seemed to take longer than expected to absorb the detail of conversion to a new aircraft; a man alleged to have been careful and safety-conscious, yet flew home on a dead radio rather than at least try to have it fixed; a meticulous man, but one who, it appeared, might well not have been taking a note of his briefing over the phone.

Peter Pardoe was next in the witness-box: the flying club secretary. Yes, he had known Frank for years. A good club member. A good pilot. Had done a lot to bring new interest into the club. A man who, despite being busy, helped other club members quite a bit. The secretary thought he was a very competent and safety-conscious man. Once Carter had established the facts and opinion of the club secretary he sat down. And the Solicitor General rose to seek to destroy the good this man had done for the plaintiff's cause.

'I am interested in one of your observations. You say Frank Newton spent time at the club in helping others?'

'Yes.'

'We know he was a very busy veterinary practitioner. Did you know that?'

'Of course.'

'Do you have other professional men in the club?'

'Yes.'

'Many as busy in their general lives as Frank Newton?'

'I suppose so.'

'And of them, did they all put in the effort that Frank Newton put in for the benefit of the club or its membership?'

'No, not at all.'

'Half?'

'No, not half. A few, maybe.'

'I see. And no doubt that didn't surprise you. After all, they were very busy men and you could hardly expect them to make the time necessary to help out to any great extent?'

'That's right. But with Frank it was a real hobby.'

'Oh, yes. I accept that. But as hobbies go, it is of a kind which makes considerable physical and mental demands. Not like an interest in model-making, something which makes few mental demands in its pursuit?'

'I agree.'

'And would you agree that the pursuit of such a hobby by a man already overstretched in his work would inevitably mean that he was pushing himself?'

'Not necessarily. He might be working very hard manually, but that wouldn't mean he was pushing himself if, after his work, he had a sort of mental hobby.'

'Indeed, one must agree. But assume he was mentally and physically tired by reason of the nature and hours of his work. Then to pursue the hobby pursued by Frank Newton as he pursued it would be pushing himself. Is that not a reasonable conclusion?'

'I am not a behavioural psychologist or psychiatrist. I can't answer.'

'Well, we will leave it. For perhaps one doesn't need to be either to draw a logical conclusion.' Satisfied with the point, the Solicitor General sat down.

John Prescott satisfied himself with a few taps to drive further home the distinction between expected levels of competence between private and commercial pilots and then he was done and Peter Pardoe's place was taken by a young policeman, Sam Coles.

Carter had been considering his approach with Sam Coles. Ground had undeniably been lost with the last two witnesses, both a disappointment. Their evidence needed a quick counter-attack, which was a pity for it had been Carter's intention to spend time with young Coles. But to do that would lose the much-needed punch now necessary to wipe out the damage. The change in tactics was immediately apparent. Suddenly, from the quiet pursuit of proceedings in a civil suit all were swiftly transported into the atmosphere of a criminal trial.

'Your name, rank and station please, officer?' And the witness was invested with the mantle of authority and credibility; a policeman giving evidence to representatives of the community who believed in the rule of law, the honesty of policemen and their integrity. The details given, Carter continued in the crisp style he had adopted. 'You knew Frank Newton, a vet practising predominantly within the area in which you are a member of the local constabulary?'

'Quite well, sir.'

'A man alleged to have been a habitually tired man. How many times did he lapse at the wheel of his car and sleep, or commit a silly offence?'

'I think he had had two speeding offences in the last few years.'

'Is speeding an offence you would normally associate with being tired?'

'No sir. If anything, it would be the reverse.'

'Quite. As a policeman you have been used to detailed and thorough training?'

'Yes.'

'You are used to observing men and their reactions?'

'Yes.'

'And you are learning to fly?'

'Yes.'

'You have flown with Frank Newton?'

'Yes.'

'As an instructor, was he good, medium or indifferent by the police standards you have been used to?'

'Good.'

'As a man in a plane, what was his approach?'

'Thorough.'

'Mentally alert at all times or not?'

'Alert.' And Carter sat down.

'You had a high regard for Frank Newton.' The Solicitor General's voice was in sharp distinction to Carter's: deliberately slow, insinuously soft, yet with a quality in it of the strength of a coiled spring. 'There is something to come' it seemed to say. And the Court was very quiet as the concentration built up by Carter's change of speed and attack was deepened by the promise in the Solicitor General's voice.

'Yes.'

'And you would certainly wish to do your best for him and the plaintiff in this case?'

'I want to see what I think was wrong put right.'

'I see. So you hold strong convictions in this case?'

'Well, er, not terribly.'

'But you take the view that Frank Newton was wrongly blamed?'

'I think that could have happened.'

'Well, let us consider how you can help. You fly?'

'Not yet, as least I have no licence yet. I don't earn the sort of money a concentrated course costs.'

'So you don't fly. I see. Did you pay Frank Newton for his help given to you?'

'No.'

'So you would consider that, if anything, you owed him a debt of gratitude?'

'No. I mean yes. But it doesn't affect my evidence.'

'No, no, no, of course not. Tell me, how old are you, er, officer?'

'Twenty-four, nearly twenty-five.'

'Hmmmm, yes. Hardly an officer with the sort of experience one might attribute to an officer of, shall we say, ten or more years standing?'

'No, but enough to make up my own mind.'

'Yes. But young people . . . but perhaps I can leave it. Let us return to flying. Have you great experience by which you can compare Frank Newton's capability as a flying instructor?'

'Well, no, but I have been taught by others and I think he was good.'

'But you haven't been taught by, say, a flying instructor whose job it has been to instruct commercial pilots?'

'No, but Andrew Cairns was in the Air Force, and I think that though older, Frank Newton was about as good, and I think both were very good.'

' "You think"? I see. It's been some years, of course, since Mr Cairns was in the Air Force?'

'Yes.'

'Police instruction, now. Do you maintain that the initial course you undertook to become a constable – with more to follow no doubt as promotion becomes a possibility – can really be equated with the course required to obtain your private pilot's licence?'

The question hung in the air until the young constable's reply took its place. 'No, sir.'

'And you are still at the beginning of the long road to a licence?'

'Yes.'

'And to promotion and further police training?'

'Yes.'

'So what little instruction you had from Frank Newton has been of a relatively elementary nature?'

'I s'pose so, but he was very good at that.'

'Oh, yes. But you are hardly in a position to be able to comment on his capability at higher levels of instruction, are you officer?'

'No, but I would think it would have been just as good.'
'But you don't know?'
'No.'
'And because of your own infancy in the sphere of flying, you cannot possibly be in a position to pass judgment on fully qualified pilots, can you?'
'No, but some seem better than others.'
'In your ignorance, that is of course understandable.' And the final comment was out and the Solicitor General sitting down before Reginald Carter could object.

Dr Wilson took the stand and did some good for the case but wasn't able to be much help. He hadn't seen Frank Newton professionally before his death for three years or so. But in cross-examination by John Prescott, the judge noted:
'Though you are a doctor, I dare say you have some idea of the sort of life Frank Newton led, and the sort of demands it would have made on him?'
'Yes.'
'Mentally, would you have said there was much the same sort of strain on busy practitioners in both fields?'
'Animals don't worry you with mental illness, and they can't talk, so you don't have to listen to their worries. But medically, of course, and because they often can't tell you about their symptoms, it must be very difficult at times. Swings and roundabouts, I'd say.'
'And you knew he was a very hard worker?'
'Yes.'
'In tiring work. Mentally tiring?'
'Yes. Could be.'
'And from a physical point of view, probably more tiring than your own work?'
'Yes, correct. Those guys sometimes have to fight at, say, a difficult calving. Beast the wrong way round. Why, I remember a night when . . .' But the QC had made his point, and his quiet 'Thank you' cut the doctor short.
He was followed by Newton's accountant. And the judge made a note 'No money worries'.

The next witness to take the stand was the Communications Technician. Without dungarees he looked oddly out of place to his friends, but in or out of them, his habits followed him wherever he went and, as he waited for the questions to begin, he gave an habitual shake of the head to get the mop of red hair out of his eyes. He had been the last man to see Frank Newton alive, except, of course, Sam Meadows, whose fleeting glimpse into the Cessna's cockpit left an image which died with him milliseconds later.

Back in a quiet, easy, style now, not displeased with the way it had gone with the policeman despite cross-examination, Carter began his examination and established the fact of the Technician's arrival at Masterton with four jobs to do; the message given him to have a look at Frank Newton's radio first. Yes, he remembered Frank. Must have been about two that he'd got to the hangar, and he'd about a couple of hours' work left to get the radio repaired, refitted and tested out.

'Was he at all put out when you told him that it was going to take a couple of hours more – this would be, I think, at about two?'

'He was all right about it.'

'Didn't press you to try and finish in a hurry?'

'No. Jist wanted to know when.'

'What happened then?'

'Gits 'is cleaning gear and starts goin' round.'

'What sort of things were you aware of him doing?'

'As I said, cleanin' and so on.'

'Pre-flight checks?'

John Prescott was on his feet in an instant. 'Really, your Honour . . .'

But he got no further as the judge indicated he had the same thing in mind. Turning to Reginald Carter, QC, he said, 'Mr Carter, surely it hardly needs me to remind someone of your experience not only to avoid asking a question of your own witness in such a way as to suggest an answer, but that if you do, then you are in grave danger of destroying the effect of his answer, if favourable. I trust I shall not have to mention it again. And particularly when one is dealing with a piece of evidence of importance.'

Carter regretted that he hadn't got away with it, but not to worry, he thought. The mechanic was not the sort of man to follow suggestions. 'I will rephrase that. Was there anything you saw or heard which led you to believe that Mr Newton was doing anything more than clean the plane at the time?'

'Yeah, I reckon so.'

'What else?'

'I 'eard 'im round the engine, few other things. Can't remember 'xactly, jist knew 'e was doin' it.'

'Doing what?'

'Like I said, pre-flight checks.'

'Thank you. Now I understand he left you for a short while at about twenty to four. Did you see him again?'

'Yeah, 'bout four 'e come out, and I 'elped 'im git the plane out.'

'Did he do anything further to the plane then?'

'No, jist gits in an' goes orf, fills her up, then dahn to the bottom of the field.'

'How do you know this?'

'I sees 'im, don't I. 'E's doin' that as I'm orf to the club-house where I left me corfee.'

'As you were drinking it, did you see him again?'

'Too true. There 'e was run up at the bottom of the field an' I'm watchin' fru the winder. Then orf 'e goes.'

'Did he hold at the beginning before take-off?'

'Yeah, I reckon 'e was on 'is finals.'

'Final checks?'

'Yeah, like I said.'

'And generally, did he seem all right to you. Tired or anything?'

'Seemed OK. Nice feller.'

The Solicitor General waived his right to cross-examine and so left it to Prescott.

'Mr Austin, you can't be sure he was doing pre-flight checks when you think he was, for if the truth be . . .' For an hour and a half John Prescott tried on the question of checks, but time and time again he was baulked by the plain commonsense of the Comms Tech. 'You didn't see them, did you?'

'No, but what else would 'e be friggin' around wiv there, you tell me, if it weren't dabbing his petrol?' and so it went tediously on.

The judge, very near the beginning, had made his note 'Pre-flight checks done' and marked the margin with a cross to remind himself much later that on this man's evidence he would base a finding of fact.

Finally, having achieved nothing save made the belief unshakable for judge and jury that if the technician identified sounds around an aeroplane then you could count on it as correct, John Prescott sat down. And the Solicitor General smiled to himself, glad he had had more sense and recognized the witness as one of a breed in whom self-doubt didn't come easily; in fact, almost never, unless you happened to have incontrovertible fact at your finger-tips to confound his self-belief. Then, and only then, would he change his mind, candidly and honestly amazed at his mistake, or dig in and call black white and be seen for the fool he was.

As Barry Austin stepped down, the judge glanced at his watch and, seeing the time as close on 4.30, adjourned for the day. As they rose, Reginald Carter, QC, felt relieved that at long last something had gone as planned for the plaintiff. And so ended the second day.

'Shall we go in here?' And the Hulmans and Charles Gray trooped off after their silk and his junior, robes billowing, into the small conference room. Seated, Carter lit his pipe and puffed for a few moments as he gathered together the things he wanted to say to the Hulmans.

'I wanted to have a chat for a moment now, because we've swum the first length and, I think, done all that we can in a general sense, to paint the picture to the judge and jury to show what sort of man Frank was. Now I won't say we aren't a trifle out of breath as it were, but by and large, I don't think it's too bad. What are your views, Charles?'

'I don't reckon we've suffered too much damage. I think Frank has come out as a nice guy, keen on flying. And all the nonsense about him being exhausted by his hobby: I reckon the jury will say "So what? The guy had interest and energy to match." But I didn't much like the Christchurch business. That, I think, was a pity. But the rest of it, to coin a phrase, is bullshit and I don't think it will matter all that much.' But what he said reflected a much greater optimism than he felt.

'Yes,' the silk murmured. 'But tell me, Grace, can you think of anything at this late hour which we might be able to use to beef up the general picture on Frank. Or you, Bill?' Grace replied for them both when she said, 'No, except maybe Marty Chalmers.'

'Yes, of course. I want to give that a bit more thought, but don't worry, I haven't forgotten him. Anything else? They thought it over, but no one could come up with any ideas.

'Right then. We'll go on again in the morning, but there is

something I want to say to the two of you. And it is something that Charles and Jeremy here,' he nodded to his junior, 'and I have given very serious consideration to. The basic problem, as we all know, is that to win we have to persuade a judge to take the view that this case isn't a statistic to chalk up as private pilot error, but something very different. It is the rare case of the lesser trained man alone being right and two experts being wrong. In setting about it we have worked hard on the basis of establishing Frank as a very special guy. But, to be honest about it, I really don't think we have quite achieved the picture we need.

'That's the first thing. And secondly, as you know, everyone is pretty short on real evidence, so statistics may play their part. Now what I would like you to think about very carefully is whether or not we ought to take our case to its strongest point, which will be at the end of our evidence, and then see if we can't settle. And by that I mean, take the money and let them water the statement down in Court just a little to something they will agree to. Now will you think about that?'

He didn't let them reply, for he wanted them to avoid a snap, blind decision based upon past obstinacy. In his own mind now he was quite certain, as were his junior and their solicitor, that it would be the best way out in the end. 'Think it over with Charles here and we can discuss it later when we've seen a bit more of the game. Now, tomorrow I plan to deal with the . . .'

The conference lasted for another twenty minutes. Then Grace and Bill went with Charles for something to eat and drink, and Charles quietly explained what the lawyers saw as the best course for Grace to take: not complete victory, but some way along the road towards it. And the gentle pressure worried Grace and Bill, and they talked of nothing else but the case that night.

Chapter Twenty

It was dark outside, but the nurse hadn't drawn the curtains to the day-room yet, and no one else had bothered. She was late because a new and very distraught patient had been admitted after supper, a young girl, victim of a brutal rape. Steve Ring had seen the girl and heard her hysteria in the ward sister's office, but it meant nothing to him. Nothing had any meaning, time was no more. The past was the future, and every today was torture, immutable but, through long habit, bearable torture; the remains of the man within weeping through life, the biblical hell on earth, the just rewards of a mass murderer. In a clearer moment (one of the few) he had thought of time and his wait for death, and the thought of only forty years to go hadn't seemed so bad. But at other times the burning floating heads would torment him beyond endurance, and it was then that he had what was noted in the ward nurses' reports as a 'weepy day'. Tears of torment torn from a tortured soul in an unbearable wasteland of despair.

He was the only person in the ward addicted to barbiturates, but it was better that way. He wouldn't have known it, but the chemically induced fog was all that retained his mind in any sort of semblance of entity. In a psychiatric bottle, in suspension; a mind reserved for the treatment which, it was hoped, would one day begin the long haul back to normalcy for Steve Ring. The trial was being carefully monitored by the consultant psychiatrist and his colleague for anything that they could use to try to allay Steve's guilt. But meanwhile, he was kept away from newspapers, TV, and the radio as much as possible, and if there was talk about it in the ward, a nurse would gently steer it away to another subject.

It was dark outside and with no curtains the glass was a black mirror reflecting the ward. Steve stared at the blackness and his mind matched the nothing he saw. Other patients were grouped complacently around the television set. Some heard and saw, others gazed starkly and would have so gazed at the blank screen. Had the nurse come then, she would have touched Steve on the arm and walked him through to the other room, away from the TV. But she wasn't around and the news of the trial filled the room. As though in a dream, part of Steve's consciousness picked it up. He shook his head to lose the voice. It was a new voice talking about his murder. At first he didn't understand, didn't realize where it came from, or hear all it said. But it became compelling. He had to listen, and as the words cleared part of his mind it was led back to the past and into the reality of the moment.

Steve listened in fear and tried to shut it out, but was held transfixed by the awfulness of this stranger's intrusion into what was privately his. He couldn't escape, and try as he might he couldn't prevent his mind grasping at what he heard. It was difficult: the meaning came in and out of phase. Bits were lost, but bits were grasped and held as flotsam in the relentless grip of a drowning man. Question and answer, question and answer. It didn't seem to make sense. He listened intently and part of it stayed in his mind. Then the voice went and something else was being discussed. He stared again at the black window.

Yet as he stared his mind fought for understanding. The words reverberated in his mind. It came slowly, but eventually he understood what it was that was meant by the words. The pilot of the Cessna had been tired, the pilot of the Cessna had been tired, tired. It was, at first, just a fact. Then the fact began its tortuous process of assimilation into his damaged understanding. A case in court. This fact, too, gradually sank in. A judge to apportion blame. Tired pilot . . . blame; that linked. Altitude . . . tired pilot . . . blame. Too high . . . a crash. His crash. His fault . . . pilot tired . . . not warned . . . too high . . . crash.

The enormity of the facts grew in his mind and caused him to freeze in horror at the realization that he wasn't to be allowed to live on undisturbed in his private hell. A living judge was going to pass sentence, and the world would join in the chorus of the flaming heads. The people of his world were going to scream silently to his face: 'You did it'. He shut his eyes to keep it all away, but heard mention of his familiar hell and knew now it was too terrible a place to retreat to for sanctuary. He opened his eyes and saw a fellow patient look at him with a compassionate smile. And suddenly he knew he couldn't take any more.

'Steve, dear.' He felt the touch on his arm and looked up. The nurse saw his alarm. 'Is anything wrong?' He looked at her blankly for a moment then shook his head. She smiled compassionately. He was a tragic boy, she thought.

'Time for bed, Steve. I want you to come along for your pills now, then straight up with you, before you begin to go to sleep.' She was holding his arm as she walked him towards the dispensary. They were joined by a few of the others. She unlocked the drugs cabinet and handed two capsules and a glass of water to Steve. 'Take them now, there's a dear.' She watched him. Steve took the capsules and was about to swallow when, from the corner of his eye, he saw the girl who had been admitted that evening. Upset and in tears, she came rushing into the dispensary, and distracted the nurse for a moment. When the nurse turned back to Steve she saw him emptying his glass. She nodded and said, 'All right, dear. Now you go on up and straight into bed.' He did as he was told. As he went to the lavatory, he flushed the two capsules down the pan.

An hour later the nurse did her rounds. Steve's door was shut, as always. She looked in, as usual. He was on his side, quiet and motionless, as always. Satisfied, she left the door to his room ajar and went downstairs for a cup of tea. It was shortly before midnight. Silent in bed, he had heard the nurse open the door, heard her breathing for a moment, heard her leave, and heard her footsteps die away. Then everything was still again. Everything except the noise in his head.

Very quietly, when he thought she had gone away, he rose from his bed. Taking his pillow out of its slip, he walked in bare feet down the passage, away from the stairs, to the men's lavatories. The doors didn't lock, but he unhooked the main door and shut it behind him before he turned the lights on. Then he went to a shower. The spray arm was above his reach. He brought a chair and, putting it in the shower, reached up and grasped the arm. It was heavy stainless steel and though it gave a bit, it took his weight. Deliberately he stepped down and out of the shower, his pyjama shoulders, face and hair a little wet from the water he had shaken from the spray. But he didn't notice. Taking the pillow-slip, he tore it down one side, then the other, then tore it again longways. He had to use his teeth to start the tears. He knotted the two lengths into a rope and tied one end around his neck. Then, on the chair again, he reached the little distance up to the spray arm and knotted it firmly there. He listened to the unbroken silence of the night, then gently, so as not to shatter the silence, he tilted the chair with his feet, holding it between them so it wouldn't fall and clatter as he took his weight on his arms by holding the spray arm with both hands. The chair fell its final distance with a little thud, breaking the silence briefly.

Death came slowly. His last conscious thought before the explosion of his ruptured brain was to pray that he wouldn't wake up again in C Ward.

The editor of the *Evening Star* arrived at his office at 8.35 on the following morning, and took the call twenty minutes later. 'You wanted to speak to me?' he asked, having been told there was a girl on the phone for him, and no one else would do.

'Yes. You the editor?'

'Yeah. Who are you?'

'My name doesn't matter, but I thought you ought to know that a mental patient committed suicide last night at Bramley.'

'Yeah, and what's so special about a nut taking a dive?'

'You know the case that's on about the crash?'

'Yeah.'

'Well, he was one of the Air Controllers on duty.'

And suddenly it was news.

The third day began quietly with the evidence of Bill Hulman. And the judge noted the following part of his evidence in chief:

'When you rang Mr Newton, what time was it?'

'A few minutes short of 6 in the morning.'

'Did you understand that he was asleep when you rang?'

The Solicitor General and John Prescott, QC, let the leading question pass without objection.

'Yes.'

'Did you have to hang on for long before he answered the phone, as you might if a man was very tired and dead as . . .'

This time Prescott moved, but the judge intercepted the objection as he said, 'Mr Carter, I fear I have to make the point again. Questions please, which neither lead nor constitute comment or suggest an answer.' Then, to the jury, gravely he said, 'You will disregard the comment made by Mr Carter. He cannot give evidence, and now is not the time for him to point to conclusions. His time for that will be during his final address to you.' He paused before adding, 'But of course if independently you draw conclusions that is a matter for you.' Then he nodded to Reginald Carter, QC, satisfied that a possible point for appeal had been adequately dealt with. But, he thought, if he'd been Carter he would have done the same.

'He answered very quickly. Almost as soon as the bell rang.'

'And his voice. How would you describe that?'

'Crisp and businesslike.'

And in cross-examination the judge noted:

'Had you rung him before, early in the morning?'

'In the past, yes.'

'And you wouldn't know whether he was a tired man or not when you rang?'

'No.'

'And in the past, had he answered quickly and briskly?'

'Yes.'

'A professional habit, perhaps?'

'I couldn't say.'

Alan Johnson, who had last seen Frank Newton in the sheep field shortly after 8.30 on his last morning, came and went. Frank had been the normal Frank. It went unchallenged.

'And now, your Honour, I call my first witness concerning the state of mind of Captain Harry James Standard.' It was said with slow, deeply penetrating effect, in a voice which said 'And now we begin to get to the meat of the problem'. The silence in Court was broken only by the footsteps of the witness approaching the witness-box. A nondescript man in a blue serge suit in his late fifties; overweight, and of less than average height. A grey little man. His voice as he took the oath was quiet, barely audible. He looked acutely uncomfortable. Charles Gray felt a pang of anxiety. Would the man come up to scratch? Witnesses so often made statements, important ones, but when it came to repeating them in court, their courage, conviction, or whatever had motivated them, sometimes evaporated and with it their evidence. 'Your name, sir?'

'Patrick Sean Bates.' It carried a marked Irish accent.

'Your occupation?'

'Caretaker at Farnham Court, the block of flats on the Terrace in the city.'

'For how long have you been there?'

'Well, I can't rightly remember . . . that is, exactly, but about four and a half years. Ever since the block had people living in it.'

'Do you remember a girl called Jenny Carol?'

'Oh to be sure, I do indeed.'

'Did she live there?'

'Oh yes, she did. Number 33 on the 17th floor. A very nice

flat with a view over the city.'

'Did you know her occupation?'

'To be sure. She was an air hostess, wasn't she?'

'And when did you last see her?'

'We had a chat a couple of days before the crash, when she came in. Late afternoon it would have been.'

'Did she live alone?'

'No, that she did not. There was Captain Standard with her.'

'How long had she had the flat?'

'Maybe two and a half, three years. This captain man moved in with her just a few months before the accident.'

'When did you last see the Captain?'

'It would have been about ten the night before.'

'Before what?'

'The last time I saw the girl. The time I told you about. But that's funny, 'cos it brings it to mind that I tell a lie when I say I last saw the girl at the lift. I remember now I did catch a glimpse of her as she drove off the next morning, but not to talk to.'

'I see. Not important, but thank you for being accurate. Now, to the Captain. How was it that you saw him at ten the night before your last conversation with the girl?'

'I came up from my flat below to do a last check, and there he was along the hall waiting for the lift. It came before I got anywhere near to him so he didn't see me.'

'Was he alone?'

'No, he was not.'

'Who did he have with him?'

'A boy – about eighteen, I would have said.'

'Did you see the Captain or the boy again that night?'

'No, I did not.'

'So you can't say when the boy left?'

'I can indeed. It was about ten minutes after Miss Carol went up the next day.'

'I will return to that in a minute, but first, did you see the Captain again at all?'

'No.'

'You say you can tell us when the boy left. How?'

'Well, as I say, after Miss Carol had gone up I decided to make my check of the parking area underneath the block. I was very careful about that. I wouldn't have any casual parkers there. Now where was I? Oh yes. So there I was, going down the front steps, and what should happen as I turned the corner, but this self-same boy runs straight into me, nearly knocking me flying. He went down, and when I went to him I saw he was in a terrible state. To be sure, it was a terrible sight for a man to see. Blood everywhere, and this great split to the side of his mouth. And his face! That was a terrible mess too. Great long scratches it had on it. He was in a hell of a state.'

'But would it not have been possible for him to have left the building the night before and returned that afternoon, after you had seen him with the Captain?'

'He could have done, but I know he didn't.'

'How can you be so sure?'

'He told me all about it. I took him in through the parking to my flat to see what I could do for him. He refused a doctor. Then he told me all about it. He said . . .'

But before the janitor could continue, the Solicitor General was on his feet. 'Yes?' the judge asked.

'As I understand it, my learned friend intends at this point to adduce evidence from this witness as to what the boy said. I object. Patently it is the worst sort of hearsay.'

'Correct me if I am wrong, but I can admit evidence as secondary evidence in this sort of case if I consider it germane and material, can't I?' the judge asked, again with it in mind that admission by counsel would scotch an appeal point.

'Yes, your Honour, but this is not a straight civil case: more in the nature of a criminal hearing, in so far as a jury is present, and I submit that since they have not got your Honour's acuity in deciding what weight which evidence should carry, I would maintain that only the strictest rules of evidence should apply in this trial.'

'I take the point,' the judge said, turning to the witness. 'Mr Bates, is the conversation you are asked about something you intend to relate from your memory, or have you some other means of helping you recall it?'

Carter said nothing; the point was well covered. The elderly man dragged a black book from the depths of his inside jacket pocket. 'I have my diary here, sir. Would that do?'

'When did you enter it up?' the judge asked.

'Within an hour or so of the young man leaving me.'

The judge nodded. 'Very well, go on Mr Bates.'

'Well, what he told me was this . . .' And he began to tell

the Court about Philip James and the way he had been wounded.

But one man in the Court hardly heard it. He was a man no one had really noticed as he sat quietly in Court throughout the trial. Now he wasn't listening to the evidence, but remembering the part he had played in the game. An ex-police sergeant, he had had a long and fairly good career before an early retirement when it became plain that his methods wouldn't make him an Inspector. As a private detective he had lived on the usual divorce rubbish, but he had a name, and unlike many of his colleagues, he did manage to get the occasional unusual and interesting case. Charles Gray had remembered him and had rung him up. The fee had been high – high enough to take him off all other work. His job: to exhaust all lines of enquiry into the lives of the air hostess, Captain Harry Standard, and the co-pilot, Sam Meadows.

He had started the investigation with not much to go on and had found out nothing of any use about the air hostess. An easy job, but out of it one thing had come up – Bates. The ex-sergeant had a nose for a slight smell, and though Bates had seemed open enough, he had come away with it in mind to go back, but next time with something to work with: fear, honesty, or money. Honesty would take Bates a little of the way, fear would be useful, but money would speak loudest. And Charles Gray had agreed to let him use it.

First he had checked Sam Meadows out and found nothing. Following the Meadows investigation, he had started in on the principal, Captain Harry James Standard. Unobtrusively, he had been down to the airport, and his story about an insurance payment being due to the Captain's old mother, if he could just clear up a few minor questions which the bloody insurers wanted dealt with, had helped him along. The manager remembered the morning that the Captain had left for Nandi. He was an honest man, the manager, so he repeated the story which he'd given to the Air Accidents Department. But he didn't want the 'insurance man' to get the wrong end of the stick. So in telling him about the phone call and the death of the Captain's father, he added the rider that the Captain had been quite OK.

'Not very upset, then. I can say that to the insurers? Nothing to worry about, him flying?'

'No. Bit shocked, I s'pose, but he was OK.'

'Do you mind if I just have a quiet word with a few of the others to confirm your opinion?'

'Be my guest.' Then two odd things, little things, popped up. He had had a word with the Senior Despatch Clerk. 'Yeah, he was upset by his dad I think. Nothing much, but you could tell.'

'This message, do you remember it at all?'

'No, not a lot. Young guy gave it. Something to do with ring a number by a certain time. Can't remember, but the guy said it was urgent.'

'The Captain was a bit upset, you think, when you gave him the message.'

'Yeah, a bit. I had to chase halfway 'cross the office to catch him. Seemed preoccupied.' And that was strange. Because according to the manager, the Captain hadn't learnt of his father's death until the phone call.

One of the girls had also said something which was a trifle odd. 'Yeah, he was always so cheerful, you know. But that morning when he came by I don't think he even saw me. Still, his dad had just died, hadn't he? So's not surprising really, is it?' 'No, not at all,' the ex-sergeant had replied. Then he drifted off and looked up the recorded deaths for that day and the day before. No Standard had died in any old people's home. After that it had been a tedious records search, until he discovered that John Jeremy Standard, father of Harry James, had died when Harry was a kid. And there the trail stopped.

So he had gone back to Bates. 'G'day, Mr Bates. Do you think we could have a little chat? And before you say no, it might just be, Mr Bates, that I could put a grand in your way, and for nothing more than just being an honest man and helping me.' And a thousand bucks was a lot of money, so they had had their little chat, and bits began to fall into place.

'Could I be having my money now? I've told you all I know.'

'Here's a ton, Mr Bates. That's for the information so far, but you will remember I said I would need your help too?'

'What's it you're wanting me to do further, then?'

'Give evidence, Mr Bates, if required.'

'Not on your bloody life.' So the ex-sergeant had decided to add fear to honesty and money.

'Think about it, Mr Bates. I can have you subpoenaed and

you'll get it forced out of you. No more money then, and I dare say you might find yourself in a bit of bother about withholding evidence. Or would you rather just have the nine hundred dollars to tell the truth? Which is better? You tell me.'

And that had led to the need to find out a bit more. The first bit had come quickly. He had started round the hotels and the first and nearest had been the James Cook. He pulled a stroke there. Flashed the old police ID. One look was enough and anyway one of the porters had greeted him as Sergeant. He'd let it ride. But the register didn't tell him what he wanted. And the girl on the desk couldn't help. But then he'd had a bit of luck.

'Can I see that, Christine?' the other girl asked as she came in. The receptionist handed the photo of Harry Standard over and the mists of memory were disturbed. At last, she'd said, 'I am sure I've seen him, or someone like him.'

'Would you have been on duty on the night of February 6th a couple of years ago?' She wasn't sure.

'How about looking at the register,' the ex-sergeant said. 'It might jog something.' A lot of names were regulars, easy to place. Then she saw 'James Barrett'. 'Of course, I remember now. It was the name Barrett. You know, Barretts of Wimpole Street. Stuck in my mind. That's right. He was funny, too. Something odd about him. But he's the man, I'm sure of it.'

As Bates had been giving his evidence, it had received a shocked reception. That no one liked it was clear. Reporters had been hard at work, and the sound of fast-moving pencils had made itself heard in the short silences between the parts of Carter's quiet and dispassionate examination. This witness's evidence, if believed, was a bomb. Earlier on, the junior to the Attorney General had been seen hastily to leave the Court.

The fact that the janitor was to be called had been no surprise. Carter had mentioned it in opening the case, but he had decided on a shock approach and had been less than specific in his opening as to the evidence Bates would be giving. Finally when, in complete silence, Reginald Carter sat down, the Solicitor General rose to his feet. But he didn't begin his cross-examination. Instead he addressed the judge.

'Your Honour, I appreciate that it is still twenty minutes to one, but I wonder whether you would be so kind as to adjourn for lunch now. There are one or two matters on which I should like to take instructions before I start my cross-examination.'

'By all means. Shall we say two o'clock?'

'Much obliged, your Honour.' So they rose for lunch. And the Solicitor General's office was a very busy place during that lunch hour.

As two o'clock struck the usher's voice silenced the noise in Court and brought all to their feet. The judge entered, sat, and nodded as he tried to make himself comfortable in a chair designed more for effect as a seat of justice, than for comfort for the man dispensing it.

The Solicitor General's first question brought a gasp from people in the Court. It was a whiplash, designed to destroy credibility at a stroke.

'How much were you paid for this information and to come here to perjure yourself, Bates?' The trick was swift, but legitimate. It was, of course, throwing the door wide open to admitting other evidence of character, but wasn't stopped by the judge, for he had no doubt the Solicitor General well appreciated what he was about. And the double question was clever. Two heart-stopping accusations to any witness, but of the two, perjury was the worst, and in dealing with the worst, the Solicitor General hoped that the lesser might draw the truth. And so it happened. Bates gasped and the colour fled from his face. 'I've told the truth, as God's my witness.'

'So you have been paid. Tell me how much, Bates? I demand to know. What were you paid?'

The judge knew he should interrupt, but decided to leave it for the time being. And Bates, his mind in a turmoil, had the answer out before clear thought. 'A thousand dollars.'

Suddenly, the Solicitor General's voice was smooth. 'A thousand dollars. And for what, may I ask, were you paid this extraordinary sum of money?'

'To persuade me to come here and have my name in all the papers. Not something I wanted at all.'

'So you are a man to require payment for the truth. Is that what you are saying?'

'It's not like that at all, but how would you like it here?'

'You don't ask me questions. But I suggest you, sir, are a liar. Tell me, when did you, er, first concoct this story of yours?'

'I didn't do any such thing.'

'But you would agree that one thousand dollars was a great deal of money to a man in your position? More than you have ever had at one and the same time in the past, eh?'

'That's not true.'

'No, of course not. I was forgetting,' and the sarcasm could have been cut with a knife, 'dearie me, yes. I forgot. There was that time when you had more than that, wasn't there?'

'I don't know what you mean.'

'No? Well, let me see if I can help you. What was your job before you became a janitor, Mr Bates?'

'I was an ambulance man.'

'Oh, I see.' It was said with such sincere surprise that Bates breathed again. 'And tell me, why should a fit man like yourself give up such a rewarding job?'

With the slickness of an answer held long in mind, Bates replied, 'I didn't like the hours. In fact, it wasn't me that didn't like them, but the wife. I would have gone on.'

'Indeed. So are you saying that there would not be a shred of truth in an allegation that you were sacked for stealing from the wallets of patients you assisted?'

With the reflex of a man fighting, and unskilled in the art, Bates shot the answer back. 'That's a lie! It's a wicked lie I tell you.'

'Your full name is Patrick Sean Bates and you are fifty-seven, correct?'

'Yes.'

'And is it not also correct that you were convicted of theft in the manner I have mentioned just four years ago? Do you need me to remind you of the details, or shall I have to rely on the records of the officer on the case?' He gave Bates no chance to answer as he turned and casually said, 'Inspector Brenner, stand up for a moment please, would you?' Then, as the officer stood, he turned his back to Bates. 'The officer on the case, I believe, Bates. But let's see what else I can help you with. Eleven charges, wasn't it, and then you asked for thirty-four other offences of the same nature to be taken into account, and you were given a suspended sentence, correct?'

As white as a sheet now, Bates stared at the officer and

remembered him, and knew that the officer remembered him. The ex-sergeant smiled to himself as it crossed his mind that old Bates was earning his keep. Somehow he had rather thought he would. And it dawned on Bates why he had been offered so much money. They'd known it would happen. The bloody sods. Oh dear mother of Christ, the bloody sods. Anger flashed across his mind. 'You knew, didn't you, you sod! You fucking, stinking, sodding bastard!' He was staring and shouting at the ex-sergeant who completely ignored the outburst. Yes, he had known, and the outburst was just what was needed to make this witness hold water. The jury would work it all out later.

The judge's voice, peremptorily abrupt, cut Bates off. 'One more word out of you, Mr Bates, except in civil answer to learned counsel's questions, and you will spend six months in prison for contempt. Keep it in mind.'

'My previous statement is correct, is it not?' The Solicitor General's voice was quiet in its persistence.

Bates nodded, and answered 'Yes.' It was just audible.

'So you aren't above lying to the Court, Mr Bates, as we have seen, when it suits you to do so? And I want an answer to that.'

'I haven't lied. I swear it on my mother's head.'

'But you have. You told lies about your ambulance career, didn't you?'

'About that, yes.'

'And money is such a strong temptation to you that you would rifle the pockets of an injured man entrusted into your care. True, isn't it?'

'I did then. But it was just then.'

'But that wasn't once, was it. Over forty times, Mr Bates?'

'I s'pose so.'

'Over a period of nearly two years. And how many pockets did you try in which there was only small change not worth bothering with?'

The judge was quick. 'You needn't answer that. And I think you have made your point, so perhaps we can get on.'

'If it pleases you, your Honour. But tell me, Mr Bates, do you earn more or less now than when these offences occurred?'

'Less.'

'Your wife was working too then. Is she now?'

'No.'

'Will you pass me your diary, please?' The usher brought it over and the Solicitor General examined it. 'Tell me, why has your diary got sellotape all along its back and not the original binding?'

'It started to break up before I had finished it. Wasn't strong enough, and that's God's truth.'

'But you will agree with me that it would have been a simple matter to have slipped an entry in, wouldn't it? No matter, I'll keep it if I may and the jury can see it as an exhibit.' He passed it to an usher, but with little pause continued. 'To be clear, one thousand dollars was a lot of money to you, wasn't it?'

'Of course it was, but they knew I wouldn't come up here for nothing. Not that I knew then that . . . but they did. Oh, yes, they did.' It was said very bitterly. 'But,' his voice took on new strength, 'I have told nothing but the gospel truth about what I told Mr Carter there.'

'That's something people will have to consider. Thank you, Mr Bates.'

The Solicitor General sat down. John Prescott resisted the urge to get in on the act. Reginald Carter let Bates go. The judge thought about it all, and concluded there was nothing against the law in paying money to a witness to tell the truth. He considered the tactic. Perhaps the jury would believe the witness. But who would have done otherwise, with that sort of record? If he had denied the bribe, who would have believed him? Very interesting, the judge thought. Must remember it for the day I start writing.

'Montague Grimes.' Carter's voice was crisp, but no less crisp than the step of Montague Grimes into the witness box. 'Your name and occupation please.'

The judge remembered the face from the past. 'Montague Andrew Grimes. Private investigator.'

'And before that?'

'Sergeant in the city CID.'

'For many years?'

'Yes.'

'And employed on this case by the plaintiff's solicitors?'

'Yes.'

'When did you first meet Mr Bates?'

'When I started to make enquiries into the backgrounds of the aircrew. Tuesday, April 28th last year.'

'And what did you talk about? I see you have a notebook.' Prescott and the Solicitor General nodded their consent. 'You may refer to it.'

'I spoke only about Jenny Carol and Captain Standard in general terms and then left.'

'Then what?'

As the evidence was being given by the ex-sergeant a young man hurried up to the Minister of Transport's office, and straight in to see Christopher Silaman. 'Well?'

'They've hit hard. Standard was a homosexual, and there may be more to it.'

'Tell me about it.'

'And after we had been talking for a bit in his flat, he said, and I quote, "Here, wait half a mo', I've got my diary. Now, I wonder where that would be?" Then he went over to an old roll-top desk and was muttering about his wife always moving things. Then he came back with the diary.'

'Is this it?'

'Yes. When he handed it to me I asked him to open it at the material point and, as you can see, I initialled it at that page, the one before and the one after. He wouldn't let me keep it, but I told him he would receive no witness fee if he didn't produce it today.' Grimes didn't mention that he had made a copy of the entry.

The Minister of Transport said 'thank you' and the young man left his office. Then, elbows on the table, Christopher Silaman leaned forward and gazed out of the window, but saw nothing. Finally he pressed the buzzer and waited. The door opened and Sheila, a girl he could trust implicitly, came in, pad and pencil in hand. He noticed them and, with a smile, said, 'No, you won't need them, but I want you to go out and personally post those letters you did for me and deliver one by hand now, the one to the editor of the *Clarion.* But the letters to the Prime Minister's office and the personal one to his residence, I want you to hold on to until tomorrow, then deliver them by hand, but not before ten. Now it's important, Sheila, not to get it wrong. So tell me what you are going to do.' She repeated her instructions, then left.

The Solicitor General had been hard at work, but had so far nothing to show for it. 'I am sorry to press the point, Mr Grimes, and I don't doubt you, but the fact of the matter is that though you say there isn't the remotest possibility of Bates having forged the diary to look like an entry for that date because he produced it during the first and only major conversation you had with him concerning Captain Standard, nevertheless it is true that you had enquired earlier about Jenny Carol and Captain Standard. Now that is correct, isn't it?'

'Yes, sir.'

'And two or three weeks did elapse between your first visit and your second?'

'Yes.'

'And a thousand dollars is a lot of money to someone like him?'

'Yes, but I would point out, sir, that there was no mention of a thousand dollars or any sum of money at all until the second visit when he produced the diary.'

'But the man's no fool. He could have sensed there was money in it. Possible, isn't it?'

'Possible, sir, but if I may say so, with respect, I have been long enough on the job not to give anything away to a villain.' And the Solicitor General had to be content with that, but didn't much like sitting down amidst the laughter which accompanied the last answer.

John Prescott rose to his feet. The case was tending to leave him out in the cold. All the points that came to his mind were being pre-empted by the Solicitor General.

'Mr Grimes, you are a man of great experience in these things, so perhaps we can rely on you. Tell me, a man who is a criminal and takes a lot of money to do something, as a policeman, would you be inclined to believe such a man?'

The judge raised his eyebrows, and waited for the objection, but none came.

'Depends on the circumstances, sir. Courts rely on such men. A villain turns Queen's evidence – it's a bribe. Evidence for freedom and freedom is money.'

'You could have subpoenaed Bates and paid nothing . . . ah, wait a moment, please.' He glanced down at the piece of paper which had been slipped along to him by the Solicitor General: 'For Christ's sake, shut up. If you don't there will be hell to pay and I, personally, will cause it'.

Colour suffused Prescott's face. 'Your Honour, my learned friend has raised a point of importance, and with your leave, I would be obliged for two minutes' adjournment with him alone.'

'Very well. I'll stay here while you clear it up.'

And the two of them marched from the Court to the nearest conference room. Before the door had closed, Prescott whirled round to face the Solicitor General, furious. 'What the devil do you mean by seeking to interfere in my case? How dare you have the bloody impertinence to write me a note like this,' he brandished it. 'What the hell do you mean by it?'

The Solicitor General drew a deep breath. 'Look, sorry about the note, Prescott. Heat of the moment and all that. I apologize. But don't you see that you take us straight over the cliff with Bates's evidence if you push the money side of it? I kept off it because to me it's as clear as daylight. It can only do us harm.'

'But it's corrupt. I want to make that clear. I want the jury to be left in no doubt about Bates.'

'Prescott, old thing, it's corrupt if he was paid to perjure himself, that's all.'

'But that's what we've got to pursue! Get it from Grimes and then have Bates recalled.'

'Look at it this way. If we had a cat in hell's chance of satisfying anyone that it was a payment to induce perjury, then it's beautiful. We would go ahead – I would have done. But what if you try and fail? Grimes is no fool. Bates is not a nice man, Prescott, and at the moment, that is clear. He's a dirty old man who enjoys writing up nastiness in his diary, and he's a man who was prepared to sit back and let the vet be blamed whilst he kept evidence secret. But, if you pursue it, you'll be in grave danger of creating a perverse sympathy for him.'

'So you want me to leave it?'

'Well, I don't think you've got a snowball's chance in hell of making perjury stick. So, yes, I'd leave it alone until we come to speeches. But I've had my say, so it's up to you.'

And now that his initial anger had evaporated with the apology, Prescott saw the other side of the coin. 'OK, I'm not sure you're right, but above all I suppose we've got to stick together.'

The murmur in Court died as the two leading counsel returned. And the judge, in mock solemnity, looked at his watch. Prescott saw it, and was quick to apologize. Then he said he had no further questions, and sat down. The judge looked at his watch again. Just after 4.15. 'Mr Carter, I am not inclined to start another long witness tonight. What do you think?'

'I have a manager of a bank here, your Honour, I don't want to detain him any longer than necessary, and he should be quick.'

'Very well, then.'

'Hamish Armitage, take the witness stand please.'

The man walked briskly to it, took the oath, and with a confident smile, turned to Reginald Carter, QC. 'Hamish Armitage, that's your name?'

'Yes, but I am not the Manager of the Southern Hemisphere branch in Lambton Quay, but the Securities Manager.'

'I see. Well I hope it won't be long before you are the Manager. But, to business. There is an account holder at your bank by the name of Rex Althrop Harrison Jones-Hillyer, a double-barrelled name, yes?'

'Correct.'

'Who holds a deposit box – correct?'

'Yes.'

'Do you have its contents with you?'

'I do.'

'And do you have a list of items put in it and the dates of deposit and is each item marked with the date of deposit?'

'Yes.'

'And the means of deposit is marked, by hand or otherwise?'

'Yes.'

'And finally, can you tell the Court whether or not any of the items deposited have been out of bank custody since deposit?'

'The client has taken four items out over the past two years.'

'But of the items you have with you, has the client had any out since deposit?'

'One of the four items was returned for deposit. It came back in the same envelope.'

'Roughly how long ago was the first deposited?'

'About a year ago.'

'Will you now produce to the Court the items you have held on deposit. And also the client's letter authorizing this step.' Sixteen items and a letter were produced and marked as exhibits. Carter then sat down.

The Solicitor General rose. 'Mr Armitage. I am, I fear, all at sea. What are these things?'

'I have no idea, sir. They are private to the customer.'

'So beyond what you've told us, you can't help at all?'

'No.' And shaking his head in bewilderment, the Solicitor General sat down. Prescott didn't rise, but then the Court did. It was the end of the third day.

The phone rang, on that third evening of the case, at nine o'clock promptly. The Deputy Premier picked it up. Few people were around in the offices; most had gone home hours ago. But the Deputy Premier was working late and he had only received the transcript of the third day's evidence about an hour and a half before. It had been a busy day for him in any event, what with the leaking and feeding into the media of all the news that was being used to minimize coverage of the trial.

'Is that you?' The Prime Minister's voice was unmistakable even at the end of a phone in Brussels.

'Yes. I was waiting for you to phone.'

'OK, what's the position?'

'Well, on the fishing side you'll be glad to hear the arrest went off well. Quite a hoo-haa about it, and thank heavens one of the protection vessel's shots hit the trawler in the bow. And on the . . .' They talked about the Press build-up for ten minutes or so. 'Sorry? Bad line. What did you say?' the Deputy Prime Minister asked.

'The case. How goes it?'

'Badly. I've just been reading the transcript. There are a number of things but the worst is that they have pretty well got home on an allegation that the DC8 Captain was a practising homosexual.'

'What did you say? Homosexual?'

'Yes, homosexual. He wasn't worried about his father at all. He died years ago. So what he had on his mind is anyone's guess and I've a feeling that whatever it was it probably won't come out in the trial. If Carter knew he'd have mentioned it in opening . . . in fact, it's all a bit puzzling at the moment.

But anyway his homosexuality seems certain.'

'And we're going to be in trouble because our people didn't know, is that it?'

'I rather think so. I think we'll just have to take the bull by the horns now.'

'How far are they going to get?'

'Oh, I wouldn't worry. There's no hint of anything more than that we got our facts wrong.'

'So we use Christopher now. Is that what you suggest?' the Prime Minister asked.

'Yes.'

'But only the last bit of the letter, eh?'

'Yes. The rest won't bother us.'

'OK, do it, but tell him how sorry I am, you know the sort of thing. And with this sex thing, I think you'd better lay it on a bit. Appalled, and all that. Terrible failure by the Minister, but a good chap to have come clean, you know the sort of thing, OK?'

'All right. It's too late tonight, but I'll hold a Press conference on it tomorrow, and release the letter and my reply.'

'Yes, do that. Now, have you got the figures I asked for on tonnage for the year . . .'

At twenty past nine the Deputy closed up shop and started to walk away from his office. As he was leaving the building, he was surprised when suddenly he was joined by the Opposition spokesman on finance. They had known each other over many years, from opposite sides of the House.

'Hello. I never work as late as this when I'm off the Treasury benches,' the Deputy Premier said.

'Going to your car? So am I. Well, what's been keeping you so late?'

'I like to have a chat with the guvnor every night.'

'Keeping tabs on you! At least our guy lets us breathe without having to tell him.'

The Deputy Premier laughed. 'That's not quite fair. Take tonight: a lot's going on.'

'Anything interesting, apart from the wool you chaps are pulling across everyone's eyes?'

'There's just a lot happening. But yes, as a matter of fact, there's something you'll enjoy. You'll know about it tomorrow anyway, but keep it to yourself tonight. OK?'

'Might have to tell the boss.'

'Yeah, but not the world. Anyway, 'cos of the case, the guvnor's handing Chris his cards.'

'Who? Chris Silaman? You must be joking! What did he have to do with it?'

'The homosexuality. His people missed it.'

'Oh. Christ, I'm glad we don't operate like that! Poor Chris.'

'Well, better the young than the irreplaceable. Oh by the way, there is something I think we should talk about. You remember the tonnage figures . . .'

They stood and talked for another ten minutes before parting. 'Yes, take care,' the Opposition spokesman said finally before walking away and thinking back to Silaman. What a thing! However, it would have been the same in his Party, no doubt. But interesting. And as he drove home an idea began to germinate. Somehow it wasn't all quite right; a sideways or even downwards move yes, but the sack . . . odd, that, really. And all a bit quick. Very strange. But perhaps it was a defuse operation, a stitch in time sort of exercise. Then a drunk wandered into his path and the shock of nearly running the man down drove the business of Chris Silaman from his mind – at any rate for that night.

Chapter Twenty-One

The day dawned bright, and the Deputy Prime Minister hummed happily to himself as he showered and dressed. It was still a nice day when he joined his wife for breakfast.

But then – such is the power of the Press – the sun suddenly went out of the morning. For there on the front page, a page strangely bare of the facts carefully seeded to minimize and squash it into insignificance, was a full report of the trial. And next to it was a report of the suicide of someone he'd never heard of, but who, he learned as he read, had been one of the Controllers on duty at the time of the accident. But that was far from the worst. For the front page also carried Christopher Silaman's open letter of resignation, and an editorial.

For a time he sat motionless, grasping at the implications. His wife, pouring her second coffee and available for brief communication with her husband, noticed he wasn't eating, which was very unlike him. It spelt crisis. A matter of minor importance he would probably have mentioned but it wouldn't have upset his appetite. 'Is anything wrong?' she asked. 'You haven't touched your egg. It'll be cold.'

'No, I'll just have coffee.' He didn't bother to answer the first question. She was a good housekeeper and didn't like waste. But she could see he was more than ordinarily troubled. 'I asked, dear, what was the matter.' For a few moments he stared at her, miles away. Then he noticed her and replied.

'I haven't worked it out yet, but yes, one way or another, there's trouble.' Then he was up and striding to the phone. It took ten minutes to get through to Brussels, and another ten to get the Prime Minister to the phone. 'Hello. What's the panic?' The Prime Minister was clearly annoyed.

'I've just got the morning papers here and, not to put too fine a point on it, we could be in trouble. Silaman's got a letter of resignation all over the front page.'

'What! How can that be? What the hell have you been doing?' He paused to get his initial flash of anger under control. 'All right, tell me about it and I'll tell you what to do.'

'He starts off OK by telling everyone that he failed – not himself but the Air Accidents people – to give you all the facts which have come out in Court. But in the first bit he uses these words, and they're the ones that stick the knife in. I quote: "It was upon the facts thrown up in the course of the investigation into that disaster that you and our colleagues had to rely". But it gets worse. In the second paragraph he says this: "It was upon a lack of complete information that you came to the personal decisions that you did", then he says "As you know, I had no part in the decisions". That's followed by a reference to the Press conference he gave, "suggested by yourself". That's you. None of that's too bad, but I'm afraid the next bit is. I won't read the lot, but in sum, what he says is to thank you for having run the Ministry of Transport in his early days. In fact, he even goes so far as to use these words ". . . when I first entered Government I knew little of politics and the detailed and personal interest you took was invaluable. Indeed, it led, by reason of your greater experience, to early decisions affecting my portfolio which would not have been mine, in my lack of experience".

'Finally, he . . .' But he got no farther as the Prime Minister's mounting anger boiled over. The Deputy had lived with it for years, let it roar on, unmoved, merely waiting for the point to arrive when the steam would run out. Which it did, as the Prime Minister said: 'What the hell do you mean by permitting this to be published?'

'Obviously his timing was perfect, with early delivery to the editor of the *Clarion* – need I say more? Now that they've printed it, so will the rest. But what line do you want me to follow? One thing's certain. Now that he's got in first, and on the terms of that letter, he's OK. Honourable resignation is mentioned by the paper. It speaks of the integrity of a man who, rather than try and hold on to his job, has the honesty to acknowledge a mistake. In fact, it very nearly whitewashes him. In my view, we'll just have to go along with it.'

'But there must be something we can do? I'm damned if I'm going to let the smug little bastard off the hook.'

'Well, frankly, I think he's shut the door on us, not just on the homosexuality bit but the lot, and done it in such a way that he has all the public sympathy. Anyway, what do you want me to do?'

The Prime Minister, having vented his spleen was coldly considering the question.

'Are you still there?' the Deputy asked.

'Of course I'm bloody well still here!' Then as his thoughts clarified, he said, 'The problem is that if we appear to accept his resignation at face value, there will be no way we can use him if the cover business gets out. Correct?'

'I'm afraid so.'

'And what do you think are the chances of any trouble on that front?'

'I don't think there's even a suspicion.'

'OK, in that case we'll just have to hope that you're right. Anyway you'd better have a Press conference and say what a good chap Silaman is, and make all the right noises.'

'Right. I'll deal with it first thing. Anything else?'

'Yes. When you see Silaman you might like to mention to him that I'll not forget this.' And the phone went dead. But the malevolence in the man's voice seemed to spread and encompass the Deputy Prime Minister, who felt very glad that he wasn't in Silaman's shoes. The fact that he had given a snippet of information to the Opposition spokesman on finance the night before had been completely forgotten by the Deputy Prime Minister.

The fourth day began as the others had, except, perhaps, that the jury were beginning to feel at home. From being twelve strangers with their cautious 'What a nuisance' smiles, they had started to talk between themselves, for now there was a feeling of comfortable corporate identity amongst them. Already most of them had decided who should be their foreman, who was probably going to talk most, and who was likely to be quietly, stubbornly, opposed to the general opinion. And also who was going to be the devil's advocate. It always happened.

Having settled himself, the judge gave a dry cough before saying 'Yes, Mr Carter?' 'Govind Singh please.' The day had begun. The small, dark barman with hair slicked into a dark helmet took his place.

'You are Govind Singh, and until recently, were employed as one of the barmen at the Gateway Hotel, a hotel near Nandi International Airport?'

'Yes, sir.'

'Would you look at these three photographs, please.' And the usher gave the witness photos of the Captain, his co-pilot, and Jenny Carol. 'Do you recognize any of these people?'

'All of them, sir.'

'Were you on duty in that bar of the hotel late on the evening of February 7th about two years ago?'

'Yes, sir.'

'And did you see the girl and the younger man together in the bar, and later the older man as well during that evening?'

'Yes, sir.'

'What happened?'

'The older of the two men came in drunk and swore at the girl and then I tried to stop it and the younger man knocked the older one out.'

'Well, now. Let's start at the beginning. You were serving behind the bar . . .'

'Rex, you had better listen to me, and listen well. We had a deal, didn't we? And do you know what I shall do if you don't keep it?' The ex-sergeant was sitting in a plastic chair in a drab room in the cheap but conveniently obscure downtown hotel. Sitting opposite him on the bed was a young man with a scar dragging down from his mouth. It wasn't that, though, which held the ex-policeman's eye, but the flicker of eyes unwilling to meet his gaze, the perspiration on the young man's brow, the perpetual rubbing of his hands together.

'But I can't! I can't now. I know I said I would but that was different. That was before Bates went in . . . I mean, Jesus Christ! They crucified him! I mean, they did, didn't they? No, I won't do it. I don't care what you do, I'm not going to do it!'

And still the ex-policeman pinned him with his unwavering gaze, but remained silent so that the boy could think about what it would mean if he didn't agree to give evidence. They had been together now for over three hours, including the flight from Auckland, and still the kid refused. The ex-policeman lit a cigarette, leaned back, and appeared to examine the little white tube with the greatest of care as he let the young man sweat it out. And while the time went by his mind went back along the path he had had to follow to get this young man here. With the lead from Bates, his first step had been to the smart Gay Lib place in town, Suivas, owned by the weirdest of guys. The ex-policeman had known him, in the line of duty, a few years back. Now, as they met, the guy was startling in full drag.

'Fancy seeing you here, of all people! Don't tell me you've gone gay in your old age!'

'Sorry to disappoint you, dear, but I need a bit of help.'

'You going to buy me a drink, then?'

'Yeah, why not.'

'Well, here's looking at you. Now what could I do for you which you wouldn't do for yourself?'

'Have a look at this, there's a dear.'

He/she had a look. In fact, he/she was a fantastic person and a great many people would have been amazed if they had known the sort of things this strange person did for others in trouble, with no hint of thanks and with no desire for recognition. 'Yeeeees, well, fancy you having a photo of little Phil. He's rather nice, isn't he?'

'Yeah, fantastic. But I want to find him.'

'Is our Phil in a spot of bother then?'

'Not so's you'd notice. Remember, I'm not fuzz any more.

But if I don't find him then yes. And so's you'd notice.'

'Bad, would it be?'

'Very. But it won't be half as bad if I can find him before anyone else goes looking. Is Phil his real name?'

'Oh, I shouldn't think so, dear. I mean, he'd want his privacy when he comes off the game, wouldn't he?'

'On it proper, was he?'

'An expert, our Phil. Pulled some awfully big ones when he was here. You'd be amazed at some of them.'

'I doubt it. But you said when he was here. Since when?'

'Oh now, let me think. Yes, quite a time ago now. You see, little Phil met with a nasty. Don't know the details, but they do say he got out too far and someone carved him up.'

'What was his game, then?'

'Bit greedy, our Phil. Went in for retirement benefits a bit, I think. Dangerous, that, really.'

'So where'd he go?'

'Is this on the level? The trouble?'

'Yes, dead level. If I don't get to him first, then he'll drown. And that's straight.'

'And what if you do get to him?'

'He'll maybe go under, but he'll come up again.'

'All right then. Try Egnaro's, up top.' Then, as though it hadn't been said, the guy in drag raised his glass and said, 'Well, cheers. Fancy you here and not gay! I just don't believe it. Lovely feller like you!' And that had been the end of the conversation.

In Auckland, the ex-policeman had been a stranger with no friends to help him. So he had quietly sat in a cafe across the road from Egnaro's and waited and watched. At four on the afternoon of the third day he had seen Phil enter the club and followed him in.

'You a member?' And ten bucks poorer, he was. At the bar he had bought a drink, caught Phil's eye, smiled, and offered him one. Twenty minutes later they had left together.

The flat door was closed and locked by Phil. 'Do you want to talk a bit first?'

'Yeah, Phil, I want to talk. And you'd better know we're not here for a fiddle.'

'Whaddaya mean?'

'How's the mouth, Phil? She hurt you real bad, but it could have been worse, I s'pose.'

‘Who are you and what do you want?’

‘You to decide to give evidence, Phil.’

‘You’ve got to be joking! Christ! Come on, out. Fuck off!’

‘It’s worth ten thousand bucks. Not to lie, or fuck some fag, but to do what is probably the only decent thing you’ve done in a long time. You only have to tell the truth. It’ll hurt, but with ten grand I dare say you won’t need to worry too much.’

And here the little sod was, thought the ex-policeman, over a year later and a thousand bucks better off, and at the last minute, after it had all been jacked up, the kid was trying to avoid going through with it. Still, he thought, as he watched the ash drop from his half smoked cigarette on to what passed for a carpet, he’ll just have to, won’t he? ‘No, Rex? Really no evidence?’

‘Just leave me alone. If it’s the grand, I’ll let you have it back, but just leave me alone. Get off my back. I’m not going to do it, not for you, for money, or anything. So you’d better believe it.’

‘What a pity. Well, I had hoped that you would be sensible. After all, say you got a couple of years in stir, so what? Ten grand’s a lot of money; good compensation I’d have thought.’

‘I wouldn’t do it for fifty.’

‘No? But you’ll do it, Phil. You’ll give evidence, see if you don’t. ’Cos if you decide not to, then, as a good citizen, I will arrest you, and if you think about it, I’ve got enough on you to see you an old man before you see the light of day again. And you’ll still have to give evidence, even if I arrest you. Do you know what this is?’ He drew a slip of paper from his breast pocket. ‘It’s a subpoena. You can be made to go into the witness-box. So either you do it all of your own free will and emerge as a young man who, seeing the error of his ways, confesses, reforms and basks in righteousness as one of society’s prodigal sons – and, of course, collect another nine grand, or I’ll make them lock you up and throw away the key.’

‘You might get me to Court, but I wouldn’t say anything. That’s my right. I don’t have to incriminate myself.’

‘That’s right. But you see, Phil, I would do it for you. You see, even though I am an ex-policeman, I am afraid I still have such a nasty suspicious mind that I make what are called contemporaneous notes of conversations with some people.

And, you may remember, you had quite a bit to say to me one way or another. And it's all bloody good stuff. So you see, Phil, I mean it when I say they'd throw the key away.'

'But that's blackmail!'

'Really! What a diabolical thought!'

By the time John Prescott, QC, for Paranational, was nearing the end of his cross-examination of the Indian barman the story of the goings on in Nandi was hot news. It was the fourth sensation: suicide, homosexuality, ministerial resignation, and now a drunken brawl between aircrew.

'You said the Captain was very drunk. Just how drunk was very drunk?'

'I would have said that if he'd had much more he would have passed right out.'

'Did you see him the next day?'

'Yes, just as he was checking out. We were short-staffed at the time and I was on the desk.'

'Would you say he looked at you?'

'Yes.'

'Did he speak to you more than was necessary to complete the business of checking out?'

'No.'

'Treated you in fact just as he would have treated a stranger on the desk?'

'Oh yes.'

'Didn't you think that was odd? He had seen you before, in fact, owed you an apology for knocking you down?'

'Perhaps he didn't want to be reminded of the night before.'

'Or perhaps he had been so drunk as to have little or no recollection. That could well have been true, couldn't it?'

'He had a cut on his face.'

'Oh yes, but a man who becomes very, very drunk, so drunk that an experienced barman thinks he is in danger of passing out, may not be surprised at a slight injury. But did you see any of the rest of the aircrew as they checked out?'

'Yes, all of them.'

'The co-pilot as well?'

'Yes.'

'And the Captain was with them. Tell me, what was the Captain's demeanour in regard to the co-pilot?'

'I didn't notice anything.'

'So his behaviour was consistent with no real recollection at all, or with very bad behaviour which everyone has decided to forget, or, of course, it would have been equally consistent with them all having made their peace earlier that morning?'

'I suppose so.'

'Certainly the sober co-pilot hadn't been hurt, had he?'

'No.'

'Nor the girl?'

'No.'

'So the only person who had suffered was the Captain, who behaved as though it had never happened. That is correct, isn't it?'

'It could be.'

'It goes further than "it could be" doesn't it? There was nothing you saw the next day which would have led you to any other conclusion, was there?'

'Well, no, I suppose not.'

'Thank you. So, to be quite clear on this, there is nothing you can say which would support the supposition that the Captain and the co-pilot in flying that plane were in any way still antagonistic to each other – angry?'

The Solicitor General cringed inside. Prescott really wasn't at his best in this case. But he breathed a small sigh of relief when, far from coming unstuck, he got the best answer he could have hoped for.

'I agree, sir.'

'Thank you.'

Carter rose slowly, and wished to heaven that this gullible and suggestible little witness had been called by someone else. Then, instead of the kid gloves approach required for his own witness, he could have been as hard as he wished to be in cross-examination. 'My learned friend suggests to you that you can say nothing to suggest that these two men and the girl weren't the best of friends as they left your hotel. But tell me, what were the words used to the girl? Tell us again.'

'I can't remember clearly, but I do remember two words, "fucking" and "slut".' 'Fucking slut.' It wasn't a question, just a murmured joining of the two in the stillness of a Court.

'And the co-pilot. How would you describe his demeanour, having heard this?'

'I think he was indeed very angry.'

'Tell me, you've seen other crews check out. Are they

usually silent? Without a word for you, or a joke for each other?'

'They're usually pretty cheerful.'

'And this Captain's crew, a cheerful bunch as they left, would you say?'

'No, silent.'

'I see. Would you have known if words in private had passed between them earlier that day?'

'No, not if it had happened in a room.'

'I see. But there was nothing to show they had made . . .'

'Your Honour, I object . . .'

'No matter, your Honour. I won't pursue it. Thank you, Mr Singh. You may go. Your Honour, at this point I think it would be as good a time as any to deal with interrogatories. An application was made to interrogate the Chief of Air Accidents, and perhaps I can explain this sort of thing to the jury, so they will understand. So, with your leave?'

'Certainly, Mr Carter.'

Turning to the jury, the plaintiff's silk began to address them.

'In a case, it very often happens that a plaintiff suspects that a certain thing has occurred, but has no proof of it. And the question of whether she has or hasn't a case may depend on discovering the answers to certain questions. But only someone on the other side is in a position to give those answers. The law likes justice, and would not like to think that a person with a good case is denied justice because someone wants to keep something secret. Now this is not a licence for a plaintiff to go on a fishing expedition, so generalized questions cannot be asked. But specific ones, material to her case, may be. And though a man may not wish to answer, nevertheless, if the Court thinks he should, then he must.

'In this case, a Mr Graham Weller has been asked and was required to answer certain questions. In brief, they will be relied upon by the plaintiff to help establish that for some odd reason, restraint was imposed on Mr Weller in the investigation he conducted. You will hear the questions and answers, but the sort of thing I have in mind is that apparently he started with some police assistance, then for some unknown reason it was withdrawn. And a number of other points emerge. Indeed, it is largely on his evidence that the case for exemplary damages rests.

'Anyway, now I will read the interrogatories.

'"At the commencement of your investigation, were you afforded police assistance? Answer yes or no."

'And the answer to that question was yes.

'Next we have "If yes, how many officers were assigned to you to so assist?"

'The answer is four.

'"Did those officers stay on the investigation through to its completion . . .".'

'G'day to you all.' And the Deputy Prime Minister strode across to the table, where he sat to face the TV cameras and the Press. 'The reason I've called you together is to give you the Prime Minister's reaction to the news that Christopher Silaman has tendered his resignation as our Minister of Transport. I spoke to him as soon as I knew . . .'

'When was that, sir?'

'I'll deal with questions later. But I will tell you that I had a long talk with the Prime Minister in Brussels yesterday evening. And when I spoke to the Prime Minister I had to fill him in on what was happening here, and in particular the trial that's now on. And I can tell you he was deeply, deeply shocked to learn of the plaintiff's disclosures. Yes, he was very unhappy indeed that it appears there was evidence which we knew nothing of. It placed him in a very difficult position.

'Now we need men like Christopher Silaman. He's done a lot in the field of transport since we took office. So the Prime Minister has had a very difficult task. However, after a lot of thought, his conclusion was that if it had been he who, as a Minister, found himself responsible for this sort of failure, then he would have acted as Christopher Silaman has done. Any man of real integrity would have done so. And if a man feels like that, then the rest of us should respect him for it, and honour his wishes. In the result, I have to tell you that the Prime Minister has accepted the resignation, but in doing so, he has particularly asked me to say that it is with, and I quote, the greatest possible reluctance.

'Now, are there any questions?'

'Trantor, *Clarion.* Can you tell us exactly why he has resigned. He won't comment, and you must know.'

'Because evidence has emerged in this trial which he considers should have emerged from the investigation.'

'Are you referring to the homosexuality issue?'

'That and others. But they are all facts still to be considered in the trial and as such are *sub judice*, so I can't comment.'

'Bartram, *Globe*. Can you tell us, sir, did he also resign because he thought he'd made a mistake in not releasing publicly in the report of the Chief Investigator of Air Accidents the fact of the trouble of the Captain of the DC8, and the fact that there had been omissions in Air Traffic procedures?'

'I should imagine that all these issues may have played a part, but I cannot comment further.'

'Sir – Haley Times, *Empire Chronicle*. Could you please clear up one point mentioned in Mr Silaman's letter. He makes it plain that he took no decisions but referred facts to the Prime Minister. Was it the Prime Minister who decided that the public weren't to be told about the then believed death of the Captain's father and the Air Traffic omissions?'

'You must understand that the task in that sort of thing is difficult. There are two things to consider in the compilation of all air accident reports. One, how much do you reveal in the public interest, and two, how much of what you have learned do you not publish because it serves no public interest, and I don't mean ghoulish interest, and which, if released, would just foul up people's lives. That's all I can say now. Glad you could all come.' Then he rose and with a small gesture of goodbye, walked out of the room. The girl's 'but you haven't answered my question' was heard by him as he left, but not noticeably so.

'. . . and the answer to that final interrogatory was no.' In the brief silence that followed the jury assimilated what they had heard, and they wondered what the Solicitor General's evidence would be which could satisfy them that there were good reasons not to have included in the published report of the Chief of Air Accidents what he had included in his report to the Minister of Transport. Why hadn't the Government let it be known that the DC8 Captain had a problem? Why no mention of the Air Traffic omissions? Why say it was all the vet's fault? And why a report which was clearly rushed through? Was it, as the Prime Minister had said, to prevent hundreds of people from waiting for a long time for settlement and an end to uncertainty and financial hardship. Or was there, as suggested by Mr Carter, more to all this than met the eye? Why had the policemen been withdrawn? Surely it was just the sort of case for skilled investigation, to help get at the truth more quickly. But what really was the truth? It hadn't been his father the Captain was worrying about, but it would be wrong, wouldn't it, to brand the pilot as homosexual because of the unsupported word of that man Bates?

Weller's interrogatories started a great deal of thought, which led to a great many questions. It was all very odd, and even odder when one thought of the answer which Weller had given, in which he had been at pains to make the point that throughout the investigation he had received the assistance of someone called Mark Simpson, a loss adjuster, whatever that might be, but who obviously wasn't anything to do with the Government. If there was anything odd, or more to it all than met the eye, surely the last thing in the world that they would have wanted was an outsider in on it – two, in fact, because there was someone from Merlin Mutual as well.

It all seemed a muddle and very strange, and a lot of people wondered who the Solicitor General would be calling to give evidence.

Well pleased with the effect, Carter called his next witness, and the jury watched the grey-haired, thin, but powerfully built sixty-five-year-old man in a quiet suit calmly take his place in the witness-box. The judge spared him a glance and immediately the words 'expert witness' came into his mind. And that caused him to frown. 'Mr Carter,' he said. 'Have we finished with the matter which you were pursuing yesterday with the man from the Bank?'

'Your Honour, perhaps you would be so kind as to permit me to reserve comment at this stage.'

The judge looked down at him for a moment. 'Very well, if you wish it, but I trust that you have not been wasting this Court's time.' As he continued to look sternly down on Reginald Carter, QC, he hoped he would reply further, but was disappointed, as Carter said, 'Take the oath now, please.' 'If I may, I would rather affirm,' the witness said.

'Very well.' And the man promised to tell the truth without dragging God's name into it. 'Terence Roy Singleton, Bachelor of Science, Fellow of . . .' And as the man's track record in support of his claim to expertise was recited, Grace passed a note along to Charles Gray. Brief and to the point, it merely said 'What's happened?' When he passed it back he had added the words 'Tell you later.'

'And so your experience covers Air Traffic Control procedures, pilot training and classification, and flight procedures, is that correct?'

'Yes.'

'And I believe you are now acting as a consultant, having last held the position of Chief Inspector Airways?'

'Yes.'

'And you have been in this Court throughout the evidence?'

'Yes.'

'In that case, we can move on fairly quickly. The first thing I wish to deal with is the question of aircrew. Quite simply, would you have permitted a Captain to fly a passenger aircraft if he was a homosexual, and maybe the subject of blackmail . . .'

'Your Honour, I protest in the strongest terms I can command. There has been no evidence in this case that the Captain was being blackmailed. I take the strongest exception to my learned friend's question.'

And Prescott was joined on his feet by the Solicitor General, who said, 'I agree entirely with my learned friend, and I will say this: it is a matter which I will certainly bear in mind should this matter come before the Court of Appeal.'

'I see. Well, Mr Carter. Are you alleging blackmail in this case?'

Carter looked down at his papers. Difficult. 'Your Honour,' he said, looking up. 'I have not called evidence as to blackmail, so perhaps I can put it on this basis. In my final address I shall certainly invite your Honour and the jury to consider that there is evidence of a phone call which clearly agitated the Captain more than just a trifle before he left Wellington. And if it be accepted that indeed it didn't concern his father's death, an event which had occurred years before, and if it be accepted that he was a homosexual and the evidence of the man Bates is accepted, well then, I shall suggest that it may well have been in the nature of a blackmail call; a matter of commonsense perhaps. Or if not that, then something equally disturbing.'

The judge snorted but held his peace. His time would come.

'However, in deference to my learned friends' objections, I

will rephrase the question.' Then, turning to the witness, he said, 'Would you have permitted a man to fly in the condition in which some of the evidence indicates the Captain was in?'

'No. Under no circumstances.'

'And with Nandi in mind?'

'With the barman's evidence in mind, I would not have permitted the Captain and that particular First Officer to pilot any aircraft together.'

'Why?'

'Because they are required to cooperate and act as a team, each checking the accuracy and performance of the other. In my view, it would be extremely dangerous for two men at loggerheads to fly together, and even more so, if one of them had the sort of problem which I think the Captain may have had on his mind, something disturbing, whatever it was.'

'I see. And what exactly would you fear as a result of two such men flying together?'

'A mistake, which goes unchecked, through lack of cooperation.'

'And in this case, what sort of mistake?'

'A QNH error. An altimeter recalibration error on descent.'

'Mr Carter, one moment please. This is important, so I would like to be clear on it.' And to the witness the judge said, 'As I understand it, your evidence so far is that there had to be a mistake in the QNH for this accident to have happened. Is that correct?'

'Unless of course one or other of the pilots was flying with an altimeter reading which he completely ignored; for instance, the vet at 4000 feet with an altimeter showing 4000 feet, yet for some reason thinking it was saying 3000, his prescribed height. But assuming no pilot was daydreaming and all were following the altitude clearance instructions, well yes – one or other of the altimeters had to be wrongly calibrated.'

'I see. So what you as an expert say to me is, I can forget fanciful errors. The only probable one in this case was either that the DC8 was too low or the Cessna was too high. But whichever was the case, it would only have arisen because someone didn't calibrate their altimeter correctly, or was lax in watching it. Is that what you say?'

'Yes.'

'And you further say I should find for the plaintiff on the

basis that though there were two pilots on the DC8 with much greater experience and very much more highly trained, I should nevertheless be persuaded that the fault was on the part of the aircrew and not the vet, an older man, perhaps tired and a part-time pilot with an aeroplane in which, if I accept the report of the Chief Investigator of Air Accidents, he was inexperienced? Is that what you say, sir?'

'Well, someone made a mistake, your Honour. On the one hand a vet with what I consider a faultless flight behind him; on the other a very unhappy aircrew and an Air Traffic Control error.'

'Yes, but again, as an expert you would tell me, would you, that the omissions on the part of the Air Traffic Control people would only have become relevant in the event of a mishearing of the ATIS which Mr Carter mentioned in opening? Or, to put it another way, if I become minded to find no fault on the part of the aircrew, the Air Traffic Control side of it is completely irrelevant. Would that be correct?'

'Yes. One follows or compounds the other.'

'Wait a moment please, Mr Carter.' And the judge began to note down the points he had wanted to clear with the expert.

And across the city three men met to discuss an intriguing situation. One of them was the Opposition spokesman on finance, another the spokesman on law, and the last was the Leader of the Opposition who, as they seated themselves, spoke first. 'OK, Jim. Let's have it.' The finance spokesman nodded briefly and outlined his conversation with the Deputy Prime Minister of the night before.

'But this means Silaman pre-empted his sacking – so he knew what was in the wind and popped it to the Press without telling his own people first. Pretty dangerous,' the Leader of the Opposition commented.

'Yes, that's why I brought it up.'

'But do you see what I'm getting at?'

'You think Silaman decided to get out now before the evidence got worse?'

'Well, I think it could be that. But if so I don't understand the about-turn at the Press conference. One minute they're going to sack him, then he does the one thing which couldn't be better calculated to upset them, by giving it to the Press before them. Yet they lean over backwards to forgive him.

God knows what's behind that.'

The Leader, who knew his opposite number pretty well, began to try to see it from his point of view. 'Tell me if I go wrong. They were going to sack him. Now I wonder quite why? The evidence that's come out is bad but I'd have thought it could have been pushed down the line leaving Silaman, if not clean, then intact, unless there's much worse to come. But they wouldn't know that. So that means they already reckoned they'd be needing a scapegoat. Might it not be that they have another worry and they wanted to sack Silaman now in preparation for heaping coals upon him, if necessary, later? Now that could be right, couldn't it?'

No one said anything as he continued thinking slowly aloud. 'Yet no leader takes kindly to a secret stab in the back and if they'd wanted to use him later why the nice chap bit today?' He pondered on it for a bit in silence. 'You know, I think it must be, (a) he knows something and they want to keep him sweet, and (b) because the way he has done it has ended any possibility of using him later. But where the hell does that take us?'

The lawyer took it up. 'Doesn't he seem to disassociate himself from early decisions? What's he say . . .' He searched for the reference in the column in the paper. 'Ah, yes. He says "Decisions . . . blah blah . . . would not have been mine".'

'Yes, I think we must be there, you know. Someone made a cock-up of some sort some time ago,' the Leader of the Opposition concluded.

The lawyer thought about it and then took it up again. 'So we've got to look at how they have handled this thing? It's been the vet all the way, hasn't it. And as far as we know the two insurance companies have forked out . . . Oh! But wait a minute. No, I've got it. Look, I am acting for the insurance company covering the vet. Would I pay up on my own without bloody good proof? No, all cases have risks, so what do I do? I say I'll take most of it, but you chaps have got to chip in. But there has never been a single mention of how much by whom. Yes, you know, I reckon why they're worried is because someone may twig that they paid into the kitty to settle this thing. And depending on the outcome of the case, the amount could become a question. What do you think?'

The Leader laughed. 'No, I don't think so.' Then an idea germinated and he paused before he added, 'No, I have a feeling it's more devious than that. Why the secrecy about the settlement? There have never been any details on it. If it had merely been a normal settlement and the PM had shelled out, say 10 or 20 per cent to stop a long case years later, what would he have done? Certainly not hidden his light of Christian charity under a bushel. It would have been an irresistible chance to capitalize with the people. No, I reckon it was a secret settlement because he faced a small problem and paid over the odds to keep it quiet. But God knows what it could have been.' He sighed, and then added, 'No, perhaps you're right. Maybe he just didn't want anyone to know how much he paid out, for if the vet is found liable whatever the PM paid out would be too much.' Again he pondered. 'And yet I have a hunch that there's more to it. I know him. He just would not have been able to resist using a Government contribution as a shining example of his humanitarian approach of life.'

The finance spokesman looked up. 'I was trying to think back. What did they do when they got in?'

'Great hoo-haa about expenditure, wasn't there? Balance of payments, public expenditure, the usual.'

'Yes. Which leads one to the next question. What could have come in for a cut which could affect this case?'

'Oh, I see what you mean. Of course, they had only been in for about five minutes before it happened, so we can forget any legislation. Well, you're the financial king. You tell us.'

'Well, it's a bit wild, but I think it links. Minister of Transport resigns for all the wrong reasons, so probably to save his political skin – a few bruises now instead of being flayed alive later. So whatever it was had to be something which, tenuously at least, could have been laid at his door, hence his letter dissociating himself. Now the only other Government involved which matters to the Ministry of Transport is the Air Traffic Control Service. Perhaps it's an insurance link of some sort.'

'But . . .' They thrashed it around for another half an hour, then went to lunch. The only concrete thing decided on was to dig around a bit on insurance and try to find out the terms of the settlement. They all agreed that the Deputy Prime Minister's slip would be useful, at least as something to beat the Government with, even if they didn't get to the bottom of the whole thing.

*

As the judge continued to make his note of the damning evidence Carter nodded to the expert, and with a brief 'Thank you' sat down. It didn't show, but deep inside he had the slightly sick feeling which overtakes the best in the profession when a strengthening case suddenly reaches an unforeseen check.

Lunch had come and gone, and the Solicitor General rose to his feet to cross-examine the expert. 'Mr Singleton. It may surprise you to know that I accept most of what you have said. So I dare say I shall not keep you for long. My concern is for the Air Traffic Controllers. A faultless performance for the vet's flight, correct?'

'Yes.'

'And you would agree that whether Airways or Arrivals Controllers made a mistake or not, it would be wholly irrelevant if there was no mistake on the flight deck of the DC8, correct?'

'Yes.'

'But I suggest to you that not even that is correct, for I think you would agree with me that it is not mandatory for a Controller to give a QNH, merely a custom?'

'Well, I would always give it, and I think most people teach it.'

'But everyone knows, don't they, that the definitive thing relied upon by aircrew is the Automatic Transmission Information Service, the ATIS? So to call the Air Traffic omissions a mistake is going too far – would you agree?'

The expert considered it. 'Well, I'm not sure. I think I would have given it.'

'I see. Well, there are all sorts of things which affect a safe landing besides the QNH – wind speed and direction, and many others, yes?'

'Some others, yes.'

'Many of which are not even, customarily, mentioned by Airways or Arrivals to an incoming plane, and why not? Because everyone knows that it is the ATIS that a pilot relies on, correct?'

'Yes.'

'And the duty of the Airways Controller is simply to make sure that the descending plane has, to use the term, "copied" the current ATIS?'

'His duty? Yes, I think I would have to agree with that.'

'Tell me, have you personally had the opportunity of hearing the ATIS in action?'

'Yes I have.'

'To a transmission made by the Tower Coordinator who was on duty at the time and who recorded weather Mike?'

'Yes.'

'Have you any comment to make on the way he records what he says?'

'I would have to agree that he has a very clear and concise voice which makes for a very good transmission. I have heard it on a receiver.'

'And have you checked to satisfy yourself that weather Mike was accurate at the time?'

'Yes.'

'And would it have been remotely likely that the Coordinator in his recording would have said, for example, QNH nine eight eight millibars instead of QNH one zero one eight millibars?'

'No, I can't imagine it happening. He would read from his record as he taped the transmission, then run it through to check back.'

'So as the plaintiff's expert, you say if the ATIS was OK, as you say it was, then the Air Traffic duty was finished when Airways had satisfied itself that it heard the vital message "We have copied weather Mike". Indeed, doesn't the transmission by the ATIS end with "On first contact with Wellington Control notify receipt of Mike"?'

'Yes.'

This was clever, for the expert would never have said yes to the first part of the question. 'Thank you.'

More than pleased with the evidence, the Solicitor General sat down and wondered what had occurred to Prescott, if anything.

'Mr Singleton, I appear for the aircrew, as one might say.' Prescott paused so that the impressive fact could come to carry its full weight. 'And one of them, as they flew towards Wellington, said "We have copied weather Mike". Now, I would like to consider that and its implications with you. In the first place, does it not mean that the pilot of the moment was not so eaten up with sheer hatred for his fellow pilot as to neglect his duty? For amongst other things it does presuppose that he had consciously set his radio to the ATIS frequency, doesn't it?'

'Yes.'

'Then he had received the transmission?'

'Yes.'

'With no one to remind him to do either, apart from his co-pilot?'

'Correct.'

'Well, let's take it from there. A clear voice, described by you as concise, speaks. Now tell me, what do all pilots have clipped in front of them?'

'A pad.'

'What for?'

'To make notes.'

'What of?'

'Amongst other things, an ATIS transmission.'

'Quite. And as facts are fed to the pilots they listen and note them one by one, and can listen to the ATIS for as long and as often as they wish to?'

'Yes.'

'Now, you have said that, for the DC8 to have been at 3000 feet when the actual local sea level atmospheric pressure was 1018 millibars, as we know it was at the time, it would have been necessary for the altimeter to have been recalibrated to within three millibars of 988 millibars, to give an error in altitude of nearly or about 1000 feet. Is that correct?'

'Yes.'

'Now when I ask you to, will you please say clearly and concisely, for us all to hear, "1018 millibars" and then "988 millibars"? And while you do so, I should like the members of the jury to conduct a small experiment. Will each one of you,' he turned to them, 'please take a pen or pencil and paper, and when Mr Singleton speaks will you each write down the figure he gives?' And he waited as they prepared themselves to do as he asked. 'Now, Mr Singleton, if you please.'

'One zero one eight millibars. Nine eight eight millibars.' He said it clearly and slowly.

'Thank you. And now members of the jury, we will go a stage further with the experiment. I will ask Mr Singleton to repeat the first figure, 1018 millibars. Will you please listen very carefully, and while listening, will you please write, not the number he gives, but 988. But listen carefully. Again please, Mr Singleton.' And it was done and they all realized how difficult it was to make the error, and more than that, it was immediately apparent, as they tried to write the three numbers when four were given, that something was so plainly wrong as to make everyone question it. 'Thank you. But let's go on. Recalibration of an altimeter. Something which, when done, is always subject to a flight deck check, isn't it?'

'Yes.'

'And throughout that journey there would have been dozens of checks carried out between the pilots, wouldn't there?'

'Yes.'

'Thank you.' He paused for a second to collect his thoughts. 'Oh, yes, there is one more thing. You mentioned that you wouldn't have let these men fly. One was a middle-aged man, and if one accepts that he was a homosexual, the probability was it wasn't new. So you wouldn't have grounded him for that, would you?'

'No, I shouldn't think so. It would be a medical psychiatric assessment, I think.'

'And they had had a row the night before, over the girl-friend or whatever. You wouldn't ground all pilots who have the odd row, would you?'

'It would depend on how deep it went.'

'If no deeper than a mere silence, perhaps a natural embarrassment after making a fool of himself the night before, and also a trifle embarrassing for a younger man who had struck his senior. That wouldn't see them grounded, would it?'

'If it was no more than that, then probably not.'

'And if a captain did get drunk on an occasion, but didn't drink for at least twelve hours before the flight, that wouldn't worry you?'

'No.'

'So it comes down to a phone call about which we know almost nothing, is that it?'

'Well, not really, is it?'

'But isn't it? If there was no phone call to consider, well, we have been through the rest, haven't we?'

'Yes, but there may be a cumulative effect.'

' "Maybe" is the same as saying "possibly" isn't it?'

And the judge noted the question and the answer 'yes', for liability rested on probability.

'So it's the phone call. But even that, is it so important? Worried, he might have been. But he had flown safely to Nandi, with dozens of checks on the way, and back again?'

'Yes.'

'Thank you.'

Carter rose to his feet and contemplated his expert for a few moments. He hated taking risks and from the beginning, years ago, had taken the age-old advice to heart 'Never ask a question to which you don't know the answer'. But he wanted to ask the question. Indeed, he knew he had to if he was to keep the thing afloat at all. So with a quiet prayer, he asked, 'If a QNH error led to a crash and you had forgotten to give a QNH, ATIS or not, tell me. Would you blame yourself?'

'Yes, terribly, of course.'

And fortunately he had got it out before the Solicitor General had realized what was happening.

'And was this or was it not a QNH error, as a matter of probability?'

'It was, in the absence of pure pilot error.' Which wasn't what Carter had wanted.

'And if you had known the facts as we know them about the relationship of these two pilots, would you have let them fly together without further investigation?'

'Under no circumstances.'

'Thank you. Unless you have any questions, your Honour?' Without looking up, the judge shook his head as he went on noting the brief re-examination.

'Thank you, Mr Singleton.'

Then the judge looked at his watch, and down at Carter. 'Is that your case, Mr Carter?'

'If your Honour will give me a moment to take instructions,' and turning to his junior behind him as Charles Gray bent forward, he murmured, 'What's the position?'

'OK, I think.'

Then, turning to the judge he said, 'I find I have one more, your Honour.'

'In that case, I'll rise now.' And so ended the fourth day of the trial. And everyone was very conscious of the fact that a man had died and a Minister had resigned since the end of the third day.

Chapter Twenty-Two

'Want to go and eat, darling?'

'You go, Bill. I just don't feel hungry.'

He looked at her with a tender compassion which had grown as the strain had increased. Now it was tinged with the beginnings of sharp concern. The death, the resignation, both had hit her hard. She had lost weight as the trial had approached, the burden of it becoming heavier and heavier as the days passed. At first, as the pattern of her case emerged she had experienced fierce pleasure that the dream had strengthened and assumed substance.

The highlight of it all had been the grave decision taken with Charles Gray and Reginald Carter, QC, a decision based not so much on the hope of an outright victory, but more on her conviction and Bill's that if only what they knew was known to the world, then people might think again and wonder whether the vet had in fact been to blame. And of course, it could go much further than that. A judgment in her favour meant a terrible wrong would have been righted.

So she came to be fighting, in the end, for the ideal of justice to her dead husband. She had become governed by the *idée fixe*, the obsession. But essentially, she was a very ordinary person. And so she suffered, torn by the strength of her obsession. Her suffering was plain for all to see. In two years she had aged ten. Her face bore the lines of conflict and was grey and sagged. Her eyes alone burned bright these days, or had until this evening. But now as she turned to Bill to tell him to go on without her, he saw a doubt in her eyes such as he had not seen before, saw it clouding the brightness of her gaze. Suddenly she looked small and defenceless, a lost child, bewildered in the presence of something awful and not understood. And then – and it was the only time Bill had known her to do it – she began to cry.

'Oh, God! Why did you let me do it? Oh, Bill, it's all been a terrible mistake! And oh, Bill, I have done so much harm!'

'No, no, no. It hasn't been a mistake, darling. And if harm has been done, it's not been by you. And you must be sensible ınd realistic, darling. I mean, we've known for a long time :hat the facts would all have to come out. That's all that's ıappened. And it's been right for it to happen. And you have ɔeen right to make it happen.' And his voice became stronger ıs he added, 'And, darling Grace, you are not going to turn ɔack now. I will not let you throw it all away, so stop it. Come ɔn, now.' And he shook her gently, but she wouldn't be com-:orted. 'Grace, we've known that all the business about the ɔilot and Bates was going to come out, so it's not that. So what is it, dearest? Why break up now, when you're so near he end?'

And between her sobs she said, 'I know, but a young man killed himself last night because of me. And . . . and that man eft the Government. I didn't want people to suffer like this. I felt so sorry for Bates, and it isn't ended yet. What are we loing? How will it all end? I'll tell you how it will end. That udge isn't going to say it was the fault of the pilots or any-ɔne else, but Frank. We will have done nothing to help Frank, but terrible things to other people, people who have got to go ɔn living. And that man Bates, he'll lose his job now. And I've ruined the name of the pilot, and that poor dead boy, ınd the Minister, and for what? Nothing, Bill. Nothing!' And she cried afresh and again asked, 'Oh, God! Why did I do it?' He couldn't answer her so he let her cry because he knew he could say nothing to help.

'I'm going to eat. What about you?' And there was no sym-ɔathy in the ex-policeman's voice. He was very tired of the grubby little room which had been their prison throughout the day and he didn't look forward to the night ahead. The young man looked across from the bed. He seemed exhausted. It had been a terrible day, a day of pleading, tears, anger, and once, violence. But nothing had moved the ex-sergeant. Except . . . could it? Could it be done, even now? And he wondered as ıe replied, 'No, I'll stay here, I'm not hungry. Lock me up, if you like. I'm not going anywhere.'

'And I'm not, either, laddie. I'll have it sent up.'

'Why don't you do what you did when you went for a crap; ıse the old handcuffs again?' Could it work? he was wonder-ıng. 'You'd like that, wouldn't you, and where could I go, tell me that, yer fucking old sod, a fucking wanked out old creep cop who never made Inspector. You poor old bastard.' He was

watching to see the effect. With a bit of luck, he thought, i
might work. 'Hey, tell me, do you keep those cuffs so you car
look at them and remember what a great guy you were, you
sad old sod? I bet you stole 'em when they kicked you out
That's right, isn't it? Couldn't bear to let them go. 'Cos wha
the hell are you anyway? Watcha do for bread? Few buck
from the State I suppose for a life spent in getting fucking
flat feet and putting your fucking great nose in other people's
shit. Then, of course, I s'pose you get the old age pension
Christ! Do you know, I feel sorry for you, I do really. A
right old has-been who just never even was. Jesus Christ, you
poor old sod . . .'

'Yeah, you can go in a moment. But do you want any food
yes or no? Just tell me before you go on feeling sorry for me.

'Aw, for fuck's sake, what are you anyway?'

'For the last time, what's it to be?'

'Get stuffed.' And he turned away on to his side as the ex
sergeant rang down for sandwiches and soft drinks. Then he
returned to his book. No, Phil thought in frustration, it hadn'
even looked like working. And he felt bitter as he realized
that there was going to be no way of escape.

Arthur Brighton drank his beer, then looked malevolently a
his son John across the supper table. What he felt at the
moment had been growing for a long time, even before the
accident. After the accident, he had looked very carefully a
the flight strip for his Airways position, and been very carefu
to see if there was anything on it which shouldn't be there, or
anything omitted. And it had seemed OK.

So the summons to the Director of Air Traffic Services
office had come as an awful shock. The welcome had been
courteous but cold. It was the Director who had done all the
talking.

'We have asked you to come here as an internal matter
Not that it will necessarily stay that way, though we hope so
You were on Airways when the DC8 was inbound, and you
made all transmissions to it. Have you heard the tape?'

'No, sir.'

'I see. Well you'd better hear it now before we go any
further.'

Then he was listening to it, and when he heard his reply
his voice was easily recognizable. The exchange was brief:

'Wellington, this is Paranational Zulu Delta crossing New Plymouth this time, flight level 35,000 feet, estimated New Plymouth south at 28. We have copied weather Mike.'

'Paranational Zulu Delta – roger. Report New Plymouth south. At Wellington weather Mike current. Initial wind as follows 160 magnetic 15 to 18 knots, swings 150 to 180 maximum 20. Over.'

'Paranational Zulu Delta – copied.'

The tape was switched off. 'Your views on that, please, Mr Brighton?' But Arthur, stunned, hadn't been able to answer immediately.

'Don't rush, take your time.'

'I seem to have missed the QNH.' Then, with all the years of experience he had behind him, he had rallied, 'But as you know it is only advisory, not mandatory, to give it.'

'That is true. But why do you think the custom exists, if not as a double check on the ATIS?'

'I appreciate that, sir. But I will not accept blame for something which is not a positive omission in procedure.'

'But you do accept that your omission was tantamount to bad procedure. If it had been to your normal high standard you would have included it, wouldn't you?' He hesitated, then was lost as the Director went on. 'Perhaps you should know that we have been monitoring you recently.'

'I see. OK, yes. I accept that the transmission wasn't in accordance with the very highest standards of procedure.'

'I am glad that you accept that, Mr Brighton. Now, I don't know where it will go from here, if anywhere. But as you know, you have been in line for supervisor, and I am afraid that is now completely out of the question.'

Arthur thought about it and realized that there was nothing he could do. 'I see. In that case, I'll get back to the Centre.'

It was on his way back that he suddenly remembered the slip of paper with the message to ring John. And with the memory had come the thought that his son had been buggering up his life one way or another for years, and now he had managed to fuck up his final promotion. He had more or less held his peace since that interview, but now, as he looked across the table at him, with it all brought back to mind again by the news on TV of the trial, it became too much for him. Suddenly he was just too angry to show anger. He spoke in the flat voice of cold, absolute finality – the finality with which death ends life. 'After you have finished your supper, John, you will pack your things and leave, and never come back unless one day I change my mind and want to see you again. You are just too much trouble for me to live with. I don't want to see or hear or ever be worried by you again.'

Rod Stringer, the Controller on that fateful day about two years ago, had been caught in a trap. He too had been called in to see the Board, headed by the Director of Air Traffic Services, and he'd heard the playback with its omission – no mention of a QNH in the brief message: 'Paranational Zulu Delta – g'day – you are identified. Continue descent to 4000 feet and home on to Porirua – expect no delay for a twin NDB approach on to runway one six.' But the fact of the failure was something which he had had on his mind ever since the crash.

Right from the time of that transmission, he had had something bugging him, as little things do when one remembers there was something one had meant to do but can't quite remember what it was. But it had flashed back to mind shortly after the event, and the knowledge of it had been something he had kept to himself, hoping it wouldn't be spotted. But as he listened to the playback and was asked to comment, he knew there was no escape. And he too had been sent away with no promise of protection, and in the miserable certainty that he would never make supervisor now.

Rod and Arthur had suffered the curtailment of their careers just five weeks and two days after the accident. Arthur eventually lost his son, who remained alive, but no longer any son of his. Rod built a cage in his mind, and tried to live within it, blaming James Barrymore for his lapse: James over his shoulder, staring at his back and distracting him at the vital moment.

At first Rod had tried to arrange shifts to avoid being on the same as Barrymore. But it always broke down. He had tried to ignore Barrymore, but the more he strove to cut him out of his consciousness the more aware he became of the supervisor's presence, and so the worse it became. Time passed, but it didn't make things easier. Rod Stringer began to anticipate the presence of Barrymore and the unease which accompanied every shift they shared began to infect his time away from work. It all came to a head one day as Rod was walking from the FIO's office into the VFR gloom. He was eturning with a cup of coffee when he bumped into James Barrymore and part of the coffee was spilt. It was the last traw, and the rest of the coffee was flung in Barrymore's face, accompanied by a near-hysterical shout from Rod Stringer. 'Get out of my way! Stop following me! Oh, for God's sake, eave me alone!'

In the quiet of the Centre the words from the overwrought man had sounded like a pistol shot. They were the last Rod Stringer spoke on duty. Once the problem was appreciated or what it was, he had no option but to resign, at least that was how he saw it. When the doors of Air Traffic Control in New Zealand had closed behind him, Rod Stringer tried to get into the same field in another country. To his amazement, he discovered that though the job was much the same the world over, it was all so badly organized and subject to vested nterests that his past status or training got him nowhere. In he end he got a job in a bank at a very much lower salary. He read the reports of the trial and cursed James Barrymore.

Grace Hulman, of course, knew nothing of these or the housand other little upsets that had attended the disaster for which the world, at the insistence of the government of the day, had blamed Frank. But even so, her unhappiness in the arms of Bill Hulman that evening took a long time for him to assuage. Later they went down to dine, and managed to gnore the covert glances always accorded the key figure in the course of any *cause célèbre*. And upstairs again, they alked and read and avoided the colour TV and the radio, for the media was now full of it.

But the judge did watch TV, and, horrified at the coverage, wondered whether to try and stop the comment which went beyond the bounds of legal permission. However, the damage was done, so what was the use? He went to bed hoping very much the case wouldn't drag on. He wished that the evidence was over and done with, for he had a feeling that his findings would not be changed.

The next day began badly for Grace. She was spotted as she was getting out of the taxi and before she had shut the door to dart across the pavement, people had swarmed around her. The first shout of 'There she is!' seemed to become lost in the first question as a microphone was thrust in her face. It was all so terrifyingly quick it bewildered her. She was blinded by the popping of flash bulbs, before being led speechless and utterly bewildered into the Court building, to be hurried into a conference room for sanctuary behind a heavy door. It was a dimension to her case she really hadn't thought about and she found it deeply upsetting. But her only comment was 'Why are people such ghouls? I just don't understand it.'

But the lawyers did. They had seen it all before. A case was a case, but with the mention of the words homosexual or blackmail, it was news. As Carter observed to Charles Gray when they met, 'Extraordinary, really. The more sophisticated the human race becomes the worse its taste. I do believe that Grace and her case are about to enter the exalted "Woman raped by gorilla" category, you know. Our client must be worth a fortune in print. Not quite in the same category as ex-Prime Ministers and their memoirs about the people they were once pleased to call colleagues and friends, but not far off it. Well, am I still to pursue the same line with the judge?'

'Yes, I think so, don't you?'

'He won't like it much, but I don't think there's much he can do about it, so yes.'

'Silence in Court. Be upstanding.' And the hearing began for the fifth day, but not with evidence, for Reginald Carter, QC, began to address the judge in an application the like of which the judge had not met before in all his long years in the law.

'Your Honour, I wonder whether I may make an application before I call my next witness. It is that his name be suppressed. And I base it on the grounds of natural justice. Should it be made common property, it will make it very difficult in life afterwards for this young man who now voluntarily offers to show himself. I intend to call him to prove that Captain Harry Standard was indeed a homosexual and worried out of his mind by a phone call taken shortly prior to his departure from Wellington.

'This young man, who has no convictions is, or shall I say was, a male prostitute and blackmailer' – Silence in Court had to be called twice before he could continue – 'and one who, er, plied his trade at the top end of the market. No doubt you nd the jury will wonder why a person of his type should villingly come forward to expose himself to criminal charges. There are two reasons. The first is that he has decided to bandon his old way of life. And your Honour may be in no loubt about this, for once he has taken his place in the vitness-box, his cover, to coin a phrase, will of course be blown. He will become known to the police, who know nothing of him or his past activity at present. The second reason s that he has been promised ten thousand dollars to come ere and tell the truth. It does not, of course, constitute a ribe, for money which changes hands to help a man do what he law requires of him carries no wrong with it. But it has been offered to help him to a new life, for he suffers the lestruction of the old one here in this Court. That is my pplication.' And he sat down.

The judge considered it for a time. 'And what do you say?' He nodded to the Solicitor General.

'Your Honour has wide powers of discretion, but certainly wouldn't wish to be seen as supporting suppression of a vitness's name on the grounds relied upon by my learned friend. Apart from that, and my amazement that in this case ve are hearing evidence which has plainly been purchased, I ave nothing to add.'

'Yes, Mr Prescott?'

'I merely associate myself with my learned friend the Solicitor General.' And he sat down, leaving the judge not a great leal wiser than he had been at the beginning.

'Mr Carter, the thought crosses my mind that if, while I am itting on a case, a man pleads guilty to an offence, then it nay be my duty to sentence him, as in a case of contempt. That would be correct, I think?'

'Yes, your Honour, but subject to the right of representaion.'

'Yes, but I can of course assign counsel to him if he has no objection?'

'Yes, I think so. And with that in mind I might mention hat I have received instructions from him to represent him ere. And if I may suggest it, I rather think it would be in he best interests of justice if the matter were dealt with mmediately following his evidence.'

'But what of prosecution? I rather think the Crown should be represented, and at the least there must be an indictment prepared by the Crown.'

'Yes, your Honour. I have had one drawn and further, I asked Inspector Hemmings here today to be prepared to file it if he would be so kind. One of the junior counsel here could be instructed to act for the Crown.'

'Is Inspector Hemmings in Court? If so, will he please come forward?'

The policeman came forward. 'You have heard what has been said? What would the police view be on all this?'

Troubled by the unorthodoxy of it, the policeman wasn't sure what to say. 'Well, your Honour, we of course don't even know an offence has been committed, but if a man confesses to an offence and gives us proof, we would go ahead on it.'

'So you would have no objection to following the course suggested by learned counsel? I confess it does seem to save a lot of trouble.'

And with the indication from the judge, the policeman agreed and filed the indictment on behalf of the police. That done, the judge indicated that Carter could go on. 'I think you had better call him . . . what was it? Philip James – yes, that's on the indictment anyway – for the time being.'

'Call Philip James.' And to everyone's surprise the slim young man sitting at the end of the row behind the lawyers rose and was in the witness-box almost before anyone had a chance to take a good look at him. But the judge did, and saw the scar on the young man's face. Then, having subjected him to careful scrutiny, he said, 'Will you write down your correct name on a piece of paper for me, please?'

It was done, and as the judge read it to himself, he nearly expostulated, 'God bless my soul!' But instead, one eyebrow merely twitched as he recognized the surname of a man who was more than a little prominent. And to avoid doubt, the young man had written his father's full name, preceded by 'son of'.

'You have heard Mr Carter. Has he expressed your wishes in the matter?'

'Yes, sir.' And many of the jury found it hard to accept that this pleasant young man could be guilty of what had been alleged.

'I see. Well, I must tell you that you are under no obligation as a witness to answer any question that may incriminate you. That is the first thing. Do you understand?'

'Yes, sir.'

'But if you do incriminate yourself during your evidence, I shall ask for the indictment to be read and for your plea to it. If guilty, then I shall hear anything Mr Carter may wish to draw to my attention in mitigation. Then, if you have no wish to say anything before sentence is passed I shall pass it upon you. Is that perfectly clear?'

'Yes, sir.'

'And can I ask you this. Do you appreciate the gravity of the offences which it is said you will wish to plead guilty to?'

'Yes, sir, I do. And now, before I get too old to put my education to better use, I want my past to be dealt with.' The young man hoped it hadn't sounded too good to be true, but it seemed to go down with the old boy OK, and Carter had done what was promised.

The judge considered it all for a few moments, then, satisfied it was all more or less in order, he nodded for Carter to begin. And step by step the jury heard of all that had happened on that late afternoon in Jenny Carol's flat. And Bates' evidence was supported, and the scar supported it all. And they heard about how a friend had introduced Phil James to Captain Harry Standard. And finally, the mystery of the phone calls to the airport was no mystery any more. And that left just one matter to clear up.

'Will you look at the exhibits labelled 7, I think; the ones produced by the man from the bank?' The envelopes were handed up, each a little bulky.

'Will you examine them?' The young man did as he was asked.

'Do you recognize them?'

'Yes, sir.'

'What is in each envelope?' And every ear strained in the silence not to miss the answer.

'Tapes.'

'Is there a tape there which concerns Captain Standard?'

'Yes.'

'Will you take the envelope and open it. The rest I would like you to give back to the usher.' It was done and the slim youth held the one white envelope.

'Open it, please.'

The tearing sound was clearly audible around the Court, and then he had a small cassette in his hand.

'What is that?'

'A tape for this business dictaphone.' And he produced a small hand Grundig.

'Has that tape a recording on it?'

'Yes.'

'I will ask you to play it in a moment, but first, will you explain how it came to be recorded?'

'The same way as the others. I would wait until whoever I was with wanted to go to bed or whatever, and then switch it on. I always made sure my jacket was by the bed, and then I would ask a few innocent sort of questions about his past which probably only he'd know the answers to, and then when we started it would go on running and I would make sure there was some talk about what we were doing. Then when I left I'd put it in the bank, which I did with this one, posted it through the door that night for safe keeping.'

'We have on exhibit sixteen tapes. Is that correct?'

'Yes.'

'And you had withdrawn three you had earlier deposited, making nineteen in all. What did you do with the three?'

'Sold them back for a payoff.'

'How much did you demand?' No one stirred in the court.

'$250 each.' It was the main risk, he thought, but how could they know and which of the old fags would speak up: none. They'd all rather forget it and write five grand apiece down to experience.

'Was that the whole of the money you had from each of the three?'

'Yes.' And who the hell was to know they'd each forked out a few earlier payments of a grand each, anyway?

'I see. And are those nineteen tapes the whole of your excursion into blackmail?'

He had thought about this a lot. None of the other tapes were in that bank any longer, and he'd used other names, other accounts, so he decided to risk it again. 'Yes, that's all.'

'And what name did you use for your account, and what bank?'

He corroborated the bank's Securities Department man.

'Now will you play the tape, please?'

It began with a slight thump, and in every mind's eye the jacket was falling to the floor. Then there was an unknown man's voice, the voice of an older man. 'Don't come over for a moment. Just . . . just stay there. I want to look at you.' Long pause, creak. 'Turn round . . . pause . . . Jesus, you're beautiful, Phil. A beautiful body, my little boy. Come here.' The fall of soft steps on carpet was heard, then a creak and rustle, a murmur too low to catch. 'Kiss me, Phil.' Silence, then the young man's voice. 'Hey, where'd you learn that, then? You been doing it long?' 'Don't talk.' 'But I want to. Go on, where'd you learn that, then? Go on, tell me.' 'Oh, all right. I was in the RAF for five years at a place called Gayden in England. V Bombers. And I had a friend . . . what was he called . . . oh come on, Phil. I don't want to talk . . .' 'Go on, tell me, I'm interested. Then I'll shut up.' 'A guy called Billy Sinclair.' 'Straight? Billy Sinclair?' 'Yes, now just shut up . . .' A pause, silence, then a creak and a rustle of the bed, then another creak. 'Ahhhh, oh gently. Oh, God, no, you'll have to stop!' The sound was sharp, staccato. Then quietly, 'Hang on.' 'What's that?' 'Vaseline, of course . . .'

The Solicitor General was on his feet and the relief of the increasing unease and embarrassment was all but palpable as the interruption cut the mounting tension. 'Turn it off. Your Honour, in view of what we have heard I think I speak for my learned friend as well as myself when I say that the question as to whether or not Captain Standard was or was not a homosexual and being blackmailed is not one I will contest further.'

'Mr Prescott?'

'Yes, your Honour. I am constrained to accept it as a fact.'

'I appreciate your intervention,' the judge remarked dryly.

'I have no more questions, your Honour,' Carter said, and sat down.

'Either of you?' And without rising they both shook their heads. Without the tapes they had reckoned they could have destroyed all credibility bought for $10,000 – or at any rate had a good go at the blackmail side of it, for who was to confirm that this witness had made that phone call? There was a silence as the judge collected his thoughts. It had all come to a very abrupt end.

'Very well. Now I must deal with you. Please put the indictment to him.'

The associate rose and cleared his throat, as he prepared to read the indictment. 'You, in the name of Philip James, are . . .' It was read in the darkest and gravest of voices, and the word 'blackmail' hung heavy in the air.

'And how say you? Are you guilty or not guilty?'

The answer came in a very quiet voice, 'I am guilty as charged and would like eighteen other offences of a similar nature to be taken into account.'

'Mr Carter,' the judge's voice was arid, 'perhaps it will save time if I tell you what I have in mind in mitigation. I dare say he could have gone on doing what he did for years, until he ceased to have youthful appeal. And as a blackmailer, because of the small amounts he demanded and because of the sort of people he was dealing with, I dare say no one would have come forward and laid any complaint against him. I am also conscious of his youth, and I rather take the view that in many ways very young men like himself are the prey and not the pursuer. And I bear in mind that he is not a criminal outside this sort of activity. I also accept that he wishes to reform, and with the sum he has, there is no question of a reversion because of lack of money.

'But all these things couldn't persuade me that he should not go to prison for a term of three years, even though he is but a young man. However, what does persuade me to be lenient is the fact that he has appeared before me to help a woman whom he doesn't know in the cause of justice. And I don't say that naïvely. I have in mind the ten thousand dollars, but clearly he could have made that amount much more easily in the further pursuit of his dishonesty than he has done in appearing before me.

'In the light of this, and the fact that he had made no secret of the other cases he wishes me to take into account, I have decided, subject to anything you may say, to send him to detention for six months. In doing so, I have in mind that he may escape attention, and at the same time I trust that he will see enough of what he could have suffered for a term of years to strengthen his resolve not to appear before a Court again.'

'Your Honour, I have nothing to add.'

The judge nodded gravely. 'And you, Philip James, do you wish to say anything to me before I pass sentence upon you?'

'No, sir. But I would like to thank you and say that I will not do it again.'

'Very well. I sentence you, Philip James, to six months in a detention centre. Take him away, please.' Then he added to the two advancing officers, 'I trust I shall not see a photograph of this young man in the papers tomorrow!'

'No, sir.'

Five minutes later Philip James was hustled out to a police car under a blanket. But they got some splendid photos of that, which were presented to avid readers the next day. As they drove away, the officer said 'Some people have jam on it, I reckon.' Philip James didn't reply. Ten grand for six months – less, with good behaviour. And a nice stash of another twenty-three tapes waiting to be used. What a bloody laugh!

'What's the joke then?'

'As you said, jam on it. But it sees me finished, you can be sure of that.' The officer merely grunted.

'And that, your Honour and members of the jury, is the plaintiff's case.'

'Thank you, Mr Carter.'

The Solicitor General quickly began his opening speech. 'May it please your Honour, members of the jury. The plaintiff's case has been put and it now falls to me to address you at the commencement of the case for the first defendants, who are sued in two capacities. The first, in the form of the Air Traffic Control Services, it being said by the plaintiff that the accident was their fault, or partly so, by reason of failure on the part of two Controllers to give what we know as a QNH. The second suit is in defamation on the basis that the Government, amongst others – but it is only the Government on trial here – failed to take reasonable care and defamed the man Frank Newton. The basis of this suit is that in knowledge of the facts then before them, they wrongly put it about that it was the vet's fault, which the plaintiff says was not justified. And further, it is suggested that there is something much graver here for you to consider. The fact that the Government deliberately entered a conspiracy of suppression and silence on all matters save to stress all that pointed the finger at the vet.

'To deal with the alleged conspiracy of silence – the last point first – in two words: arrant nonsense. And plainly so. Mr Carter, for the plaintiff, read interrogatories to you, administered on the Chief Investigator of Air Accidents. In one answer it became plain that the investigation was not a closed book but attended by one Mark Simpson, a man who had nothing to do with the Government, and who in fact was there specifically to protect the interests of the vet. I will say no more. In a word, there plainly was no conspiracy of suppression or silence.

'But what about defamation by the Government in, in effect failing to do all that was reasonably required to dig up all the facts we now have?' The Solicitor General paused and hitched his robes before continuing. 'On the latter point I can be brief. In this case a woman works for two years to dig for a case. Her purpose has been to try and avoid blame for one man, a different purpose than that of the earlier investigation, which was to take an impartial look at the whole thing, not with it in mind to prove liability, but to see if there was anything wrong. And in this they were successful. They found that the DC8 Captain had a problem, and they found the Air Traffic omissions. All that this plaintiff has managed to do extra is to show that the nature of the Captain's problem was different. And in doing this she has caused untold misery, you may think, without achieving a single thing.

'The death of the father, I suggest, is a trifle more awful to a man than a demand for $250. In effect, no one is any further forward. They discover a disagreement in a hotel in Nandi. So what? you will say: people have them every day. Was it serious? On the evidence of the barman, the answer must be no. The plaintiff says it must have been, for they weren't jolly as they all left together. But remember, they did leave together, which indicates toleration at least. So you may also think the silence on the part of the Captain was that of a man who has made a fool of himself, and who is waiting, maybe a trifle bashfully, for forgiveness, as the first step to re-establishment of his old position. The co-pilot? He hits his Captain. Bit of a facer, that, for the younger man. Would he, after that, have walked up and slapped the Captain, hail fellow well met on the back? No, he would quietly wait to see how deeply he had hurt the older man's feelings. Finally, on this, it may be suggested the young man couldn't stand the older because he had learned from the girl what we know now. There is no evidence for this at all, indeed all the flight checks required co-operation and militate against this, and you are not allowed to speculate.

'So, no damages for a conspiracy of silence – remember

Mark Simpson. And no element of damages on the basis of unreasonable failure to discover all that the plaintiff discovered, which leaves mistake, as it were. And the question is, was it a mistake to blame the vet, which turns on did the aircrew mishear the ATIS? And on that, remember my learned friend's cross-examination of the plaintiff's expert. When he asked you to write your figures down, that demonstrated, convincingly, you may feel, how unlikely it would be – indeed how very difficult it would be to make that mistake.

'So where does that take us?' He paused again to let the rhetorical question sink in. 'To the point where it becomes clear that this accident didn't happen by reason of the alleged mistake on the part of the aircrew, who worked well through countless checks together during that long flight to the accident. And if that is correct then the omissions on the part of the Air Traffic Control people are wholly irrelevant. And this was the view taken by the Government. So they rightly attached no weight to either the fact that the Captain had a problem, or to the omissions, both being irrelevant in the absence of a mistake on the part of the aircrew. So I suggest to you that the plaintiff's case, even on the basis of defamation by an error of judgment and/or failure to take care of the vet's reputation falls to the ground. Rightly the Government took the humane view that to publish facts irrelevant to the cause of the crash was not the correct line. It is a view which I suggest will recommend itself to you. For to have published those facts would have been harmful and misleading. It may have tended to mislead, for it would have been said by people "Why say the pilot had a problem, if it is irrelevant?" As it was, for there was no mistake in the air. And why point to omissions if irrelevant, as they were, in the absence of a QNH error? So, you may feel rightly and humanely, the Government didn't publish either matter. And of course that left the vet. But think about this. Has it been said, ever, "It was the fault of the vet"? No, indeed it hasn't.' He paused. 'All that was done was to mention material facts. His inexperience was considered to be material, the Captain's problem not material, likewise the ATC omissions weren't material.

'So, you know, there can be no possible question here of the gravest damages claimed to punish the Government. I won't waste time on it further. The plaintiff, with others, drew conclusions. For her personally, they were sad conclusions. But her grave mistake has been to fail to recognize the probable truth of them, so in anger and frustration, she unwisely brings this action. And it will fail. Not necessarily because his Honour will say it was the vet, but more probably because, as I will suggest, it is one of those cases to which there will never be an answer. And if that is so, she fails. For to succeed, the burden lies on her to persuade the learned judge to say that as a matter of probability, not possibility, it was the fault of the aircrew. And on the evidence, that will not stand up – or so will be my submission.

'I now turn to the evidence I shall call. Briefly, it will merely be to satisfy you on Air Traffic Control matters. In doing that, I shall be calling . . .'

Grace had listened with growing unease; there was something terribly wrong with it all. Then it clicked into place and she scribbled a note for Charles Gray, 'Why haven't we called Marty Chalmers and Tichfield?' And when the reply came back Gray had written 'Too dangerous. If it got out that he knew all about the suppression of the two things, it would kill the defamation side stone dead. The jury will simply say why the hell didn't someone cause a public stink if it seemed wrong at the time? By the time you came to see me it was too late, all finished and done with. So we saved our shot and kept our powder dry for the case. Don't worry about his opening: I doubt whether poopoohing it all will have cut much ice and Carter has another go later.' But it didn't bring her much comfort.

The Solicitor General came to the end of his opening and, on looking at his watch, turned to the judge who answered the unspoken question. 'Yes, well I think that rather than be left with a partially heard witness over lunch, it would be better to start him at 2.15.' But before he rose he passed a note to the associate who then passed it over to the three leading counsel. The note said 'I would like to see you all, please.'

As they entered the judge's chambers, he stopped pacing back and forth and began without preamble. 'I have four options open to me in this case. The first is to decide that the plaintiff fails, not because I find it was the fault of the vet, but because the burden of proof that it was someone else's fault hasn't been satisfied; in effect, an inconclusive and unsatisfactory state of affairs, but which will still lead to the jury having to consider defamation – in fact I will be passing the buck to them.

'Or I can find the vet to blame, in which case I would direct the jury to find for the defendants on defamation.

'Or I can find the aircrew at fault, or the Air Traffic people. But it leaves defamation open.

'Or I can find against both defendants. But you know, if you think about it, whatever I find it is going to do a great deal of damage. To be blunt about it, wouldn't it be better if you chaps settled this thing now, before it gets worse?' He clasped his hands together before he continued.

'A man has died, another gone to prison, a Minister has resigned, Bates will be out of a job. What more bloodshed do your clients want? The only possible reason for continuing is *amour-propre,* and pride is the very worst reason for a case to go on. You, Carter, hasn't your woman had her pound of flesh yet? And your people,' he was speaking now to the Solicitor General, 'surely it must affect their attitude that in the course of their investigation they missed something as important as this man's homosexuality and blackmail? They can't be unmindful of it. And frankly, the pilot must have been horrified when faced with blackmail. Can't you do anything with them? And Prescott, there were Air Traffic Control problems, and plainly in cross-examination Carter here is going to do a lot of harm.' He shook his head. 'But what also worries me is the effect all this is going to have on the public, and you must all have this in mind, you as well, Carter. It'll inflict even greater damage if it goes on, as confidence will be shaken. It's bad, very bad. Yes, I think the time really has come to go to your clients and do something about it. Now please try to do so. You are all leaders at the Bar and it lies with you to make people see sense and be objective about what they are doing. Do I make myself clear?'

'Yes, judge.' The senior of them, the Solicitor General, spoke for them all.

'Now, there is something I should like to say to Carter alone. Do either of you have any objection to my doing so? But before you reply I will tell you that it would be a mistake to draw any inference from it, and I shall require no reply from him.'

As the Solicitor General and Prescott left, it came to the minds of both of them that Carter was about to have a strip torn off.

'I ,want to say this. Your woman may pay dearly if she is too stiff-necked about this. You know that. I hope she does. Think about it, Reggie.' Carter nodded and left.

After leaving the judge, Reginald Carter, QC, saw his client and her husband with their solicitor and his junior. Brusquely, he bade them follow him. When they were all seated in the Conference room he decided to be blunt.

'Our case is now at its strongest point. From now on the probability is that it will weaken. You, Mrs Hulman, have now made your point publicly. To pursue it further, will I believe, lead to disaster. There is too much doubt about the whole thing. In my view the judge will decide on the liability issue that you have not satisfied him that it was a fault on the part of the aircrew or the Air Traffic people which caused the accident. I think he will leave it, to all intents and purposes, blank. If he does, then the jury will have to consider defamation. You won't persuade them of a conspiracy against your husband. At best, they will say that there was an error of judgment in not making all the facts known so that the public could make up its own mind. If so, when it comes to an award it will, I believe, be derisory. And, make no mistake about this, they could find against you.

'If all this comes true you will be devastated. Now, my advice is to settle now. If you do decide to do so, I will try and ensure that at least some sort of statement is made in Court by the other side. Last night I drafted what I think they may accept. I would like you to listen .to it. "The first defendants accept that during the course of the investigation facts remained concealed which, had they become known at the time, might have persuaded them to attach sufficient importance to them to warrant a decision to make those facts public. It is also accepted that in the absence of publication a biased picture was presented to the public which might have reflected unduly adversely on Frank Newton's part in the air disaster which occurred. Finally, it is accepted that the facts referred to were within the capacity of the Ministry of Transport to discover. That they were not discovered is regretted." Now, before you give me instructions, does anyone wish to say anything?'

Charles Gray broke the silence. 'I confess, Grace, that I do think it would be in your best interest to let Mr Carter try and settle on those terms – with the money of course.'

'Well, I bloody well don't!' Bill was on his feet in his agitation. 'The whole thing is a bloody carve up. She should go on and . . .'

'No, Bill. I must make this decision.' Her voice was quiet and decisive. 'And I can see that what Mr Carter says is right. If he can do it, we will at least have done a lot of what I wanted. Everyone knows the facts now.'

And suddenly the weight of the damage she had caused others by bringing the case was too much for her. Her voice broke as tears started to her eyes, but she managed to finish by saying 'And I can't bear to go on and make it all worse for everyone. It's too selfish.'

Carter left the room with his junior to meet his opponents in the Robing Room.

'Oh, there you are. I think we can probably settle this thing now. All it needs is for you to go a little along the way with us and make a pretty neutral statement in Court. We will forget the defamation side and take the $120,000 offered. Would you like to see the statement?'

It was the Solicitor General who replied. 'Reggie, that offer isn't open any longer. You, you may remember, refused it. And a lot of water has flowed under the bridge since then. In a nutshell, the damage which we hoped to avert has been done. Both of us think we will win now. So, no settlement. The best we will do is to let her withdraw and we will all bear our own not inconsiderable costs. Sorry, but there it is.'

Deep inside Carter had feared this very thing. With pity in his heart for the woman who had just lost it all, he nodded, sighed, and closed the conversation.

Back in the Conference room, he looked at her with compassion, as he said simply, 'I am afraid that it is too late. They won't settle. They offer to pay their own costs if we withdraw. They take the view that they will win and there is no more damage to be done.'

The tears had steadied Grace to an attitude of near-fatalism.

As Reginald Carter, QC, had left them it had all been over. The thought had left her drained. She heard Carter, and slowly understood what he had said. 'Oh, God. No settlement,' she said as though to herself. 'And they said all the damage has already been done?' The thought revolved in her mind. The rest of them were no longer actors in the play. For this act the stage had to be hers, and hers alone the final decision.

'If we stop I pay my costs. That will be a lot, won't it? I mean, it will be more than theirs, with all the work done by that detective and so on.' They heard her voice gain strength. 'If we don't go on, I pay mine, and if we do, I pay theirs as well. But if I stop now – withdraw, as you put it – it will be acceptance of it being Frank's fault, won't it?' She was more or less talking to herself. 'No, I won't do anything which people could say I did because I accepted that. And all the damage? Done?' Then she fell silent and pondered; then broke it with a quiet question. 'Bill? It's your money too. Would you mind?'

'No, darling. Whatever you decide is right by me.' He wanted to say what he had in mind: 'Go on and go down fighting, don't give up now, die believing it but don't die knowing you turned your back on it' but held it in check. The final decision had to be hers.

'Mr Carter, are you telling me it is hopeless?'

He sighed. 'Hopeless? No, not entirely hopeless, no. If you instruct me to go on, then on we will go, and if I can take them apart, you may count on me doing it. But you must appreciate our case was never very strong. But then, no one else's is. Our difficulty is simply that it is up to us to prove our case . . . no, that's too strong. We have to satisfy blame as a probability. We can go on trying, but our chances are not good.'

'I may not take your advice, but what do you advise?'

'If money were in any way important, I would probably say cut your losses.' And he had what the judge had said in mind. After it was all over, he would tell Gray, but just now he had decided to keep it to himself. It would be distressing and achieve nothing. And the pressure he had brought to settle was his responsibility as her counsel and it was not in keeping with the traditions of integrity of the Bar to become a mere messenger boy passing on a message from the Bench. It was for him to agree or disagree, and then advise as he thought fit.

'In that case, Mr Carter, I think it more important to be able to go on looking myself in the face in the future than to save money. Selfish, I know. But will you please go on and do the very best you can for us? If we fail, I won't blame you or Charles. You have both been wonderful.'

They both nodded in acceptance of the tribute, and mentally prepared themselves to fight on. It might just conceivably go their way. There was more evidence to come. But if it was lost, then it would only be so after fighting every inch of the way. And both were aware of the fact that though a case might be lost, nevertheless the losing of it could be almost an apparent victory, the loser honoured for trying.

Back in Court the Solicitor General opened his evidence. He had decided not to deviate from his plan of campaign, a campaign to build up the gulf between the amateur as a pilot and the professional. A campaign to roll over the plaintiff's case and flatten it by the sheer weight of the expertise he was to call. A campaign designed to take each member of the jury and the judge into an aeroplane like the DC8 and then demonstrate the reality of cooperation needed to fly the thing, and from that he intended to show that the simple message 'We have copied weather Mike' was infallible, could mean no mistake, and was the definitive Air Traffic guidance. And conversely, it was a campaign to belittle the giving of a QNH by Controllers at the Centre into an insignificant little nicety in the patter used by a Controller; part of the jargon, but like most jargon in the world, used more to add the comfort of exclusivity to the user than to convey anything important, a mere ego boost. Something so trivial that when said by the Airways and Arrivals Controllers as part of their patter, it wasn't even repeated by any commercial pilots if they had had the benefit of an ATIS. He had tapes to demonstrate it.

It was a dull afternoon. The judge took few notes, for much of what the two captains and two co-pilots said was mere repetition, a gathering of weight which was supported by the commercial flying instructor called. And Carter's cross-examination, of necessity, had to be repetitious too. But the judge noted the first short burst in full. It was to the first captain.

'What is your duty if you are ill or disturbed mentally and

find yourself asked to fly?'

'To ground myself until a doctor takes over and declares me fit.'

'If you received a phone call blackmailing you because you were a homosexual just before a flight, what would you do?'

'I don't know. But I suppose I would ground myself until I had sorted it out.'

'Why would you ground yourself?'

'Because a guy with a problem can do something stupid or forget something, particularly if the guy is the captain.'

'A matter of safety?'

'Yes.'

'Is getting your QNH right on descent a matter of safety?'

'One of the most important things on a trip, especially if visibility is bad.'

'The crash occurred in cloud.' After the flat statement, he paused to dissociate the next question.

'The ATIS is your definitive guidance information on approach to land?'

'Yes.'

'But of the information given, there are two vital pieces? QNH and wind conditions?'

'Yes.'

'And as normal practice they are always given by the Airways Controller and certainly the QNH by the Arrivals Controller as well?'

'Yes.'

'Why?'

'Why! Well, I guess, well, to check there's been no mistake in copying the ATIS I s'pose. But frankly, if there was any conflict I would go back to copy the ATIS again. That's always accurate and it's changed when there's even a two degree change in the ground temperature. Very accurate and kept right up to date.'

'But the mere fact of a repeat of QNH recognizes the possibility of pilot error in copying the ATIS?'

'Well, anything is possible.'

'And if the man flying that plane in descent through cloud crashed, you would consider that possibility as the cause – a mistake in copying the ATIS?'

'What's his co-pilot doing? He'd check too.'

'For the sake of the question, please disregard him. A man

under blackmail. In cloud. Just recalibrated his altimeter. Crashes. In the absence of any other explanation, you would say he had probably got the ATIS copy wrong, wouldn't you, Captain?'

'Yes, but here the guy had a co to help and then there was this Cessna. He's much more likely to have got lost, worried that he had crook gear on the deck, begun to feel he was flying in a circle in cloud. It's what it feels like. Maybe worried about hitting the ground, edged up a bit. I'd think of all those things before I thought of the ATIS copy. And as fact it's almost impossible, I'd say, not to copy the ATIS right. No one, like here, could mistake 1018 for 988.'

'But your answer to the question was yes. Assume if you would that the small plane just flew properly on in that cloud. Then you would say even if the DC8 pilot got the ATIS copy wrong, nevertheless, it would be corrected by his co-pilot, correct?'

'Yes, I would expect that.'

'Tell me, if you were told that a co-pilot had fought with his captain the night before an intended flight and knocked him cold, would you let them fly together?'

'If they were friends again I'd let them.'

'But if they weren't. Would you let them fly together?'

'No.'

'Why not?'

'Might be a break-down in cooperation.' Terribly uphill work, Reginald Carter thought.

'Quite. So it comes to this. If a man was subject to blackmail and crashed in the circumstances I mention, you would think, "Probable copy error from the ATIS transmission, but no worry for the co-pilot is there." But if they had fought, then of course, it might be that there was, in effect, no co-pilot because of a failure in cooperation, right?'

'Yeah, could be. But I'd add this. These guys had been flying for hours, so they must have cooperated. But even if not, I reckon that it was the vet. Private pilots in cloud can be dangerous. Nothing like the training and experience . . .' Carter's 'Thank you' cut him off. And Carter sat with the thought that many a long climb ends in a cliff, but it could have been worse, he supposed – just.

And it had gone much the same way with the rest of them. Then the judge rose for the day. The end of the fifth day of the trial. But before the judge left his chambers, a note was passed in for him. It said 'Not stiff-necked'. That they hadn't come to terms had been annoying, but he had very much regretted his few words to Carter. If it ever got out then there would have been a fine old row, and anyway, it had not been quite the right thing to do.

He smiled as the note was crumpled up and dropped in the waste-paper basket on the way out. At least Carter would know that his attitude had been neutralized by the note, and when, or rather if, he had to give judgment against the plaintiff, it wouldn't be because of a mistaken attitude of mind. Yes, he thought. He was rather pleased Carter had sent it in. And while he drove home he also felt rather pleased that he wouldn't have to think of giving judgment before the break at the weekend.

Chapter Twenty-Three

After the Hulmans had come back to the hotel, Grace had wanted nothing more than to check out, leave the whole awful business behind her, and go home. But not to be seen in Court in the days to come would look like an admission of defeat; it would say in the clearest possible terms to the public, jury and judge, 'I quit.' The night that followed was the worst night of her life. Even worse than the night of Frank's death, when she had been a healthy woman subjected to terrible shock. But now her health and strength were exhausted. The mounting stress of the last two years had been too much. She spent the night in helpless weeping and not even Bill could comfort her.

On the sixth day, Friday, the jury filed in and took their places. Some of them noticed that Grace Hulman looked very ill. 'Be upstanding in Court. Silence in Court.' The usher liked to move the words around a bit sometimes. But the judge didn't notice as he strode in to do his job, a job that suited him well, exercising an intellect that liked exercise. He nodded to the Solicitor General to begin.

'My next witness, your Honour, will deal with the ATIS. I

hink that, having heard so much about it, the jury may like
o hear the machine and appreciate its intrinsic value as some-
hing not subject to the frailties of man. Mr Allan Bell, please.'

At the mention of the ATIS the jury's eyes turned to the
rey machine on the table in the well of the Court. It looked
hat it was, the simplest of simple tape recorders. Smaller
han the average one in home use, within its plastic lid could
e seen the head mechanism, and the rollers, bounded by the
ape; a closed circuit loop which would go round and round
ndlessly repeating its message to anyone who cared to listen.

While the oath was administered to Allan Bell, the jury was
truck by the clarity of his voice, which didn't quite seem to
o with his slightly scruffy appearance. A tall, rangy man.
You are Allan Arnold Bell of 146 Steely Road, Miramar,
mployed as a grade 5 Controller within the Air Traffic Con-
rol Service?'

'Correct, sir.'

'And have you been in the Service now for some nineteen
ears?'

'Yes.'

'And on the afternoon of February 8th some two years ago,
ou were on duty in the Control Tower at Wellington Inter-
ational Airport?'

'Yes.'

'In what capacity, that afternoon?'

'Coordinator.'

'Which means?'

'Controller in Charge, with one other Controller and an
ssistant responsible for the immediate approach and take-off
one for the area, and regulating the airfield ground activity.
And apart from that, there was the wider responsibility for
he Automatic Transmission Information Service.'

'Let us turn to that. What is it?'

'The machine is there,' he gestured to the table, 'and it
imply keeps transmitting the local conditions. Weather condi-
ions.'

'If it malfunctioned, what would be the result to an incom-
ng passenger aircraft?'

'They would listen, hear nothing – or something out of the
ordinary – and not be able to copy. It has happened. A tape
broke once, and split on another occasion.'

'But could it distort an element of information or give

wrong information?'

'No.'

'You have heard that in this case the pilot said "We hav copied weather Mike"?'

'Yes.'

'What weather was current from say about 4 o'clock o that afternoon?'

'Weather Mike. It would have been picked up by the DC about 175 miles out at 4.15 or so and before the first tran mission to the Wellington Airways Controller, which I believ was timed at 4.28. It was, I think, during that transmission, a 4.28, that it was said "We have copied weather Mike".'

'Did you make the recording for weather Mike?'

'I did.'

'Have you your records with you?'

'Yes.'

'And what QNH did you record in your recording o weather Mike?'

'One zero one eight millibars.'

'Are you sure?'

'Positive.'

'How can you be positive?'

'Because the creed,' and he held up a strip of paper, 'ha that QNH on it. That strip comes out of the machine in th Tower. As the Met office chap writes it on at his end, it i copied on the machine in the Tower by singeing the paper which is fed out as it is done. I then took it – it announce itself by a noise when operating – and copied the informatio on to the ATIS record. Having done that, I dictated from i and listened to the re-run to make sure it had gone on pro perly. As I listened, I checked each item against the record t check that I had made no dictation mistakes. Then when I wa happy with it I signed the ATIS log.'

'You say you put the new information on the ATIS. Coul this not lead to a tape having part of the old message left o it, for instance an old QNH?'

'No, a tape is only just long enough to take the one messag before it is at the beginning again. The QNH appears pretty well in the middle of the recording and when one is checkin it one always listens to it right through, and back to the star again.'

'You say a tape could become damaged?'

'It has happened but the actual tape which was in use on
ne ATIS on February 8th is still on it. After the accident it
vas taken for the investigation.'

'It would be nice to be sure about that. Could you play it
ere?'

'Yes, it is wired up to a speaker. But the recording won't be
Aike. The weather had changed a bit – a two degree change
n temperature; the afternoon was getting on and I noted the
vind was then 20 to 25 knots.'

'But apart from that, the message we are about to hear will
e identical with that which led to the DC8 pilot saying "We
ave copied weather Mike"?'

'That is correct, but of course, it will now be called weather
Vovember.'

'The QNH will be the same?'

'Yes.'

'Said in the same way?'

'Yes.' And he laughed as he added, 'We develop a sort of
rofessional patter. Each guy always sounds the same.'

'Very well. Would you please be so kind as to operate the
nachine?'

Allan Bell stepped down to the table and switched the
nachine on. 'Good afternoon, this is Wellington Terminal –
Vovember – runway one six – surface wind one sixty degrees
nagnetic 20 to 25 knots – visibility 25 kilometres reducing to
5 – occasional light rain – cloud 7 opters at 2500 feet – tem-
erature 14 degrees – QNH 1018 – expect twin NDB
pproaches – the 2000 foot wind on 180 degrees magnetic 38
nots – on first contact with Wellington Control notify receipt
f November . . . Good afternoon, this is Wellington Terminal
– November – runway one six – surface wind . . .' 'And so it
goes on,' he said above the recording.

'Thank you. Now I would like to pass to . . .'

The Leader of the Opposition motioned to his two colleagues to sit down. The clock on the mantelpiece chimed the
hour. Eleven in the morning. Not far away from where they
sat, Allan Bell continued his evidence.

'Right, what's the score? Come up with anything?' The
man who aspired to become Minister of Finance in the next
administration savoured the moment before he said, 'Believe
it or not, yes I have.'

'Well, let's have it.'

'Jimmy Furlough. Merlin Mutual Board. He'd like to take over the Chair. He came across after I'd made a few noises about possible changes when we get in next time. Now he doesn't know any more than the Merlin Mutual side of it, but what he does know is they agreed to carry 25 per cent of the claim on a non-disclosure, no liability basis and binding regardless of any later action, with Government adding something. Now we all know that Merlin Mutual Ltd had chipped in – all that balls about the "hands across the table" stuff. But no one, no one at all has been told that the dear old PM chipped in.'

'Well, well! Fancy that!' the Leader of the Opposition murmured.

'Interesting, isn't it? Anyway, I've drafted a few questions for answer in the House. First: "It has been understood in respect of the claims for damage suffered as a result of the air disaster of two years ago that all have now been met by the two insurance companies who, to quote the Honourable Prime Minister, permitted their hands to be joined across the table by Ministers. Would the Honourable Member disclose the total sum paid out in respect of the said claims and the proportions borne by each of the said companies?" Now, of course he won't answer, but unless he says that the Government chipped in too, then I think we've got him.

'Here's the second question: "From the fact that the Honourable Prime Minister has not disclosed the information sought in the earlier question, is it correct to assume that the claims are considered to be solely the concern of insurance companies, and so the reason for the Honourable Member's reticence is to avoid public comment on private commercial matters of no concern to the Government?" To which I reckon he'll say yes in one way or another. If so, then we come to the third question, when we go all out and hit him

'"It has come to the notice of the Opposition that the Prime Minister has misled this House, and done so by reason of repeatedly making it plain that the Government played no part in the settling of claims earlier referred to, save to act in the capacity of mediator, it being implicit in earlier answers that the sum total of the claims was fully borne by Merlin Mutual Ltd and by the Dominion and Commonwealth. It is understood that in fact, far from acting solely as mediator he Government made a substantial contribution in payment o the total of the claims. No doubt the Honourable Prime Minister will make a statement on the matter." '

'Then I reckon we go balls out for a vote of no confidence. Grand slam! We'll be home and dry.'

The legal man spoke for the first time. 'The idea's good but we can play it better than that, I think. But proof – have you got anything we can produce – our percentage contribution or something?'

'No, not yet, but Furlough reckons he can get hold of what we want.'

'That is all very well, of course, but it all turns on this case, doesn't it?' The Leader of the Opposition's voice was speculative as he continued. 'Let's see . . . if the judge blames the Air Traffic people, the Government comes out of it very well – better than very well, don't they? They will have paid out only a percentage when if they had waited for the trial it would have been 100 per cent. And if he blames aircrew, the Government still won't look too bad. Sure, they paid out a percentage but it was a reasonable thing to do: risk, association and so on. But we could at least make a stink on that. But if he blames the vet, well, then, and only then, can we go o town. Is that right?' He glanced sharply at the lawyer.

'Yes, that's it. We could almost certainly get a vote of no confidence through. Any contribution when there was no need o part with a cent would be beautiful. Jesus, we could cause a row! But if it's the Air Traffic people we'll just have to forget it. In fact,' he added, 'in that unlikely event we couldn't even use the secrecy bit. We'd just be met with millions of dollars saved.'

'OK, chaps.' And turning to his spokesman on finance, 'You get the necessary bumf from Furlough. You didn't actually promise him anything, did you?' The Leader was suddenly concerned.

'No, of course not, not really.'

They smiled as the Leader of the Opposition continued, 'Good. Now you'd better sort out the questions, so we'll be ready directly the case ends and while the issue is still good and hot. OK?'

The lawyer nodded as he said, 'Right, but dear Lord, please don't work a miracle now and let the plaintiff win!'

'Don't worry, she'll lose – has to on the evidence.' And they

broke up in a happy frame of mind. Things were beginning t
look promising.

Carter rose to his feet and just stood there for a bit. It wasn
often that he found himself at something approaching a los
but the case, if indeed there was really much of a case lef
lay against the aircrew. He was almost certain that the judg
would find, in any event, that the words 'We have copie
weather Mike' would let the Air Traffic people off the hook
He shuffled his papers for a moment and almost sat dow
again, for really there was nothing to challenge the Tower Co
ordinator with. And had it been a judge alone that he wa
dealing with, he would have sat down and done his case n
harm. But a jury was a different thing from a judge. Fail t
question one witness and they might read all sorts of thing
into it: doubt about his own case, a withdrawal of attack o
the Air Traffic people. A jury wouldn't adequately distinguish
between acceptance of one piece of evidence, the ATIS, an
the rest of the attack.

So, finally, he decided that it would be better to mount a
fishing expedition in water with no fish, than to have no ex
pedition at all. And one never knew, he thought, there migh
be a minnow somewhere.

'Mr Bell. Tell me, was it a busy day in the Tower?'

'No, not terribly.'

'And what may I ask does that mean: "not terribly"?'

'Well, we weren't run off our feet, so to speak.'

'Not run off your feet. I see. Perhaps quiet. Was it quiet?'

'Fairly quiet.'

'I see. So we have a not terribly busy, yet fairly quiet tim
there. How on earth can it be both? Busy, even if qualifie
by not terribly, is still busy, isn't it?'

'Well, er. Well . . . yes, I suppose so.'

'And quiet, even if qualified by fairly, is still quiet, isn't it?
And he was carrying quiet menace in his voice. But he hope
the jury didn't realize that it was a toothless tiger which
threatened. Really rather shaken by the unexpected attack
Allan Bell hadn't recovered his wits as he replied, 'I . . .
s'pose so.'

'Quite. So you say it was busily quiet, do you?' The sarcasm
was patent.

'Of course not.'

'But you have told us it was both. I was merely trying to ssist you out of your dilemma.' It was the trick of the non-uestion to leave a witness floundering with nothing to answer. And so, to stop it, the judge stepped in.

'Was that a question, Mr Carter?'

'Well, your Honour, I was affording the witness the oppor-unity to try, at this late stage, to remember that afternoon.' Then to the witness, 'But if the truth be known, you don't emember it, do you? It was as thousands of others. Un-emarkable until the crash happened and you weren't told of hat till later, were you?'

And the witness was caught in the ambiguity of a 'yes' to he first part, which could equally be 'no, you are wrong, I do emember' and the 'no' required to the second part. And Carter pressed to further confusion. 'Wasn't it?'

'Yes.'

'Yes what?'

'It was like other afternoons.'

'So you can't really remember it. And all this evidence about he ATIS really all boils down to what you think you must ave done, but you cannot remember doing it, can you?'

'I do remember that afternoon.'

'Well, I suggest you don't. But tell me, an ATIS may sound plendid to you as you hear it play back while you're check-ng what you have said into it. But what of reception on board a flight deck? Static in the air and that sort of thing. You vouldn't know anything about that, would you?'

'No.' Then he suddenly remembered. Of course! 'But,' he dded strongly, 'I certainly do remember that afternoon. It vas the afternoon that the ATIS had its monthly check-over.'

'Was it malfunctioning?'

'No, it wasn't. But every month it has a service.'

'Not by you, I presume?'

'No.'

'Have you mentioned this to anyone else at all before to-lay?'

'It must be known. It would be in the records.'

'I see, so if it turns out from them that it wasn't routine, it vould probably have been because there was a fault in the nachine, hmmm?'

'But it was the regular check. They would have contacted ne if the ATIS had developed a malfunction.'

'Ah. So this paragon of metallic virtue doesn't always behave impeccably. It does go wrong from time to time?'

'Well, it can.'

'And does sometimes?'

'Very occasionally it breaks down and stops transmitting.'

'Of course. And a breakdown could explain a QNH problem, I suppose?'

'No, the pilot wouldn't have said it had been copied, would he?'

'That, Mr Bell, may depend upon the state of mind of the pilot.'

The judge had listened with what he considered to be remarkable patience, but decided now that this had to be stopped. 'Mr Carter, where is all this leading us?'

'A crash occurs. A QNH error I suggest, and now we find that the ATIS is not infallible. Your Honour, I think it relevant.'

'Very well, but if you would confine yourself to specific lines of enquiry, it will save confusion, and I may be able to take some sort of note.'

'Indeed, your Honour.' But Carter's mind was working hard. He thought he detected a fish lurking somewhere amongst all this, by instinct rather than by sight. Anyway he had at least managed to justify being on his feet. 'I think I would like to explore this business of the service further with you. At what time did it take place?'

'I think at about 4.'

'Really? And in your estimate the DC8 would have taken the message at about a quarter past?'

'Yes.'

'Could it not be that the technician altered the ATIS?'

'Not possibly. He is an expert. I could see him all the time. And I would certainly have heard if he had dictated anything on to it. It is only feet from my chair. And anyway, the DC8 said quite clearly that it had copied Mike, so no.'

'When did you dictate Mike?'

Allan Bell looked at the log. '3.47.'

'And when did you change it to November?'

Again he looked at his records. '16, or rather 4.45.'

'I see. Tell me, can you remember whether the DC8 was the only aircraft which would have had recourse to the ATIS during that time?'

'I am afraid I can't remember.'

'Would there be any way of finding out now?'

'The airline might still have its flight schedules, I don't know. The investigation may have noted it, but again I don't know. And one can't always know whether the ATIS is used by an inbound plane or not. Big ones, yes, but the others, well, I don't know.'

'Can you remember whether another DC8 came in?'

'Yes. No, it didn't.'

'You mean yes, you remember?'

'Yes.'

'And the DC8 we are concerned with was the only one?'

'Yes.'

'And the only thing to affect the ATIS during that time was to receive attention from a man who serviced it?'

'Yes.'

'And this was minutes before the DC8 would have relied on the receipt of Mike?'

'Yes.'

'Which you changed to November about half an hour later?'

'Yes.'

'I see.' He paused in thought. Then turning to the judge he said, 'Your Honour, all this is new to all of us. But my case is finished. However, I do think that you and the jury should have the benefit of seeing this technician.'

'Some of your evidence, Mr Carter, was I dare say a trifle new to the Solicitor General and Mr Prescott, and as you have rightly said, your case is at an end. Do I understand you are asking me to instruct this witness to appear, as is my prerogative?'

'Yes, your Honour.'

'I see. The answer is no. This case is already over-long, and I am not disposed to add a witness who, as I see it, couldn't be material. Mr Bell has cogently summed up for me on this. The DC8 had copied weather Mike after the ministrations of the technician. I take the view that to call him would be a waste of time. However, if the Solicitor General calls him so be it.'

The Solicitor General was looking at the technician's earlier statement to the Air Accidents people, and was coming to the conclusion that since part of the plaintiff's case was about secrecy, it would be wise to be seen to be entirely open. And in any event, it would be no bad thing for the technician to jump on any suggestion of trouble with the ATIS. So as the judge finished, the Solicitor General rose to say: 'Your Honour, the last thing in the world I would seek to do is take straws from my learned friend's grasp. If he wants the technician, I am only too happy for him to come here to help.'

Plainly annoyed, the judge rapped out, 'Very well. After lunch then.' And he was nearly out of the Court before the usher could collect himself enough to take a breath for the stentorian call he was paid to make.

Carter didn't see Grace or Bill when he came out, but on catching sight of Charles Gray, he breezily said, 'It's bricks without straw, but at least we're still going.'

'Frederick Joseph Kilson, please.' The Communications Technician had been found during the lunch hour enjoying the sun and unconcernedly eating his sandwiches, at peace by himself. The sudden appearance of the policeman startled him; being dragged off to the witness-box with no time to collect his thoughts and without even a chance to change out of his working clothes did nothing to soothe his nerves.

As he stood in the box waiting for the ritual to begin, he felt as scared as if he'd been a criminal. Rising to his feet, the Solicitor General realized the need to put the man at ease and out of his fear, a fear made patent by the trembling hand which held the Bible, by the catch in the voice and the sheen of perspiration on the upper lip. In that state he'd be dangerous, if handed over to the tender mercies of cross-examination by Carter. The judge also saw the witness's condition. 'Mr Kilson, there is no need to be alarmed. You have done nothing wrong. You are merely here to see if you can help the Court for a few minutes. It is something quite simple, but it needs your expertise to help us. Do you understand?'

'Yes, sir.' It was gulped out, but he was beginning to feel steadier and his heart was beginning to return to its normal pace.

Taking his cue from the judge, the Solicitor General set about calming the witness to a point where self-possession returned and he could safely be handed over to Reginald Carter, QC. And confidence began to flow back into Kilson's mind as he went over familiar ground, and strengthened as he was asked about various aspects of the apprenticeship he had served: the sandwich course, his experience, and the road to his present grading.

'So in a nutshell, you are well experienced for your age, would you say?'

'Yeah, I reckon.'

'Now I would like to turn to the question of the ATIS. In front of you is a bundle of papers. Would you have a look at them, please?'

'Yeah, the ATIS service log.'

'Would you look at page 27. They are numbered, I think?' Having numbered them himself during the lunch hour with the help of his junior, he knew they were, but it was another 'Yes' for the sake of confidence. 'Do you see your signature on that sheet?'

'Yeah, it was the day I serviced the ATIS. February 8th.'

'And what was the serial number of the machine you serviced? Would you please read it out?'

'D/877461/69 Mk. III.'

'Would you now go to the table and read the serial number on the machine there?' He went, and tilting the machine up, read the number.

'Thank you. Return to the witness-box please. So may we take it that the ATIS there is the one you serviced on that afternoon?'

'Yeah, has to be, don't it?' He was beginning to feel at home, self-confidence re-established.

'What's the purpose of the service you were required to carry out?'

'Give it the once-over, that's about it. Nothing to it, really. Can't get anything simpler.'

'Was there anything at all wrong with it?'

The Comms Tech looked at the service log. 'No, routine service.'

'A completely routine task with a simple piece of equipment done in no hurry. Is that how you would describe the task?'

'Yeah.'

'Thank you. My learned friend may have a few questions for you, so stay there.' Prescott indicated that he had no questions.

Carter got to his feet. 'Mr Kilson,' he began, 'would I be

right in saying that such a job as this was almost so simple that it hardly needed a man of your expertise to perform it?'

'All part of the job.'

'Yes, I appreciate that, but a part well beneath your technical level?'

'Yeah, you could say that I s'pose. But someone's got to do it, haven't they?'

'Oh, yes. But in getting someone of your competence to do it, it was rather like asking a consultant surgeon to put an elastoplast on a child's graze. Do I make the point?'

'Yeah, I see. Yeah, you could say that.'

'Such a simple task that it really needed hardly any thought at all from someone like yourself used to complicated communications equipment?'

'Yeah, do it blindfolded, I should think.'

'Yes. And I suppose this sort of under-employment of expertise must annoy people like yourself at times. Piffling little job. Something requiring the sort of level of expertise one might consider a first-month apprentice to have?'

'Yeah, he could do it.'

'Not something requiring the same level of concentration as, say, the servicing of the 25-channel Philips, or is it Decca monitoring recording apparatus in the Centre?'

'Shit, no.'

The judge was on it in a flash. 'Please remember where you are, young man, and moderate your language!'

The Comms Tech looked startled for a second, then smiled as he said, 'Yeah, sorry about that, judge. Won't happen again.'

Carter, very well pleased at the over-confidence, decided to come in for the kill, even if it was such a tiny kill. Anything was better than nothing. 'Tell me, are you familiar with the saying "Familiarity breeds contempt"?'

'Heard it.'

'Would you agree that it is just in this sort of task that a mistake can be made because it's all so easy and requires so little thought?'

'You can't make a mistake on an ATIS.'

'How can you be sure of that?'

'There's nothing to go wrong. Just clean it, more or less.'

'I see . . .' He didn't get the next question out before the 'ech, flooded with sudden anger, burst out, 'An' if you're aying I fuckin' well don't do the job, I'll bloody well 'ave the Jnion on yer. I'm a skilled man and proud of it . . .' But the udge cut him off.

'Mr Kilson! Language of that nature in my Court is not omething I will tolerate. Use it again and I shall consider 'ou in contempt and fine you. And speak to Counsel like that gain and you will also be in jeopardy. And be clear: whatver the power you may ascribe to your Union, I assure you t has none here. Bear that in mind and answer the question sked.'

Carter continued. 'Yes, a skilled man doing a job beneath im at the end of a hard day. Well, we will leave it.'

'But, Mr Carter, I don't quite understand where all this leads s,' the judge interposed. 'Are you saying this man was lax nd made some sort of mistake? If so, what? What possible nistake could he have made? We know the pilot of the DC8 aid "We have copied weather Mike" and that, as I undertand it, was current at the time. So where is all this taking s? Surely, to create vague innuendo without any substance an do your case no good at all, apart from pinpointing its veakness. Now, what do you say?'

'Your Honour, I am much obliged. Perhaps I can be more pecific in a moment.'

'I very much hope so. Now please get on with it and don't vaste any more time.'

'Of course not, your Honour.' But although Carter had, in act, no criticism to make, it was all part of a new campaign. 'aced now with a case which had no hope, he was at work on enerating grounds for Appeal. Clear evidence in the subseuent transcript that the judge had been swayed by ill-temper vould help. Probably wouldn't win the Appeal, but might nake the defendants think twice before letting it go to Appeal, nd so a settlement might yet be won.

So, unperturbed by the judge's outburst, and in the hope of etting him more up-tight, he carried on with the waste of ime. 'Now, Mr Kilson, would you be so very kind as to go o the table and we will pursue the matter further.'

But the judge intervened. 'Mr Carter, we have heard the ATIS. Surely that is enough?'

'With respect, no, your Honour.' Then turning to the witness, he indicated that he should go to the table. With ill grace the witness did what he was told to do. The judge's annoyance was plain.

'Now. The Tower is how many floors up?'

'Mr Carter. What possible relevance can that have?' the judge snapped.

Turning to the judge Carter blandly replied, 'Oh, I think your Honour will see it soon.' Then turning back to the witness, the judge containing himself with some difficulty, he repeated the question.

'Two or three I suppose,' was the reply.

'Really? You only suppose? But I thought you'd done this job before.'

'Yeah, but not often.'

'When was the time before?'

'Aw, I'd done it the month before. I see'd that from the log. Before that I was on other things. In fact I only came down here 'bout a couple o' months before.'

'I see. So you climb the final flight of stairs to the Tower where the ATIS is, correct?'

'Yes, of course.'

'And where is it in relation to you as you get up there?'

'Mr Carter.' The judge's voice was astringent. 'Waste further time and I shall be obliged to take a grave view of it. I trust I make myself crystal clear?'

'Obliged your Honour, indeed you do,' was Carter's quiet reply. Someone giggled nervously, but it was lost in Carter's repeat of the question.

'On a thing to the right. Controllers and the rest ahead and left.'

'And when you enter, it would be operating?'

'Yeah.'

'Turn it on then, please.' And as the witness did what he was told the tape started where it had left off – '. . . one sixty degrees magnetic 20 to 25 . . .' 'Will you turn the volume down, please.' And the slightly metallic sound went down to a monotonous background noise. 'Thank you. Now, would you please go through all that you would have done.'

'I would like to know the relevance of this before you go further, Mr Carter.' The exasperation in the judge's voice was now very plain to hear.

'If your Honour will bear with me just a moment longer I'd

be obliged,' was Carter's yet blander reply. 'Now, Mr Kilson, you were going to show us,' he said as he turned back to the witness.

'How can I, I haven't got me gear.'

'Don't worry, Mr Kilson. Pretend you have.'

'Mr Carter!' The judge's voice was a whiplash in the Court. 'This charade has gone quite far enough! If you have anything cogent to ask, then ask it – otherwise sit down.'

With silky smoothness and with an assumption of great surprise, Carter said, 'Your Honour, do I understand that you are seeking to prevent me from adducing evidence which I consider it necessary to adduce in the course of the presentation of my client's case?'

'No, Mr Carter, I am not. However, I am mindful of the costs of this case, the fact that it keeps the members of the jury from their business, and the interests of your client. I trust I make myself clear?'

'Oh perfectly, your Honour. Indeed, I am most grateful for your Honour's guidance. Indeed most grateful.' Then turning to the witness as though nothing had happened, he said, 'And now, Mr Kilson, please continue, and tell us what you are doing.' In the background, 'Good afternoon, this is Wellington Terminal – November . . .' could be heard, and there was a strangely hypnotic quality about it.

'Well, I come up to it, having told the guy why I was there, lift the lid, like this, and stop the tape like this.' And as he turned the knob the last 'November' seemed to echo in the sudden quiet. 'Then I take the tape off like this,' and the small loop was in his hands, 'and then I start to clean the heads and the rest of it. Then when that's done I pick the tape up and put it back on, like this, and she's all ready to go.'

'I see. A very simple operation, in fact, just as you said.'

'Yeah, kid's play.'

'And do you leave it then, or what?'

'No, I switch it on again, to check.'

'I see. I suppose the tape could be in a different position when you put it back?'

'Yeah, I might have turned it a bit so it'll start up before or after where it was.'

'Yes. Oh well, let's complete the exercise, shall we? Turn it back on again, please.'

'Yeah.'

The judge opened his mouth, then thought better of it. He rather thought he saw Carter's tack and was determined now that the silk would get no further help from him in that little game. And once again the tape started along its perpetually closed run. '. . . knots – on first contact with Wellington Control notify receipt of Mike. Good afternoon, this is Wellington Terminal – Mike – runway one six – surface wind . . .' And then the message was suddenly lost.

The first person to react was a member of the jury. He gave a gasp, and suppressed it immediately. He must have been mistaken! Then from the back of the Court someone said something indistinct. Then those who had been listening closely gave voice to their surprise, and their voices merged with the shout of the usher 'Silence in Court. Silence. Silence in Court.' And finally there was silence – silence save the metallic voice, which twice in each message, clearly said 'Mike'. And everyone listened in fascination to something that couldn't be happening.

The judge eventually spoke. 'Mr Carter, I don't understand. What is this? What has happened?'

'Your Honour, I don't pretend to know. But one thing is clear. An ATIS which was transmitting November a few minutes ago has been touched and now transmits Mike. Well, Mr Kilson?'

'It can't happen, it just can't happen. It's a single-track machine. Can't carry two messages, I mean . . .'

And suddenly something clicked in Carter's mind. The man's hands – the tape – the laying of it down in front of the machine – the picking of it up.

'Mr Kilson, I suggest it is simply that when you replaced the tape you put it back upside down as it were. So that the top edge of the loop became the bottom, and what we hear now is the loop in reverse, correct?'

Silence followed the question. 'Yeah,' the witness began hesitantly, 'but even so, it's a one-track head. If it went the other way round it would be rubbish. That's one thing I check for at the end, the message going backwards. It doesn't make . . .'

'But it would, and does, if the recording head, or that part of it, that sensitive part, a narrow longitudinal strip set in the head, was off centre in relation to the centre of the tape. That would explain it, wouldn't it?'

Again silence as it sank in: offset, reverse, so a parallel ack. 'Yeah, yeah. You're right. Yeah, it would.'

'So what we are hearing now is the Mike weather put on ıe tape just before your servicing of it on February 8th, but ever erased by the subsequent November, for that was corded, as we have all heard, on the other track of the tape. the result, Mr Kilson, had it fallen to you to come to rvice this machine yet again in a further month's time, and ıen, as now, and as you did on the afternoon of the 8th, you ırned the tape over, then from the time you did that until e new weather was dictated on to the ATIS, any plane rely- g on the ATIS would be listening to the weather last put on before you turned the tape over on February 8th, preserved r the intervening month until you turned the tape again. hat must be it, mustn't it?'

And as the full impact hit him, the young Comms Tech ent white as a sheet and all that was heard above the tape as his whispered 'Oh, Christ! Oh, Jesus Christ!'

'Are you all right?' There was genuine concern in Carter's ice as he added, 'I don't think it's your fault. The position- g of the head wasn't something touched by you. And when u checked it after service you didn't hear what you would ve expected if you had inadvertently turned the tape over – unintelligible noise. Now, are you OK?'

In a daze, he nodded. Then, having turned the tape off, he ent back to the witness-box, as he was asked to do. 'Now, Ir Kilson. You have in front of you the ATIS service log. hen did you service it the month before?'

Still shocked, he looked at it, then concentrated, and the gures began to make sense. 'January 8th, started at 2.15.'

'Will you turn now, please to the ATIS records of trans- ission for that day – it's the papers to your left.'

The young Comms Tech fumbled through them. 'Yeah, it as made up 2.05.'

'So in the sequence we think may have happened, it would ve been that weather which had been preserved for a month our turning the tape, which was brought back into trans- ission at about 4.15, or a few minutes before, on February h for the DC8 to hear. Would that be correct?'

'Yeah, must be, sir.'

'Tell me, would I be right in saying that the weather which u preserved on January 8th for its next transmission at

4.15 on February 8th to the DC8 was weather Mike?'

The young man looked at the sheets again, and his answ was hardly audible as he said, 'Yes, it was Mike.'

'And let me guess – far from being the local weather wi a high pressure reading of February 8th of 1018 millibars, w it not a day of low pressure, with a QNH of 990 odd?'

Again the young man looked at the records, then toneless answered, 'It shows here that it was 987.'

'I see.' And Reginald Carter QC, without movement, starte to consider the implications. But the case, as such, hard featured in what passed through his mind.

Grace hadn't fully understood what had or was happening. was something terribly important which she couldn't qui grasp. And suddenly she could bear it no longer, and forge ting where she was she said out loud, 'But what's it mean What's it all mean?'

The judge looked down on the woman and decided t answer the agonized question – shatteringly clear in the ele tric silence.

'To you, Mrs Hulman, it means that your husband, Fran Newton, was in no way to blame for this accident.'

Epilogue

Carter became a judge shortly after the case, the Solicit General suffered a stroke, and John Prescott still hopes to joi Carter on the Bench. Whether the judge will ever make th Court of Appeal is speculative; but all in all, he did fair well.

Of course, because it was all the fault of the Air Traffi Services people, the Opposition never did table their question and since the insurers sold more silence for more cash th Prime Minister was OK. Chris Silaman, poor man, was la heard of on a visit overseas, and may or may not be heard c again.

Mark Simpson looks like ending up as senior partner i Stanley's; a good loss adjuster, Mark.

Anthony Carnegie got a rise all right and has just joine

he Board of the Dominion and Commonwealth; he'll probably be taking over the General Manager's spot soon. Rumour has it that the fat man's off to a bigger job in New York. Of course, to take forty-five per cent was an awful balls-up. Still, on what he thought he knew, he played his cards pretty well.

The ex-Sergeant is now ex-everything, having been hit by a car two days after the case was over. Had it happened earlier, it might have seen things turn out a little differently, but that's life.

Charles Gray when last encountered was still a guy without enough ambition to bugger up his life. He has become a regular visitor of the Hulmans now. Marty was pretty cut up about his part in it all, but when he went to make amends to Grace and Bill they understood and are still friends.

Graham looks like shaping up well as a vet. Most of his father's old clients have found him good, though as yet Bill doesn't use him on horses! And Helen – well, she and Graham are to be married and Grace is delighted.

As for the other Graham, the whole thing was one hell of a shaker for him. Of course he was protected by the Government, but he's rumoured to be thinking about an early retirement. Being bound by the Official Secrets Act, he'll never be in a position to rock the boat, and anyway he'll be kept in line – something to do with his full pension rights.

Philip James, or whatever his name was, did his time, hasn't been in front of the Court again, doesn't rely on Dad, yet runs a new Merc though he hasn't been on the game so far as anyone can find out. Odd, that. Almost as odd as the recent suicide of a pillar of the Church.

And Bates, poor old Bates. In fact, not so very poor, because Grace had him sent 25,000 bucks.

James, the Supervisor, retires next year. He and Mary were very upset about young Steve, but these things happen.

Rod is probably going to come out of it all right in the end. He's just been made manager of a branch, though he mightn't be everyone's choice.

Sadder is the fact that John, Arthur's son, is now in prison and his dad won't go and visit him.

As for Dirk, last seen in hospital, he made out with a girl called Clarry. They're very happy now and have a child of their own.

So life goes on – though it has taken Grace and Bill a bit

of time to get over it all. Incidentally, the case settled and Grace agreed to accept $100,000 for the defamation bit and $135,000 in respect of Frank's death, and also her costs. The money hasn't been particularly important, but Bill was, and has become more so. In fact, they are very happy, so what really, can one say? Perhaps the last few paragraphs of chapter five say it all, if one adds the touch of wonder each of them often feels that life has treated them so well.

;eoffrey Jenkins

;offrey Jenkins writes of adventure on land and at sea in me of the most exciting thrillers ever written. 'Geoffrey nkins has the touch that creates villains and heroes – and en icy heroines – with a few vivid words.' *Liverpool Post* style which combines the best of Nevil Shute and Ian eming.' *Books and Bookmen*

Bridge of Magpies

Cleft of Stars

Grue of Ice

he River of Diamonds

cend of the Sea

he Watering Place of Good Peace

Herman Wouk

One of the most talented novelists writing in America toda
All his novels have been highly praised, and *The Cai*
Mutiny won the Pulitzer Prize.

His books include:

Don't Stop the Carnival

Aurora Dawn

The Caine Mutiny

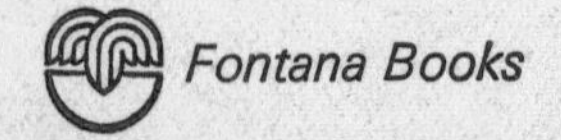

esmond Bagley

r Bagley is nowadays incomparable.' *Sunday Times*

e Enemy

e Snow Tiger

he Tightrope Men

he Freedom Trap

unning Blind

he Spoilers

he Golden Keel

yatt's Hurricane

igh Citadel

he Vivero Letter

andslide